THE HOSTAGE HEART

Forthcoming Titles in this series by
Cynthia Harrod-Eagles from Severn House

DIVIDED LOVE

THE HOSTAGE HEART

Cynthia Harrod-Eagles

This first world hardcover edition published 2017
in Great Britain and in the USA by
SEVERN HOUSE PUBLISHERS LTD of
19 Cedar Road, Sutton, Surrey, England, SM2 5DA
First published 1997 in Great Britain under the title *Dangerous Love*.

British Library Cataloguing in Publication Data
A CIP catalogue record for this title is available from the British Library.

ISBN-13: 978-0-7278-8736-8   (cased)

All Severn House titles are printed on acid-free paper.

Severn House Publishers support the Forest Stewardship Council™ [FSC™],
the leading international forest certification organisation.
All our titles that are printed on FSC certified paper carry the FSC logo.

MIX
Paper from
responsible sources
FSC® C013056

Printed and bound in Great Britain by
TJ International, Padstow, Cornwall.

With love to Angie and Wendy,
who took such good care of my mother.

Author's Note

Dear Reader

When I was a little child, I was mad about ponies. Unfortunately, we lived on the top floor of a council flat in London, far away from riding stables and green fields, and my parents couldn't afford riding lessons anyway. So it was down to the local library for pony stories.

Ruby Ferguson, the Pullein-Thompsons, Monica Edwards – I gobbled them up. And when I had read every pony book in the library system, there was nothing for it but to write my own. Thus was born my impulse to write. Between the ages of ten and eighteen I wrote nine pony novels. Then at eighteen I left home and went to university, and when I discovered adult life held just as many disappointments, it was natural for me to start writing adult novels.

After winning the 1972 NEL Young Writers' Award with *The Waiting Game*, I began to develop ambition. I wanted to write a great literary novel; I wanted to win the Booker Prize; I wanted to feature in works of reference, for my books to be studied in universities.

But between a one-book Young Writer and great literary status there would obviously be a long and stony road. I was offered a contract to write three modern romances, and accepted it gratefully. A second publisher offered me a contract for another three, and a third for four more. I was developing the skills that can only come from *doing*, and making a name for myself in the publishing world as reliable and professional; and when that won me the contract for the Morland Dynasty Series, I was finally able to give up work and become a full-time writer.

This year will see the publication of my ninetieth book. I have come a long way from those first romances. I have not won the Booker Prize or written the great literary novel, but I have learned a lot, earned my living, and I hope, in my small way, given people pleasure. I still write two books a year. The compulsion to write is as strong as ever: life will always hold disappointments, and the escape into fiction is a comfort, for the writer as well as the reader.

This book is the work of a very young me; but it's the product of an energetic, enthusiastic and optimistic self in what seemed a simpler world, and I'm very pleased to see it back in print. If you know my later books, I hope you will uncouple your expectations, and just enjoy reading it as much as I enjoyed writing it.

Chapter One

The third time Emma saw the advertisement, she stopped and read it more closely. It had appeared in the *Guardian* and the *Times Educational Supplement* without causing her more than an amused glance, but finding it again in the trade journal she wondered if it could be serious after all.

It was the word 'governess' that intrigued her: so very Jane Austen, so unexpected in the nineteen-nineties.

Governess wanted to teach and care for girl aged 10. Large house. Other help kept. Excellent pay and conditions for dedicated person. Mrs Henderson, 3 Audley Place, W1.

It was the 'large house', she thought afterwards, that made her decide to write off. Not because she had ambitions that way, but because in conjunction with 'girl aged 10' it seemed to her infinitely pathetic. She pictured a poor little only child rattling round in a vast, echoing mansion. She had grown up one of seven – an unfashionably large family even in those days – in a three-bed terraced house in Hoxton. She shared a bedroom with her two younger sisters; her four younger brothers had the large bedroom; and Mum and Dad had the smallest room, which was only just big enough to take a double bed, so that their wardrobe had to stand out on the landing, a hazard to shins in the night when you had to go to the bathroom.

Downstairs was a front room – designated the quiet room

where homework was done – a back room where everything else happened, and the tiny kitchen. Outside in a minute square of garden the grass struggled unequally against an army of tramping, scuffing feet, for it provided the only play area apart from the street.

In this confined space they had tumbled over each other, played and quarrelled, helped and hindered each other; nine mouths jabbering, eighteen eyes precluding privacy, thirty-six limbs always in the way whenever you tried to move. Noisy it was, inconvenient always, exasperating often – but lonely, never. In moments of high irritation with the brothers who made a noise like a Panzer division when she was trying to revise for an exam, or the sisters who borrowed and spoiled her tights and her lipstick and her favourite sweater, she would cry out for peace and quiet and a room of her own. But she always knew how lucky she was to belong to so many souls. The old saying was: Home is the place where, when you go there, they have to let you in. When you had six siblings, you knew there would always be a lot of places you could call home.

So she thought how sad it must be to be a child, aged ten, in need of a governess. Was Mrs Henderson disabled in some way? Or was she away from home a lot? Perhaps she was in the Diplomatic Corps: Audley Place was Mayfair, where a lot of embassies were situated. A poor little rich girl, presumably. Well she would send off a letter and her CV, and see what happened. It would be interesting, at least.

Her flat-mates did not see it in quite the same way.

"Are you crazy, or what?" Suzanne said, staring at her over the coffee-tray she was bringing in. She was thin, dark and intense, with eyes that bulged slightly behind her rather John Lennon-ish, wire-rimmed glasses, and fine, straight hair that was always slipping out of its pins.

2

"What's crazy about it?" Emma said mildly.

"Going into service is crazy," Suzanne said, banging the tray down on the coffee table. "This is the twentieth century. Governess! You're not Jane Eyre, you know."

"Oy, look out!" Alison said, annoyed. She was painting her fingernails, her left hand laid out flat on a pile of books on the table which Suzanne had jogged. "You'll have the bottle over."

"Well, you shouldn't do that in here," Suzanne retorted. "It's disgusting. Some of us eat on that table."

"Blimey, I'm only painting them. It's not contaminating," Ali said. "It's not like Rachel cutting her toenails in the bathroom and leaving the bits all over the floor."

"One bit, once. Don't exaggerate," Rachel said, without looking up from the stack of homework she was marking. "I missed it. It wasn't deliberate."

"What is that colour anyway?" Suzanne said, staring now at Alison's hand. "It's nauseating. You aren't going to work like that tomorrow?"

"Of course I am," Ali said. "It's the latest thing: Amazon Green."

"Gan Green more like," Suzanne said. "Are you taking sugar or not today, Rache?"

"Yes. No, wait – make that no. I'll try without again." Rachel dieted on and off, though nothing she did seemed to make much difference one way or the other. She was a full-bodied sort of girl: not fat, but no Kate Moss either. Emma thought she worried too much, but Suzanne and Ali were both walking twigs, and Rachel looked at them wistfully when they swapped size eights and passed by the bra department without pausing. She took the mug from Suzanne and sipped it flinchingly. "Ugh! I wish I could get used to the taste."

"You don't persevere, that's your trouble," said Alison, waving her hand about to dry it. "Put two in for me, Suze. Anyway, go on, Em, what's all this about?"

3

Emma, who had been waiting patiently for all the sidetracking to end, passed the copy of the advert round for them to look at.

Suzanne frowned over it. "I'm sure I know that address."

"This Mrs Henderson a mate of yours, then?" Alison asked innocently. She liked baiting Suzanne.

Suzanne rose to it. "No, of course not. You don't think I mix socially with the types who live in Audley Place do you?" She had fiercely left-wing principles, and sometimes had difficulty in squaring them with her job with a top interior designer, where inevitably her customers were drawn from the ranks of the wealthy.

"Perhaps you did a job for her?" Rachel suggested soothingly.

"Maybe," Suzanne said, still frowning. "I'm sure I know the address, but Henderson – no," she shook her head. "It doesn't mean anything to me."

"So you've got nothing against the Hendersons personally?" Emma said.

"I don't need to have," Suzanne said. "You'd be mad to have anything to do with this. Even if it's genuine—"

"Why shouldn't it be?"

"Why should it be! Nobody has governesses nowadays. Nannies or childminders, maybe, for when they're little. Then the kid goes to school. Either there's something wrong with it, or the whole thing's weird. I wouldn't touch it with a bargepole."

"It's probably white slavers, Emma," Rachel remarked conversationally. "They'll drug your tea and whisk you off to the nightclubs of South America."

Suzanne raised her brows. "You think that sort of thing doesn't go on? I could show you an article—"

Alison intervened. Suzanne always had an article on every kind of human exploitation. "Well, anyway, you wouldn't want a live-in job, would you, Em? I mean, it'd make you like a servant. You'd probably get roped in for housework and all that sort of thing. You know how people treat their au pairs."

"And running about after some horrible bratty rich kid," Suzanne put in, "who'll treat you like dirt—"

"Why should she be horrible?" Emma asked, amused.

"Bound to be," Suzanne said briefly.

"I agree with Suze," Alison said. "You'd be no better than a servant."

"Better a servant to one kid than thirty," Emma said. "Whatever this child's like, it can't be as bad as being a class teacher. I've had my fill of that, thank you very much."

Rachel looked up at that point. She and Emma had taught at the same school for three years, but Emma had given in her notice to leave at the end of this term. Neither of them had been physically assaulted yet, but they had endured most other things from the increasingly unruly children. "I know you want a change," Rachel said in her gentle way, "but isn't this a bit drastic? I mean, living in and everything, your time won't be your own. The kid'll be sick in the night and you'll have to change the sheets and all that sort of thing."

"Oh well, that'll be nothing new to me," Emma said lightly. "You forget I had six brothers and sisters. Anyway," she tired of the argument, "this is all a bit previous—I haven't got the job yet. I probably won't even get an interview."

And with that she changed the subject firmly, and a little while later when the conversation had picked up between the other three she slipped out of the room and sought the privacy of her own room.

Each of the girls had a bedroom to herself in the large, shabby flat in Muswell Hill, and they shared the living-room, kitchen and bathroom. The lease was in Rachel's name, but they shared the rent and the bills equally, and on the whole the arrangement worked very well. Of course, they had their quarrels. Suzanne tended to use other people's things without permission; Alison was very bad at clearing up after herself and had to be nagged to do her share of the

5

housework; both of them tended to put upon Rachel, who was mild and gentle and would always sooner clean the bath herself than have an argument with the person whose turn it was; and all three thought Emma was neurotic because she couldn't bear dirt or mess in the kitchen.

But none of the arguments was serious, and the four girls rubbed along happily enough. Emma loved the flat. After her overcrowded childhood, it was paradise to have all this space, a room of her own where no one messed with her things; and after eight raised voices, three constituted peace and quiet to her. There was a big garden out at the back which strictly speaking belonged to the ground floor flat, but in which they were allowed to sunbathe and eat al fresco in the summer. And best of all, there were the wide green spaces and towering trees of the Alexandra Park right on her doorstep, so to speak. She was a Londoner by birth, a real townie, but she liked a bit of nature as much as the next man.

She could see the tops of the trees from her bedroom window, as she sat on her bed and started to prepare the next day's lessons. Her heart wasn't really in it, and she had to struggle to keep her mind from wandering to more enjoyable subjects. So she wasn't too upset at being disturbed when there was a tap on the door and Alison appeared.

"Are you busy? Can I come in?"

"Yes, if you like."

Alison leaned against the chest of drawers and fiddled with things. She was thin and red-haired and rather kooky-looking, given to wild clothes and outlandish makeup. Today she was wearing a leather miniskirt and a sort of sleeveless vest in purple lycra, and her hair stood out round her head in the through-a-hedge-backwards style which was currently fashionable amongst the bright young things. She worked for an very exclusive clothes shop in Bond Street which catered to the 'Daphne's' set, and blackish-green lipstick and nail varnish were nothing out of the ordinary there.

"Did you want something?" Emma asked at last.

"Oh, not really," Alison said, and wandered over to the window. "Did you get the *Guardian* today?"

"Yes, did you want to borrow it?"

"No, I just wondered."

Emma waited patiently. Alison was never direct about anything. She was one of those people who, when you asked if they wanted a cup of tea, would answer, 'Well, are you having one?' Obviously there was something on her mind, but it would take a while to get to.

At last she said, "You know Phil?"

Phil was Ali's boyfriend. "That's a rhetorical question, I take it?"

"Well," Ali went on, "you know Phil works for British Airways? Well, he's got a friend who owns a travel agency."

"Really?" Emma said politely. Alison turned from the window.

"Em, you're not really going to apply for this job, are you?"

"Yes, I really am."

"I wish you wouldn't. I mean, I know you want a change and everything, but — well, why not make a real break, go into something else? I mean, teaching is bad enough, but this job you're talking about — I bet the pay's lousy, and the hours'd be terrible. What you want is a job that'll let you get out and about and meet people."

"And you've got something in mind?"

Alison looked eager. "This friend of Phil's — he's doing awfully well and he wants to take on an assistant."

"In the travel agency?"

"Yes. OK, he might not pay great bucks to start with, but it'd be an opportunity, because when he opens another branch, you'd be in line for manager. Plus you'd get all the cheap travel and holidays."

"And you think he'd take me on?" Emma said drily.

"I know he would, if Phil put in a word. They're great

mates." Alison's eyes pleaded. "Only, if you go for this other thing, you'd be living in, wouldn't you, and you'd leave the flat, and we'd have to get someone else."

"Ah," said Emma significantly.

"Well, that's not the only reason," Alison said indignantly. "We all get along so well, it'd be terrible to break us up. I mean, we'd miss you. And I want you to be happy, do the right thing. Will you think about it at least?"

"I'll think about it," Emma promised. "Thanks, Ali."

Alison idled her way out, and Emma stared out of the window, thinking in surprise that she hadn't realised Alison cared that much.

Only a few minutes later there was another knock on her door, and this time it was Rachel who came in.

"Am I disturbing you?"

"No, it's all right." Rachel came in and stood looking at her, chewing her lip anxiously. "Have you come to reason with me too?"

"Oh dear, I suppose I have. Emma, have you really thought about this? I know it's none of my business, but it's an awfully big step to take. You'll lose your seniority, and then there's the pension and everything. Teaching can be tough, but you've got security, and jobs aren't easy to come by these days."

"It's nice of you to worry about me," Emma said, "but I've given in my notice now."

"Oh, but Mrs Petherbridge would let you withdraw that," Rachel said eagerly. "She was asking me today if I thought you were determined to leave. She doesn't want you to go. I don't either."

"Thanks. But I've thought it out carefully. It wasn't a sudden decision, you know. I really do mean to leave."

"Oh. Well, if you're sure. It was just I didn't think you'd be happy being a governess after teaching at a proper school."

"I haven't got the job yet," Emma pointed out patiently.

"No," Rachel said, brightening. "That's right. You haven't. Well, goodnight, then."

"Goodnight," Emma said, and as the door closed behind Rachel she thought, whatever next?

Emma was the first up next morning, as usual. She was in the kitchen making tea when Suzanne appeared, which was not at all usual: Suzanne did not normally get up until half past eight, and was always last through the bathroom, since she didn't have to be at work until ten most days.

"Hello," Emma said. "Want some tea? It must be a shock to your system seeing the early morning light."

"Don't get smart with me," Suzanne said in mock exasperation. "Because of you I didn't get a wink of sleep last night."

"What, lying awake worrying about my welfare?"

"No, lying awake trying to remember why I knew that address in Mayfair. I just knew it rang a bell, but I couldn't put my finger on it."

"And you've got up at the crack of seven o'clock to tell me that?" Emma laughed.

"I knew if I didn't tell you I'd forget again and it would drive me crazy. It's Akroyd."

"What is?"

"Not Henderson, Akroyd. The people at 3 Audley Place. We did it up just before Christmas, but it was one of Simon's jobs, so I didn't have anything to do with it really, I just heard him talking about it."

"Akroyd, eh?" Emma said.

"You know about Akroyd, don't you?" Suzanne said suspiciously.

"Not a thing."

"Ignorant! Akroyd Engineering. You must have seen the name on motorway bridges."

"Oh, that Akroyd!"

"Yes, and *she*'s Lady Susan Stanley, the Earl of Cheshunt's

9

daughter. So they're rich as Croesus on both sides, I hope you realise." Her voice wavered between triumph and disapproval.

"Look, I haven't got the job yet," Emma said for the nth time. "So who's this Henderson person?"

"Search me. But anyway, at least you can let me know what you think of the house. It was a no-expenses-spared job and Simon raved about it. If you get to see inside, I'd be interested to hear your opinion."

"At last, someone willing to use the word 'if'," Emma laughed.

"I meant 'when' really. They're bound to want to see you," Suzanne corrected herself.

"Oh really? Why?"

"Because you'll be the only person bonkers enough to apply, that's why," Suzanne said, turning round and heading back to bed. "*Governess!* I ask you!" She turned at the door for a parting shot. "And if you get white-slaved, don't come running to me."

"I won't," Emma promised cheerfully.

Chapter Two

It seemed as if Suzanne's cynicism was justified, for Emma received a very prompt reply to her application, asking her to come to Audley Place. The letter was signed by Mrs Henderson and Emma liked the way it was phrased. It didn't sound at all like a job interview.

'I should be glad if you would come and have tea with me at five o'clock next Tuesday. If that should not be convenient, please telephone me, and we'll make another date.'

"Tea!" Suzanne snorted. "How fraightfully naice! What kind of way is that to recruit staff?"

"I don't know," Emma defended, "if you're going to have someone living in your house, it's important that you like them personally. Maybe you'd be more likely to find that out over tea than in an interview situation."

"She still doesn't say who she is," Suzanne went on. "I loathe that kind of inefficiency."

"Maybe she owns the place," Ali said. "Maybe *you* got the name wrong, have you thought of that?"

Suzanne gave her a dark look. "Not likely, is it?" she said, and stalked out.

"I wish you wouldn't tease her," Rachel complained gently. "You know how touchy she is."

"Oh, never mind that," Alison said blithely, "we've got more important things to worry about."

"Such as?"

"Such as what Emma's going to wear to her interview."

11

They both turned to look consideringly at Emma, who immediately felt nervous. "My suit, of course," she said. "What else?"

"Your navy suit?"

"Yes."

"With the red, white and navy scarf, I suppose?" Ali said witheringly.

"What's wrong with that?"

"It makes you look like British Airways ground staff, that's what."

"It was a very good suit," Emma protested feebly.

"When?" Alison asked cruelly.

"It's classic," Emma said. "It never goes out of style."

"True," said Alison. "What was never in can never go out. Why don't you let me lend you something?"

Now Emma laughed. "Have you looked in the mirror? I'd never get into anything of yours, Stick Insect."

Alison looked her over. "True. You are a bit of a Muscle Mary. Well, what can we do with her, Rache?"

"The suit's all right," Rachel said judiciously, "if she had it dry-cleaned. But she needs something better underneath it than a polyester blouse and that old scarf."

Alison's eyes gleamed. "Right, we can soon sort that out. Come up and meet me at work tomorrow and I'll find you something. And you must buy some decent shoes. Shoes are a dead giveaway, you know. If you've got decent leather on your feet, you can get away with murder, clothes-wise."

"Why, you dear old-fashioned thing," Emma smiled. "My grandmother used to say that back in nineteen fifty-five."

"*And* some decent tights," Alison went on firmly, ignoring her. "It's the first thing this Henderson dame will look at, if she's a real Upper."

"Just don't let Suzanne hear you talk like that," Emma warned.

In her room that night when she was getting ready for bed, she paused to study herself in the mirror. It was something she didn't often do. Usually she was rushing to get somewhere, and only glanced to see she was tidy, without really seeing what she looked like. She was accustomed to herself, comfortable with her looks; but now she stared and tried to see what a stranger would see. 'Muscle Mary', Alison had called her teasingly. Well, she did go to the gym twice a week, and she liked to keep fit, but she didn't think she was over-muscled, just nicely trim. And she had curves: she wasn't skinny like Ali and Suzanne, and sometimes beside them she felt practically gross, but in her heart of hearts she wouldn't want to be stick-like, however fashionable it was. She had nice legs, she thought. She would have liked her neck to be a bit longer; and she wished her hair was either dead straight or properly curly, rather than wavy and inclined to go fuzzy in damp weather. But it was a nice colour, what her mother called strawberry-blonde, which meant shades of wheat and barley and honey, naturally sun-streaked, and with threads of pure copper in it which gave it a reddish tinge in certain lights. Her nose was straight enough, her mouth wide, her eyes hazel. She was too used to it to know whether anyone else would find anything beautiful about it. She thought it was a pleasant face rather than a pretty one.

And besides, however much you might admire someone else's looks, you couldn't really imagine yourself looking like them; deep down, you couldn't really want to, because then you wouldn't be you. But she had to admit that clothes looked better on the stick-insects of this world, and there was nothing, she told herself with a sigh, to be done about that.

Audley Place was only a short walk from Marble Arch tube, and for a wonder it neither raining nor windy, so Emma had some hope of arriving looking tidy. She was glad Alison had persuaded her to improve her 'interview outfit'. The blouse she had on under the suit was pure silk crepe, beautifully cut and with a double-stitched collar and cuffs which enclosed her neck and wrists softly and neatly. It gave you, she thought, a sense of confidence to be wearing something that felt as good as it looked. It was the same with the tights: she wouldn't have thought there could be so much difference in a pair of tights, but what she was wearing now was a world away from the usual old Marks and Sparks multipack jobs that she usually wore. Her legs thought all their birthdays had come at once.

The blouse had been horribly expensive, even with the discount Ali had managed to wangle for her, but just at the moment it felt worth it. Ali said that as long as she didn't spill anything on it she could probably take it back the next day: apparently it was called 'unshopping', and lots of people did it. Emma thought it didn't sound honest – and told herself that she could really do with having one decent blouse to wear with the suit on important occasions.

As she advanced into the residential streets of the most expensive real estate in the land, however, some of her confidence began to seep away. There was something *about* Mayfair! The houses looked so immaculate and so private; the little shops were so exclusive; and the further she got from Oxford Street the more select it became. The pavements looked cleaner, the cars more expensive – the very air seemed nicer to breathe. By the time she reached her destination she was feeling quite demoralised.

The red and white house was obviously freshly decorated, the enormous double front door under the pillared porch as glossy as dark water. Emma felt the house was staring at her with those tall dark windows, saying, 'What are you doing here? You're out of your league, girl – go back to Muswell Hill where you belong.'

Drawing her courage up from the toes of her shoes where it had slithered, she walked up the steps and rang the doorbell. She wasn't sure what she expected, but it certainly wasn't to have the door opened by a maid in a black dress and small white apron. A *maid*? She was really stepping out of her sphere.

While she stood trying to gather her scattered wits, the maid smiled pleasantly and helped her out. "Good afternoon – Miss Ruskin, is it? Please come in – Mrs Henderson's expecting you."

Inside the house was cool and dim, and smelled faintly and deliciously of beeswax. The floor was of polished wood, covered in the centre with a Turkish rug; the walls were panelled, and a staircase with a beautiful carved handrail curved upwards ahead of her.

"This way, please." The maid led the way directly upstairs. Underfoot the carpet felt like velvet, the handrail was so deeply polished it felt frictionless – it almost wasn't there at all. Emma was enjoying the sensations of the house so much she had forgotten her nerves, and when the maid opened a door on the first floor and announced, "Miss Ruskin, madam," Emma stepped over the threshold with an expression of confident eagerness which, though she didn't know it, gave her face a most engaging look.

She had only time to note that the room was well-lit from two large, tall windows, draped in voile, and observe the delicate pieces of antique furniture scattered about, before her attention was drawn to the woman seated in an armchair by the fireplace. She stood up with a ready smile, and at the same moment a clock on the mantelpiece chimed silverily.

"Ah, perfect timing! I do like punctuality."

"So do I," Emma said, smiling in response.

"Come and sit down, Miss Ruskin. I'm Mrs Henderson. Yes, you can bring up the tea now, thank you, Pam," she added to the maid, who nodded and went out.

Emma advanced across what felt like an acre of soft carpetings towards the slim, smiling woman, who extended a welcoming hand and took Emma's in a cool, firm grip. Mrs Henderson was probably, Emma thought, in her early forties, but was so exquisitely well-groomed she might have been either older or younger. She was dressed in a cocoa-brown jersey skirt and jacket over a silky blouse of gold-coloured fabric boldly patterned in black. Her dark hair was styled as only a hairdresser can do it and her make-up had been applied by a skilled and subtle hand. She wore no jewellery but an expensive-looking gold wristwatch and a plain gold wedding-band; and, applying the Alison test, Emma noted that her hosiery and shoes were impeccable.

Most of all, Emma noticed that Mrs Henderson *smelled* expensive. The air around her was sweet with the subtle tones of her make-up, her perfume, and the new smells of her clothes and shoes. No matter how scrupulous you were in your personal habits, you never got to smell like that on a teacher's wage and living in a shabby furnished flat in Muswell Hill.

"Do sit down," Mrs Henderson said, seating herself. "Tea will be here in a moment. Five o'clock's rather late for tea, I know, but I thought you probably wouldn't be able to get here earlier, if you were coming after school. What time do you finish?"

"Twenty-five past three," Emma said.

"And did you have far to come?"

"No, my school's only ten minutes from where I live."

"Well, I'm sure you must be ready for something after a long day coping with children. What ages do you teach?"

Emma had sent this information with her application, but she guessed that Mrs Henderson wanted to hear her talk, so she answered the questions easily, aware that she was being discreetly scrutinised by the woman opposite. But she was impressed that Mrs Henderson had arranged the interview so that she didn't have to take time off work, and had guessed she would be an aching hollow by the time she got here. Such thoughtfulness argued kindness, and Emma was comforted by that; and as the conversation advanced and she told her questioner more about herself, she felt that Mrs Henderson liked her, and was glad to have her here.

16

The maid came in with the tea-tray, followed by another bearing a cake-stand. Emma stared, bemused, at the kind of tea she had read about but which had never actually come in her way before: sandwiches cut into symmetrical fingers, hot scones wrapped in a napkin, and on the cake-stand squares of gingerbread, slices of Dundee and Battenburg, and a variety of small cakes.

"How do you like your tea, Miss Ruskin? Will you have a sandwich first, or a scone? A scone? Yes, it seems a shame to let them get cold, doesn't it? And which jam would you like? There's strawberry, raspberry and greengage. The cook makes them, down at Long Hempdon – that's our country place. Mrs Grainger is a cook in the old style, wonderful to say! How she finds time to make jam as well as everything else she does I don't know. We're always terrified she's going to be head-hunted and leave us, but somehow it never happens.'

Emma murmured an appreciative comment, and Mrs Henderson went on, taking over the burden of conversation so that Emma could eat and drink uninterrupted. "Well, I'm sure you'd like to know a little about the family. Mr Akroyd travels a good deal on business – he's Akroyd Engineering, you know – but the family lives permanently at Long Hempdon. That's in Suffolk, not far from Bury St Edmunds. Do you know Suffolk at all?"

"I'm afraid not."

"It's a lovely county. Will you have another scone? They're bought, I'm afraid. This house is really only a pied-a-terre, so we don't keep a full staff here."

"So it's Mr Akroyd who's advertising for a governess?" Emma prompted.

"Yes, for his youngest daughter. Ah, you're wondering how I fit into the picture. I wonder that myself sometimes," she laughed. "I was originally Lady Susan's social secretary – Lady Susan is Mr Akroyd's wife, did I mention that? When the family moved down to Suffolk Lady Susan didn't need a full-time social secretary any more, but over the years I've added various other duties to my repertoire, including dealing with the staff. It's hard to define my position, really – a sort of house-steward, I suppose. I deal with all the things Lady Susan doesn't care to do herself. How is your cup?"

Mrs Henderson plied the teapot again, and then resumed. "The child who needs the governess is the youngest, Arabella. She's very much younger than her brothers and sister. The eldest, Gavin, is twenty-eight – he was the son of the first Mrs Akroyd. Then there's Zara, who's seventeen, the twins Harry and Jack, who are fourteen, and Arabella, who's just ten. They're all Lady Susan's children. So you see Arabella is rather isolated, especially as the boys are away at school."

"Wouldn't it be better for Arabella to go to school?" Emma asked, forgetting for the moment that if the child went to school there would be no job for Emma to apply for.

"Normally I would agree with you," Mrs Henderson said, examining Emma with her bright, curious eyes, which made Emma think of a Persian cat, "but Arabella is rather a special child."

Oh dear, Emma thought, here it comes. Everyone thinks their child is uniquely complex and difficult to understand. 'Highly strung' used to be the phrase – now it was 'sensitive'.

"She's very sensitive and highly strung," Mrs Henderson went on. "She was very unhappy at her last school, and fell far behind in her work, and what with one thing and another ended by making herself ill. What we need for her is someone able to 'cram' her so that she catches up, but that's not all. She needs someone to spend time with her, understand her, love her, and give her back the confidence she has lost."

"Yes, I see," Emma said, though she didn't, quite. What Mrs Henderson seemed to be saying was that Arabella needed a mother, and the question that naturally arose was, why wouldn't Lady Susan do? But she didn't quite know how to ask that. There had seemed some little reserve in Mrs Henderson's manner when she spoke about Lady Susan, which warned Emma not to probe.

After a moment, Mrs Henderson said, "I think I can tell you, Miss Ruskin, that I am looking very favourably on your application. Your qualifications and experience as a teacher are excellent, but more importantly I like you as a person. You come from a large family, and you obviously like children, and you come across to me as warm-hearted, affectionate, and level-headed. I think those are qualities Arabella needs. She's in danger of becoming a 'poor little rich girl' – of substituting material values for human ones. Your background – forgive me – is very different from hers. I think there's a great deal she could gain from you."

There was a silence while Mrs Henderson stared thoughtfully at her clasped hands in her lap, and Emma finished off a piece of Battenburg and wondered what was wrong with the family and whether the 'sensitive' little girl would turn out to be a monster. Then Mrs Henderson spoke again.

"I've painted the picture for you as faithfully as I can. Now tell me, have I put you off?"

Emma said, "No, you haven't put me off. But I have to be honest with you: until I try, I don't know whether I can do any good for the child."

"But you'd like to try?"

"Yes," said Emma. "I'd like to try."

Now Mrs Henderson smiled. "Oh, I am glad! Because I want very much to offer you the job."

Later that evening back at the flat, Emma told the other three about the interview. About the child, she said only that she was ten years old: she didn't want a lecture at this stage about spoilt brats. Alison was impressed with the size of the salary that had been mentioned; Rachel by the friendliness of the reception; Suzanne wanted to know what she thought of the decorating job. But none of them was convinced that it was the right thing for her to do.

"Well," Emma said at last, "it has to be on a trial basis at first, until we see if I like the kid and she likes me. So if it's no good, I've lost nothing. I'm not committed."

"You'll have given up your job," Rachel said unhappily.

"I'd have given that up anyway. Seriously, Rachel, I don't want to go back to school, whatever happens."

"What about the flat?" Alison asked.

"I won't give up my room until after the trial period," Emma said. "I can afford my rent, don't worry. And while I'm away, if you want to use my room for overnight guests now and then, I don't mind. But this is still a bit previous. Mrs Henderson wants me, but I have to meet the rest of the family first."

"And when does that come off?" Suzanne asked.

"I'm going to spend Easter with them, and if we like each other all round, we'll finalise details them. If the worst comes to the worst, I'll have had a weekend in the country, all expenses paid."

"You sound happy," Rachel said. "You're really looking forward to this, aren't you?"

"Yes, I am," Emma said.

"Even the living-in bit?" Suzanne said curiously.

"Oddly enough, especially that. I like the idea of having the child all the time, not just for a few hours a day. If it works out, I can really make a difference."

"You're broody," Alison accused. "I know what it is — it's all a throw-back to Chris, isn't it? Getting so close to being married and then breaking it off. You want a substitute child."

"Shut up, Ali," Rachel said, unusually sharply for her. Emma was looking uncomfortable. It was eight months since she had broken up with Chris, but Rachel knew how much she had been hurt, though she never spoke about it.

But Emma said lightly, "It's all right, there's a grain of

truth in what Ali says, I expect. It'll be quite nice to be a surrogate mother for a bit: at least I can get out of it if I don't like it, which is more than you can do with the real sort." The moment passed. Alison wanted to discuss whether Emma's wardrobe would stand the strain of a weekend in what she insisted on calling a 'stately home', and Suzanne wanted to tell Emma all the ways in which a rich child could be uniquely horrible, and soon they were all outdoing each other in bizarre fantasies about Emma's forthcoming stay in the country which wouldn't have been out of place in an episode of *The Addams Family*.

Later, alone in her room, Emma thought about what Alison had said. She had been very much in love with Chris, the first really serious love of her life. And she had thought he felt the same about her. At first everything had been wonderful: he had wanted to spend every minute with her; had planned a whole future with her; paid her extravagant compliments; told her he loved her a dozen times a day. He had never known anyone like her, he said; she was the embodiment of everything he had ever wanted in a woman.

But then he had changed, had started to blow hot and cold. One day he was wrapping himself in her arms, the next accusing her of stifling him. He began to hedge about getting married, asking what all the rush was. Emma, bewildered, could only stick to what she knew: that she loved him, and thought he loved her, and that if two people loved each other like that, they got married. That was so simple and natural, she couldn't understand what he found difficult about it. But on the day he first said he didn't think he was ready to make a commitment, she felt the iron enter her soul. These days, the word 'commitment' spelt doom to any relationship. It was the buzz-word of the emotionally irresponsible. Bit by bit, he detached himself from her, and in the process, painted her as a monster of possessiveness who had made life impossible for him. In the end, he believed his own propaganda.

21

Having broken off with him, Emma then had to draw back all the tendrils of love and trust she had put out to him, and learn to be without him – or, perhaps more accurately, to do without loving him. She had not been out with anyone since. When she was asked for a date, as she was from time to time, she made excuses. She did not want to go through all that again, and she didn't know, now, if she would ever be able to trust a man again. If she got fond of someone, and he said he loved her, how would she be able to believe him? Better, she thought, to stay single, and safe.

And in that case, going to live in a large house in the country might not be a bad idea, for she would be well out of the way of both harm and temptation. She had wanted a complete break, both from her work, and her social situation, and this job offered both. Some people might call it running away, but to her it looked like a sensible regrouping of her forces.

Chapter Three

Emma was the only person to get off the train, and there was only one person waiting on the platform, so there was no difficulty about their identifying each other. He was a little man like a jockey, in a dark blue suit; walnut-faced, with grey hair slicked back, which had a sort of dent in it all the way round his head, product of years of wearing a hat. So it was no surprise to Emma when he pushed himself off the wall against which he was leaning and said,

"Miss Ruskin, is it? Yeah, I'm the shofer, sent to meet you. Atkins is my name. Is that all your luggage? Right you are, then. Car's outside. This way." Emma was looking about for a ticket collector, but Atkins said, "Nah, don't bovver about that. Most o' these stations are unmanned 'cept in the rush-hour."

She followed him out through a wicket gate and into a narrow, green, damp, overhung lane. He chatted as he walked, as if he knew she needed reassuring. "Keep expecting 'em to close this station altogether, but we hang on by the skin of our teeth. Nearly lost it a few years back, but then our local MP got made a cabinet minister and the line got upgraded. Now we're starting to get commuters from Cambridge moving into the village, so I suppose we're safe. Good thing, too. 'Er ladyship wouldn't like it if they closed us down. She ain't been on a train in twenty years, but she'd have something to say all right. 'Ere's the jalopy."

It was an elderly beige Rolls, vast and stately as a ship, immaculate inside and out. Atkins opened the rear door

23

and the car exhaled the smell of well-tended leather and freshly-cleaned carpets. Emma felt intimidated.

"Um, would you mind if I sat in front with you?" He looked at her, and she added defensively, "I sometimes get carsick in the back."

"Just as you like," he said, as if he knew she was lying, and opened the nearside front door for her and closed it noiselessly after her. He stowed her bag in the boot and then climbed in, picking up his peaked cap from the dashboard and putting it on with a just-audible sigh.

"Don't bother on my account," Emma said.

"Gotter wear me 'at. 'Er ladyship wouldn't like it," he said; but he seemed pleased by her remark, and set the car in motion with a faint smile lurking about his lips.

Emma felt she ought to use the journey to get to know him a bit better. After all, if she got the job, he would be part of her new life. "Is it far to Long Hempdon?" she asked to set the ball rolling.

"Five miles to the gates," Atkins said. "Then another mile to the 'ouse."

"Wow," Emma said, surprised. "It must be a big place. I wasn't expecting anything like that."

"Stately 'ome," Atkins said, and she couldn't tell if the comment was proud or derisive.

"Is it — was it — perhaps it was in the family, Lady Susan's family?" Emma hazarded.

"Nah!" he said robustly. "Guv'nor bought it fifteen year ago, give or take. Dead old, it is — Chooder mostly. *She* don't like it — draughty 'ole she calls it. Wanted a modern 'ouse. But *'e's* dead set on being lord of the manor. Wants 'is son to inherit the family seat and all that sort o' thing. He'll probably get a title from the Government next time round, see — services to industry, get me?" he added with a sidelong wink, "— so 'e reckons 'e might as well have the place to go with it."

"I see," Emma said. He seemed to be being pretty

24

indiscreet, considering she was a stranger, but it was all very revealing and she didn't want him to stop, so she asked, "What's it like, the house?"

"It's all big beams and little winders. All right if you like that sort o' thing," Atkins conceded. "I don't mind a bit of 'istory meself, as long as I've got central 'eating. Of course, we only use one wing. The family what owned it ran out o' money and it stood empty for years, going to rack and ruin. So the guv'nor got it cheap – he loves a bargain – and did one wing up. Going to do the rest up eventually, make it a show place. So he says. I wouldn't 'old me breath."

"And it's got big grounds, you say?"

"Any amount. Park land mostly – not much in the way of a garden. The eldest girl, she rides a lot, or she did before she went to college. Guv'nor always said she could ride all day and never leave her own grounds."

"The eldest girl – that's Zara, isn't it? What's she like?"

"'Oly terror. Like 'er ma."

"Oh," said Emma.

Atkins looked at her sideways, sizing her up. "New to you, all this, ain't it?"

"I've never had a live-in job before."

"It's different," he conceded. "Different way o' life."

She judged there was a gleam of sympathy there for her, so she said, "Tell me what everyone's like?"

Atkins faced forward again. "The Guv'nor's all right. I've known him donkey's years. I used to be a foreman at his first factory, down Chadwell 'Eath way. Then when he started to really make it big, he asked if I'd like to be his driver. I done that for about fifteen years, but it started to play on me 'elf, the long hours and everything, meetings till all hours then 'ome to pick up a bag and straight off to the airport. I got sick and 'ad to pack it in. But it was just about then that the Guv'nor moved down 'ere permanent, so he asked if I'd like to come 'ere as shofer, drive 'er ladyship about and whatnot. Well, it suits me all right. I got me own place and the work's nothing. So 'ere I am."

"It's nice to know that Mr Akroyd rewards loyalty," Emma said.

"Oh, he's all right," Atkins said again. "And 'is son's all right – Gavin – once you get used to 'is little ways. But—" He left the sentence tantalisingly open, and then deflected himself to nod towards the view from the front windscreen. "This is the village now, Hempdon Green. Not much to it, just the church and one pub. Used to 'ave a couple of shops, till they opened the big Tesco's over at Chevington Ash." They passed a village green, and came to a small humped bridge, beside which a road-sign said, 'River Ash'. It was a very small river, hardly more than a trickle, Emma thought.

"Runs into the Kennett," Atkins said. "Used to be fish in there – dace, chubb, pike as long as your arm. Now they got all them new fact'ries outside Bury, there ain't even any water in it. Took it all. No fish now."

"What a shame," Emma said.

They crossed the bridge. "All this is new," Atkins remarked. His mouth turned down. "Commuter-land."

He hardly needed to tell her that, as the last of the old cottages ran out to be replaced by raw-looking houses and bungalows with picture windows and open-plan lawns. And then they were out of the village altogether, and there were green verges and hedges to either side.

"Nearly there now," said Atkins.

Emma realised her chance to get information was running out. "What about the little girl?" she asked anxiously.

"Eh?" said Atkins vaguely.

"The little girl I'm supposed to teach. Arabella, isn't it? What's she like?"

"Poppy," he corrected. "Everybody calls her Poppy, except her ma. Yeah, she's all right. She can be a pain in the neck, like all kids, but there's no real harm in her."

He broke off. "Here's the park gates now," he said, turning the car in.

Emma looked eagerly about her as they drove up the tree-lined road. On either side there was grassland dotted with large trees. My own private Alexandra Park, she thought with an inward smile. At least I won't feel homesick. Then they rounded a curve in the road and the house came into sight. Emma gazed with some awe on the enormous, rambling Tudor mansion, not showing its disrepair at this distance. She felt dwarfed by the size of the house and park and the strangeness of the situation; and even Atkins seemed to have withdrawn into a grave silence, as if his alliance with her could not survive beyond the park gates. An enormous house; a 'her ladyship' who was a holy terror; a 'sort of housekeeper' — Mrs Henderson; a chauffeur and a cook, and so, presumably, other servants. She had never lived in this kind of way, and hadn't the least idea how to behave or what to expect.

Oh well, she thought, I'm only on trial anyway. I probably won't get the job, so what does it matter?

"'Ere you are, then," Atkins said, drawing up in front of some wide, shallow steps up to the front door. "You get out here — I've got to take the motor round the back. Don't worry about your bag — it'll get took up."

Another moment found her standing quite alone before the house and already visualising difficulties. Was she supposed to ring the doorbell or just walk in? How did she address people? Would she count as a servant or one of the family or what? She stood staring at the door and wishing she had never come; and while she was hesitating, the noise of a car's engine which she had been hearing in the background but which, being a Londoner, she had been ignoring, grew rapidly louder. Then a bright red Elan SE sports car shot out of the avenue with a noise like a growling dog, whirled into the open space before the house and screeched to a halt so dramatic that

27

a handful of gravel was sprayed like machine-gun fire over the steps.

The engine was abruptly silenced, the door opened, and the driver extracted himself and strode, long-legged, to where Emma was standing. He eyed her up and down briefly and coldly and said, "I'm sorry but this house is not open to the public. You want Hempworth Manor, about a mile further down the road. That's the National Trust house."

Emma should have felt shrunken and humiliated by this display of cool arrogance, but oddly enough she didn't. She looked up at the extremely handsome young man with interest. She had never in her life seen anyone who looked so like a Gavin, and had no doubt that she was being addressed by the Young Master himself.

He was wearing a tweed sports jacket over a dark blue, open-necked shirt and beige cavalry twill trousers, all very expensive-looking, and showing off his fine figure to perfection. His hair was blonde, thick and springy like a Pantene advert. His skin had a golden tint that she felt was its natural colour, not the result of sun-bathing. His eyes were a vivid blue, the colour picked up and enhanced by the shade of his shirt; his features were exquisitely well-cut, firm and Grecian.

All in all it added up to just about the most handsome man Emma had ever seen, on or off the screen; and, boy, she thought, does he know it! His arrival in that car — and of course, it would be bright red! — with the screech of gravel, told just what sort of a bloke he would be: in love with himself, and expecting every woman to fall for him on sight. But Emma was quite unsmitten. He was so handsome he hardly seemed real, and she was simply enjoying looking at him. In fact, she probably stared at him for longer than was really polite. His nostrils grew a little white, and he said tautly, "I'm sorry, did you want something?"

Emma's sense of humour asserted itself. "Not really," she said. "I was just admiring your front."

He blinked. "I beg your pardon?"

"I've never seen anything quite like it." She paused just one beat and then nodded towards the house. "Your façade. Tudor, isn't it? Very handsome."

She could see he didn't know what to make of her. Tall, handsome, athletic and wealthy, he had probably spent his whole life receiving homage from other people, and being fawned over by young women; the idea that someone could be making fun of him, Emma thought, would throw him.

He seemed to take refuge in icy politeness. "You're Miss Ruskin, I suppose? Have you just arrived?"

"How clever of you to guess." Emma could not help herself, though she knew it was unwise to bait him further. She added hastily, "Atkins just this minute dropped me off. He's taken the car round the back."

"Then perhaps it would be a good idea for you to go inside," he said. "Allow me—" And he strode up the steps and held the front door open for her commandingly. She went meekly up and walked past him into the large, dark panelled hall; and saw, to her relief, that Mrs Henderson was coming down the main staircase towards her.

"Ah, Mrs Henderson, this young lady has just arrived," Gavin greeted her, with a hint of disapproval in his voice.

"I thought I heard the car," said Mrs Henderson with a welcoming smile to Emma. "Did you have a good journey?"

"Yes, thank you," Emma said.

Gavin cut across this impatiently. "Have Atkins put my car away, will you please," he said to Mrs Henderson. "I shan't want it again today."

"Certainly," Mrs Henderson said, and added quickly as he was about to turn away, "Have you been properly introduced, Miss Ruskin? This is Mr Gavin Akroyd. Gavin, Emma Ruskin, who we hope will be Poppy's governess."

29

Gavin inclined his body a fraction from the vertical in Emma's direction, but without meeting her eyes, and then took himself off without another word.

Mrs Henderson didn't seem at all put out by his coolness, and said to Emma, "Now Miss Ruskin, let me show you your room." She led the way up the stairs, chatting as she went about the train journey and the weather and so on. On the first floor she opened a door and said, "We've put you in here for this weekend, but of course if you do come here permanently other arrangements will be made. This is a guest room, you understand."

It was a charming room, beamed and low-ceilinged but quite large, with three leaded windows that looked out over the front of the house. The oak floorboards were wide and darkly-polished, the walls were painted pale primrose, which contrasted pleasantly with the dark wood, and the curtains and bedspread were a darker yellow, which made it all look very springlike.

"What a lovely room," Emma said with sincere pleasure.

"Yes, it is nice, isn't it? You have a fine view, too," Mrs Henderson said, walking over to the windows and pushing one open. It stuck a little, and she laughed. "You'll find out as you learn your way around that everything in the house is slightly skew-wiff — walls, floors and everything. It's impossible to hang a picture straight. But I always think it's part of the charm of an old house like this. And through here," she added, opening a door on the other side of the room, "is your bathroom — something the Tudors didn't have, and which I think is part of the charm of a modern house, don't you?"

Emma agreed. A bathroom to herself — what luxury!

"And now, my dear," said Mrs Henderson, "I expect you'd like to settle in and unpack and so on. Dinner will be at seven-thirty — you'll hear the gong at a quarter past. We'll gather in the drawing-room then for sherry — that's the first door on the right as you reach the bottom of the stairs. Now, is there anything you want before I leave you?"

There were a lot of things Emma wanted to know, but she didn't know how to ask them. It all sounded a little rich for her system – sherry, drawing-room, gong and all. Would it always be like this, or was this a special ceremony for her initiation? She couldn't think of a polite way to put that question, so she asked instead something more urgent.

"Should I change?"

Mrs Henderson eyed her skirt and blouse with understanding. "We don't dress," she said, "but perhaps you'd feel more comfortable in a frock."

Delicately put, Emma thought, and said, "Thanks," with a grateful smile, and Mrs Henderson left her.

At first she amused herself with examining her room. They seemed to have thought of everything for her comfort: a water carafe and glass, a box of tissues on the bedside table, magazines on a table by the window (*Country Life* and *The Lady*) – even a basket of cotton-wool balls on the dressing table. There were even plenty of hangers in the wardrobe; and an en-suite bathroom – just like a luxury hotel! She looked out of each window in turn and admired the view. Then she decided to have a bath, to use up the time until dinner.

In the bathroom she propped up her wristwatch where she could see it so that she shouldn't be late, and then relaxed in the hot water. There seemed to be no shortage of that, thank heaven! She had been afraid that staying in the country might be a bit short on comfort, but the plumbing all seemed to be up to scratch, which was a great relief.

Anyway, here she was, and in a short time she was to meet the rest of the family: her (possible) future charge – and why Poppy, by the way? – and her (possible) future employers. And Gavin. Hmmm. At any rate, it would be nice to have something around that was good to look at, though she hoped he would thaw out a bit, and not keep on

31

frosting her. She liked to be on friendly terms with everyone – but perhaps she shouldn't have begun by teasing him. It probably wasn't what he was used to, and especially not from someone he'd only just met. She reminded herself to be on her best behaviour at dinner – talking of which, it was time she got out of this lovely bath.

Drying herself, she caught sight of her reflection in the mirror, and made a face. "And now," she said aloud, "for the fray!"

Chapter Four

Emma walked across the hall and with a very slight hesitation entered the drawing room. She got the immediate impression of a large number of eyes turning on her; there seemed to have been no conversation going on, and she wondered for a hot and embarrassed moment if she were late and they had all been waiting for her.

But Mrs Henderson came immediately towards her with her hand outstretched, as if anxious to leave her no time to feel out of place. "Ah, Miss Ruskin! Do let me introduce you to everyone. Lady Susan Akroyd, Mr Akroyd, Mr Gavin Akroyd you've already met of course, and this is Arabella. And Miss Akroyd isn't down yet, I'm afraid."

"She's late," Mr Akroyd growled, and then approached Emma with his hand out. "How d'e do, Miss Ruskin. Can I interest you in a drink?" He took her hand in a hard grip and pumped it economically once up and once down, as if that was all he allowed. He was a short, stout man with the red face of a person who does himself well, but his expensive suiting and hair-dressing rendered the shortness and stoutness acceptable. There was perhaps a trace of Gavin's good looks in there somewhere, but they were spoiled by lines of bad temper or discontent. He was smiling at the moment, but it seemed a perfunctory smile, and his voice was harsh. He had a marked Lancashire accent which she somehow hadn't expected.

"Oh, yes, thank you," Emma began, but without waiting for anything further Mr Akroyd turned away saying,

"Sherry?" as he poured it out from a decanter on a small table. He put the glass into her hand with an air of having done all that was necessary, and retired to the other side of the room with his own glass, which was a heavy, short tumbler which obviously contained a large and undiluted whisky.

Emma wondered whether she ought to shake hands with Lady Susan, but being at a distance from that lady she needed some encouragement to cross what looked like a hundred yards of thick, soft carpeting. Encouragement was not forthcoming. Lady Susan, splendidly attired in a dress of blue silk and three rows of pearls, had not glanced at her. She was looking at her husband now with an expression of lofty tedium. Her style of clothes, hair and make-up made her look of an age with her husband, but stealing a sidelong look at her face, Emma thought she was probably quite a bit younger. Under the makeup she had classical features, but there was no animation in her face to make them beautiful.

Gavin was standing by the fireplace with a sherry glass in his hand, and his expression was only a little less unwelcoming than his step-mother's, though he had looked in her direction and bowed his head slightly when Mrs Henderson had performed the introductions. Now he stood broodingly, looking into the middle distance as if posing for a sculptor.

But there was someone else in the room who interested Emma more at the moment. The little girl had her eyes fixed on Emma's face with an expression of intensity, and so it was to her she went, holding out her hand and saying "How do you do," aiming for a manner that was friendly without being patronising.

The child took her hand after a moment's hesitation, seeming pleased with the grown-up attention. She was very small and thin for her age, and would have been pretty if it were not for the drawn look about her face, as if she had been ill for a long time. Her skin was transparently fair, which showed up the dark shadows under her eyes; her hair was almost white-blonde, thin and fine and straight, and flat to her head. The hand Emma took in hers was damp, and the nails were bitten to the quick, but there was a little dab of pale pink nail-varnish on what bit of the nails remained.

Emma smiled down at her with a sudden piercing sympathy. "I'm very glad to meet you," she said, and meant it.

The little girl said abruptly, "I don't usually stay down for dinner. It's only because of you coming."

"Oh, well, then, I'm honoured," Emma said.

Unsmilingly, Arabella went on, "Zara said she didn't see why she had to eat now just because you were coming. That's why she's late. She wanted to have her dinner in her room and watch television."

Gavin said sharply, "Don't tell tales, Poppy."

Mr Akroyd coughed. "You'll find our Poppy a bit outspoken," he said, but it was not in apology. He looked at Emma defiantly to see what she'd say.

"Truthfulness is a good quality," Emma said, diplomatically.

"Hmm," he said, still staring at her. "Well, there's truth in what Poppy says. We don't often eat together when it's just family, but Mrs H thought it'd be the best way for us all to have a look at you."

"That wasn't quite how I put it," Mrs Henderson protested laughingly.

"Aye, well, that's what it came down to," Mr Akroyd said indifferently. "So if we're going to do it, let's get it over with. Gavin, ring the bell and let's go in."

"Surely we are to wait for Zara?" Lady Susan said. It was the first time she had spoken, and her voice was light and faint, but the disapproval was quite clear in it.

"Zara can damn well be on time, or go without," Mr Akroyd said. "I'm not waiting *my* grub for her." And he strode across the room and flung open the doors to the dining-room. Emma thought she saw where Gavin got his assumption of superiority from. Mr Akroyd disappeared into the dining-room, but no one else had moved, and Emma felt very awkward, and didn't know if she was supposed to do anything or not. Mrs Henderson stepped in, smoothing things over, which Emma was beginning to gather was her main role in the household.

"Yes, well, it is half past, so I think we should go in, don't you? Gavin, won't you escort Miss Ruskin? Lady Susan, shall we go in? Come along, Poppy."

They passed through into the dining-room, which was dominated by a long mahogany table which would have seated twenty without a squash. It was laid now for seven, which meant that once seated they were so well spaced out that conversation was almost ruled out. Mr Akroyd was already seated at one end, and as Emma came in with Gavin walking stiffly at her side he called out, "Come on then, Miss – er – Whatsname, come and sit down here. Poppy, you plonk yourself down there opposite, then you can size each other up."

Gavin pulled out the indicated chair for her and Emma sat. She was on Mr Akroyd's left; the little girl took the chair opposite, on his right. Gavin then went to pull out the chair at the other end of the table for Lady Susan; Mrs Henderson sat on her left, and Gavin then took the chair next to Emma. Two maids came in to serve the soup, and the first deadly silence fell.

Even before everyone was served, Mr Akroyd had taken the first mouthful of soup. Then he paused with his spoon half way to the bowl and looked round the table; and, as if deciding that something was required of him, he said to Emma, "Well then, Miss – er – I suppose you want to tell us all about yourself. That's what all this fedaddle is about." Emma hardly knew how to reply, but he didn't wait for an answer. Instead he caught at the maid's arm as she passed him on her way out and said explosively, "Where is that girl? Julie, go up to Miss Zara's

36

room and tell her to come down right this minute, d'you understand?"

"Yes, sir," the maid said, and left the room hurriedly.

"Now then, where was I? Oh yes, tell us about yourself, Miss – er," Mr Akroyd went on, filling his mouth again.

"Herbert, must we talk business over dinner?" Lady Susan said severely from the other end of the table.

"Well, I don't know when else you think I'll get to see the girl," Mr Akroyd said, and put down his spoon with a gesture of exasperation. "In any case, I don't see why we have to have this fuss and nonsense. If Jean says she's all right, that's good enough for me."

"I'm glad to know you have such faith in my judgement," Mrs Henderson said, "but—"

"Right, then," Mr Akroyd interrupted. "Just ask this Miss Whatsname if she wants the job and be done with it."

"Ruskin!" said Gavin explosively, glaring at his father. "Her name is Miss Ruskin!"

Emma glanced sideways and saw his nostrils flare and a spot of colour appear in his cheeks. He was not leaping to her defence, Emma decided: he was angry and embarrassed by his father's rudeness.

"Whatever her damned name is, it's women's business to vet her, not mine. You just get on with asking what you want to ask and leave me out of it." And with that he attacked his soup again and had nothing more to say.

Lady Susan was ignoring the whole thing: she might have been alone in the universe, let alone at the dinner table. Arabella was moving her spoon about aimlessly in her soup, looking down at her plate with an air of withdrawn misery. Gavin and Mrs Henderson met each other's eyes across the table.

"Miss Ruskin has been teaching in a state school," Mrs Henderson said brightly and conversationally.

Gavin caught the ball from her. "That must have been

37

interesting," he said, turning to Emma. "What age group did you teach?"

"Middle school," Emma answered. "Tens to fourteens."

"I should think that must be very hard work," said Mrs Henderson.

"It is," Emma said.

"And demanding," Gavin added, looking at Mrs Henderson: *your turn.*

"But interesting," she said desperately. Lady Susan and Mr Akroyd continued to ignore everything.

Emma was wondering, half appalled, half amused, how they had ever got together in the first place, they seemed so ill-suited. She thought it was time she made a contribution, and said to the little girl, "I understand you are always called Poppy – why is that?"

She looked up briefly, and then down again. "Daddy called me it when I was little," she said in a small, embarrassed voice. "I don't like Arabella, so he said I didn't have to be it."

"Where the devil is that girl?" Mr Akroyd said suddenly, finishing his soup and slamming the spoon down in the empty bowl. It was impossible to tell if he had been listening or not. "Jean, ring the bell, will you? If she thinks she can just—"

At that moment the door opened and the missing member of the family walked in. She was slim and blonde, and would have been pretty except that her face was set in lines of sulky discontent. She had evidently taken a great deal of care over her appearance, which surprised Emma a little, given what Arabella had said about her not wanting to come down at all. She was wearing a very smart black evening skirt and pink lurex top, and her make-up was extremely elaborate for a family dinner. Was it possible, Emma thought, that she was trying to impress her? But why should she care what a potential governess thought?

"And where the hell have you been? You're late!" Mr Akroyd bellowed.

"I know," she said pertly, giving a defiant stare to Gavin, who was looking at her. She flounced in, sliding her eyes sidelong at her mother, who paid her no attention.

"Well, you'll get no soup now," Mr Akroyd said. "I'm not waiting for you."

"Good," she said. "I hate soup." And deliberately ignoring Emma, she walked round the table and sat down.

"Zara, this is Miss Ruskin," Mrs Henderson said, still trying to hold the evening together.

"Yes, I know," Zara said with elaborate indifference, shaking out her napkin. Emma, who had been prepared to say how do you do and be pleasant, subsided with amused despair. Was there no one with normal social manners in this household? Just then the maids returned to clear the soup plates and put on the second course, so there was an excuse for no one to speak for a while. Emma saw that Poppy had eaten nothing so far but a small piece of bread, and when she was served with a chicken breast in mushroom sauce she looked at it with something like despair. Had she been ill, Emma wondered? As soon as possible she must get Mrs Henderson alone and find out what was wrong with the child. But then she remembered she hadn't got the job yet.

With the chicken there were new potatoes, young carrots and asparagus: a simple, well-cooked meal. Emma was quite happy just to eat: she'd only had a sandwich for lunch and she was very hungry. Mrs Henderson seemed to have given up trying to make conversation for the moment, and Gavin was eating with savage concentration, his brows drawn down in a forbidding frown, while Zara was eating with elaborate unconcern. Emma looked at Poppy. She had made a pretence of cutting up her meat and was pushing it round the plate unhappily. She cut a small piece of potato and forked it to her lips, but then let it fall off back onto the plate. At that moment she caught Emma's eyes on her; Emma smiled wryly – *that'll get you nowhere, you know* – and the child suddenly blushed guiltily.

"Now Miss Ruskin's here, can I go riding again?" she asked, as if to distract attention. She added quickly to Emma, "I haven't been for ages because there was no one to take me and I'm not supposed to go out on my own."

Emma could not ignore such a plea for help. "Do you have your own pony?" she asked.

The pinched face lightened a little. "Yes, he's called Misty and he's white—"

"You mean he's a grey," Zara said witheringly. "You don't talk about *white* horses – you ought to know that at your age."

Poppy's face reddened. "I don't care. I shall call him white because he *is* white," she said defiantly.

"Well, you'll just show your ignorance, then," Zara said. "Anyway, I don't suppose for a minute she can ride," she added, with a flick of a glance in Emma's direction. "Why should she, where she comes from?"

Poppy turned an eager gaze on Emma. "You can, can't you? I bet you can."

"I did learn to ride when I was a child, but I haven't done it for ages. Still, I don't suppose it's something you forget, is it?"

"Where did you learn?" Mrs Henderson asked, hoping to keep the conversation polite.

"In Epping Forest. I had a course of lessons at a riding school when I was about twelve."

"I knew you could," Poppy said gratefully. "So I can go riding again, can't I? She can come with me?" She looked from mother to father, neither of whom was listening, and then appealed to Mrs Henderson. "Can't I?"

Zara jumped in sharply. "And what do you think she's

going to ride? I hope you don't think she's going to ride *my* horse?"

"Well, why not?" Poppy said defiantly.

"Don't be ridiculous. She couldn't manage him. Besides, I might want him."

"But you haven't taken him out for weeks."

"She couldn't possibly ride well enough. I'm not having Barbary's mouth ruined by a beginner."

Emma raised her eyebrows at this unprovoked rudeness, but she said peaceably, "Perhaps I could come with you on a bicycle?"

Zara addressed her directly for the first time. "We haven't got any bikes," she said with childish triumph.

"I'll *buy* a bloody bike!" Mr Akroyd bellowed suddenly, making everyone jump, and Lady Susan drew an audible breath of disapproval. He glared up and down the table. "Now let's have an end to this bloody yattering and arguing! You're like a pack of hyenas, the lot of you! Julie, clear these plates away."

The table was cleared and Emma found herself being offered a choice between raspberry sorbet and chocolate pudding. She was about to ask for sorbet when Zara said loudly, "Good heavens, the sorbet, of course. The pudding's kid's stuff. It's only meant for Poppy."

Some devil in Emma made her say to the maid who was hovering by her, "Chocolate pudding for me, please. I love all pudding, but chocolate's my favourite." The maid served her with, Emma could have sworn, a smile hovering about her lips.

"Good lord, how vulgar," Zara said, staring down the table at Emma's plate.

And immediately Gavin said, "I'll have the pudding as well, please."

"But you never eat pudding!" Zara cried, as though cheated.

"I can change, can't I?" Gavin said.

41

"You haven't changed. You don't like pudding," Zara insisted suicidally.

"Then I must have some other reason. I leave it to you to decide what it might be," Gavin said.

He levelled a very frosty look at his half-sister. Her cheeks reddened, and she opened her mouth to retort, but Mr Akroyd looked up from his plate and said, "If anyone else says the word 'pudding', they go out of this room. It's like a bloody madhouse in here tonight."

In the silence which followed Emma realised that Lady Susan at the other end of the table had not yet announced her choice, and for a breathless, almost hysterical moment she imagined what would happen if her ladyship opted for the chocolate pud. But of course she did nothing so vulgar. She merely waved the maid away and snipped herself some grapes off the elaborate stand of fruit which decorated the table.

The meal soon came to its close; they all filed through to the drawing-room for coffee, and Emma wondered how soon she could escape to her room. The Family From Hell, she thought to herself: the scenes over dinner had been so grisly it was almost funny. Mr Akroyd evidently felt he had done enough of the polite, for he bolted his coffee and with a muttered excuse hurried out of the room. Zara went over to the hi-fi in the corner and began fiddling about with CDs, looking for something to put on – presumably something that would annoy as many people as possible, Emma thought.

Lady Susan, having received her coffee, suddenly looked towards, though not at, Emma, and said, "Do you hunt, Miss Ruskin?"

Emma couldn't help herself. "Hunt what?"

Zara turned and threw a contemptuous look in Emma's direction. "Oh my God," she muttered sneeringly.

But Emma had no desire to join the tribal rite of rudeness, so she corrected her reply hastily to, "No, I'm afraid not. I've never had the chance."

Lady Susan digested this without emotion. She tried again. "Are you by any chance related to the Norfolk Ruskins?"

"I'm afraid I don't know," Emma said. "My father came from Hoxton. That's where I was born."

"Hoxton?" Lady Susan enquired with a vague frown. "And where—?"

"It's in the east end of London," Emma told her. Lady Susan's eyes widened slightly as if she had said something indecent, and then she turned her head away and began talking to Mrs Henderson in a low voice. Snubbed again, Emma thought. She was growing almost merry on discomfiture, as though it was intoxicating.

And then suddenly Gavin was by her side, sitting, coffee cup in hand, on the sofa beside her and saying politely, "I wonder, Miss Ruskin, if you would care to come to church with us tomorrow morning? The car will hold one more. We go to the parish church in the village, and it's always rather a nice service on Easter Day."

"Yes, thank you, I'd love to," Emma said, glad of a kind word at last.

"Are you a churchgoer?"

"Well, I'm C of E as far as I'm anything, but I haven't been for years," Emma said. "I don't think people do, much, in London."

"What has London got to do with it?"

"Oh, I don't know – it's just a different sort of life from the country, isn't it? I mean, in a village, the church is part of the way of life. You don't have that sort of community in London."

"And do you think that's a sufficient reason for going to church?" he asked. She couldn't tell if he were disapproving or not.

"Everyone has to work that out for themselves," she said. "I shall enjoy the singing and the atmosphere – that will be reason enough for me to go."

"You're very straightforward, aren't you?" he said, but again, neutrally.

"I try to be. It saves a lot of time and confusion," she said. "But isn't bluntness an Akroyd trait? So your father was saying, anyway."

He didn't answer that, only looked at her with a faint, speculative frown. Blotted my copybook again, she thought. Oh, the hell with it!

They were interrupted by Mrs Henderson. "I think it's time Poppy was in bed now," she said, standing up. "You look rather tired too, Miss Ruskin," she added, giving Emma the chance to escape. Emma took it gratefully, and said goodnight all round. Zara and Lady Susan did not respond, but Gavin stood up politely and said, "Breakfast for churchgoers is at eight. Please let Mrs Henderson know what time you'd like to be called and she'll arrange it."

"Thank you," Emma said, and followed Mrs Henderson and Poppy out of the room. At the first floor their ways parted. Emma looked down at the little girl's peaky face and said, "Goodnight, then, Poppy – may I call you Poppy?"

Poppy nodded. "Will you still be here tomorrow?" she asked.

"Yes, of course. Didn't you hear me say I'll be coming to church?"

"Yes, but people say things," she said cryptically, "and then they don't do them."

"I will certainly be here tomorrow. I'll see you at breakfast."

Poppy regarded her face seriously for a moment, and then nodded again, with satisfaction, though unsmiling. "G'night then."

Alone in her room, Emma could not immediately settle. She paced up and down, going over the evening in her head and trying to sort out the impressions of this most unfamilial family. What a bunch of charmers! she thought. You'd have to be mad to want to be part of this set-up.

Then she thought of the pale and miserable child making circles with her spoon in her soup. No one seemed to care for her, she thought; and she felt a fierce longing to make things right for her. But she had probably blown her chances of the job. She'd be on her way on Monday evening with a flea in her ear – if they didn't throw her out tomorrow.

There was a tap on the door of her room, and she went to open it, and found Mrs Henderson standing without, looking embarrassed. "Oh Miss Ruskin, I'm glad you're still up," she said in a rush, as though she wanted to get it over with. This is it, thought Emma. She's going to ask me to pack my bags. "I – I do hope you didn't get too bad an impression of us," Mrs Henderson said. She laughed nervously. "I'm afraid it wasn't the most convivial of evenings."

"Oh, no, really," Emma began, trying to find a polite response. "I – er – the dinner was very nice."

Mrs Henderson hurried on. "The thing is, Poppy really took to you. She was talking about you while we were walking upstairs, and she was quite excited at the idea of having you for her governess. And the poor child really does need someone of her own. I do hope – I mean, I suppose – have you come to any conclusions about the job?"

"I didn't think I needed to," Emma said. "I was sure I wouldn't be offered it. I didn't make much of an impression on Lady Susan."

"Oh, I shouldn't worry about that, if I were you," Mrs Henderson said. "Lady Susan won't really trouble herself about it, and you heard Mr Akroyd say that he would abide by my decision. It's Gavin who will really have the final say."

Emma was so surprised by that she didn't manage to ask why. Mrs Henderson hurried on. "If you were to be offered the job, would you still consider it?"

"Oh yes," Emma said, "I'd certainly consider it." She surprised herself a little with how firmly it came out.

"I'm glad," said Mrs Henderson, and said goodnight and turned away and left her.

Chapter Five

After the emotional turmoil of the evening before, Emma slept badly, and woke with the frightening sense of someone being in the room. A moment later the curtains were drawn back with a sound which, in her state of half-wakefulness, was like the ripping of metal foil. It made her sit up with a gasp of shock.

"Oh, sorry miss, did I frighten you?" It was a young woman, a stranger. Emma stared at her blankly, hardly knowing where she was. "It's half past seven. I've brought you some tea."

"Oh! Yes, thank you." Reality slowly tuned in. She was at Long Hempdon, and she was being woken up by a maid. Imagine! With memories of old books she had a sudden horrible doubt whether the maid would want to lay out her clothes, but she only smiled and went out, closing the door soundlessly behind her. Emma reached for the tea and sipped gratefully. Outside the sun was shining, and several thousand birds seemed to be cheeping and whistling and chirruping in satisfaction over the fact. It was a far cry from Muswell Hill, where the birds had to compete with the traffic noise.

"Why did I ever live in town?" she asked herself as she jumped out of bed and headed (oh sinful luxury!) for her own private bathroom, which would not have any of Ali's tights dripping from the shower-rail, or Suzanne's talcum powder coating every surface.

When she reached the breakfast table she found Mrs Henderson, Gavin and Poppy already seated and eating.

Gavin was reading the business section of the *Sunday Times*, and Mrs Henderson was listening to Poppy who was describing the Easter eggs she had found at her bedside when she woke.

"I've eaten two Rolo mini-eggs already, and a whole Buttons egg *and* the buttons, and half a Cadbury's creme egg," Poppy was saying as Emma came in. "It's nearly as good at Easter as it is at Christmas!"

"You'll be sick, you little horror," said Gavin without looking up from the paper.

"I'm never sick with chocolate, only with dinner and spinach and liver and things like that," Poppy said.

"Good morning, Miss Ruskin. Did you sleep well?" Mrs Henderson noticed her at that point. With a friendly nod she indicated the empty place beside Gavin.

"Yes, thank you," Emma said, taking the seat, and wondered why people always asked that and why you always lied when you hadn't slept well. Gavin only flicked a glance at her and returned to the paper, as though determined not to notice her; Poppy gave her a shy smile and concentrated on pushing her spoon into her boiled egg without letting the yolk spill over.

"Can I pour you some coffee?" Mrs Henderson offered.

"Yes, thank you." Emma felt it was up to her to make some polite conversation. "Isn't it a lovely day? I was thinking when I woke up how nice it is to be in the country on a day like this."

She thought that must be unexceptionable, and Mrs Henderson smiled and seemed about to make some polite reply, but Gavin folded his paper to a new page with a great deal of rattling and said coolly, "I'm afraid your reading of the weather signs is not quite accurate, Miss Ruskin. We will certainly be having rain in an hour or two."

"Oh, surely not," Emma protested brightly, deciding he was just being perverse. "With that blue sky and those pretty white clouds—"

48

"A sky that colour is not to be trusted at this time of year," he said without even looking at her, "and those pretty clouds are from the west, which always means rain."

"Perhaps Miss Ruskin doesn't have much opportunity to study the weather, living in London," Mrs Henderson said soothingly.

Gavin looked at her with a raised eyebrow. "Are you trying to suggest that they don't *have* weather in London?"

Mrs Henderson frowned at him, and Emma said cheerfully, "I don't even know which way west is." If they wanted her to be an ignorant townie, then she would act up to them.

Poppy looked shocked. "Oh, but you must know that! East is where the sun rises and west is where it goes down. Everybody knows that. I've known that since I was *born*, nearly!"

"I only know east from west on a tube map," Emma said.

"What's a tube map?" Poppy asked blankly.

"There you are, you see, even you don't know everything," Mrs Henderson said to Poppy reprovingly. "You may be at home in the country but you'd be lost in London. Do you like a cooked breakfast, Miss Ruskin?" she hurried on, as if determined to change the subject. "I'll ring if you would like bacon and eggs or anything of the sort."

Emma was going to say no, rather than be any trouble, but sensing that Gavin was looking at her, waiting for her answer, she decided, what the hell, she'd be as much trouble as possible and enjoy herself. If he was going to disapprove of her anyway, she might as well get something out of the weekend.

"Yes, please. I like to breakfast in style on a Sunday. I don't generally have time on school days for more than a piece of toast."

The breakfast was excellent, and Emma wolfed everything, while Gavin worked his way through the paper, Mrs

Henderson described the architecture of the local church, and Poppy wriggled with boredom. Emma was happily crunching toast and marmalade when the door opened and Zara came in.

"Morning. Not too late, am I?" she said, dropping into the seat beside Poppy, who was staring at her with unconcealed amazement.

"Too late? No, of course not," Mrs Henderson said, seeming a little surprised herself. "Shall I ring? Would you like something hot?"

"Good God, no!" Zara exclaimed with a theatrical shudder. "What kind of person d'you think eats all that bacon and eggs muck these days? Just shove me over a piece of toast, will you?"

"I'd happily shove you over the nearest cliff," Gavin said, glaring at her over the News Review section. "What are you doing down at this time of the morning, anyway?"

Zara looked defiantly at him. "I'm coming to church with you, of course. It *is* Easter."

"Oh Zara, you never go to church," Poppy said reproachfully. "When Gavin got cross with you last time, at Christmas, you said it was boring and stupid, and he said well then there was no point in you going if you felt like that, and you said—"

"Shut up, nobody asked you," Zara said quickly.

"Maybe they didn't, but she has a point," Gavin said. "Why the sudden change of mind?"

Under his steady scrutiny Zara coloured a little. "What does it matter why I've changed my mind? I have, that's all. Anyway, you're always so holy about it, you ought to be glad I want to come."

"Yes, well, normally I would rejoice over the return of a sinner to the fold," Gavin said drily, "but you know perfectly well Dad's gone out in the Mercedes and Atkins has taken the Rolls over to Cold Ashford. We're going in Mrs H's Mini, and that only takes four."

"Well, that's all right," Zara said, concentrating on buttering her toast, "Miss Whatsername can stay at home. I don't suppose she really wants to go. She said last night that she never does normally."

Poppy opened her mouth to point out the illogic, but Gavin spoke first. "The fact remains that there are only three spaces in the car," he said calmly, "and Miss Ruskin laid her claim first."

"Laid her claim? What on earth are you talking about?" Zara said scornfully. "Last night she said she wanted to go because there was a spare place in the car. Now there isn't a spare place in the car, she can stay at home. What's all the fuss about?"

There was a brief silence while Emma wondered what she had done to earn this resentment from a girl she barely knew, and struggled against the urge to say she would stay home, just to avoid more argument. Gavin began to fold up his newspaper with an air of finality.

"There's no fuss at all. If you really want to go, you can go in the Mini with Mrs H and Poppy, and I'll take Miss Ruskin in my car."

He pushed back his chair and walked briskly from the room before anything more could be said. As he passed Emma's chair she saw the tightly compressed lips and frown of annoyance, and thought, with a sinking heart, what a jolly drive they would have of it. Though it was Zara's doing, he was bound to blame her for the disturbance of his peaceful breakfast and the nuisance of having to take two cars. She had not made a good impression on this family so far – but, really, who could have?

Zara had the grace to look a little subdued at her brother's exit, but Poppy was wide-eyed and garrulous. "Oh, it's not fair! Oh, you lucky thing! I've been asking Gavin for ages to drive me in his car but he won't take me. He drives ever so fast, and Mummy says he'll kill himself one of these days, but I bet he won't."

"Shut up, Poppy," Zara growled.

"Well, he won't," she said defiantly. "Daddy says no son of *his* is a bad driver, and he's had the Elan a year and never got a scratch on it, so he must be good, because the Mini's got dents all over, and Daddy says that's because of Mrs H touch-parking. What's touch-parking?"

"Poppy, stop gabbling and drink your milk," Mrs Henderson said, catching Emma's eye and suppressing a laugh.

Poppy stuck out her lip. "I don't like milk. Why can't I have tea?"

"Because milk's better for you," Mrs Henderson said with the weary air of one who has covered this ground before. Emma noticed that very little of the boiled egg had gone down Poppy's throat, and wondered whether it was because of all the chocolate eggs, or from the same cause as last night's uneaten dinner. But Poppy was gathering herself for an argument, and Emma thought she ought not to be there to witness it, in case it turned Poppy against her as well.

"I think I'll go and tidy up, if you'll excuse me," she said, and fled the fractured family with as much dignity as she could muster.

Her forecast of the journey to church was right: Gavin drove in grim silence, his eyes never straying from the road ahead, as if he was determined to get this tiresome task over with. Emma's sense of mischief roused itself. She *would* make him talk! She began to ask him questions about anything that came into her mind: what are those birds over there? Oh, I see, and what's the difference between a rook and a crow? And is a west wind one that blows from the west or to the west? And what sort of trees are those?

Gavin answered her as abruptly as possible, until she over-reached herself and asked what were those flowers, pointing at random and happening to alight on a verge full of blowing yellow trumpets.

"Daffodils," he said shortly, glancing at her sidelong.

52

"I suppose you want to tell me you don't have those in London."

"Oh, but you see," Emma said brightly, "country daffodils are so much bigger than town daffodils."

A flush spread across Gavin's beautiful cheekbones, and his eyes were fixed on the road again. "I don't know what sort of game you think you're playing, but I suppose you think it's clever to amuse yourself at others' expense. We may live in the country, but we're not exactly stupid, you know."

"I didn't think you were," Emma said, half contrite, half annoyed. "It was just a joke."

"Oh, a joke, was it?" Gavin swung the car backwards into a space alongside the churchyard wall. "Pardon me, but I thought the point of a joke was that it was supposed to be funny."

Emma's contrition died the death. What a pompous prig, she thought. He got out of the car without another word and came round to her side to let her out. No one is at their best struggling up from the low seat of a sports car, but she would not take advantage of his offered hand. She extricated herself with as much dignity as she could muster, waited while he put the hood up on his car, and then walked ahead of him into the church. They sat side by side on a pew near the front, waiting for the others to arrive, while the organist played a voluntary; and she resolved she would not bother to talk to him again unless she had to. The whole weekend was a disaster, and if it really was Gavin who had the final say, she obviously wasn't going to get the job.

But the church was very beautiful, and it was Easter Sunday after all, and she felt she ought not to be sitting here in this resentful frame, so she cleared her mind of all negative thoughts and concentrated on enjoying the sights and sounds around her. Out of the corner of her eye she saw Gavin glancing at her out of the corner of his, and

53

wondered whether he was sorry he had made so much fuss. Well, she wouldn't give him the satisfaction! But no, that was negative again. She composed her expression and looked at him, ready to be friendly, but he was looking straight forward again and would not meet her eye, so she shrugged inwardly and dropped it.

When they came out of the church after the service, Emma found to her surprise and annoyance that Gavin had been right about the weather. His prophecy had been fulfilled. The whole sky had clouded over, and the rain was just beginning, driven in large scattered drops by a brisk wind – a west wind, presumably, she thought sourly.

"Oh blast," Poppy said. "I wanted to show you the stables and my favourite ride this afternoon."

"It's going to tip down any minute. It's a good job I put the hood up," Gavin said pointedly; but Emma thought he was entitled to an *I told you so* and that this was a pretty restrained one in the circumstances.

"We're holding up the traffic standing here," Mrs Henderson said, coming up behind them in the porch. "I think we ought to get moving. Where's Zara?" She was lingering behind talking to a friend. "Poppy, go and ask her to come along, would you?"

Zara came up to them with two other girls of her own age, both pretty and smartly dressed, and with eyes that seemed drawn to Gavin like pins to a magnet, no matter who they were addressing. Well, it was natural, Emma thought. He was extremely easy on the eye.

"Natalie and Victoria are coming back with us for lunch," Zara announced brightly as she reached the group.

"It's awfully nice of you to invite us," Natalie said. "It's awful at home on Sunday afternoons, isn't it, Vic?"

"Awful," Victoria agreed, gazing at Gavin. "It's much nicer at your house, Zara."

"Well, I'm afraid you'll have to wait here until I come

54

back and fetch you," Gavin said. "The Mini will only hold four."

"Oh, now, Gavin, don't be stuffy," Zara said at once, petulantly. "What's the point in making two people wait instead of one?"

"And which one had you in mind?" he asked grimly. "Yourself, I suppose?"

"Don't be silly, I haven't got a coat. Besides, I have to go with Nat and Vic, they're my guests. You can take Poppy back in your car and Mrs H can drive us girls, and Miss Ruskin can wait here. She'll be quite all right under the porch," she added hastily as Gavin's brows drew down alarmingly.

"You know perfectly well your mother doesn't want Poppy to ride in my car," he said. Emma felt a surge of impatience. For heaven's sake, doesn't this family do anything but argue? She was tired of being discussed like an inanimate object.

"It's all right, I can walk home," she said. "I need some fresh air. And I'd like to see a bit of the countryside."

"No, you wait here and I'll come back for you," Gavin said, accepting the inevitable.

"There's no need—"

"I said, I'll come back for you. It's raining and it's colder than you think, and you don't know the way. Please don't argue!" he added wearily as she opened her mouth to protest again, and she shrugged and closed it again. Gavin seized Zara's arm and was hurrying her towards the car, and the others followed, keeping well enough back not to hear what he might be saying to her. Emma waited until they had gone, and then started to walk, as she had always intended to. She wasn't going to be told what to do, especially not by God's Gift to Women. It wasn't very far, and it was a straight road. It wasn't as if she could get lost.

Maddeningly, Gavin was right about the cold. Emma had

55

only been walking a few minutes when she realised it, and was sorry she had started to walk. It would have been better to stay in the church porch and be picked up. But no, she had to be pig-headed and prove that a Londoner was equal to a little weather and a few country lanes!

But a country village on a Sunday in the rain was about the deadliest place imaginable. Every house was shut up tight, and there wasn't a soul in sight, not so much as a dog or a passing car. In London the streets were never deserted in daylight; there was always somebody about. Now the rain was coming down harder, and she could have sworn the drops were wetter than London rain. She turned up her coat collar and looked about for shelter, but she was just leaving the village and there wasn't so much as a tree in the hedgerow. The clouds were heavy and dark, making it seem like late afternoon, and the country lane stretched before her uninvitingly, flanked by tall wet hedges which shut out the view. I hate the countryside, she thought fervently, and stuffing her wet hands in her pockets for warmth, trudged on.

There was no sign of Gavin. He ought to have got back to her by now, even driving at a normal speed. She thought wistfully of bright lights and a roaring fire – well, to be honest, even the flat in Muswell Hill with the radiator full up and the telly on would be heaven compared with this vista of wet useless fields under a wet dark sky. Still no Gavin. She bet he'd forgotten her. He was having cocktails or something and being purred over by those girls. Or maybe he'd decided to let her walk and teach her a lesson. Either way, she reckoned she was on her own. The road ahead of her was curving now in what she decided was the wrong direction. She remembered the road they had come by had not been straight, and she reckoned she would shorten her walk by a good bit if she were to cut across the fields instead of walking round two sides of them by the road. And if Gavin did come back for her and missed her, he'd know she must have taken a short cut.

Anyone living in London, she thought, with all those twisty streets, must have a good enough a sense of direction to cross a few plain, straightforward fields. There was a gate in the hedge to her left, and she saw a field beyond of short, rather thin grass, and another gate on the far side. Brilliant, she thought. No problem to a genius like me.

She was half way across when she heard someone shouting. She thought perhaps it was Gavin, and walked on, ignoring it loftily. The shouting was renewed, louder this time, and she realised belatedly it was not Gavin's voice.

"Hoi, you! What the hell d'you think you're doing? Stop right there!"

She looked round and saw a large man in gumboots hurrying round the edge of the field towards her. He was waving an angry fist, and under his other arm he carried what looked suspiciously like a gun.

"Trampling all over my young wheat, you bloody trespassing vandal! I'll have the law on you! Stand still, damn you!"

Only now did Emma see that where she had walked there was a dark track through the thin green vegetation. Oh dear, she thought, her face hot with shame: not grass after all. The man was coming closer. Under his flat cap his face was red and angry, and it was definitely a gun he was carrying. Was he allowed to shoot trespassers? And if not, did he know he wasn't? She didn't feel inclined to find out. She was close to the gate now, and going back would be as bad for his wheat as going on, she reasoned, so much better she avoid the confrontation. She ran for the gate, to renewed yelling from the man behind her, and scrambled over in frantic haste, glad she had always been agile. In the field beyond the grass looked like grass, but she was taking no chances – and besides, crossing the middle of the field she'd make too good a target. She turned aside and began running as fast as she could along the side of the field, keeping close to the hedge.

She couldn't see another gate, apart from the one she had

just come over, at which the man with the gun had now appeared and was inviting her to come back so that he could teach her to trample people's crops. Pass on that one, she thought. The hedge she was jogging beside was rather threadbare in places, especially at the bottom, and after a bit she came to a place where she judged it would be possible to squeeze through. She managed it, with a struggle and some damage to her appearance, and found herself in another field, which had a gate on the far side, through which she could see a road. Getting her bearings, she decided triumphantly it was the same road, and that she had definitely cut off a wide loop. All the same, she was now very wet, cold and dispirited, and would be extremely glad to get back to civilisation.

This grass really was grass, she decided, short and ragged and bitten down. Besides, there were cow-flops about, and that meant it couldn't be a crop, could it? Pleased with her powers of deduction she hunched her shoulders against the suddenly heavier rain, and hurried on.

Then she saw something move out of the corner of her eye. She looked, and through the mist of the driving rain she saw the black and white beasts gathered by the hedge, and realised the significance of the cow-dung. Well, cows were all right, she told herself firmly; cows didn't hurt you. She was not going to behave like someone out of a Carry On film and run away from cows thinking they were bulls. She might be a townie but she wasn't that green. She walked on steadily.

One of the creatures had left the others and was walking towards her. Its path would intersect hers just before she reached the gate. Why would one cow want to inspect her when the others didn't? She began to feel a little nervous. The cow hurried up a bit and got itself between her and the gate, and it stopped, turning a little so that she saw it sideways on for the first time. That was when she noticed that it didn't have an udder.

She turned cold, and stopped dead, frozen to the spot.

A cow without an udder couldn't be a cow. That meant it must be a bull. She was alone in a field miles from anywhere, with a bull between her and the only gate.

The bull stared at her, and tossed its head. Sizing up where to gore her, was her panicky thought. Oh, what a fool she'd been! Why hadn't she listened to Gavin? Why did she have to go and prove herself?

Mustn't run, she thought. Above all, mustn't make any sudden move. Keep calm, and keep still. It was just staring at her. Maybe if she inched away very slowly to the right she could get to the hedge and force her way through. Slowly does it. Slo-o-wly.

And then a small red car drew up in the road beyond the gate, and to her unmingled relief the familiar form of Gavin Akroyd stepped out and came up to the gate.

"What in blazes do you think you're doing?" he asked in his most supercilious, but at that moment welcome, voice. The bull looked round at him and then back at Emma, and moved a step away from him, which brought it closer to her.

"Don't shout!" she implored in a strangled voice. "Don't startle it. You'll make it charge me."

"Make it—? Oh, for heaven's sake!" In one fluid movement he vaulted over the gate, and the bull gave a snort and a sort of curtsy, and bounced away from both of them, pausing a little way off to turn and look at them again. Gavin ignored it and walked over to her, gripping her upper arms as he realised her legs were about to give way.

"What on earth are you doing, standing about in the middle of a field like a halfwit?" he asked her unamiably. "What are you doing in a field at all, for that matter? I thought I told you to wait in the church porch."

"You told me, yes – and then you didn't come," she retorted through clenched teeth. She was beginning to shiver uncontrollably, from cold or reaction, she didn't know which. "What was I supposed to think?"

59

"I'm sorry, I got held up. But you should have waited. You didn't think I'd just leave you there?"

Put like that, it did seem unlikely – and insulting to him, really, to suppose it. She muttered something ungracious.

"Come on, let's get you to the car. I'm surprised at you, being afraid of a mere cow."

Here it comes, she thought, the poor ignorant townie bit! "I'm not afraid of cows," she said shortly through her chattering teeth. "But any sane person is afraid of a bull – except, apparently, the great Gavin Akroyd."

"That wasn't a bull, you ignoramus," he said, amused.

She pulled her arm free from his grip and turned to face him angrily. "Now look here, don't try and get smart with me," she said, almost crying. "I know a bull from a cow when I see one! Cows have udders!"

He was grinning now, shaking his head with amusement. "Is that how you figured it out? You poor mutt, they're all heifers in this field. Maiden cows. Their udders haven't developed yet."

"Well, how the hell was I supposed to know that?" she shouted in a temper.

He lifted his hands as if to hold her off. "Pax! It's not my fault you decided to plunge into the Great Outback. Besides, even if your little friend there had charged you, she couldn't have done you much harm. They've all been de-horned."

Well, so they had, she saw now. Why hadn't she noticed that before? Her humiliation complete, she walked beside him in silence back to the car, not even comforted by the fact that he was managing quite creditably not to laugh. He let her in, went round the other side and climbed in beside her, and started the engine. "I'll put the heater full up," he said kindly. "You must be frozen, you poor thing."

It felt wonderfully warm inside the car, and the smell of new upholstery was comforting, essentially a smell of civilisation.

"Thanks," she said gruffly. He drove off, and she felt a

little remorseful. A puddle was gathering at her feet. "I'm making a mess of your nice clean car," she said in a small voice. "I'm sorry."

"Don't worry about it," he said. For some reason, she saw, glancing at his profile, he seemed to be enjoying the situation. "When we get back, you'd better go straight upstairs and have a hot bath. You don't want Zara's chums seeing you like that."

Now that was sheer kindness. She looked at him in surprise, and saw a smile directed towards her so different from anything she had seen on his face before that it made her insides turn over.

"Thanks," she said. She felt confused. Something was happening here, she thought; some contact was being made between them which she had not at all expected. She knew nothing about him, and yet she could feel herself liking him, as if they had known each other a long time; and him liking her, which was even more odd and unlikely. "Um, look—" she began hesitantly.

"Yes?"

"About that cow—?"

Now he was positively grinning. "I won't tell a soul," he pledged. His eyes met hers, full of warmth and, the last thing she expected to see, some uncertainty. "But on one condition," he added.

"Which is?"

"That you take the job as Poppy's governess."

She hesitated. "I haven't been offered it yet."

"You will be."

"How can you be sure?"

"I'm sure. Look here, Poppy likes you – she told me so – and she doesn't like many people. And I think you'll be right for her. So will you take the job? Please?"

Afterwards, she was always sure it was that 'please' that decided her. It seemed so unlike him, and she was a sucker for novelty.

Chapter Six

Since Emma was available, there seemed no reason not to start her trial period at once; so on Monday she went back to London to pack up her belongings. Gavin said he would be in London himself that afternoon, and to her surprise he offered to pick her and her luggage up at the flat and drive her back. She was pleased, not only because it would save humping cases to the railway station, but also because she'd be able to show him off to her flatmates. And then she caught herself up sharply. Show him off? He was her potential future employer's son, that was all!

Atkins drove her to the station for the earliest train. "I'm glad you're coming back," he said. "Makes one more human being in the house. Score one to our side, eh?"

"After the reception I got the first evening, I was surprised they wanted me," Emma said.

He glanced at her. "Did their best to put you off, did they? But the Guv'nor's all right, his bark's worse than his bite. Her ladyship don't like nobody, that's a cross we all have to bear. And Zara's a spoilt little cow that wants smacking, that's all. Don't let 'er bother you none."

Emma didn't say anything, but she felt embarrassed. Ought they to be discussing the family behind their backs, especially in these terms? If she agreed with him, would her words get back to her potential employers?

He seemed to understand her thoughts. "Don't worry, I wouldn't say nothing. Had a go at you, did she? Her trouble is, she's jealous of everybody and everything. Keep an eye on her, is my advice. She'd stab you in the back as soon as look at you."

She thought she might as well get the full low-down while she could. "What do you think of Gavin?" she asked.

"He's a bit of a stuffed shirt, but he can't help that. That was the way he was brought up. And he's had females buzzing around him all his life, so he can't help thinking he's God's gift. I've known a score of young ladies mad about him, but he's never cared a jot for anyone but himself, as far as I can see – and why should he? He don't need anybody. He's straight enough with me, that's all I care about; but then I've known him since he was a kid. He knows he'd get short shrift if he give me any of the old acid."

This was not encouraging, though it was what Emma had suspected about him. "He was the first Mrs Akroyd's son, wasn't he?"

"That's right." He glanced at her again, to gauge her interest. "She wasn't a nob any more than the Guv'nor. Childhood sweethearts, they were. Lived next door to each other when they was kids. Nice woman, she was, too – no nonsense about her. She doted on Gavin. But then when Mr A started to get rich, nothing would do for him but Gavin had to go to public school and mix with other rich kids. So they packed him off to some posh boarding school. It nearly broke his mum's heart, but she wanted the best for him so she went along with it. Then while he was away at school, she died. He was only nine."

"Oh, I am sorry! Was he very much upset?"

"Bound to've been, I should think; but he never shows his feelings much. I reckon that's what made him so stiff and stand-offish, anyway; especially when his dad married Lady Susan so soon after. You know what kids are like."

"I suppose he'd see it as a betrayal of his mother."

"Yeah. Well, it stands to reason he must've known his mum was only a common woman, dunnit?"

"But surely nobody minds about that sort of thing any more," Emma protested.

"Don't they?" he snorted. Emma thought about the first evening and realised she was dealing with a different kind of world now. "Well, him and Lady Susan have never got on, though they're always polite to each other, of course. And there's no love lost between him and Zara. He likes the twins all right, but they're away at school most of the time. And Poppy—"

Just at that interesting moment they pulled up at the station entrance, and Atkins interrupted himself to say, "'Ow about that for timing? That's your train coming in now! Better step on it – they don't hang about for passengers these days. Got your ticket?"

"Yes, thanks." Emma gathered her bags. "Thanks very much for the lift."

"S'my job, ennit? Be seeing you, then."

"Yes, very soon." .

"I knew it! They've thrown her out! She's come back to us!" Suzanne cried as she opened the door to Emma.

"Well, yes and no," Emma smiled, pushing past her. "I smell something cooking! I'm starving."

"What, they didn't even feed you? The way the rich treat their servants is shameful," Suzanne pretended indignation.

"Is that you, Em?" Alison said, coming out from the sitting-room. "You're early. Chucked you out, have they?"

"What's that?" Rachel appeared from the kitchen. "They did what? Oh, poor Emma!"

"You're all very eager for me to fail my first job interview," Emma complained. "But I might as well put you all out of your misery. They liked me, I'm on a month's trial, and I've just come back for my things."

"Well, congratulations," Rachel said. "Come into the

kitchen and tell us everything. I've got a cake in the oven. It should be ready any minute."

"Are they filthy rich?" Alison asked.

"Strinking," Emma said, sitting down at the kitchen table and easing off her shoes. "Oh, this is comfortable!"

"Tired of the high life already?" Suzanne asked with a cynical smile. "What's the house like?"

"Rambling and Tudor. They only live in one wing. It stands in a huge park – a mile from the gate to the house, just like in all the stories – and they've so many servants I haven't counted them all yet."

"Fantastic!" Alison said.

"I suppose you have to live in the servants' hall and sleep in an attic?" Suzanne said.

"No, I shall have my own room and bathroom, and I'm supposed to be one of the family, but as far as possible I mean to have my meals with Poppy – that's the little girl's nickname. Oh, thanks," she added as Rachel put a mug of tea in front of her.

"Why the segregation?" Suzanne asked. "Didn't you like them?"

Emma frowned. "They're not a happy family. Mr Akroyd's a bit of a rough diamond. 'I'm a plain man and I know what I like': that sort of thing. But I don't think there's any real harm in him, and he'll be away a lot anyway. There are two little boys I haven't seen yet, but they're away at school most of the time. Lady Susan's as cold as charity, hardly speaks and never looks at you. And Zara, the elder girl, has got a chip on her shoulder, is rude and sullen, and has taken an instant dislike to me."

"How lovely for you!" Suzanne said. "Just what you need to make you feel at home."

"Poor Emma, isn't there anyone nice there?" Rachel said, getting her cake out of the oven.

"Poppy seems like a nice little thing, but rather nervous and down-trodden. She's been though some kind of emotional trauma and she's got a food-phobia – hardly eats a thing – but she seems to want to be friendly, which is the main thing."

"It's not what I'd call the main thing," Alison said. "What're you going to do for a social life?"

"Oh, I might be able to get the occasional game of darts in the village pub," Emma said airily.

"You can't bury yourself in the country like that," Alison said, looking shocked. "How are you going to meet any men?"

"I'll come up to London on my days off and you can line them up for me," Emma said.

"Oh well, it's only for a month, anyway," Suzanne said firmly.

Emma laughed. "That's my girl! Never look on the bright side! That cake smells heavenly, Rache. I suppose there's no chance of a piece for a starving traveller?"

"Of course. I don't mind cutting it now. Or would you like something more substantial?"

"No, thanks all the same, just a piece of cake. I haven't got long. I've got to get my things together. Gavin's calling for me in about an hour."

There was a brief silence, and then the three of them said with one voice, "Who's Gavin?"

"Oh, didn't I mention Gavin?"

"No, you didn't," Rachel said.

"Now I wonder why the omission?" Alison added with heavy irony. "A bit of a Freudian slip, that. Significant, wouldn't you say?"

"Not a bit. He's the son of the house. Late twenties. Very superior."

"In what way?" Suzanne asked suspiciously.

"Aloof and proud," Emma said.

Alison and Rachel exchanged a look, and Alison sighed. "Pity. I thought for a minute—"

"Not for the fraction of a minute," Emma said warningly.

66

It was comfortable to be back at the flat, to be able to wander round barefoot and not be on one's best behaviour, to be able to say what one liked without being afraid of being misunderstood or snubbed. Home, however shabby, certainly had its advantages. She was almost sorry when the doorbell rang to announce Gavin's arrival – almost, but not quite. It was going to be an adventure, and she was ready for an adventure.

The other three had been watching the afternoon film in the sitting-room. "I'll get it!" Suzanne yelled, and beat Alison off the mark. By the time Emma got into the hall, Suzanne was gone, the flat door was standing open, and the other two were standing about expectantly.

"She's gone down to the street door," Rachel said. "Maybe it got stuck again."

"Or maybe your Gavin doesn't understand about buzzers. P'raps the upper classes don't have them," said Ali.

"I hope you're not going to shame me and make embarrassing remarks like that in front of him," Emma said severely. "Look, come into the sitting-room, for heaven's sake. You can't stand about here like a WI committee."

They followed her reluctantly and seated themselves, watching the sitting-room door like children waiting for the conjurer. And when Suzanne appeared, her cheeks unexpectedly pink, she behaved like the conjurer, almost waving him in as she announced largely, "Girls, let me introduce Gavin Akroyd!"

She stepped aside, and Gavin filled the doorway. Even Emma, prepared for his amazing good looks, was stunned by the sight of him – for he was *smiling*! Not just a small, polite quirk of the lips, either, but a full, open and friendly smile. It made him look even more handsome; she wondered he didn't know that, and make more use of it.

"Now, let me introduce everyone," Suzanne said quickly, with a proprietorial air, as though afraid someone else might get there first. "This is Alison — she works at Sartoriana, d'you know it? In Bond Street. Yes, I thought you might. And this is Rachel — she's a teacher." By the tone of her voice, she might just as well have said 'She's *only* a teacher.' "And this is Emma — oh, silly of me, of course you know Emma."

"Not as well as I hope to," Gavin said, which effectively silenced her for the next ten minutes. He said hello to the others, and went on, "I hope I'm not barging in on you. I expect this kind of thing is a bit of a nuisance. What's the film like, any good?"

He was all pleasant smiles as he advanced into the room, looking as though he only wanted an invitation to sit down and take his shoes off with the rest of them. Suzanne and Alison both answered at once, clashed and stopped each other, and Rachel filled the gap by saying, "Can I offer you a cup of tea,. Mr Akroyd? I was just going to make one."

"Oh, Gavin, please. Yes, I'd love one, if it's no trouble."

He sat down on the sofa. Rachel went to put the kettle on, and the other two sat down nearby, perched well forward on their seats, and fixed him with eager expressions.

"I was just telling Gavin that my firm did the decorations for his house," Suzanne said, getting the name off with telling ease.

"It was a very nice job, from what Mrs Henderson told me," Gavin said. "She's the housekeeper. It's mostly her and Dad who use the London house. I haven't seen it, actually, since it's been done."

"Nor has Suzanne," Alison said nastily.

"No, but I've seen the plans and the samples," Suzanne said, colouring. "You live in the country, then?" she asked Gavin hastily, to cover her retreat.

"When I'm home. I'm away a lot, though not as much as Dad."

"What do you do?" Alison asked. "I suppose you're going to inherit the family business?"

68

Emma frowned at her, thinking it sounded rude, but Gavin didn't seem upset.

"Yes, but that sounds a bit feudal. I didn't want to take a seat on the Board without knowing anything about the business, so when I finished at university I went and worked for a time at each of the plants, to get to know the processes from the ground up. And then I went on a management training course, partly here and partly in Brussels. Dad didn't like the idea, but I told him someone had to understand what was going on in Europe, and he said in that case it had better be me. He hates the whole idea of Europe."

Emma couldn't get over the difference in him. Before long Suzanne and Alison were sitting back and relaxing, and conversation was flowing easily. Rachel brought in tea and the remains of her cake, and they all chatted about such diverse subjects as films, restaurants, the merits of streaming in schools, whether mugs were preferable to cups, rail privatisation, and which cars gave the best performance on country roads.

Emma joined in very little, preferring to listen and observe. There wasn't a hint of coldness or stiffness about him. What had wrought the miracle? Could it be that he felt at ease here, whereas at home he felt constrained? Or was he like this with everyone except her? Maybe she brought out the worst in him. Well, she had started off by mocking and teasing him; but then he'd started off by freezing and snubbing her. Perhaps they were doomed to rub each other up the wrong way, she thought gloomily.

He seemed to have settled in for the duration, but she knew the contents of the communal larder, and didn't want the girls to have to ask him (and her) to stay and eat, so at last she interrupted. "Don't you think we ought to get going?"

For an instant Gavin actually looked disappointed; then he looked at his watch and his expression registered concern. "I didn't realise it was as late as that! Yes, we better had make a move."

"You must come again," Suzanne said quickly. "Any time you're passing."

"Yes, any time," Alison added. "No need to ring first – just drop in. You're always welcome."

Oi, what about me? Emma thought. Can I come again? But she was as moon to sun, as far as her friends were concerned, with Gavin Akroyd in the room.

They said prolonged goodbyes standing in the hall, and then at last Gavin picked up her bags and they were off. As they drove away along Muswell Hill Road, Gavin said quietly, "What fun it must be, living in a flat like that."

"I'm sorry?" Emma said, wondering if she had heard him right.

He hesitated, as if not sure whether to go on or not; and then he said, "I envy you, living in a flat like that. The freedom. The friendship. The good times you must have had."

"Well – yes," she said, thinking it an odd comment. Hadn't he had fun like that? "Surely you shared a flat when you were at university?"

"No," he said. "I stayed at home and commuted in. I went to Cambridge, you see."

"Oh. Nice," Emma said blankly.

He glanced sideways at her. "I went to Cambridge so that I *could* commute," he said. "With Dad away so much, he wanted me at home to take care of things."

"Oh, I see," said Emma. That seemed rather unfair, denying him the usual student jollies, putting responsibility on him so young. "But I suppose it was nice for you to be at home, in a way," she said, "with your brothers and sisters."

He didn't answer at once, and then he said, "I'm very fond of Poppy."

"She's a very sweet kid," Emma answered at once; but

70

reflected afterwards that his comment had been remarkable for what it didn't say. She thought of Atkins's words: Him and Lady Susan have never got on and There's no love lost between him and Zara. To be made perpetually responsible for a family you didn't like must have been a burden indeed. She felt sorry for him.

"Tell me about your family," he said after a bit; and there was nothing she was happier doing. The atmosphere grew warmer and more lively. When she had told him something of her life, she slipped in a question or two about his. He told her about his love of the countryside: described solitary walks along the beach at Aldeburgh; birdwatching at Dunwich; sitting up all night in the forest watching for badgers; riding through the deep Suffolk lanes; sailing on the Orwell; hunting on crisp winter mornings. Through his words she was transported to a world so different from hers in London that it sounded like an Arthurian legend, a magical place of improbable beauty.

"God, you're so lucky!" she said at last. "How can you possibly envy me? It's me who should envy you!"

"How can you say that?" he asked, the light in his eyes fading a little. "What can you envy about my life?"

She felt this was going a little far. "Come," she said crisply, "you've had every advantage money could buy."

"Oh, money," he said. "Yes, I had that."

"It's all very well sneering at it," she said, feeling a little cross. "You can afford to say money doesn't matter as long as you've got enough of it. Privilege is easy to belittle when you've got it."

"Yes, I am privileged," he said. "But you've had a different sort of privilege, and one that I'd have been happy to swap mine for. But I don't suppose you'd believe me if I told you so."

"No, not for a minute," she said. She tried to say it lightly, teasingly, but he didn't smile.

"At least you can be sure that when people say they like

you, it's you they like," he said in a low voice, almost too low for her to hear.

"What do you mean by that?" she asked.

"Oh, nothing," Gavin said, and he sounded quite depressed.

The change seemed to start then. The animation left his face, and he said nothing more. Emma, looking at his non-committal profile, wondered whether he was thinking of Zara's girl-friends throwing themselves at him. We should all have his problems! she thought. She couldn't help feeling that being spoilt for choice was better than having Hobson's choice, and that the anxieties of having too much money must be easier to bear than those which came with having too little.

The rest of the journey was accomplished in almost complete silence. Emma would have liked to chat, but somehow she couldn't find the right words to begin. When she did broach a subject, he answered her too briefly to get the conversation going again, and after a few such snubs she gave up. His aloofness, or grimness, whichever it was, seemed to intensify the nearer they got to Long Hempdon. What a Jekyll and Hyde character he was turning out to be, she thought to herself. Was it the proximity to home that affected him so adversely, or was it her? He had been so relaxed and easy at the flat, but now after a period alone with her, he had gone back to his usual withdrawn and chilly manner.

Oh well, whatever the cause, she told herself with a shake, it hardly mattered. Her duties were with the little girl, Poppy, and she didn't particularly have to get on with Poppy's big brother. She would be unlikely to see much of him, spending most of her time in the schoolroom and nursery; and in any case, hadn't he said that he was away a lot? No, Mr Gavin Akroyd was not likely to have much effect on her day-to-day life – and that was probably just as well, she thought, glancing briefly at that icy, uncommunicative profile.

Chapter Seven

It was one of those glorious early summer days in May, and the soft air coming in through the open window of the day-nursery (now the schoolroom) was sweet with the scents of grass and flowers. It was hard to concentrate on lessons, even for Emma, so she could hardly blame Poppy for fidgeting and staring out of the window when she should have had her mind on arithmetic. Both pairs of eyes seemed to be inexorably drawn to the brightness outside every few minutes. They usually took a break at half past ten, but at a few minutes past the hour Emma decided to bow to the inevitable.

"I think we'll take our break now – what do you think?" she said, closing the book. "Shall we stop or go on? It's a bit early, but—"

Poppy shut her own book smartly and beamed with relief. "Oh yes! Break, please."

"Perhaps we can take our elevenses outside. It's such a lovely day. Have you got another favourite spot you'd like to show me?"

As far as possible, Emma had been letting Poppy show her round the house and grounds, a small act of empowerment that she felt the little girl badly needed. In the time she had been here, Emma had discovered a great deal she didn't like very much about Poppy's situation. The Akroyd family was what she had learned at teacher-training college to call dysfunctional; the members seemed to perform their own separate orbits, entirely detached from each other, never intersecting. Mr Akroyd was away a good deal, and when he was at home was usually shut up in his study haranguing someone on the telephone. When he was with his family, his temper seemed on a very short fuse, and when he went away again, Emma couldn't help feeling relieved.

Lady Susan led an even more mysterious life, in the sense that Emma had no idea what she did with herself all day. Sometimes she went out in the car, driven by Atkins, shopping, or to visit friends; less frequently a friend visited her for lunch or tea. When Emma met her about the house, she drifted past without looking at her. She didn't seem to interest herself in Poppy at all, and certainly never came near the schoolroom. Perhaps she didn't care for so many stairs, Emma thought to herself with grim humour.

Gavin she found very difficult to fathom. She didn't have much to do with him, and when she came upon him unexpectedly in the house, he was usually cool and aloof, merely nodding to her or greeting her formally. At dinner he rarely spoke; but just once or twice, in the drawing-room after dinner, when his father had been called away to the telephone, Zara was out about her own amusements, and Mrs Henderson was occupied with keeping Lady Susan from the tedium of her own company, Gavin had seated himself beside Emma and engaged her in conversation. And it had been pleasant, stimulating, and had given her a glimpse of a hidden person she felt she would have liked to get to know better. But it never lasted long. The next time she saw him he would be distant with her again, as though trying to backtrack on any advance in intimacy she might presume upon. She always felt that he was very aware of her status as an employee in the house, and kept her at arm's length because of it. He would talk to her for as long as it amused him, and then drop her. That was the way, she supposed, he was with women. After Chris, it didn't surprise her.

And yet he interested her. He seemed so much the odd one out of the family; and Poppy spoke of him with such wistful affection. If Poppy liked him, Emma thought, he couldn't be all bad. And she was aware that, little as they had to do with each other, there was something about her that interested him. Often she would catch him looking at her, during those silent dinners; his gaze would be hastily withdrawn as soon as she looked up. But she couldn't flatter herself it was the interest of approval; a fascination of loathing was just as likely.

She had made the brief acquaintance of the twins Harry and Jack in their short time at home between their Easter skiing holiday and their return to school. They were tall, handsome boys with cut-glass accents; beautifully dressed, and with beautiful manners and more self-possession than seemed natural in fourteen-year-olds. All the other boys of that age Emma had ever known were at their most awkward, by turns shy and surly, childish and aggressive; greasy, spotty, violently untidy, strangers to the bathroom and unable to carry on a normal conversation with anyone but their own compadres. Harry and Jack were so unlike this template Emma found it hard to believe they were human.

The difference their presence made to their mother was the greatest revelation to Emma. For a few short days, Lady Susan became animated. She beamed, she attended, she asked questions and listened to the answers. She evidently doted on the boys, and if they were not dancing attendance on her she pursued them to their haunts, forever wanting to touch them, and seeming riveted by their slightest utterance. The boys took this in good part, but in the opportunities she had to observe them she could not see that they felt any great affection for their parent in return. They bore with her because they were too polite not to, but they were glad to get away from her.

They were polite to Emma, too, with that delightful courtesy of well-brought-up children towards those they hold in utter indifference. They lived only for each other, and had elevated the skills of escaping to be alone together into an art-form. Emma felt very sorry for Poppy, who was even more eclipsed by their sudden glamour; and could not help noticing how differently Lady Susan behaved towards them as opposed to Poppy. Emma supposed she was one of those women who only cared for their sons and thought their daughters nothing. Poppy would have liked to be with the twins, join their conversations and go with them on their jaunts; but they would not have her. They were kind to her in an off-hand way, but they did not her company.

When the boys went back to school, Zara did too, for her last term. Emma was glad to have her out of the house, since she was invariably rude and contemptuous and had many small ways of making Emma's life uncomfortable. Emma wondered how she would manage when Zara came back for good: there was no prospect of her going to university, it seemed, and in fact her present school was of the finishing rather than the academic variety. She supposed Zara would be launched into society and lead the same kind of life as her mother. Emma hoped she would be able to inculcate some harder ambition in Poppy's breast than being a clothes-horse and getting married. She could only assume that was what she had been hired for, though she sometimes wondered whether it wasn't just to keep the child out of her mother's way.

At the very least, though, she could give Poppy someone of her own to pay attention to her and offer her affection. The isolation in which the child had led most of her life so far seemed terrifying to Emma.

Now, in answer to Emma's question, Poppy said eagerly, "Can we go down to the kitchen? Mrs Grainger said she was making Chelsea buns this morning and they'd be ready for elevenses."

"Did she indeed? I love buns."

"Me too! They're the best!" Poppy said eagerly, relief flooding her face that she was not to be denied the treat.

"She won't mind our going down there?"

"No, she likes it. Really," Poppy said earnestly.

"OK then, let's go."

It was the first time Emma had been 'below stairs', and she was intrigued when Poppy led her into a part of the house she had not seen before, through a concealed door which looked like part of the corridor wall, and down what were evidently the backstairs. They were of bare wood, uncarpeted and dusty, but the smell of food drifted up them like a friendly ghost. Poppy pattered down with evident familiarity, all the way from the top to the bottom of the house, emerging into a dim, flagstoned corridor lined with panelled cupboards, and pushing through another door into the kitchen.

It was warm and full of the smell of baking; sunlight streamed in through a high window. The walls were of rough whitewashed stone and the floor stone-flagged, wavy with centuries of footsteps. There was a large old-fashioned deal table, and an ancient built-in pine dresser, but otherwise everything was modern: strip-lights in the ceiling, modern cupboards and units, a huge steel industrial cooking-stove, racks of stainless steel pots and pans overhead, an enormous dishwasher and a big American-style larder-fridge the size of a wardrobe. Under the vast Tudor chimney a four-oven Aga looked almost lost, and in front of it Mrs Grainger was sitting with her feet up on a stool, having a cup of tea and reading the *Daily Mirror*.

She looked up and smiled as they came in. "Ah, there you are. Let you off, has she?" she said to Poppy.

"You did say," Poppy answered defensively, out of her chronic anxiety.

"I did say," Mrs Grainger agreed economically.

"I hope we aren't disturbing you?" Emma put in.

"Not a bit. I was hoping to meet you, and I knew They'd never bring you down. So I told Poppy I'd make some buns." She nodded towards the Aga, on top of which the promised

77

Chelsea buns were cooling on a wire rack. "Can I offer you a cup of tea, Miss Ruskin?"

"Emma, please. Yes, I'd love one, thank you."

"Me too?" Poppy pleaded.

Mrs Grainger looked sidelong at Emma. "You're supposed to have milk. It's better for you."

"I don't like milk. Please can't I have tea, Emma? I always do down here."

"Tattle-tail, giving me away!" Mrs Grainger chided her.

Emma thought of her own childhood home, where everyone drank strong orange tea from babyhood upwards. It never did them any harm. "I won't tell. And tea is supposed to be good for the heart, now, isn't it?"

"Is it? They're always changing the rules, aren't they?" Mrs Grainger said placidly, pouring the tea. Poppy and Emma pulled up chairs, and the buns were transferred to a plate and dredged with sugar. They were soft, fragrant, sticky, bursting with fruit, and more delicious than anything Emma had ever tasted before. Shop buns were the palest, feeblest imitation beside them, and Emma said so.

"I'm glad you like them," Mrs Grainger said, looking pleased. "I really enjoy baking, you've always got something to show at the end of it. Yeast baking especially. But I get precious little chance these days, unless the boys are home. Mr Akroyd likes his cake hearty, but he's never here; and her ladyship only wants the dainty stuff if she has afternoon tea."

"Well count me in, any time you've got buns to get rid of," Emma said. "This is sheer heaven."

"And how are you settling in? Finding your way around all right?"

"Yes, thank you. Poppy's showing me everything, bit by bit."

"I was hoping to get to see you. I said to Bill to ask you to come down for tea some time—"

"Bill?"

"Bill Atkins, the chauffeur."

"Oh yes. Sorry, I didn't know his first name."

Poppy finished her first bun and asked if she could have another. "Yes, as long as you don't spoil your lunch," Mrs Grainger said. Poppy took another and began nibbling it in a circle, unrolling it as she went. "Take it with you and go and see the kittens, why don't you?" the cook suggested beguilingly.

"Can I? Are they still in the boot room?"

"Yes, but watch you don't let them out. And mind Tigger doesn't scratch you."

Poppy disappeared, bun in hand, through another door. Mrs Grainger turned to Emma. "I didn't want to talk about her while she was listening, but I wanted to say how much better she's been since you've come. There was a time I was really worried about her. She would hardly eat a thing except sweets, and it was making her ill."

"She's still very thin," Emma said.

"Yes, but Anna and Julie tell me she's eating much better now. They always keep an eye on her plate for me and report back. She's been a very unhappy child, you see."

"I understand she was at school for a while."

"Yes, but she didn't fit in there. The other girls teased her, and the teachers didn't stop it. Anyway, Poppy got really unhappy and even tried running away, but her dad gave her a lecture and said she'd got to stay, so she just went into a decline and made herself ill. Came back at the end of term like a shadow, and then Jean Henderson stepped in and said enough was enough and persuaded Gavin to make Mr Akroyd to let her stay home."

"Gavin?"

Mrs Grainger looked at her, eyebrows raised. "Oh yes, he loves that kid. Ever since she was born, he's doted on her. He's practically like a father to her, and she worships the ground he walks on, as I expect you know. Trouble is, he's got so much else to do, he hasn't got the time to spend with her. And he's been away from home so much in the past couple of years, he hasn't been able to keep an eye on her."

"I'm surprised," Emma said. "I mean, I'm very pleased that she has someone who cares for her, but I wouldn't have thought Gavin would be the type to—" She paused, not wishing to offend.

"Oh, there's a lot of good in that young man," Mrs Grainger said. "I know he can seem stand-offish, but he's had a lot to put up with one way and another, and he's very shy, though you mightn't think it." Emma didn't. "Harry and Jack are all charm and easy manners, but Gavin's more serious-minded. He can't just be social like them."

"I suppose they learn that at public school."

"That's part of it. Oh, I'm no snob, I think Eton does them a lot of good. It's a pity Gavin never had the chance to go there. He went to boarding school, but it was quite a different sort of place; but then Mr A didn't know what he knows now. He hadn't married into the nobility then. You know Gavin was the son of Mr Akroyd's first wife? Yes, well, there's always been a lot of family tension. Her ladyship hasn't got any time for him, despite the fact that it's him that keeps everything together – the estate and everything. But of course she resents the fact that it will all go to him and not one of her own boys." She looked at Emma defensively. "I suppose I'm speaking out of turn a bit, but you'll find out for yourself sooner or later. And of course he's got no respect for her, especially over the way she's treated Poppy – or not treated her, really."

"It seems a very unhappy household, one way and another," Emma commented. "I wonder he doesn't leave – set up on his own somewhere."

"I expect he would have, if it hadn't been for Poppy. He doesn't trust anyone else to look after her. He doesn't want her growing up like Zara, you see – wants her to get exams and have a career and everything, so she can be independent."

Emma decided to satisfy her curiosity on another subject. "Tell me, why does Zara dislike me? As far as I know, I haven't given her any reason to."

"Zara?" Mrs Grainger smiled at her. "Oh, that's easy! I should have thought you'd have realised—"

At that interesting moment the kitchen door from the main part of the house opened and Mrs Grainger broke off abruptly. It was Gavin.

"Mrs Grainger, have you seen Poppy?" he began, and then saw Emma, and frowned. It seemed, she thought resignedly, his natural reaction to her "Ah, Miss Ruskin. You're here, are you?" His voice sounded cool and disapproving. "I was wondering where you were. I went up to the schoolroom, expecting to find you there, but of course it was empty."

Checking up on me, she thought indignantly. She stood up. "We were having our morning break, Mr Akroyd," she said with dignity, "but I was just about to go back. Poppy's through there looking at the kittens."

Gavin's face seemed to flush slightly – with anger, Emma decided. "Don't let me drive you away," he said. "I'm surprised to see you here, but what you do during your break is your own affair."

She thought he was being sarcastic. "Our break is over, Mr Akroyd," she said stiffly. "It's time we got back to work. Thank you for the tea, Mrs Grainger." And without waiting for any further comment she made her escape, bristling indignantly, through the door Poppy had taken before her.

She always had breakfast, lunch and tea with Poppy in the day nursery, but dinner was taken with the family. It wasn't a very cheery meal, but at least she got to chat to Mrs Henderson, who could usually be relied on to be sociable.

On this particular evening Mr Akroyd was absent, and Gavin took his place at the end of the table. Lady Susan

81

was silent as usual until about half way through the meal, when she suddenly laid down her fork and addressed Emma out of the blue, cutting across a rather rambling account Mrs Henderson was giving of some alterations to the gardens.

"I understand that you took Arabella down to the kitchen this morning."

Emma looked at her, surprised, and just managed not to say, "What, me?" Instead she said, "Yes, that's right."

"I should be glad, Miss Ruskin," Lady Susan said with something approaching animation, "if you would never do such a thing again." Her eyes were fixed on a spot somewhere beyond Emma's left shoulder. Emma felt her blood rise. Out of the corner of her eye she could see Gavin eating steadily with his head bent over his plate, his whole attitude redolent of guilt. Oh, I see, so that's what this is about, she thought. Sneak! Tell tale! Getting his mother to do his dirty work, is he?

"May I ask why?" Emma asked, her voice rising a little with resentment.

Lady Susan's eyes brows went up. Clearly she was not used to being questioned. "Because I don't wish her to be there. She is too fond of associating with the servants as it is. She must not be encouraged by you. That is all."

Emma had never heard anything so archaic. "I see. You think she'll be corrupted, or pick up bad habits, I suppose?"

Lady Susan was so astonished at Emma's answering back that she actually looked directly at her for an instant. But she spoke in the same, languid tone as always. "I will not be questioned in this way, Miss Ruskin. You will adhere to the rules I lay down concerning my daughter's upbringing, or you will seek another position."

Emma opened her mouth to say she would do just that, when she caught Mrs Henderson's anxious eye across the table. The housekeeper gave her a pleading look and a little shake of the head; and Emma thought of Poppy, and how the little girl needed her, and knew she must not sacrifice her for the sake of her own temper. So she swallowed her retort and bent her head to her plate instead, and forked in some food to prevent herself from speaking.

In the silence she heard Gavin clear his throat, but it was Mrs Henderson who spoke, reverting to the broken topic of gardens, and so the meal passed on.

As they were walking out from the dining-room later, Mrs Henderson said to Emma with an attempt at cheerfulness, "What are you going to do this evening?"

Get out of this house for a bit, at the very least, Emma thought; but she phrased it more politely. "Oh, I thought I'd go out for a walk, see a bit of the neighbourhood. I haven't set foot outside the park since I arrived here."

"What a good idea," Mrs Henderson said. "Are you heading anywhere in particular?"

Emma hadn't actually thought, but she said now, more or less at random, "I think I'll go down to the village and have a drink at the pub."

She hadn't realised Gavin was right behind her until he said, before Mrs Henderson could speak, "I'd rather you didn't do that."

It was the wrong way to put it, for the mood Emma was in. She turned, bristling. "And why not, may I ask?"

His face was grave. "It's not a very nice place," he said.

"Not very nice?" she repeated coldly. Like the kitchen, she supposed.

"It's rough. It's not suitable for someone like you."

Contamination of members of the household by the lower classes: that's what he was afraid of, the beastly snob! "You forget," she said, poison-sweet, "that I come from Hoxton. I expect it will seem nice enough to me."

"I doubt it," he said coldly. "Anyway, I would prefer you not to go anywhere near it." He said 'prefer', but the tone was a tone of command.

"Really, my dear," Mrs Henderson jumped in as Emma

drew breath to answer, "I think perhaps you'd better give the pub a miss. I tell you what, why not stay in tonight, and tomorrow evening early, go in to Cambridge on the train? You could go to the theatre or a movie and have supper there — there are some nice restaurants and bistros. Much more suitable."

Emma didn't want to have a row with Mrs Henderson, who was only trying to keep the peace, so she just said, "Very well," and left them, going up to her room. But inwardly she was seething. Did they think they owned her body and soul, just because they paid her wages? They didn't want their precious child's governess mixing with the lower classes — or their precious child mixing with servants, either. Really, these people! What world did they live in? Then she caught sight of her expression in the mirror, and laughed, her brow clearing. If she stayed here long she'd become as left-wing as Suzanne!

All the same, she wasn't going to be dictated to. If she wanted to go to the pub for a drink she'd go. She changed into slacks, put on her coat, took her handbag, and went out; down the backstairs to avoid bumping into anyone, and across the back hall. The evening was fine, and it was still light, and though it was a long walk into the village, she was glad to be out, and enjoyed the fresh air and the smells of grass and earth and evening dew.

By the time she reached the village, she was ready for a drink — and a sit down: country distances somehow seemed further than town ones. The pub, called the Dog and Duck, looked picturesque from a distance, a cob cottage with a thatched roof and crooked mullion windows, and there was a group of cheerful locals standing outside enjoying their evening ale *al fresco*. As she came closer, however, she found her enthusiasm waning a little. The place had a definite air of seediness about it: paint was falling off it in chunks, the thatch was infested with weeds, and the tarmac surrounding it was full of holes. Pop music was blaring out of the open door, and the men standing outside were not genial, ruddy-faced farm lads off the set of a BBC costume drama, but a bunch of scruffy and extremely disagreeable-looking youths such as might be found hanging about any inner-city street corner – or, these days, the centre of any rural town.

They were watching her approach, and with the emptiness of the dark countryside behind her, she began to feel very exposed, and to realise how conspicuous she must look to them. The Dog and Duck did not look like the kind of pub a lone female would enter for fun; indeed, she wondered whether in this benighted place women ever went out alone. The youths were obviously talking about her, making remarks which she couldn't quite hear, but which made them laugh raucously amongst themselves.

Her footsteps slowed. Part of her wanted to turn tail and run, another part could not bear to be thwarted of her legitimate desires by a bunch of brainless yobs.

"'Ello, darlin', 'ow about a drink, then?" one of them called to her. She said nothing, but her heart sank, and her footsteps slowed still further.

"You out on your own?" another asked. "Ain't you scared, goin' about on yer own on a dark night like this?"

"Ne' mind, we'll look after yer, won't we?"

They all giggled and shoved each other, but their eyes were predatory.

"Well, say summink, can't yer? Wojjer want to drink, then?"

"She don't want to 'ave one wiv you – do yer, darlin'? She fancies me, dun't she. Come an' 'ave one wiv me."

"Nah, she don't mind – she'll 'ave one wiv all of us – won't yer, love?"

They roared with laughter at that, but they had drawn closer together and were now blocking the entrance to the pub, so that if she did want to go in, she would have to push past them, or ask them to move. Instinctively she knew

85

that in either case, they would not let her by, and physical jostling would follow, which was what they wanted. They were five and she was one, and they had absolute belief that they could do anything they wanted, and no-one could touch them for it.

But if she walked on past the pub, they might follow her. They must know by now that the pub was where she had been heading. If she walked by, they would know they had scared her, and would be elated by their power over her, and would certainly follow. And where else could she go? The few buildings nearby were in darkness. If they followed her into the darkness and caught her . . . She *must* go into the pub, even if it meant shoving past them, fighting her way in. Inside there would be a landlord and a telephone. It was her only chance of safety.

But while she had hesitated, they had grown in confidence. They were moving towards her now. They meant to keep her out of the pub, then. She began to feel really afraid. Would anyone inside hear if she screamed – or pay any attention if they heard? Would it make the yobs more or less likely to do her harm? She swallowed and licked her lips, searching for something to say to turn the situation, as they inched nearer, their eyes seeming to glitter like animals' eyes in the dark.

And then the sound of a car engine broke the tableau, the gutteral roar of a twin-exhaust sports car approaching at speed. The eyes flickered away from her for an instant; then headlights swung round the corner and washed over the pub façade, and the yobs ducked a little and put their hands up to shield their eyes from the dazzle. Emma turned, hardly daring to hope: but yes, it was Gavin's car, and it pulled up beside her with a squeal.

"Get in," he said tersely, leaning over to open the passenger-side door.

She didn't argue. She hurried round to the other side and got in, aware of the derisive hoots of the disappointed pack. Gavin barely waited for her to shut the door before gunning the engine, performing a tight and violent u-turn, and speeding away down the road. Emma was flung about, jerked backwards in her seat, and now had her hair blown forwards into her eyes.

"Do you have to drive like this?" she protested; but turning to look at him, she saw that he did. His lips were grimly closed, his nostrils taut and arching with fury. If he didn't take it out on the road, she thought, he'd probably take it out on her.

Then he did anyway. The words burst out of him like a major dam being breached. "What the hell do you think you're doing? I told you not to go to the pub! Did you think I was talking to myself?"

In the relief of being rescued, her own anger revived. "I don't see what business it is of yours where I go in my free time!" she retorted.

"Of course it's my business! In my father's absence I'm responsible for everybody in the house, even if it means protecting them from themselves! What d'you mean by prancing about the countryside in the dark like that? And going to the pub? Good God, Zara gives me worries enough, but even she knows better than that!"

This interesting reference passed Emma by in her fury. "I am not your sister, and I can take care of myself, thank you very much!"

"Oh, that's very evident! What did you intend doing about that gang of yobs? Wrestle them to the ground single-handed? I suppose you've got a black belt in karate you haven't told us about? Don't you know what would have happened if I hadn't turned up when I did?"

A slight tremble in his voice on the last words made her wonder if he had been really worried about her, as opposed to merely miffed that she had disobeyed him. Together with the realisation that he *had* rescued her from a horrid fate, it softened her a little.

"Look," she began in a more reasonable tone.

But he was not yet ready to be reasonable. "You were told not to go out. You were told the pub was rough. Yet you still went there. Are you stupid, or just infantile?"

Her anger flared again. "You *told* me, yes! You're very good at *telling* people what to do! You know all about what's suitable and what isn't. Maybe if you'd tried talking to me instead of issuing orders, I might not have assumed that it was just another example of your beastly snobbery!"

As soon as the words were out she trembled for her own rudeness – not that she cared if he sacked her, but she would be letting Poppy down. But instead of being furious, he seemed only surprised.

"Snobbery? But I'm not snobbish," he said in a voice that sounded genuinely puzzled.

"Not much, you're not!" she retorted. "You forbade Poppy from talking to Mrs Grainger, who's as kind a soul as I ever met, just because you didn't want a sister of yours mixing with servants!"

Her genuine grievance sounded clearly in her voice. Gavin threw a look sideways at her. "You don't think I had anything to do with that, do you? That was my stepmother's ban, not mine."

"But who put her up to it? You were the one who came in while we were there, and made it very clear you disapproved. You practically ordered me out of the kitchen."

To her surprise, Gavin stopped the car at the side of the road and turned to survey her thoughtfully. "No," he said quietly "you're quite wrong there. I wanted you to stay; I wanted to make conversation. But you were off like a scalded cat. I thought you disliked me so much you couldn't bear to be in the same room with me."

Emma was thrown off balance. "Then who——?"

"Who told my stepmother? I expect one of the maids mentioned it. But it was she who objected, not me, I assure you."

Emma couldn't think of a thing to say. He seemed to be taking pains to justify himself to her – and when she had just falsely accused him of an ignoble sentiment. He studied her face in the moonlight filtering through the trees at the side of the road, and she stared back defiantly, feeling herself weakening.

"So that's what all this was about?" he said at last. "You were punishing me by ignoring my advice about going out. Well, I honour the intention, if not the method. Will you shake hands and call a truce? I *was* right about the pub, wasn't I?"

"Yes," Emma said, and, determined to do the right thing if it killed her, she added, "I apologise for causing you trouble."

"I apologise too," he said.

"For what?"

In the dark he reached for her hand, and as his warm fingers closed round hers, the sensation made her start, and then almost tremble. He was very close to her in the confines of the car, and she felt his presence like a kind of radiation, as though she had come within the range of a great fire.

"For whatever I did to make you feel I wanted to drive you out of the kitchen. I assure you it was quite the opposite. I would have liked to talk to you, but—"

They looked at each other for a long moment, and Emma suddenly knew with absolute certainty that he was going to kiss her. The tension of the moment made all her nerve-endings tingle, and she found herself leaning towards him, everything inside her fluttering with anticipation. Her eyes began to close as his face came nearer, nearer; she could smell the fresh tang of his aftershave, and underneath it, the warm scent of his skin . . .

And then there was a roar, a blaze of light, the howl of a horn, and a car flashed past them at high speed, the headlight beams throwing the trees and hedges suddenly up into sharp relief, unreal, like a theatre backdrop. The wind of passing blatted briefly against the Elan, rocking it, and then swirled away with a scutter of leaves and grit as the car disappeared round the bend with a wag of its red tail-lights.

Gavin had dropped her hand, startled; and now did not reach for it again. The mood was broken. He re-started the car and drove on in silence. It was not exactly an unfriendly silence, but it was an awkward one. Emma could not think of anything to say to break it, and in the renewed tension she began to wonder if she had been mistaken in thinking he wanted to kiss her. That made her feel uneasy and embarrassed. She had made a big enough fool of herself over the pub; she didn't want to add to it by assuming more wrong and silly things about Gavin.

When they reached the house he stopped at the front to let her out, and she said quickly, "Well, thanks for the lift. Goodnight," and got out before he could say anything. She hurried up the steps, aware that he was sitting there watching her go. What was he thinking? Did he guess what she had expected and feel contempt for her because of it? Or had she just snubbed him again? She wondered what it was about Mr Gavin Akroyd, and whether she would ever manage to get her behaviour towards him right.

Chapter Eight

Over the next few days Emma found herself thinking more often than she was comfortable with about Gavin. Her mind continually strayed to the drive home, going over and over the words that were spoken, trying to recapture his tone of voice and expression. Most of all she kept thinking about that electrifying moment when she had been sure he was going to kiss her. Had it been pure imagination on her part? The more she thought about it the less she could be sure. Was it just wishful thinking? Maybe she had made a monumental fool of herself. Most likely he didn't think of her at all. She was just an employee, and a rather troublesome one at that.

But he *had* been worried about her. Surely that meant something? The tendency of her questions to herself made her realise that whatever his feelings, she was attracted to him. Maybe it was just because, shut up here in the house miles from anywhere, he was the only male within reach, and she had to be interested in somebody? Well, that was possible; but whatever the cause, she found herself looking forward more each day to the evening meal, the one time she might see him. Every evening she dressed herself with care, feeling that pleasant flutter of anticipation as she walked downstairs towards the drawing-room. And every evening there was the same disappointment. Gavin behaved towards her exactly as always, with calm, unemotional politeness. He joined in the conversation between her and Mrs Henderson, looked at her no more or less than before, called her, when he called her anything, Miss Ruskin. She might tell herself that there was a little more warmth in his eyes than before, but she could not be sure.

And really, she was glad not to be sure. It gave a spice to her days which was otherwise lacking. If she was sure he did not care for her at all, life would have been dull; but if she was sure he was interested in her, it would have meant she'd have to make up her mind about how she felt about him, and after Chris, she wasn't sure she wanted to.

But her preoccupation with the subject lasted only a few days; for after that Zara came home, and it was necessary to be careful to reveal nothing to the sharp eyes of disdain and jealousy: Zara would have been only too glad to make her life a misery if she thought for a moment Emma had dared to fancy her brother. And beside, Zara's return home shortly preceded her eighteenth birthday, for which there was to be a huge coming-of-age celebration. It was to be the grandest of grand affairs – both Mr Akroyd and Lady Susan, for different reasons, were determined on that. There was to be a ball to which most of the county would be invited, a vast buffet laid on by caterers, stewards and waitresses specially hired, champagne by the lakeful, and a cake of architectural proportions and elaboration.

Mrs Henderson told her more about it one afternoon, coming up to the schoolroom just after the end of lesson hours.

"It all sounds wonderful," Emma said. "Zara's a lucky girl. Is there anything I can do to help?"

Mrs Henderson looked relieved. "Oh my dear, I'm so glad you asked. Of course, I couldn't have imposed on you, but the whole thing falls on my shoulders, and there's an absolute mass of work involved."

"Well, I'd be delighted to do anything I can," Emma said. "You needn't have been afraid to ask – I'd like to think I was a full member of the household."

No sooner had Mrs Henderson educated Emma fully in

92

the plans for the birthday party, than she had to tell her that, after all, Mr Akroyd would not be present.

"It's the greatest nuisance, but he has to go away on business."

"Oh, really?" Emma was surprised.

"He's going to China of all places! Apparently the Chinese government is about to award a contract for a huge bridge somewhere up-country, and it's so important Mr Akroyd feels he must go himself. It could be worth a great deal of money, you see. And for the same reason, he can't put the trip off. If someone's ready to commission work on that scale, you can't keep them waiting on your convenience – especially not the Chinese, I understand. They're very touchy. If he offends the wrong person, the contract could be lost, not only to Akroyd Engineering, but to Britain."

"But couldn't Zara's party be postponed?"

"It could," said Mrs Henderson with an equivocal face, "but Zara won't hear of it. She says it doesn't matter if her father is there or not. Between you and me," she lowered her voice, "I think she thinks there will be a more relaxed atmosphere without him. I wouldn't be surprised if she weren't thinking of inviting some people she knows he wouldn't like."

Since Mrs Henderson was in a confiding mood, Emma dared to go a little further. "I'm surprised that Mr Akroyd is willing to let the party go on without him. Won't it seem rather odd, it being her coming-of-age?"

Mrs Henderson shrugged. "Frankly, my dear, I think he's in such a tizzy about this China business that he hasn't time to worry about a birthday party – even an eighteenth. And of course, she will be 'brought out' in London later in the year, so I suppose he thinks that will be the important date. But it does put more responsibility on the rest of us – especially Gavin. If anything goes wrong, it'll be him that takes the blame."

Emma could not think what might go wrong that Gavin

would be blamed for. What did they have servants for? Surely if anyone spilled wine on the carpet or made a glass-ring on an antique commode, Mr Akroyd wouldn't bend Gavin over a chair and give him six of the best for it?

Poppy was excited about the party, and chatted animatedly about the arrangements whenever Emma let her. "I'm not being let to go to the ball," she said, "but I don't care. Zara's friends are really boring, and dancing's stupid. But I'm having a new dress anyway, and Mrs Grainger's making the cake and she said she'd let me help her decorate it."

"Well, that should be interesting."

"Yes. But when I'm eighteen, I'm not going to have a dancing sort of party. I'm going to make everyone come on horseback and have a 'normous gymkhana in the park, and a picnic, and a barbecue with hamburgers and everything, and races and games. And my birthday cake will be all chocolate!"

"Isn't it wonderful to hear her talk about food so enthusiastically?" Mrs Henderson said, when Poppy repeated all this in her presence. "You've done her so much good," she added to Emma, fondly.

Preparations for the party took Emma away from the schoolroom a good deal in the following weeks – Lady Susan not only gave her blessing to the use of Miss Ruskin as a spare secretary, but did not hesitate to use her herself. Emma was frequently sent on errands for her ladyship, driving into Bury or Cambridge in the Mini to collect things, while her ladyship looked after Poppy. Generally when Emma returned she would find that Lady Susan had wandered off on business of her own, and Poppy would be discovered in the kitchen, kneeling on a stool and messing about with pastry or measuring ingredients for Mrs Grainger. Emma wondered if the child's mother knew where she inevitably ended up, but thought her ladyship would probably sooner even have her child tainted by servants than be inconvenienced herself.

Mr Akroyd departed for Beijing, whence he would travel into the interior in a group made up not only of technicians from his company, but representatives of the Board of Trade, the Foreign Office and a leading High Street Bank. Emma couldn't help wondering whether there would be any danger involved – China was not yet a completely civilised place. Lady Susan wondered anxiously whether he would have time to shop for her in Hong Kong on his way back. Zara wondered urgently whether he would give her her birthday present before he left – which in fact he did. It was a car of her own, a Peugeot 206 with all the gadgets, which Zara received with shrill delight: she actually flung her arms round her father's neck and kissed him, so excited was she. Emma noticed, however, that Gavin did not look pleased, and wondered why. She would not have expected him to be so petty as to begrudge his sister a car.

On the day of the party there were no lessons for Poppy. Emma was up early and put herself at Mrs Henderson's disposal, and it was while they were checking lists together that Mrs Henderson revealed that Emma was expected to attend the party.

"Oh, I couldn't. I didn't expect . . . really, I'd much rather not," Emma stammered in confusion.

Mrs Henderson raised one perfectly groomed eyebrow. "But my dear, you said you wanted to be a full member of the household. I should have thought you'd want to be there."

"Oh—" Emma was embarrassed. "It really isn't my sort of thing. I mean, I'm not one of the family, just a member of staff. I really don't think—"

"Well, I shall be there. And you've worked as hard as I have to make it a success. I really think you will have to put in an appearance. It will be expected."

"But I haven't anything to wear!"

Mrs Henderson laughed. "That's more like it! I thought you really didn't want to go, and I should hate to think we'd knocked all the fun out of you already! Of course, it will be long evening dresses for the ball, but I expect a cocktail frock would do."

"I haven't got either," Emma said.

"Oh dear!" Mrs Henderson seemed really put out. "I wish I'd thought to mention it to you before. I just naturally assumed . . ."

"Look, it really doesn't matter," Emma said firmly. "I would feel very awkward about joining in with the dancing and so on anyway. I'll just pop down at some point and wish Zara a happy birthday, and then disappear. No one will notice."

Mrs Henderson still looked unhappy. "I hate to think of you missing all the fun, especially when you've done so much of the work."

"I really don't mind. Honestly, please don't worry," Emma said as persuasively as she could. The thought of Zara sneering at her, and of Zara's glamorous, predatory girlfriends clustering round Gavin, was not tempting. And an evening spent watching Gavin dance with a succession of gorgeous county females and – worse – enjoying it was not high on her list of fun things to do. She might mean nothing to him, but she didn't have to have her nose rubbed in it.

Zara, looking extremely elegant and, unexpectedly, just a little nervous, stood in the hall welcoming her guests. She was wearing a long dress of yellow silk, and the double strand of pearls which had been her mother's gift to her, and her hair was done up in an elaborate swirl which had taken the hairdresser a couple of hours that afternoon to achieve.

Lights blazed everywhere, and huge flower arrangements lent colour to usually dark corners; stewards and maids buzzed round discreetly, carrying trays of champagne and directing ladies to the cloakroom; the orchestra was playing quietly to itself in the room that would later be full of young people dancing.

Gavin was very much in evidence, filling in the gaps in

Zara's attention span, helping his mother to greet the older guests, making the County feel welcome. The County was arriving in huge Rollers and Bentleys, and was swathed in furs and glittering with diamonds; the younger set zoomed up in BMWs and Range Rovers. Gavin chatted charmingly with them all, young and old, but Emma noticed that he frequently looked about him with a faintly lost air, as though he were expecting someone in particular who hadn't arrived. One of Zara's smart set, Emma supposed, as she watched with Poppy from their hiding place on the first floor landing. Gavin, she thought, looked exceptionally handsome in dinner jacket and black tie: he seemed moulded into it, whereas some of the young men arriving looked as though it was wearing them rather than vice versa. She watched him bow over the hand of a plump pink female in a regrettably short skirt, and his smile did terrible things to her pulse. But his very elegance and beauty eased her in an odd way, because it convinced her, if she needed convincing, that he was way, way out of her league, and that there was nothing for her but to admire him from a distance.

Poppy wriggled with excitement, and whispered to Emma the names and principal habits of those guests she knew, sometimes leaning out so far for a better look that Emma kept a hand on her belt in case she had to grab her. Emma responded with a "Really?" and "Does she?" which was all Poppy seemed to need – fortunately, since Emma's attention was all taken up with watching Gavin and waiting for the guest he seemed to be expecting. At last her vigilance was rewarded. A female arrived whom he greeted with every sign of particularity. It was not one of the Nats and Vics of Zara's set, but an older woman, a tall, dark-haired beauty in a sheath-like dress of turquoise silk.

Emma sighed with sheer admiration, which was almost without a pang. She was glad that it was someone so superior, someone with whom she could not have hoped to compete. She wouldn't have liked Gavin to throw himself away. The dark girl was slim as a withy, very beautiful, elegant, sparkling at throat and wrist with diamonds, and with a lovely smile, to which Gavin responded with tender warmth. He took both her hands with an ease and an eagerness that proved he had known her long, and loved her well, and led her straight away into the the room where the band was playing.

"Who was that girl?" Emma asked, turning to Poppy.

"Which one?" Poppy asked.

"The dark-haired lady that your brother just led away."

"Oh, did he? I wasn't looking." She craned through the banisters. "No. I can't see him. I s'pose it was one of Zara's friends."

"She looked a bit older than Zara."

"Oh well, I don't know then." Poppy was evidently not much interested. She had more important things on her mind. "Emma, can we go down and get something to eat now? I'm abs'lutely *dying* of hunger, and everyone must be here by now. We could sneak down without anybody seeing us."

"I'm afraid not," Emma said. "Not now. It's time you were in bed, and I have to go down and say happy birthday to Zara."

"Oh blow!" Poppy said crossly. "Do you have to? Honestly, she won't care if you do or not."

"I'm sure she won't, but it's the polite thing and I have to do it. But if you're still awake when I come back up, I'll bring you up something from the buffet."

"Oh, brill! What will you bring?"

"I don't know — whatever I can carry most easily, I suppose."

"Sausage rolls," Poppy pleaded. "And cake — chocolate cake."

"I'll see what I can do," Emma promised.

Fifteen minutes later Emma came down the stairs again, feeling like a fish out of water, and hoping not to attract attention. The 'receiving' stage was over, Zara was no longer in the hall, and Lady Susan had retired into the drawing-room with the friends of her generation. But there were still plenty of people standing about the hall, talking, sipping champagne, smoking, laughing at each other's jokes. Emma slipped between them, and was glad to note that they paid her no attention, any more than they noticed the waitresses who drifted about supplying them with full glasses. In her short dress, Emma supposed, she must look like a member of staff – which of course she was – and therefore not to be spoken to.

In search of Zara she went into the dancing-room, and was rewarded – or punished – by the sight of Gavin dancing with the dark-haired girl. He was holding her closely, and they revolved in perfect harmony, not even speaking, his cheek resting against the dark, sleek hair. Despite herself, Emma felt a lump in her throat; and as his head began to turn towards her, she backed hastily out, and went across the hall to another room where there was the sound of bright laughter and talk. There she found Zara in the middle of a group of young men and girls, all shrieking at once and having a whale of a time.

Emma would not have disturbed her, but as she happened to catch Zara's eye and the latter raised an enquiring eyebrow, she decided she'd better get it over with and walked across.

"I just came to wish you a happy birthday," Emma said, "and to hope that you have a wonderful evening. Everything seems to be going OK, doesn't it?"

"Oh yes, thanks," Zara said, looking her up and down. The friends all turned away to give them privacy, apart from the bosom pals Natalie and Victoria, who simply stared as though they couldn't believe their eyes.

"Good," Emma said, trying to shove some warmth into her smile. "Well, I only popped down just to say happy birthday, so I won't keep you any more."

"Oh, but *surely* you're going to stay and have a dance?" Natalie said with heavy irony.

"Oh yes," Victoria added, "I'm sure Zara can find you *someone* to dance with." And she whispered something to Natalie – the name of some poor nerd they despised, Emma supposed – and they both sniggered and clutched each other, thrilled by their own humour.

The only thing was to respond with dignity, Emma thought. "No, I can't stay – I'm not dressed for a formal party," she said. "I'm going back upstairs now."

Zara threw her friends a look, and then grabbed Emma's wrist, turning her away so that Nat and Vic shouldn't hear her words. "Yes," she said in a low voice, "and see you *do* go upstairs. No hanging around Gavin looking like a sick spaniel, because he's just about polite enough to feel he has to ask you to dance. I don't want him bothered by you, d'you understand?"

Only too well, Emma thought. You've got him marked down for one of your giggling friends. Well, I think I can spoil your evening for you. "You needn't worry, Gavin wouldn't ask me to dance. He's very well occupied, dancing with a very lovely girl, and I'm sure he doesn't know anyone else exists."

Zara frowned, and Emma had her moment of triumph. "What girl?" Zara asked crossly.

"Tall, dark and slim, in turquoise silk. They make a lovely couple."

"Oh but that's—" Zara stopped abruptly, and then a canny look stole across her face. "No, you're right, he's sure to be very wrapped up in *that* partner," she said, and turned abruptly away, leaving Emma to pick her way back to the door, glad to have got an unpleasant duty over with. Behind her she heard a burst of shrill laughter, which she had no doubt was Zara and her bosom buddies indulging their fabulous wit again at her expense. As if she cared!

Busy showing she didn't care, Emma did not look where

she was going, and bursting out through the door into the hall she ran full tilt into a dress-shirt and had to be held up against the force of the collision. Warm, strong hands gripped her upper arms.

"Steady! Where are you rushing off to?"

Emma's gaze travelled up from the neat, pleated shirtfront to the face that was rarely out of her thoughts these days, and found him smiling, his eyes very bright – left-overs, no doubt, from turquoise-and-diamonds, she thought viciously.

"I wasn't rushing, I was just going back upstairs," she said, trying to sound neutral. She wasn't sure she had succeeded. Gavin set her carefully back on balance, but he did not remove his hands from her arms. She was torn between not wanting him to, and worrying about what the effect on her might be if he didn't.

"Going upstairs? What for?"

"What d'you mean, what for?" she said, annoyed that he was being stupid about it. It must be obvious. "I'm not part of the party. I only came down to say happy birthday to Zara, and now I'm going back up."

"But you mustn't," he said. "I haven't had a dance with you yet, and I've been promising myself that for days. I *wondered* where you were. I kept looking for you. I thought you must be off dancing with some other lucky blighter."

He'd been *looking* for her? He'd been looking for *her*? Emma stared up at him in astonishment. Could he really mean it? But no, she told herself, don't be so simple. You saw how he seized on the turquoise girl the moment he saw her. He's just making a fool of you, being sarcastic.

"I haven't come to the party to dance," she said. She wished he would let her go – it made it hard to think. "You can see I'm not dressed for it."

"Why not?" he argued.

"Oh come," she said shortly, "you can see I'm in a short dress and everyone else is in evening clothes. There's such a thing as being too gallant, you know."

101

He laughed. "Ah, now I feel more at home! I don't feel quite right without Miss Ruskin telling me off about something." She blushed with a complex mixture of vexations, and he said, "Look, please dance with me. I promise no one will notice what you've got on. Honestly, they're all too preoccupied with how they look themselves."

Doubt overcame her. He really seemed to mean it. He really wanted to dance with her. She could no longer feel he meant to make a fool of her; there still remained the likelihood that he was just being polite. She went straight to the bottom line, and said, "But your sister doesn't want me to dance, and it's her party."

"That's the worst excuse you've given me so far." He ran his fingers down her arm and took hold of her hand. "I don't care a fig what Zara thinks, and I don't believe you do, either. Come, please, come and dance."

He led her across the hall to the dancing-room. The band was playing a slow tune. "Good," he said. "I hate that jiggling on the spot stuff. It's no fun unless you can get your arms round your partner." And he drew her to him and stepped away with her to the music, holding her close. Emma tried very hard to tell herself that it meant nothing; but just for that moment, she didn't care. She was going to have this, and enjoy it, and to hell with what came after. She let herself relax into him, feeling the warmth and strength of his body, breathing in the scent of him. How long was a dance tune? Five minutes? Six? Well, if that was all she would ever have, she'd make sure she enjoyed every second of it. He drew her just a little closer, squeezing her hand, not seeming to want to talk, for which she was grateful. They stepped slowly, swaying in sweet harmony, as if they had been dancing together all their lives. Emma closed her eyes in bliss, and time very kindly ceased for a little while to exist.

The dance was over. Sanity flooded back painfully into her

blissed-out brain as the couples around them broke up into chattering groups and began to jostle their way off the floor. She was a member of the household staff, dressed in an unsuitably short dress, and batting right out of her league. She ought to get herself out of Gavin's hair before her glass slippers turned back into clogs and tripped her up.

"Well, thank you for the dance," she said abruptly. "It was very kind of you."

Gavin, who had been smiling, suddenly looked taken aback, and she realised that in her effort to sound matter-of-fact she had in fact sounded cold and sarcastic, as if she *hadn't* enjoyed the dance and *didn't* think it was kind of him.

"I didn't ask you to be kind," he said.

"Well, it was kind, especially as I wasn't dressed properly," she said, "so thank you anyway." It sounded belligerent.

He drew back from her. "It's I who should thank you," he said politely.

Now she had offended him, she thought. Worse and worse! All the warmth had evaporated, and they were suddenly like strangers, trapped by politeness and longing to be elsewhere. How could she be so awkward? She'd better make her escape before she accidentally knocked him down.

"I must go," she said hastily, pulling her hand away from his.

"Oh, not yet, surely?" he said. "Stay and have another dance. No one will mind about your dress. Zara's not even in the room."

"No, I have to go upstairs. I – I promised to look in on Poppy."

"Yes, I see," he said. "Well, I don't want to hold you up, as you're in such a hurry." And he gave an awkward little bow, and turned away.

Emma watched him go. His gait seemed a little offended; but it was better that way. Another dance with him and she might have started to believe her senses instead of her common sense. Arguing herself into a more stable frame of mind, she wriggled away through the crowds and made her way to the buffet. There were already people around it, but she managed to sneak in at one end and, with a nod of complicity at the nearest waiter, who recognised her, she took a plate and loaded it with whatever delicacies were nearest at hand. Then she made her way upstairs, wondering why she could not behave like a normal human being around Gavin Akroyd. She was like a school kid, alternately blushing and surly. The poor bloke had danced with her out of kindness – hadn't he? – and she had snapped at him as if he had insulted her. Oh well, she thought philosophically as she turned the stair, it didn't matter. She was an employee in the house, he didn't have to like her. He'd just think her a bit mad – if he ever thought of her at all, which was unlikely.

As she passed her own room first, she thought she'd stop in and get into her nightdress and dressing-gown before looking in on Poppy. That would prevent her from having any pathetic thoughts of going downstairs again – not even as far as the first landing for a sneaky look at Gavin over the banisters! Quickly she undressed and put on her nightie and the 'sensible' dressing-gown she had bought in case of night emergencies – a full-length, high-necked, woollen thing with big pockets – and taking up the plate of goodies again she went out into the passage and along towards Poppy's room.

The sounds of the party were very faint and far away, for this was the opposite side of the house from the main reception rooms. A good thing, too, she thought, or Poppy would never get to sleep. As she went into the day-nursery, through which she had to pass to get to the night-nursery where Poppy slept, she saw a band of light in the further room, showing at the bottom of the closed door. The floorboards creaked under her feet and the light was quickly doused. Poppy reading in bed, she thought. But she didn't need to be so guilty about it: Emma had said she'd come up and see her.

Quietly she opened the night-nursery door, expecting to see Poppy curled up in bed pretending hard to be asleep. Instead, in the dark room – for it was a moonless night – she could just make out that the bed was empty.

"Hello? Where are you?" she said. The child must be hiding, for a game. "Come on out, I've got the food for you. Lots of goodies!"

She stepped one pace forward into the room, and, just as all the hair rose on the back of her neck with the realisation that there was someone behind her, there was a soft rush of movement and someone grabbed her. Hard hands, adult hands, bruised her, meaning business, and before she could scream something soft was clamped over her mouth. She struggled wildly, thrashing to and fro; the plate of food flew from her hand; she dragged her arm free to grab at the wrist in front of her, trying to tear it from her face, for she was suffocating.

A vile, sickly smell was in her mouth and nose, clinging, cloying, choking. The pad which was pressed over the lower part of her face was impregnated with the stuff. She felt faint, dizzy, she wanted to vomit; she jerked her head against the restraining hands, but she was aware that her struggles were weakening, that she was slipping away from herself. A feeling of nausea and deep despair washed over her, a desperate, desolate sense of being lost; and then a black hole seemed to open under her feet and she fell into it, and down, down into oblivion.

Chapter Nine

Emma drifted back to consciousness slowly and reluctantly. Something had happened, and she didn't want to know what. She floated just under the surface of waking, gradually becoming aware of pain: a raw burning around her mouth and nose; a bitter, biting pain in her wrists and ankles; cramped, bruised soreness from every part of her body that touched the hard, ridged surface she was lying on.

The pain focused her mind, and at once the fear came in, like a radio being switched on. *Danger, danger, danger*! She opened her eyes, but it was pitch dark. As her senses sharpened, she realised that there were voices nearby: two people talking in low, urgent voices. She could hear them strangely muffled, through a heavy, growling noise that transmitted itself through her aching flesh and bones.

"You said it was gonna be all right," someone was complaining. "You said nobody'd hear us. You said everyone'd be on the other side of the house."

"Oh, shut your face! We got the kid, didn't we?"

"Well, I don't like it. What about *her*?"

"She must be the kid's nurse or something. She'll come in useful."

"But suppose they come looking for her?"

"Why should they? She's in her nightie, isn't she? They won't start looking till they don't show up for breakfast. We got hours yet. Now shut up and gimme a fag."

The voices stopped. Now she understood her situation. The growling noise was a motor engine. She was in the back

106

of a van of some sort, lying on the bare floor, her wrists and ankles tied, and some kind of cloth over her head. She had been kidnapped, along with Poppy. Presumably Poppy was also in the back of the van, somewhere near, probably tied up too. Oh God, what would they do to her? What did they want? Money, presumably. Mr Akroyd was rich. If it was money, they would take good care of Poppy, wouldn't they? They wouldn't hurt her. Oh, she prayed not. She hoped it was money. Mr Akroyd would pay to get Poppy back. But what of her own case? Suppose the criminals decided she was expendable? What might they do then? Her stomach curdled in fear.

The van picked up speed, and every time it went over a bump some part of her hit the ridged metal floor. There seemed to be an awful lot of bumps. It was agony; but at least the pain kept her mind off her fear. Then suddenly the front left corner of the van dipped, and the floor heaved up under her. She heard one of the men say, "Look out!" and at the same moment her trussed body was flung sideways, her head struck something hard and sharp, and she slithered sickeningly into unconsciousness again.

Gavin decided to give Emma five minutes, and then go up after her. He blamed himself for the misunderstandings between them. OK, she was very touchy, but after all, as an employee her position was not as straightforward as his. It was up to him to make the situation clear. He was sure she was attracted to him, but she obviously couldn't afford to assume anything, and in his wretched shyness he had failed to make it plain to her that he was interested in her. He must tell her so in words of one syllable, and take it from there.

It was difficult for him to get away from the party, for every few steps he was waylaid by another guest, and he couldn't just brush them aside rudely; but he worked his way as quickly as he could across the hall, and once he got to the foot of the stairs he was home free. He hurried up to the nursery floor. Emma had her own room there, just along the passage from the schoolroom and night-nursery. Her door was shut but the light was on, so at least she had not gone to bed and to sleep already. He knocked; waited; knocked again. He called out, close to the door, "Emma, it's me, Gavin. Can I talk to you?" But there was no reply.

Then he remembered she had said she'd promised to look in on Poppy. Maybe she was there still. He went along the passage, through the day-nursery, and opened the door to the night-nursery. A single glance showed him the bed was empty. He snapped on the light, and in one second had taken in the state of the room: the bedclothes flung back and dragged half off the bed; the framed photograph of Misty on the bedside locker knocked over; the bedside rug rucked into a heap as though by dragging feet; and on the floor in front of him a plate broken into three pieces and various bits of party food scattered about, some of them trodden into the carpet.

The truth scalded into his brain. He turned and ran back to Emma's room, flung the door open, saw that the room was empty and undisturbed, and ran for the nearest telephone. Having summoned the police, he went back down to the first floor landing, almost to the same spot where Emma and Poppy had hidden earlier in the evening, looking for a servant. Better still, he saw Mrs Henderson come out of the room below him, and leaning over the banisters he called urgently, "Jean! Up here!"

She looked up, and saw from his face that something was wrong; so that when he beckoned she obeyed instantly and without fuss, making her way through the guests and quickly up the stairs to him.

"What is it?" she asked. Quickly he told her what had happened. She frowned. "But why d'you think they've been kidnapped? They may have slipped out on some little expedition of their own."

"Emma wouldn't take Poppy out at this time of night. And you can see from the room there's been a struggle. No, I tell you they've been snatched!"

"Shouldn't we at least search a bit before we call the police?"

"I've already called them. If they've been taken, every second counts – you must see that."

She capitulated. "Yes, of course. What do you want me to do?"

Gavin looked relieved. "I don't want the guests to know until they have to, but they mustn't leave the house. Can you quietly round up the servants and post one on each door? And put someone reliable on the front stairs, to stop anyone coming up to the nursery floor. I'm going back up to keep guard, to make sure nothing's touched."

"Yes, all right. What about the police?"

"I've told them to come to the back hall, and no sirens. When they arrive, can you bring them quietly up the back stairs?"

She nodded and went away, and blessing her quiet efficiency, Gavin went back up to the nursery, where he stood at the door, contemplating the real reason why he was sure it was a kidnap. A piece of cake which Emma had brought up to Poppy had been squashed into the carpet, presumably during the struggle, and it bore quite clearly the ridged imprint of a large, man's boot.

When Emma regained consciousness, the van was bumping less violently. They must be on a smoother, better road. She had been thrown or rolled against the side of the van, and now she found that by bracing herself against it and pressing with her heels on the floor, she could steady herself a little, enough to stop herself rolling back and forth. It was very tiring, though, and she couldn't keep it up continuously. Her hands and feet were going dead from lack of circulation, and her head was throbbing abominably. She wanted to drift off to sleep again, and struggled with herself to stay awake and alert. Something might happen; she couldn't just give up.

They were cruising steadily and, from the engine noise, fast. Then she heard one of the men say, "Oh shit! Oh no, oh shit, shit!"

"What?"

"Fuzz, coming up behind us."

"Don't panic. They can't be onto us already."

"What'll we do! What'll we do!" The van lurched under sudden acceleration, and Emma groaned weakly as her head hit the floor again.

"Christ, slow down, you maniac!" the older man said. "D'you want to draw attention to us? I tell you they can't be after us yet. Just drive normally."

"I can lose 'em," the other one pleaded. "Lemme lose 'em!"

"In this thing? Calm down, I tell you! We'll bluff it out."

Emma's heart had risen at this exchange. The police were after them already! She must concentrate, keep conscious. When they were stopped, she'd make such a noise the police would have to hear. They'd be rescued! Oh thank God, thank God!

After a tense silence, the younger voice rose in elation. "They went straight past! They weren't after us!"

"I told you so, you dummy!"

"Thank Christ for that. I thought we'd had it."

"I told you it'd be all right. You panic too easily. All the same, they've seen us now. We'll have to dump this thing."

"But you said—"

"Sooner or later they're going to put out an alert on the van, stupid, and then those coppers'll remember where they saw us." A pause, then the older man went on, "There's a place up ahead. I'll tell you where. We can dump it and you can go out and nick something."

110

"Aw, Boss—!"

"Stop whining. We'll be OK. Just take it easy. Put the radio on."

Emma's heart sank again. She was so desperately disappointed, her eyes filled with helpless tears, which she struggled against. It was hard enough to breathe, without being choked up with tears. The men went on talking in low voices, but she could no longer hear what they said over the noise of pop music.

Now the motion of the van changed again. She felt it slow, then a hard turn to the left, and then a slow but agonising progress over bumps and hollows. She guessed they had turned off the main road onto a track of some sort. The floor of the van bucked under her like a horse, and she could not brace herself enough to avoid being thrown about. She gritted her teeth, and wondered how Poppy was faring. She had made no sound yet. Was she still unconscious?

At last the van stopped, the engine was cut, and there was blissful stillness. Emma drifted into unconsciousness for a few minutes – she couldn't help it – and when she came to again, it was quite silent. The men must have got out. She wondered if she could do anything to improve the situation – get this cloth off her head, at least – then she could breathe more easily, and see where Poppy was, and whether she was all right. The cloth was a bag of some sort, she thought. If she rubbed it against the floor of the van she might be able to drag it off. The problem was that her head hurt so much, and any movement made the throbbing worse. But she had to try. Slowly, painfully, she worked at it; and as she rubbed and rubbed, she thought about the kidnappers. Two of them, one older and well-spoken, though his accent slipped a bit now and then; the younger one with an ordinary London accent, who sounded a bit stupid – probably he was the strong-arm man. It was he who had been driving, certainly. Was that all, or were they part of a larger gang? And what was going to happen now?

The bag came off at last, and Emma drew in a few gasps of fresher, colder air. But that was the only reward for her hard work and pain. It was still pitch dark; she couldn't see a thing. And she was still helpless. She began to cry softly from weariness and fear.

"Now we're getting somewhere," Superintendent Moss said, putting down the phone. "The caterers say one of their vans is missing from the depot. Now if your man at the gate is reliable—"

"He is," Gavin said.

"I'll take your word for it. *He* says nothing came out but catering vans, and all the other vans are accounted for, so it's got to be the one."

"And where does that get us?" Gavin asked. Continuous anxiety was making him weary, slowing his thought processes.

"Well, sir, we've got the van's number now, you see. We can put that out over the radio, so every patrol car will be on the look-out; and thanks to your prompt action we've got the road blocks in place. They won't have got far."

Gavin nodded, but found no comfort in the words. He tried to keep his mind on what had to be done, and what could be done, like fending off enquiries from friends and guests and trying to get hold of his father; but it would keep straying to horrible contemplation of what the villains might do to Poppy and to Emma.

Emma heard the sound of a car engine approaching. For a wild and wonderful instant she thought perhaps it was the police. But it slowed and stopped, and then went whiningly into reverse, then forward again; her imagination supplied the picture of it performing a three-point turn in the track. Then a car door opened and slammed; and then the van doors were abruptly and noisily flung open. There was a breath of fresh, cold air, and light – not much of it, only starlight, but enough, after the pitch blackness, to see by.

A middle-aged man stood there, with a battered-looking face, gold-rimmed glasses, close-cropped grey hair, a dark overcoat.

"All right, let's get 'em out. You take the woman, I'll take the kid."

Behind him the younger man appeared: tall, heavily-built, wearing jeans and an old, padded anorak. He bent towards Emma, and stopped, peering into her face. "She's awake," he said.

"She's got the hood off," the older man said in a tone of menace. "You are a total—" He added an obscenity, which sounded odd in his cultured accent.

"I put it on all right, Boss," the other protested whiningly.

"Yeah, yeah! Well, it's too late now. You'd better gag her, though."

The younger man dragged a handkerchief out of his pocket. Emma eyed it with horror and despair.

"Please," she croaked. "Please don't." The younger man paused, looking at the Boss questioningly. "Please," Emma said again. "Let me breathe. I promise I won't shout."

The Boss looked at her for a moment consideringly, and then he nodded. "All right," he said. Emma saw no compassion in his face; she thought he probably judged she couldn't have shouted if she wanted to.

The younger man climbed up into the van and disappeared behind Emma's line of sight, to reappear a moment later carrying Poppy. She was hooded with what looked like a sugar sack and her arms and legs were tied. The younger man handed her down into the Boss's arms; she made no sound, and was ominously limp.

"What have you done to her?" Emma cried, her voice cracking weakly. The younger man looked down at her with what might have been a faint thread of pity.

113

"Doped," he said briefly. "She's OK."

"Andy, shut your mouth," the Boss snapped, and walked off with his burden.

"All right, babe, your turn," Andy said. He bent over Emma, pushed his hand under her body, and used the rope around her wrists to jerk her up into a sitting position. She moaned as the rope cut into her already damaged flesh. Still holding her up, Andy climbed out of the van and dragged her towards him until she was on the edge. Then he pulled her round to face him, put his shoulder to her midriff and swung her up. He was very strong, and seemed to make nothing of her weight.

Dangling there, face down over his shoulder, helpless, all Emma could see was the grass over which he was walking. She could smell his sweat, and the tobacco smoke which impregnated his clothes. She tried to turn her head a little, saw thin, scrubby pine trees and gorse bushes. Then she saw the car, a blue saloon, a Rover, she thought. It came closer. The back door was opened. Poppy was lying curled on the back seat, unmoving. Then Andy swung her down, sickeningly, and bundled her in onto the floor. She groaned again as he pushed her legs in, and he muttered, "Shut it! It won't be long." Another little thread of sympathy? But then he threw a blanket over her, and she was alone in the stifling dark again.

She remembered little of the rest of the journey. Cramped, in pain, and starved of oxygen, she was unconscious for much of the time; and when she was conscious, she was hardly aware of where she was or what was happening. At last the car stopped, the engine was cut, and into the stillness there came the sound of birdsong, the massed trilling of the dawn chorus. The door of the car opened, the blanket was drawn away, and light flooded in. Someone was whistling cheerfully. The sound cut through her headache like an ice pick. It was Andy. He reached in and lifted Poppy out, and presumably handed her to his companion; then he stooped over Emma and cut the rope round her ankles and said, "All right, babe, you can walk the rest."

He manhandled her out and tried to put her on her feet, but her legs would not hold her and buckled under her. The world swung dizzily about her; the pressure in her head was agonising and she felt sick. Now the blood was beginning to return to her feet, and the pins-and-needles and the burning pain in her ankles made her moan again, feebly.

"Here, Boss," Andy said, gripping Emma under the armpits, "this one looks a bit rough. And there's blood on her face."

"Hit her head on something, I expect," the Boss said, his voice suddenly close, but without pity.

"Shouldn't we call a doctor or something?"

"Jesus! I wonder how you manage for brains," the Boss sighed in exasperation. "Call a doctor! What did I do to get lumbered with a dickhead like you? Will you hurry up and get her indoors, before the neighbours come round?"

Andy heaved her up roughly, taking it out on her, perhaps, for his telling-off. "Walk, you cow," he snapped, shaking her. She stumbled forward, most of her weight taken by him, her feet flopping and dragging stupidly as she tried to control them. Through a daze of pain and dizziness she caught a glimpse of the house, grey stone and creeper, coming towards her. She felt dimly that she ought to be trying to notice things in case it might help, but the darkness was swaying back towards her like a big, soft, welcome cloud.

Only half-conscious, she was dragged into the house, up the stairs, and into a room, where there was a bed pushed up against the wall. Poppy was lying on the bed, unhooded but still tied. Andy threw Emma down on the bed beside her, rolled her onto her side, cut the rope round her wrists, and said, "There you are, babe. You can untie the kid. She's all yours."

Emma was aware of him leaving the room, heard the door close and the click of the lock, but for the life of her she couldn't move, not an inch, not a muscle. She ought to get up and untie Poppy, she knew, but the blackness was swirling back, and she had no strength to resist it.

Chapter Ten

Someone was kicking her, and calling her. It seemed unkind. She didn't want to wake up: she knew that, though she didn't know why. She tried to tell them to leave her alone and go away, but all that came out was a gutteral noise.

"Wake up! Wake up!"

She tried to roll over, away from the nuisance, and pain shifted inside her head like a rock sliding down a slope. "Oh no," she muttered. "No, don't."

"Emma, *please*! Please wake up! Oh, please speak to me!"

It was Poppy's voice. Understanding slowly seeped in. Poppy was nudging her and calling her. But why? Was she late for breakfast? She tried to open her eyes but the light stabbed the inside of her skull and made her cry out. And then she remembered why she so deeply, definitely didn't want to wake up. They had been kidnapped. And, oh my God, Poppy was still tied up! How long had she been sleeping while poor Poppy cried and called to her? She must wake up, she must help her.

She rolled onto her side, tried to get her elbow under her and push herself up. The pain smashed around inside her head as if someone was playing squash with it, and as she opened her eyes a slit, nausea came rushing up like an eager crowd on the first day of the sales.

"It's all right," she muttered thickly. "All right, Poppy. Just wait a minute."

"Oh, Emma, I thought you were dead!" Poppy cried, a

117

lifting voice of relief with a sob in it. Emma, hanging her head, feeling like death, was able to imagine how frightened the child had been, with her only protector lying like a log beside her. Emma managed to get her eyes open a little further, managed some species of smile, though the throbbing, blinding pain in her head was something that had to be felt to be believed. Poppy's tearstained face was a few inches from hers, her cheek to the pillow, her hands still tied behind her back. "You were so white and still, and I called you and called you, but you wouldn't wake up. I was so frightened!"

The memory of her fear set her sobbing again, though perhaps it was partly relief. Emma managed to reach out a hand and pat the nearest bit of Poppy to her.

"It's all right," she said again. "It's all right now. Just give me a minute, and I'll untie you."

It took a good five minutes before Emma was able to move herself. Then she inched herself round so that she could lean against the wall, and Poppy wriggled round to present her back to her. The knots had pulled tight, of course, and Emma's fingers felt like uncooked sausages — thick and limp, useless for the task. While she worked away at them, slowly and doggedly, Poppy asked her what had happened.

"We've been kidnapped," Emma told her. There seemed no point in sugar-coating it. "Two men came and took us away."

"Where are we?"

"I don't know. They took us in a closed van. I couldn't see anything. And you were drugged."

"I remember now," Poppy said with a dry sob of fright. "I was waiting for you to come up, and I must have fallen asleep, and then suddenly there was somebody there, standing by the bed, and I tried to scream but they put something over my mouth and there was this awful smell—"

"Yes, I know. Chloroform, I think. But that wouldn't keep

you unconscious all that time. They must have injected you with something, I suppose, once you'd stopped struggling."

"It's horrible," Poppy whispered. "Why would anyone want to kidnap us?"

"Well, you for money, I should think. They'll ask your father for a lot of money to get you back."

"Daddy's very rich," she said.

"And they took me because I disturbed them. I came up with your goodies from the buffet and they grabbed me from behind and chloroformed me, too. I woke up in the van, tied up and with a bag over my head."

"Poor Emma," Poppy said.

"Poor Poppy," she replied. "Ah, at last, it's coming. Yes – there. Done!"

Poppy pulled her arms forward, and then at once began to writhe in agony. "Oh, they've gone dead! Oh Emma – oh—!"

Emma did her best for her, rubbing her arms as vigorously as she had strength for. She knew the agony of returning blood, and the horrible feeling of a dead limb flopping about like a landed fish at the end of one's body. "Keep flexing your fingers," she advised. She needed to rest. "Can you rub for yourself now?"

When Poppy was sufficiently recovered to sit up, still rubbing her forearms with her hands, she looked at Emma with wide, grave eyes and said in a small voice, "What's happened to your head?"

"I bumped it in the van," Emma said vaguely. "Why?"

"You've got blood all in your hair."

Emma reached a careful hand towards the centre of pain and found her hair partly sticky, partly wet. She felt queasy, but tried to make light of it for Poppy's sake.

"It probably looks worse than it is," she said, but she swayed dizzily. Poppy's hands came up to her shoulders.

"You lie down. I'll do the other rope myself. I expect I'm better at knots than you anyway. My fingers are smaller."

Emma didn't argue. The exertion had made her sweat. She lowered herself gingerly to the horizontal and closed her eyes. After a bit Poppy said, "Don't worry, I bet someone will rescue us soon. I bet Gavin will come after us. As soon as he knows what's happened, he'll come."

Emma didn't speak. Poppy's faith in her brother was touching, but what likelihood was there that anyone would discover they were missing until morning? And by then the trail would be cold. It would be a matter of waiting until they were ransomed. But Mr Akroyd was in China. Could Gavin authorise the payment? It would depend how much was demanded, she supposed. Otherwise, they would have to wait until Mr Akroyd came back. Did the kidnappers know he was away from home?

It was a fruitless area for conjecture. She turned her mind from it and contemplated her injuries instead. How bad were they? A cut scalp and concussion from the blow on the head. Deep bruises and ragged abrasions on her wrists and ankles from the ropes. Bruises on hips, ribs and elbows from being tossed about in the van. A sore, chapped area around her mouth, like sunburn, from the choloroform. And oh, she was thirsty!

"Wish I had a drink of water," she muttered. Poppy had finished untying her legs and was rubbing the life back into her feet. She looked at Emma, and was frightened. She looked very bad. Suppose she died? No, she mustn't die! But Emma was helpless: it was up to Poppy. She mustn't panic, she must think logically, just as if it was Misty who was hurt, and depending on Poppy to help him. She tried to remember what she knew about first aid. All that blood in Emma's hair looked very bad, but hadn't she read somewhere that head injuries always bleed a lot? And that it was better if it did bleed, rather than blood collect inside? She was sure she'd read that somewhere. She leaned over Emma and gently touched her head. Emma made a small noise, like a grunt.

"It's only me, don't worry. Just let me feel your head," Poppy said. She probed and peered through the matted hair, and found the gash, which looked rather sickening, but seemed more or less to have stopped bleeding. Well, that was a relief, anyway. But perhaps it ought to be bathed. And Emma had wanted a drink of water. "I'm going to make them come and bring us some water," she said aloud. "You just lie still and don't worry." It made her feel much better, much less frightened, to be taking charge like this, taking care of Emma. Emma needed her, so she must be brave.

Emma didn't answer – she seemed to have gone to sleep again. Poppy got off the bed and examined the room. It was quite bare, except for a wooden kitchen chair, and the bed, which was made up with blankets but no sheets, and just the one pillow, covered in striped ticking, but no pillow case. The walls were plain plaster, painted white. The floor was bare boards. There was one window, small, dust-caked, and with bars over it, and in the wall opposite the window was a plain door of unpainted wood with a brown plastic knob. The room was roughly eight feet by six, but an odd shape – the walls weren't parallel.

Poppy went and tried the door without any hope, and it didn't budge at all – in fact the door knob didn't even turn. She knelt and put her eye to the keyhole but could see nothing but blackness. She crossed to the window and pulled the chair under it so she could stand on it, the better to see out. The window was only about twelve by eighteen inches, and was set on the outside of the wall, while the bars were fitted to the inside, so the whole thickness of the wall – about a foot, Poppy thought – was between the bars and the glass. Through the dusty panes she could see the branches of a tree waving gently in the breeze, and the blue sky beyond. They were not on the ground floor, then.

So much for that. There was obviously no way out except by the door. Poppy went to the door and began to bang on it with her fist. After a while her fist started to get sore, so she changed to kicking it and yelling.

It was a long time before she got any response, and she was growing both tired and discouraged. But at last there was a loud thump on the outside of the door, which startled her, and a voice, curiously muffled, said, "Stop that bloody row! Whaddya want?"

"Lots of things," Poppy shouted back boldly. "Food and water and bandages. My friend is sick. Open the door and let me talk to you."

There was a pause, and then the voice said, "Stay back from the door. Go and sit on the bed."

Poppy retired as ordered, and after a moment the door opened a crack, and a tall, heavy young man sidled through, closing it behind him. Poppy saw with a thrill which was not all fear that he was holding a gun, pointed towards her.

"Is that a real gun?" she couldn't help asking. "I bet it's not a real gun."

His eyes narrowed. "Don't get bloody smart with me," he said. "You got a lot of mouth for a kid in big trouble."

"It's not me that's in trouble," Poppy retorted. "It's you that'll get it when they catch you."

"Forget that – they ain't gonna catch us."

"They always do," Poppy said, trying to sound matter-of-fact. "What's your name?"

"Andy." He leaned against the door, and jiggled his gun up and down. "I know yours, Miss Arabella Akroyd. What kind of a name is that?"

"It's as good a name as yours."

"It's a bloody mouthful. Whadda they call you for short? Arry?" He grinned at his own joke.

"You can call me Arry if you like," Poppy said. "Now can we get down to business?"

"Whatever you say," he said, seeming to be enjoying the exchange. "What d'you want?"

"First, some hot water and disinfectant and clean cloths

to clean my friend's head wound. I think it might need stitching."

"It can go on wanting," he said harshly. "Whajjer think this is, a game?"

"You don't want her to die, do you?"

"I couldn't give a stuff. It's not her that's worth a fortune." But he looked sidelong at Emma as she lay, white-faced and unconscious on the bed. "That's a lotta blood," he muttered.

"If she dies, you'll be in worse trouble when they catch you," Poppy urged.

"Stuff all that 'when they catch me' business." He looked uneasy suddenly. "What are you up to? D'you know something?" He looked round the room as though he might find some clue. And then he seemed to reassure himself, and laughed. "Listen, if you think someone's going to come and rescue you, you can forget it. They'll never find us here – and even if they found *us*, they'd never find *you*."

He sounded so sure that Poppy's small courage sank. He saw it, and his grin widened.

"All right, Arry, mate, I'll bring you some grub. And I'll see what I can do about water and rags and stuff. I don't promise, but I'll see what I can do. Now sit down on the bed and don't move."

When he had gone, she jumped up and went to examine the door more closely. She found that one of the knotholes was in fact a spy hole. She put her eye to it but could see nothing – she supposed it only worked one way. But it meant there was no chance of rushing him when he came with the food. She went back to the bed and looked down at Emma, worried. Emma opened her eyes.

"You were brilliant," she murmured. "I don't know how you could be so brave."

"Oh, he wasn't so tough," Poppy said airily. "I'm not scared of him."

"Well, be careful," Emma said, closing her eyes again.

Poppy was one of the television generation, for whom, Emma feared, reality was always one pace distant, a pale shadow of the silver screen. "That's a real gun, you know."

"He won't shoot me," Poppy said confidently. "Not if he wants the money."

Emma felt that, on the whole, it was better for Poppy to keep her spirits up, so she didn't say any more. There were other things that could be done short of shooting, some of which might make shooting seem almost preferable.

"We've found the van," Superintendent Moss said with quiet pride. "Abandoned in some scrub woodland on the edge of Thetford Forest. The locals call it Pratchett's Wood – d'you know it?"

He addressed his remark to Gavin and Mrs Henderson: Lady Susan was keeping to her room in a state of collapse, and Zara was keeping out of everyone's way, though Gavin could not be sure what her feelings about the affair were.

"Yes, I know it," he replied.

"I told you they wouldn't get far," Moss went on. "One of our mobiles went past it shortly before the general alert went out. They remembered it, and went back to check."

"But you said it had been abandoned?" Mrs Henderson queried. "You mean you haven't found Poppy and Emma?"

"No, the van was empty" Moss admitted. "Forensic are going over it now for anything that might help us. But there are tyre tracks of a car there as well, so we're assuming they transferred them into another vehicle at that spot."

"So you've lost them." Gavin's voice was blank with defeat.

"It's not as bad as that. You see, a neighbouring small-holder has reported his car stolen—"

"But—" Gavin began the obvious objection.

The Superintendent put up his hand. "Bear with me. The tracks of the second car showed that the tyres didn't match –

it had three of one design and one of a different pattern. We checked with the smallholder, and his car had three Dunlops and a Michelin. We're checking the tyre patterns, now, but we're pretty sure it was the same car, which means we've got a description and a number."

"When was the car stolen?"

"Ah, that's the interesting bit! The smallholder came in late from the pub, about half past twelve; and owing to the amount of beer he'd sunk, he had a restless night. Got up to go to the bathroom around three o'clock, and glancing out of the window, saw the car had gone. So it gives us a time period during which the car must have been nicked. Also, it proves—"

"That changing to the second car wasn't the original plan," Gavin supplied.

Moss nodded. "You're quick! Yes, otherwise they'd have had one ready."

"But where does it get us?" Mrs Henderson said unhappily. "They've still got away. They could have gone clear to the other end of the country by now."

Moss almost grinned. "I don't think so. The smallholder tells us that the petrol tank was almost empty – he'd meant to fill her up today. He reckons there was only enough to do about ten miles at most. We're checking now to see if they filled up anywhere, but with the two victims in the car I think it's unlikely. And if they didn't, we've got them inside a pretty small radius. We'll throw a net round them and gradually draw it closed. They won't get away, I can promise you that."

"God, I hope not," Gavin said. He felt miserably responsible. With his father away, it had been up to him to keep everyone safe. They had never particularly worried about security. They had guarded against burglary, but kidnapping had never entered anyone's head. He saw now that they should have thought of it, especially on a night like that of Zara's party, when dozens of people, many of them strangers, were coming and going about the house. What would his father say when he got back?

As if picking up on Gavin's thought, Superintendent Moss said, "Have you had any luck in contacting your father yet?"

"We know where he is now, and we've sent a message. We're waiting to get confirmation that it's reached him," Gavin said. "I expect he'll start back as soon as he gets it, but it will take time, a day at least, probably longer. Until then—"

"Yes sir," Moss said soothingly. "I'm quite happy to deal with you."

Gavin met his eyes. "But will the kidnappers be?"

In the afternoon, when Emma had slept a little, Andy returned, but this time with his boss. His demeanour was subdued, and the interview was much less friendly, and Poppy kept close to Emma all through it, evidently beginning to feel something of the danger they were in.

There was nothing humane or approachable in the Boss's face. It was lined with experience, but the experiences were evidently not happy ones. His nose had been broken and set badly at some point, and there was an old scar running up the side of his forehead and into his hair; but the lines from his nose to his mouth corners were harsher than scars, and his eyes behind the glasses were as cold as a snake's.

"Right, girls," he said, swinging the chair one-handed under him and sitting on it backwards, with his arms folded along the back. Andy leaned against the closed door, covering Emma and Poppy with his gun. In the small room Emma could smell Andy's anxious sweat and the Boss's overdone aftershave; but more than that she could feel the menacing presence of the two men so acutely it was like a third and more overpowering smell. It made her shiver. And there was nothing pleasant about the way he called them 'girls'. It was hard and contemptuous: as if he

126

were emphasising the fact that in his position he could call them whatever he damn well liked.

"Right, girls, let's have some straight talking. You know the score, I imagine. We've borrowed the kid for a bit, and we expect her old man to pay a nice little fortune to get her back in one piece. We know who *you* are," he went on, nodding at Emma. "You're the governess and you're a bloody nuisance, but since you've stumbled into this you can make yourself useful by looking after the kid. Right?"

Poppy, pressed against Emma's side, was trembling, but she spoke up now in a mixture of fear and anger. "You won't get away with this! They'll find us soon, and then you'll go to prison!"

"Shut your face!" the Boss snapped. His eyes chilled Emma. "You, you'd better keep her quiet if you know what's good for her. I don't have much patience with lippy kids."

Emma found Poppy's hand and squeezed it warningly. Andy was just stupid and would do what he was told, but this one, she thought, was the real criminal. He would probably enjoy hurting people.

"Better," the Boss said, scanning them stonily. "Now listen. If you give us no trouble, you won't get hurt, understand me? You'll get food, water, whatever you need. And you won't be touched. I want your old man to get you back in the condition we found you. But if either of you try anything, or make trouble, or if *you*—" Poppy shrank from the cold gaze that rested on her, "give me any lip, you'll be sorry you were born. So take your choice."

He seemed to be waiting for an answer, so Emma, pressing Poppy's hand, said quietly, "We won't give you any trouble."

"Sensible girl," the Boss said with a smile that did not warm Emma in the least. "Wise of you to realise that you're expendable. And you'd better get it into the kid's head that, OK, we want to keep her in mint condition, but if she does anything to annoy us, we can still shoot you. Not to kill, necessarily. We can just shoot you where it'll hurt. You get me? She messes up, *you* get it. Savvy?"

Poppy was trembling like a leaf now, and Emma put her arm round her and held her close. "All right," she said with a spurt of anger, "I said we wouldn't give you trouble. Can't you see you're frightening her?"

"Quite the mother lioness protecting her cub, aren't we?" the Boss sneered. Andy grinned, knowing there was a joke without necessarily understanding it. "All right, you can write the note, since you're the woman of action. We want the kid's old man to know we've got you safe and sound."

A writing pad and biro were produced, and under dictation, Emma wrote:

The kidnappers have Arabella and me securely hidden. We have not been harmed, and no harm will come to us if you follow instructions. They are demanding a ransom of a million pounds—

At that point, Emma looked up in surprise. The Boss met her eyes with quick understanding.

"Didn't know he was that rich, eh? Well, when you go back, you can ask him for a raise – if you get out of here in one piece, that is."

The rest of the dictation covered the details of how the money was to be paid. It was, as far as she could tell, a straightforward deal: they seemed only to want the money, and to have no interest in hurting either of them. She hoped it was true, and drew what comfort she could from it; and hoped, also, that the Boss had his facts right about Mr Akroyd's fortune. She signed the note, and then Poppy signed underneath 'Arabella Akroyd'. By unspoken agreement, neither of them had revealed that she was always called Poppy. They didn't quite know why, but it seemed something they should keep to themselves.

When he had examined the note carefully, the Boss tucked it away, gestured to Andy, and they both left. Alone, Emma and Poppy sat in silence for a long time, their arms round each other. Poppy had discovered that things in real life had a particular hardness and reek that television did not portray. Emma was trying to rack her aching brains for something they could do that would help.

They seemed to her particularly helpless because they weren't even dressed. Poppy was in her Rupert Bear pyjamas, Emma in her nightdress and dressing-gown. Fortunately it was warm in the little room, even a little stuffy. They had no possessions of any sort, she thought – until, putting her hand in her dressing-gown pocket for her handkerchief, she found the curved, hard shape of her nail-scissors. She'd forgotten about them. On the morning of the party she'd had her bath, and then put her dressing-gown on and sat by the window while she cut her finger- and toenails. She must have put the scissors into the pocket without thinking, and there they were still.

For no very good reason, the discovery cheered her a little. It was hardly conceivable they could be used as a weapon: the short, curved blades would not put anyone out of action, even if she could get near enough to use them. But somehow, some time, in some way, they might be useful. Emma felt strangely better for this small secret as she returned the scissors to her pocket, and hoped that the men would not think of searching her.

Chapter Eleven

Andy brought them a meal of bread and butter and tea in the evening, and left them without a word, having hardly looked at them. Perhaps the Boss had told him to keep his distance. Certainly they were being careful: the bread and butter was brought in Andy's hand and simply put down on the bed – no plates or knives – and the tea was ready-poured in two big plastic mugs. Nothing that might possible serve for a weapon.

Neither felt hungry, but both were very thirsty, and drank the tea gratefully. Guessing there would be nothing more that night, Emma warned Poppy to sip the tea rather than gulp it – it would be more thirst-quenching that way. When they had drunk, they felt their hunger, and ate the bread; and then, since there didn't seem to be anything else to do, they lay down on the bed. At first Emma tried to keep up a conversation, thinking it might do them good to talk, but she couldn't think of anything but their predicament, and without any input from Poppy the attempt soon failed, and they lay side by side in silence, staring at the ceiling.

From the light outside, Emma guessed it to be about eight o'clock. There was no light in the room, so presumably after sunset they would be left in darkness. She thought that would be unpleasant; then she wondered if any use could be made of the fact. But it all boiled down to the impossibility of jumping the man with a gun. Her eyes roved aimlessly over the ceiling. It was odd for a room to be built without a light; there was no scar in the plaster where a fitment had been taken out, so it must always have been like that. It was an odd room altogether – too small for a bedroom, too big for a cupboard, and such a strange shape, like a bit of a room snipped off at random.

A bit of a room. The idea meandered round her brain. Could it be that the wall with the door in it was a false wall, built across an existing room to cut this part off? But for what purpose? No light, not even an electric wall socket; even in a box-room you would want a light, wouldn't you? OK, it had daylight, but you couldn't guarantee you'd always come looking for your old football boots or photograph albums in daylight.

She got off the bed and went across to examine the wall, tapped it here and there with her knuckles, scratched at it with a fingernail, applied her eye uselessly to the peephole and keyhole. She tried the other walls, examined the window closely, and then stood, staring in thought.

"What is it? What are you doing?" Poppy asked lethargically from the bed.

"Oh, I was wondering about this room. I think perhaps it was purpose-built for us, by putting up this wall across the corner of a bigger room. The plaster's different from the other three walls, and the paint looks new. And that window's obviously very old. Say they had a room with a barred window already in it, and they just made this – this cell by partitioning it off?"

"Why would they do that?"

"Well, to make it secure for one thing. There's nothing in this room, nothing at all, that we could use." Not even a light flex to hang themselves with, she thought, but she didn't say that to Poppy. "And for another – we don't know what it looks like from the outside – out in the other room, I mean."

Poppy sat up, looking interested. "A secret room!"

Emma nodded. "Maybe."

"It must be!" Poppy said. "Andy said even if the police

131

found *them*, they'd never find *us*. That must be what he meant – that we're hidden in a secret room."

"Poppy, listen," Emma said, turning to her suddenly. "This wall doesn't sound solid to me. I think it's only lath and plaster. I think I could make a hole in it with my nail scissors."

"Big enough for us to get through?" Poppy's voice was an excited whisper.

"No, that would take days with only the nail scissors, and they'd notice it before it got anywhere near big enough, to say nothing of the mess. No, I just meant a small hole, just big enough to see through."

"What good would that do?" Poppy said, disappointed.

Emma looked helpless. "I don't know. At least we'd know what was on the other side. Whether they live in there or in another part of the house. Whether anyone else comes in."

Poppy's expression said she didn't think much of that for a plan, but she said kindly, "Well, if you think it'll help . . ."

"It's a choice between doing that or doing nothing," Emma said. Baldly, that was it.

"Anyway, Gavin's sure to find us soon," Poppy said comfortingly. "Are you going to start now?"

"Yes. I'll do it in the corner and down near the floor, where it won't be so obvious. You put your ear to the door and tell me if you hear anyone coming."

It was harder than she had expected to make any impression with her inadequate tool; and bending down made her head ache again. When it grew dark she gave up the attempt. They got into bed and slept almost at once, for they were more tired than they knew.

Emma slept heavily and dreamlessly, and woke at first light with Gavin's name on her lips. She didn't know at first where she was. She thought she was back in Muswell Hill, and listened for a half-awake moment for the traffic noises. Then she came slowly to the realisation of the truth, and it rolled heavily onto her heart. The flat seemed so far in the past – two lifetimes away, since Long Hempdon was one lifetime. What was happening out there? What were the police doing? Were they on the trail, or were she and Poppy entirely lost? What was Gavin thinking, feeling, doing? Would she ever see him again? She thought back over the time she had known him, and in particular of that last night, when they had danced together. Looking back with the clarity her present situation had brought to her, she knew that he cared for her, and that she had long been falling in love with him. She had wasted the opportunity of Zara's party, thrown Gavin away with both hands because of her – what? Pride? Touchiness, more like: a ridiculous, monumental chip on her shoulder, legacy of being dumped by Chris. If she had danced again with him as he had asked her, and relaxed, and gone with the moment, who knows what might have happened?

That thought gave her pause. If she hadn't run off upstairs in a huff, or whatever she had run off in, she would not have stumbled on the kidnappers. She would not have been here now, but home safe in bed. But Poppy would be here alone, terrified, at the mercy of whatever the kidnappers chose to do to her. Well, to be honest, she was not much safer with Emma there, but at least she was infinitely less frightened. Emma would not have had her face this alone for anything, not even for her own life. Her leaving Gavin as she did had served its purpose.

She squeezed her eyes shut to keep back the tears. He would have come to the same conclusion. And he loved Poppy like a father. He must be frantic with worry, raging with helpless frustration. Had he been lying sleepless, thinking of them – of her? Was that why she had woken saying his name?

If only she could get a message to him; if only she could get a message out of the house, that someone might find and take to him. Could she perhaps break the window and throw something out? But she had no paper, in any case, and no pencil. She had nothing in the world but a handkerchief and a pair of scissors . . .

The idea came to her, and she rejected it at first, but then came back to it with reluctance. She looked at Poppy, and saw that she was still sleeping peacefully, and then got up carefully, so as not to disturb her, and went over to the window where the light was better. She sat down on the chair and took the handkerchief and scissors out of her pocket. She looked at the point of the blades, and at her hands, and finally at the torn and bruised places on her wrists. With a shuddering sigh she picked up the scissors and gritted her teeth.

It was hopeless. After an agonising few minutes she had to admit it was hopeless. Had she had paper, it might have worked, but on the cotton of the handkerchief her blood just spread in blodges and smears. It was impossible to write a legible word. She shook her aching wrist and bit her lip, trying not to cry. She had the ridiculous feeling that Gavin was out there somewhere near at hand, and that if she didn't get a message to him he would walk past and never know she was there.

She looked again at the scissors and the now brown-spotted handkerchief; and after a moment her expression lightened. She dug the point of the blade into the cloth and began to cut carefully. It was difficult, more difficult than she had expected. She had to make the letters large to make them recognisable one from another, and that meant she could not make many of them. But by the time the sun came round into the room she had cut the words HELP POPPY out of the handkerchief. When it was crumpled up nothing was visible, but spread it out on a flat surface and the letters were shaky but legible. She rolled the frayed scraps together and thrust them, with the handkerchief, into her pocket. She still had to think of a way to break the window.

134

Gavin had a restless night, and finally fell asleep at about three o'clock, to be woken, feeling heavily unrested, by the dawn chorus. At once his mind began to churn over the problem all over again. Yesterday had been a full and tiring day; but at least his father was on his way home, and should be arriving this morning. Gavin would be glad to have someone to share the burden. Jean Henderson did all she could, but she was not family, the responsibility could not be hers. Lady Susan was useless, of course. The very thought of intruders in her house threw her into hysteria, and though she was enough of a mother to be worried about Poppy, her anxieties, it transpired, were far more centred on the twins. The one time she had appeared downstairs yesterday had been to beg the Superintendent with tears and a voice almost off the scale to put an armed guard on the boys' school, in case the kidnappers decided one was not enough. Moss had taken it very calmly, and assured her that he had already thought of that, and that a plain-clothes man and a uniformed patrol were even then setting up operations around Jack and Harry. Lady Susan had taken a great deal of reassuring. One minute she had begged Gavin to go and fetch the boys home, the next she had wanted them shipped off to Scotland to her father's shooting estate; and she could hardly be satisfied without an open telephone line to the school with a constant running commentary on the boys' safety.

Yes, it had been an emotionally full day, he thought wearily, turning over in search of a rest that eluded him. Particularly stimulating had been the conversation he had had with Superintendent Moss on the subject of Emma. How much did Gavin know about her? How had she been recruited to the household? Had her references been taken up? Who were her friends? Had she had any visitors since she'd been here, or been seeing anyone regularly? Had she written any letters, made any phone calls, and who to?

"Look here," Gavin had said at last, "I know what you're

suggesting, but it's ludicrous. Emma Ruskin is a good, kind, sensible, honest person. She loves Poppy and Poppy loves her."

Moss regarded him steadily. "I'm glad to have your opinion on that, sir," he said, and Gavin felt riled.

"Look, I know her and you don't!"

"You've known her for – how many weeks? Not quite a month yet, is it?"

"Some people you know in a very short time. I tell you she has nothing to do with this! In any case, they've taken her too, don't forget!"

"Yes, well that would be what you'd expect, if she was involved. Otherwise she might end up with some difficult questions to answer," said Moss reasonably. "You must admit, it's funny that this happens just after she joins your household—"

"Coincidence, that's all."

"Maybe. But we're pretty certain there was an inside connection somewhere. The kidnappers knew the layout of the house, knew that the party would be going on—"

"Good God, half the County knew the party would be going on!"

"Quite. But the timing, the route, the stealing of the catering van, taking them out down the backstairs – it all smells of an inside job to me. And your Miss Ruskin's got all the information needed, she's new, and she's never been a governess before, so you said. Funny a school teacher should suddenly give that up for a live-in job, don't you think?"

"No, I don't think it's funny at all," Gavin said angrily.

Moss nodded sympathetically – or was it pityingly? Got it bad, his expression said. "Well, maybe you're right. But I think we'll have a little look into Miss Emma Ruskin's background anyway, see what we can find out. Ruskin – is that an Irish name?"

"Not as far as I know," Gavin said. "What are you suggesting?"

"Kidnappers sometimes want other things than money," Moss said non-committally.

For the rest of the day, the news had only been negative. No reports of the smallholder's missing car being seen. No reports of it filling up anywhere, or of anyone within the radius buying petrol in a can. Nothing of any use discovered by the forensic team from the dumped catering van. No idea of who the kidnappers might be. No contact yet by letter or phone with a ransom demand. It was horribly frustrating.

Gavin abandoned the attempt to go back to sleep, and sat up. He had left his curtains open last night, and the early light streamed in, and the birdsong was fading now to daytime levels. He went to the window and threw it open, and smelled the marvellous freshness of damp earth and grass and clean morning air. Where were they? Were they all right? Would he ever see them again? The sweetness of the morning should have restored him, but all he could think was how Emma was a town girl, and whether he would ever have the chance to teach her to love the countryside.

For the prisoners, the day passed slowly. Nothing broke their solitude but the visits of Andy with food – and dull food it was, nothing hot except mugs of tea. There was bread and butter and slices of Spam for breakfast, bread and butter and corned beef for lunch. Emma asked for some fruit, and got a blank look and a shrug from Andy. If they had to stay here long, Emma thought, they would get spots.

In between they were left alone with their thoughts, their fears, and the tedium. The boredom was hard to bear. There was nothing to do; and Poppy was at the age when children are full of physical energy which needs burning off by running about and romping. Being shut up in this tiny room with no space to stretch her legs was torture to her. Emma did her best to devise ways of passing the time. She did lessons with Poppy from memory; they played 'I Spy' and 'Twenty Questions' and 'Nebuchadnezzar', sang songs and recited what poetry they could remember by heart. But still the hours dragged, and they grew more and more tense, waiting for news, waiting for danger.

For Emma the worst thing in this time of waiting was the lack of toilet facilities. They were not allowed outside the room: Andy brought in a bucket with a lid. It was dreadful to Emma to have to use it there in the room with Poppy gallantly turning her back and humming loudly to give Emma what privacy was possible. It didn't bother Poppy, but Emma was not a country girl, and had no history of 'going behind a hedge'. She found the whole thing distressing and humiliating, and begged their guard to let her go to the WC, offering every safeguard she could think of, but he would not let her out.

Time crawled by. They felt dirty, tired, restless; afraid when they were not bored, always helpless and frustrated. Emma had not thought of a way to break the window. It was too far behind the bars to reach, and the bars were too narrow even for Poppy's arm to go through. She thought of trying to wrench a leg off the chair and break the glass with that, but it was too sturdily made and she hadn't the physical strength. The hole in the wall did not prove a success. All she could see through it was a few feet of floorboards, and she did not dare start another further up for fear it would be noticed. Already she was in dread that Andy would see the first one, for she had no way of concealing it: if she had moved the bed, he would have been bound to want to know why.

Mr Akroyd arrived home mid-morning, grey with exhaustion and worry. He clasped Gavin's hand in a moment of silent sympathy and support.

"This is the devil of a business," he said. Gavin bowed his head.

Lady Susan actually came downstairs to greet her husband, and clung to him, pouring out her fears and griefs.

He bore with it patiently for a time, but then caught Mrs Henderson's eye over her shoulder and gestured to her to take his wife away. Then he went to closet himself with the Superintendent to talk about the ransom demand which had arrived.

"I'm ready to pay," he said at once. "I want that understood. I don't care what it costs, I want my little girl back."

"They're asking for a million," Moss said non-committally.

Akroyd blanched a little, but swallowed and said, "It'll take a bit of getting – I don't keep money idle. But if that's the only way—"

"We'll see," Moss said. "There's no harm in starting your arrangements, but we hope to get them both back without that."

"I don't want any chances taken," Mr Akroyd said sharply.

"I quite understand your feelings, sir. Nobody wants any harm to come to the hostages, but we have a proper method for dealing with these things. You must leave it to us. If the time comes when we think the money should be paid, we'll advise you accordingly, but for the moment we haven't come to the end of our enquiries. If we can get them back, *and* nab the villains, without the money, I take it you'd be even better pleased?"

"That goes without saying." Mr Akroyd mopped his sweating upper lip with a handkerchief. "I worked hard for every penny I own, and I don't fancy giving it away to some layabout who's never done an honest day's work in his life, I can tell you that."

When he had finished his interview with the Superintendent, Mr Akroyd went to find Gavin, who was poring over an ordnance survey map, as he did hour after hour.

"What's all this about that female?" Mr Akroyd demanded without preliminaries.

"What female?" Gavin said warningly. "If you mean Emma Ruskin—"

139

"This bloke Moss seems to think she'd got something to do with it. Is that right? If you and Jean between you have brought some criminal into my house and put my little girl in danger—"

"She's not a criminal."

"Oh, and how would you know, Mr Smartarse? I said all along Poppy should go to school. If she'd gone to school, none of this would have happened."

"She went to school and got ill – you know that, Dad. Emma's got nothing to do with it. Don't you realise she's in danger too? Probably more danger than Poppy. If they've got any sense they won't hurt Poppy, because they expect you to pay good money for her, but the same doesn't apply to—" His voice broke and failed him, The thought of what they might do to Emma was his worst nightmare, and something he didn't dare allow into his mind, or it would unfit him for anything.

Mr Akroyd softened, and laid a hand on his son's shoulder. "There, lad," he said gruffly. "She'll be all right. I dare say you're right, and she's got nothing to do with it. It's all fallen on you, this, hasn't it?"

"I feel so helpless," Gavin said bleakly. "If only there was something I could do."

Mr Akroyd nodded sympathetically. "Aye, well, the police are onto it. We just have to let them do their job."

Superintendent Moss came in looking a little more cheerful. "Now we're getting a fix on them! The post office says the ransom note was posted in Hockwold – that's a little village about fifteen miles away on the edge of the fens—"

"Yes, I know it," Gavin said.

"You do?"

"I know the fens and the forest very well. I've ridden for miles all over the area," he said shortly. There had been many, many days when he had needed to get away from the tensions and humiliations of home; and from horseback you saw the country – like your own problems – much more clearly.

"Right," said Moss. "And we've found the stolen Rover dumped on the back road between Hockwold and Feltwell. We've also got a car reported stolen in Weeting, which is about the same distance from Hockwold, but on the other side."

"What's that got to do with us?" Mr Akroyd asked impatiently.

"Bear with me," Moss said, and led them over to the table where Gavin's map was spread out. "You see, I think they've realised they can't get petrol for the Rover without giving themselves away, so Chummy, the driver, has been told to post the ransom letter, dump the Rover, and steal something else, but not all in the same place. Feltwell to Weeting is about seven miles by road or, say, five across country. Two hours on foot. He drives to Hockwold, posts the letter, drives on towards Feltwell until the petrol runs out, and then – this is the really cunning bit in his tiny mind – doubles back on himself before he steals the new motor. That way he thinks we'll never connect the two."

Gavin stared. "Can he really be that stupid?"

"You'd be surprised," Moss said feelingly, "how stupid the average criminal is. Good thing too, or we'd never catch 'em."

"But if he'd stolen the new car before he posted the letter, he could have posted it a lot further away," Gavin pointed out.

"Well, evidently he didn't think of that," Moss said. "I wonder, though, what his boss is going to have to say about it."

"His boss?" Mr Akroyd queried sharply.

"Chummy didn't plan the thing – he's too dim for that. I reckon he's just the driver – the muscles. Someone with a bit more nous is behind it. And that someone's not going to be too happy that Chummy posted the letter so close to home."

"Home?"

"Feltwell is about twelve miles from Pratchett's Wood where the Rover was stolen, and the Rover had very little petrol in it – only about ten miles' worth, the owner says. Well, there's always a bit more in the tank than you think, but not much. So the place where they've got the hostages stashed can't be far from Pratchett's Wood."

"But now they've got a new car," Gavin said, "they can move them again. They could be anywhere by now."

"I don't think so," Moss said. "In my view, the plan would have been to hole up in some deserted place, an isolated house, hidden in a wood maybe. The house would have to have been chosen and prepared beforehand, so I don't think they'll lightly abandon it. The more you drive your victims around the country the more likely you are to be spotted. No, I think they'll stick as close to their original plan as possible. The place they've chosen must be well hidden, and they'll be confident we won't find it."

He sounded so smug that Mr Akroyd gave him a sharp look. "Are you on to something? If so, spit it out, man! Have you got something you haven't told us yet?"

Moss smiled triumphantly. "Yes, we've got a pretty good idea who we're dealing with. As I said before, the driver of the car's a stupid man, luckily for us. He's also a heavy smoker. OK, every kid burglar these days knows enough to wear gloves, and there've been no finger-prints on the van or the dumped car – everything wiped clean. But on the floor of the Rover we found an empty cigarette pack and the cellophane wrapper from a new pack. The old pack is clean, but there's a beautiful set of nice greasy fingermarks on the cellophane." He positively grinned at Gavin, who, using his imagination, got the point at once.

"He finished a pack," Gavin said, "threw it down, tried to open a new pack, found he couldn't get the wrapper off with gloves on—"

"And took them off!" Mr Akroyd finished, getting there half a second behind.

"Exactly," Moss said. "We've run them through the computer and found they belong to an old chum of ours, Andrew Joseph Luckmeed. Got a record as long as your arm. The interesting thing about him is he's not long out of Blundeston, finished a stretch there in February. And while he was inside, he was keeping very close company with one Henry Gordon James, a felon very well known to us for various kinds of criminal activity. Gentleman Jim, he's known as, owing to his ability to put on a posh accent and mingle with the nobs on their own terms. And Harry James, alias Gentleman Jim, finished his last stretch in April – came out and promptly disappeared."

"You think he's the brains behind this?" Mr Akroyd asked. "Why? Has he done this sort of thing before?"

"Not kidnapping, no. Fraud, protection, gun-running, large-scale burglary, he's had his fingers in all of them. But he's always been one for elaborate plans – that's what lets him down. And snatching a little kid who couldn't fight back would be just up his alley. It'd look like easy money; and he's getting to the age when he'll be wanting to go for the big one and retire on the proceeds to Argentina. They all dream of it, your 'master criminals'." He invested the words with a world of contempt. "Moreover, he's a local lad, grew up in Thetford, first got into trouble as a teenager knocking off stuff from the base at Lakenheath. So he knows the area. All in all, I'm confident he's our man, all right."

On the evidence, Gavin was inclined to agree with him. "So, if it is this man, do you think – I mean, he doesn't sound too dangerous?" he said hopefully. "He's not likely to do anything violent, is he?"

Moss's face grew grave. "I don't want to frighten you. But I wouldn't want you to think this man's a soft option.

No, he's a cold-blooded bastard, like all these habituals; and the only violence he'd want to avoid is violence to himself. He's dangerous all right." He made an obvious effort to be cheerful. "But we'll get him, don't you worry."

Chapter Twelve

Gavin had pored over the map so often that its details were now engraved on his mind. The area they had now marked down as likely was a fairly unpopulated one, most of it in the Thetford Forest and the Hockwold fens: woodland, scrub and bog, a few scattered villages and farms and very few roads.

"It's narrowing down very nicely," Superintendent Moss said. "Obviously their hideout has got to be an isolated house, where they can come and go without being seen. Nosy neighbours would be no good to them. You can't shift two struggling prisoners up the front path of a council estate semi without being noticed."

"True," said Gavin.

"And that gives us about ten possibles. It's a matter of having a look at them and making discreet enquiries." He tapped the map thoughtfully. "Meanwhile, of course, we've got other lines to follow up."

"I suppose you mean Emma's past history?" Gavin said hotly. His father snapped an enquiring look at him, which was not lost on the Superintendent.

"Oh, we've gone into that, sir," Moss said easily. "Talked to her flat-mates, her previous headmistress, and her mum and dad. Well, we'd have had to let them know what'd happened anyway. Pretty upset, they are. Seem very nice people. Not what you'd expect."

"What does that mean?" Gavin snapped.

"Oh, nothing against the girl," Moss said. "No, she checks

145

out clean as a whistle. But it's a long way from where she started to a place like this." He waved his hand to indicate the handsome house and large park, taking in by implication the antiques, paintings, servants, cars and stables on the way.

Mr Akroyd, still watching Gavin's face, said quietly, "Come to that, Superintendent, it's a long way from where *I* started to a place like this."

The Superintendent coughed. "Quite so, Mr Akroyd. Yes, indeed. Well," he went on hastily, "if it wasn't Miss Ruskin, and it wasn't any of the servants – which we're pretty sure it wasn't – I'm at a bit of a loss to know who the inside contact was. I don't suppose either of you has any further suggestions?"

Mr Akroyd shook his head; Gavin's face was a careful blank.

The day dragged by. On one of Andy's visits, Emma tried to get talking to him, hoping perhaps to get him onto their side.

"What are you doing mixed up in something like this? You don't seem such a bad bloke, really," she said.

He looked at her unsmilingly. "Thank you very much, princess," he said. "Whajjer think I'm in it for? The money, of course. That's what we all want, ennit?"

"Don't you have any conscience about it?"

He eyed her derisively. "What do you care if her old man has to flog a few shares to get her back? Why should he have money and me none?"

Poppy looked up fiercely at that. "My father earned that money! He started off with nothing and earned every penny of it! What've you ever done?"

He only laughed at her. "Go it, Arry mate! What I done is I got you. I don't want you – he does. He's got money. I ain't. Fair swap, ennit?"

"You won't get away with it!" Poppy cried.

He grew bored with the conversation. "Oh shut your

mouth! You talk too much, both of you," he said, waving his gun at them idly. "I'll give you a friendly warning – keep it zipped when the Boss comes to see you. He ain't a patient man like me. If you start rabbitting on at him like that, you might get something you don't like."

"Is he coming to see us?" Emma asked, suddenly afraid.

Andy saw her fear, and grinned, enjoying it. "Yeah, later today. Summink to look forward to, ain't it, princess?"

The Boss's visit was short and chilling.

"We haven't had the response we wanted from the kid's dad," he said without preamble. "I'm afraid he's not taking us seriously, so we're going to have to send him a little something to concentrate his mind. Andy?" He held out his hand for the gun. Andy passed it over and then pulled something out from his pocket. There was a click, and a thin, viciously sharp blade appeared in his hand. He started to approach them, and Poppy screamed and flung herself into Emma's arms.

"No!" Emma cried, clutching the child against her. Poppy started sobbing with terror. "Don't you touch her, you monster!"

"Shaddap!" the Boss shouted. "Bloody women! Shut your noise. He wants a bit of her hair, that's all. Let her go. Get to the other end of the bed where I can see you. Move it, or I'll put one through your leg and see how you like that. Move it, I say! I've got no brief to keep you in one piece."

Reluctantly, keeping one eye on Andy and the other on the gun, Emma detached Poppy's arms from her neck. The child sobbed louder, and Andy suddenly said, "It's all right, kid. I only want a bit of your hair. Tell her, princess."

In terror the two of them watched the glittering blade approach Poppy's head; Emma knew there was nothing she could do to protect her, and yet every instinct screamed at her to fight. Andy grabbed a loose hank of Poppy's hair. Poppy screamed again. The knife flashed, and then Andy was stepping back with the knife in one hand and a hank of thin blonde hair in the other. Poppy began to sob again, but at a lower pitch, putting her hands up to her head. Emma gathered her in again, watching the two men like a cornered fox.

The Boss surveyed the two of them with eyes of utter cold indifference. "This goes in the second letter. If there has to be a third letter, it won't be hair, it'll be a finger."

Poppy cried out, and pressed so hard against Emma, it was as if she were trying to burrow her way in. Emma folded her arms round the child's head fiercely. "Go away! Leave us alone!" she cried uselessly. The two men went, locking the door as always, but she could not think it was on her command. When they were alone again, she and Poppy both burst into tears; and cried their eyes out for ten minutes or more, after which they curled up together on the bed and fell into an uneasy doze.

Zara looked up as Gavin came into her room. She was pale, nervous and distinctly guilty, and she took refuge in attack as the best form of defence. "Can't you knock? Get out of here. This is my own private room."

"You can talk to me here, or you can talk to me in front of Dad – take your pick," he said, closing the door and standing in front of it with his arms folded.

"I've got nothing to say to you," she snapped. "Get out."

"Zara, you know something about this. I know you do. I've known you all your life, and you've got guilt written all over you. Now you tell me what it is, or I go to Dad, and he and the police can get it out of you."

"I don't know what you're talking about," she said, but her eyes slid away from him.

He let his voice soften a little. "Don't be a little idiot. For God's sake, they've got Poppy! Your own sister. I don't expect you to care particularly what happens to Emma—"

Zara's eyes flashed. "Oh, Emma is it now? That little

tramp's had her eye on you since the minute she arrived. I knew what her game was the moment I saw her—"

Gavin crossed the room in three swift strides and grabbed Zara by the upper arms, and shook her. "It's your game I'm interested in! What do you know about this business?"

"Nothing! Let me go!" She tried to turn her face away from him, but he grabbed her jaw and turned it back.

"Look at me! Tell me!"

"It wasn't my fault. I didn't know what he wanted," she said, her eyes darting. She saw his expression change and grew genuinely frightened. "It was a bit of fun, that's all. We went to this club—"

"Who's we?"

"Vic and Nat and me."

"What club?"

"Bunter's. In Cambridge. It was just a bit of fun."

An expression of distaste crossed his face. He knew Bunter's – loud, noisy, and filled with rough youths and sluttish girls. "Slumming," he said in a flat voice. He let her go. "I suppose that gives you a thrill."

"You needn't look like that," she said, rubbing her arms where he had gripped her. "It's something different to do, that's all. It's all right for you – you're a man. I never have any fun. I'm always supposed to go out with 'nice' boys. Well, nice boys are boring, let me tell you. And stuck away here in the middle of nowhere, it had to be nice boys, 'cos they're the only ones who have cars."

"That's why you kept nagging at Dad for a car," Gavin said. "I knew it was a bad idea."

"Well, I got one, anyway, so there's nothing you can do about it."

"How did you get to the club before?"

"Vic's dad's car. Well, he never knew. He was never bloody well there."

"Don't swear. You're just adding to your sins."

"Sins!" she jeered.

"And crimes. Driving without insurance, and without the owner's permission. I don't suppose you'd want the police to know about that."

"I'd only get a fine," she muttered, "and Mummy'd pay it."

"Tell me about this man," Gavin said. His eyes were cold and remote, and they frightened her rather. "What was his name?"

"Billy Metcalf. I met him at the club. He came up to me, said was I Zara Akroyd. He said he'd seen my photo in *Country Life*."

"When was this?"

"Ages ago, the first time. Last year – September or October. I – I didn't like him at first. He was a bit of a tough, if you want to know. But there was something about him. Kind of scary. He wasn't like the dorky men we usually get to meet. He bought us drinks, and we danced a bit, and he chatted. Then he asked if he could drive me home, and I said no. And that was that."

"Go on."

"The next time was a couple of weeks later. He came up to me again, like before; then I started bumping into him at other places. Well, I was bored stiff so I let him hang around with me. Vic and Nat were wild about him. They said they betted he was a crim. I kept asking if he had any friends for them. But actually, it wasn't as exciting as they thought. Mostly he wanted to talk, about the house, and Mummy, and what Dad did, and all that kind of thing. He never even wanted to fool around or anything. He only kissed me once, and that was—" She paused, remembering it. It had not been pleasant, not romantic or sexy or anything. He had kissed her as if he knew she was expecting it and it simply amused him to give her something she wanted, but that he knew she wouldn't like. It was a kiss like an insult.

Gavin could see it all. "And when did you bring him here?"

She flushed. "Just before Easter. Dad was in Sunderland and you'd gone to Exeter about that legal case, and Mummy was taking Poppy to see the specialist in London, and Mrs H went up with them so there was nobody here. Billy'd been on at me for ages to take him to my home. He told me to let him know when there'd be no one around – gave me a telephone number. I thought he wanted—" Her blush deepened. Gavin's lips tightened. "Well, anyway," she went on, "he didn't want anything like that. He wanted to see over the house. I showed him everything. He was really interested. He seemed to know a lot about buildings and stuff." She caught Gavin's expression and hurried on. "And he asked about my birthday party as well. Wanted to know every detail of what was going to happen on the day. I thought—" her eyes suddenly filled with tears, "I thought he was going to buy me a birthday present, something really expensive. I hinted like mad for a few things I fancied and he seemed to take it in. He said – he said he was planning a real surprise for me. I knew I'd never be allowed to invite him officially, so I told him how he could get in through the boot room. I said if he wore a DJ no one'd know."

"Oh my God, Zara!"

She gulped. "But after that visit I never saw him again, and when I rang the number he'd given me, it was discontinued. And then when the police said there must have been inside information for the kidnapping, I realised—"

Gavin closed his eyes wearily. "You've behaved like an absolute idiot, you know that."

"It wasn't my fault," she said with spirit. "It's all right for you, you can do what you like. I'm always told I can't do this and I can't do that. Everyone's on my back. I never have any fun. I just wanted a bit of fun."

Gavin held his tongue. There was no point in telling her off. It was done now. "You'll have to come and tell all this to Superintendent Moss."

"No! It's my own private business."

151

"Yes! You fool, don't you see if they can find this Billy Metcalf, he can lead them to the kidnappers?" Still she resisted. "If you don't come this instant," he said in a hard voice, "I'll carry you down there."

She got up sulkily. "Are you going to tell Dad?"

"He'll have to know. But at the moment, he's only interested in getting Poppy back."

She managed one last sneer. "And your precious Emma."

"I hope so. Oh God, I hope so."

"We've got him," Superintendent Moss said, putting down the phone. "He was hanging around one of his usual haunts. So confident we'd never find out he had anything to do with it, he didn't even go into hiding. He's an old friend of Harry James — if 'friend' is the right word. Anyway, he's been to see him a few times at Blundeston. The way I see it, he stumbled on Zara at this club, realised who she was, and cultivated her friendship while he told Harry about it and waited for him to work out some way of using the contact."

"You still think Harry James is the master-mind?"

"Oh yes. Billy Metcalf is no thinker. His part was to provide the initial information; and I suspect he was watching the drop site as well, so he could tell James when the money was there." Moss rubbed his hands with satisfaction. "Now we've just got to get out of him where the hideout is."

"Let me have ten minutes alone with him, and I'll get it out of him," Mr Akroyd growled.

"If we were allowed to use those methods, we'd get it out of him ourselves," Moss said. "Unfortunately there's such a thing as the PACE Act. But we'll put the pressure on him other ways."

"Meanwhile, we sit here and twiddle our thumbs?" Mr Akroyd said. "That second letter—"

Moss looked sympathetic. "Yes, it's an unusual situation. Kidnappers generally like to talk about it on the 'phone, and that gives you a chance to argue. Doing it by post is most unusual, and it ties our hands a bit. We can't tell them we're getting the money but it'll take time, or demand proof that the hostages are still all right, or any of the usual dodges to keep them busy. But that takes nerve on their side. Gentleman Jim must be very confident this time. We've got to find them, to be able to take any action—"

"Well, find them!" Akroyd suddenly shouted. "Bloody find them!"

"We're doing our best, sir," Moss said courteously.

"I've got an idea," Gavin said tentatively. "About where the hideout might be."

The Superintendent looked up receptively. "Let's have it, then."

It was early in the morning. No one had slept. Billy Metcalf certainly hadn't, but he was still resisting the questioning.

"I was going over the map again," Gavin went on, spreading it out on the table, "and thinking, how would these people have got hold of a house? It would have to have been for sale or to let, and if they've only been planning it since October, they couldn't have banked on the right sort of house just happening to come empty at the right time."

"Go on," Moss nodded.

"There's a place, about *here*—" He put his finger down on the map. "I know it from my riding expeditions. It's a house called Sparlings." Moss looked down, and then up, enquiringly. "No, it's not marked. It was empty for years because it was supposed to be haunted, and then the Forestry Commission bought the land and the house with it, and it's just been let go. I don't know what condition it's in now, but when I last saw it, about a year ago, or a bit more, it was still in reasonable shape. I mean, it had a roof and walls and doors, though most of the windows were broken. You could live in it, if you weren't too particular. There wouldn't be any electricity or water, of course, but it had a well in the garden, and a person could always take a camp stove to boil the water on."

"Hmm," Moss pondered. "And Harry James is a local man . . ."

"So he'd be bound to know about it," Gavin said, following the thought. "When I was a kid it was a 'dare' place for boys, because of being haunted. And older lads used to go there to smoke or mess about."

"I think you've got something," Moss said. "We'd better take a look at this Sparlings place. In fact, I think I'll go myself."

"Please – let me go with you!" Gavin begged, his eyes naked. He needed so desperately to do something. The waiting and the inactivity were torture.

Moss smiled. "I was thinking of it," he said. "I need you to show me where it is, apart from anything else. But listen to me," the smile disappeared. "No heroics, you understand? You stick close to me, do nothing but what you're told to do: these people are dangerous. Above all you *say* nothing, no matter what the provocation. Keep your mouth shut, and your eyes and ears open, and tell me afterwards if you notice anything. Agreed?"

"Agreed," said Gavin.

Sparlings stood amongst trees, and what had once been its garden was overgrown with brambles and ivy. By the time Gavin and Moss arrived with two uniformed constables, three other officers were already in place, hidden in the trees and bushes: one at the front and two at the back.

The man watching the front of the house made room for them silently. "All right, Gardner? Anything?" Moss asked.

Gardner removed the field-glasses from his face and handed them to Moss. "There's someone in there all right. I saw a movement at one of the upstairs windows about ten minutes ago. Nothing since."

"No sign of the hostages?"

"No, sir."

"No idea how many of 'em are in there?"

"No, sir."

"Hmm," said Moss. "You don't know much, and that's a fact." He surveyed the house closely. Gavin looked too, with his unaided sight. The windows of the ground floor had been boarded up, but the upstairs windows had been reglazed since he had last seen the place. It was a simple, square house – rather like a child's drawing, with a window at each corner and a door in the middle, a pointed roof and a chimney. An old and very thick creeper grew over the face of it, and there was a tumbledown collection of sheds and lean-tos to one side. Round to the rear, as Gavin knew from his past explorations, there was another short wing to the house, making it effectively an L-shape cradling a small yard at the back, with more sheds and old stables.

At last the Superintendent lowered the binoculars. "All right," he said, "I think I'll go and have a word with them."

"Sir—" Gardner said, in warning or protest. Moss looked at him impatiently. "It could be dangerous. They might be armed, sir. Why not go in in force, take 'em on all sides at once? We can get the Armed Response Unit here in fifteen minutes, no sweat. Overpower 'em before they've got a chance to make plans."

Moss looked pained. "No, no, no. Let that lot in with their hormones on the rampage? D'you want to start a shoot-out? I don't want bullets flying around when we don't know exactly where the hostages are. Besides, we don't know yet that we've got the right place. Let's find out what we're dealing with first. The whole thing could be legit, and then we'd look like prize prawns, sending the ARU in against a bunch of woolly squatters."

He stepped out of the shelter of the bushes and looked the house over carefully.

"I still think it would be better to try and take 'em by surprise," Gardner tried one last protest.

"Too late for that, laddie," Moss said, seeing a movement at a window. "They already know we're here."

He turned to his uniformed companions. "All right, Simpson, Clarke, come with me. The rest of you keep out of sight. Yes, all right, Mr Akroyd, you can come too. Stick close and keep your mouth shut – remember what I told you."

Gavin nodded, and the four of them started out towards the front door. "Let's keep it nice and relaxed," Moss said as they neared the house. "We don't want anybody frightened into doing anything rash." And he stepped into the porch and rapped on the door. Gavin pointed out the old-fashioned iron bell-pull, and he pulled on that, too, and they heard the bell ringing somewhere in the depths of the house.

Gavin didn't think they would get any response, and was surprised when after only a short delay the door was opened. Before them stood a middle-aged man with close-cropped grey hair, a lined, pale face, and very watchful eyes behind wire-rimmed glasses. He was dressed in grey trousers and a white shirt without a tie. He looked neat and tidy, but tired and unwell. Seeing him standing there, apparently unarmed, and the bare house open behind him, Gavin wanted to rush him, grab him, pin him to the wall and make him tell them where Poppy and Emma were. Behind him he almost felt the uniformed officers stir, as if they, too, felt the same urge.

But Superintendent Moss was a monument of calm. "Well, well, well," he said with cold geniality. "If it isn't Gentleman Jim! And what might you be doing here, may I ask?"

"Hullo, Superintendent," the man said without pleasure. "I was about to ask you the same thing."

"I asked first," Moss insisted.

"I'm a local. Born and bred in Thetford. Why shouldn't I be here?"

"Just answer the question."

James shrugged. "I got to live somewhere. I've just come out of gaol, as no doubt you're aware." Moss nodded impassively. "I've got no money, nothing to live on, and I knew this house was empty, so — I sought shelter. Everyone's got the right to basic shelter, haven't they?"

"Every honest man, maybe."

James managed to look pained. "I hope you aren't going to harass me, Superintendent. I've paid my debt to society. I'm a respectable law-abiding member of the public now."

"Haven't laid a finger on you," Moss said smoothly. "Yet. On your own here, are you?"

"Of course. Who were you expecting?"

"We're looking for a friend of yours. Andy Luckmeed."

"I haven't seen him. I told you, I'm only just out."

"He came to see you in gaol, Harry. We know that."

"I haven't seen him since I came out. What d'you want him for?"

"Broken his parole. Hasn't checked in. Don't want the lad to get in trouble, do we?"

James looked past Moss's shoulder at the uniformed men. "All this just to look for a missing parolee? What are you up to, Moss?"

"*Mr* Moss, if you don't mind. Well, if Andy's not here, and you're not up to anything, you won't mind if we come in and have a look round, will you?"

Gavin was aware of the increase in tension in the Superintendent as he put this question. But James did not flinch, or whip out a gun, or take to his heels. He merely smiled — a slow, spreading, unpleasant smile.

"Not at all," said Gentleman James silkily. "Be my guest. I'm sorry I can't offer you anything, but I'm living here under rather Spartan conditions."

He stepped back and extended his arm, inviting them past him; Moss's face was far from happy as he walked in.

* * *

157

Climbing into the back of the police car beside Gavin, Moss said, "Smartarse little bastard! I'd like to take him to pieces!" He fumed for a moment or two in silence, and then asked Gavin, "Did you see anything?"

"There was nothing to see, was there?" Gavin said, depressed.

"I knew there wouldn't be, or he wouldn't have asked us in." He shook his head again. "Bastard! He must've moved 'em. I suppose Andy Luckmeed's got 'em holed up somewhere else. Damn it, now we've got to start again from scratch."

"Can't you arrest him, make him tell us?"

Moss shook his head. "Nothing to arrest him for. I've got nothing to connect him to the snatch except that he knows Luckmeed and Metcalf – but so do lots of people."

"But he's trespassing, isn't he? Can't you get him for that?"

"He's squatting, and to get him out I have to have a court order proving criminal damage."

"But—"

"It wouldn't make him any more likely to tell us where he's stashed 'em, would it? No, no, we need him on the loose, so that he can give himself away and lead us to them. He was very bold, showing us round, Mr Harry James – very confident, but he wasn't happy about it. He knows we'll be watching his every move now. He thought we'd never find him in a deserted house in the middle of a wood, and he must have been pig-sick when we turned up at the door. If we keep the pressure up, he'll panic and give himself away, or make a break for it. Then we've got him."

"And if he doesn't?"

"Well, to get the money he's got to communicate with one of his mates, hasn't he? And they're not over-endowed with brains. They're his weak spots – them, and his own over-confidence."

But meanwhile, Gavin thought, Poppy and Emma are

in danger, frightened and alone. There must be some way he could help them. And there was something about the house that was bothering him. He didn't know what, but something.

Chapter Thirteen

Andy, going idly to the window to see what sort of day it was, had seen Moss and his companions arrive. He sprang back from the window like a scalded cat, and then rushed to the Boss's room.

"The cops are outside! There's a police car! They're coming to the door!" he babbled. "What're we gonna do, Boss? Shoot it out?"

The Boss was just finishing shaving, with difficulty, in a tiny bowl before a hand-mirror propped on the dado-rail. He scowled. "*Shoot it out*? What's the matter with you? Pull yourself together, for God's sake! You've got a brain like a colander."

"A what?" Andy said blankly.

"Skip it. I've told you we're quite safe here. What I'm going to do is invite them in—"

"*What*?" Andy almost shrieked.

"Shut up! I'll keep them talking at the door for as long as possible, but then I shall invite them in. They'll look round, and they'll find nothing, and then they'll leave."

"But Boss—!"

"Don't you see, you idiot, it's the only way to convince them we haven't got the kid here? They've got nothing on us. They can't touch us. What you're going to do is go to the room, lock yourself in with 'em, and keep 'em quiet at all costs. You'd better gag them – the girl is capable of risking getting shot for the sake of getting the kid rescued." He said it without admiration. "If there's no other choice, cold cock 'em, but try not to damage the kid. When it's all clear, I'll come and knock."

Emma and Poppy had still been asleep when Andy came in, which allowed him to get the gag on her before she really knew what was happening.

"Sit there on the bed," he told her, "put your hands on your head; don't move an inch, or make a sound, or I'll belt the kid with this." He gestured with the gun. Emma stared at him, eyes wide and confused above the gag.

"What're you going to do to us?" Poppy whispered, her eyes filling with tears of fear.

"Shut up," Andy snapped. "I'm not going to hurt you. Now turn around."

He turned her with a rough hand on her shoulder, and gagged her too. Emma's mind was clearing. There's someone out there, she thought. Someone's come to the house — the police? Someone's traced us, and if I don't do something they'll go away and never know we were here. She stood up, regardless of the danger, but Andy took a step forward, gun raised, his face pulled into an ugly sneer.

"Don't even think it! You make one false move, princess, and I'll knock you out. D'you want another head wound? Sit down, hands on your head. *Sit down!*"

Emma sat, miserably, on the edge of the bed, and Andy thrust Poppy down on her knees in front of and facing Emma, effectively blocking any movement.

"That goes for you too, Arry," he said, rubbing the muzzle of the gun against the side of Poppy's face to get her attention. "You move or make a sound, and I'll hit *her*, right where she got it before. You get me? Now *shut up!*"

They waited, Emma sitting, Poppy kneeling and pressed against her knees, Andy standing behind Poppy and holding her by her hair. Tears rolled freely down Poppy's face, soaking the gag. Andy was braced and taut, listening, sweating rankly with fear. Emma listened too, her heart thumping like a trapped bird in her chest, hoping and fearing.

161

Oh find us, please find us! she thought desperately. There were footsteps and bumps, now near, now far, now on the floor above their heads. *We're here*, she cried in her mind, willing them to come, trying to call them telepathically. But after a long time, the footsteps went away, and eventually perfect silence reigned. And then there was a knocking on the door, which made them all jump. But Andy sighed with relief, and she knew it was not rescue.

"All clear," he said, backing to the door and taking the key out of his pocket. He unlocked it, and the Boss came in, looking pleased with himself.

"Well, that's that," he said. His hard eyes met Emma's above her gag. "The police have been here – in force, I may add. They've been here, searched the house to their hearts' content, and gone away again, perfectly satisfied that you aren't here, and never have been. Brains, you see, will always overcome brawn." He grinned. "Your would-be rescuers stood only feet from you, and walked away again."

Poppy was crying dismally, and Emma stared at their tormentor with hatred. He didn't need to come and say those things. He did it because he wanted to hurt them. He didn't just want the money. He wanted power over people, and when he had that power, he would use it to be cruel. She realised then that they had been lucky so far not to be hurt; that luck might not hold in the future. If the money was not forthcoming, he might very well want to prove himself by taking it out on them. Her heart sank to its lowest level yet. Did the police really think they had never been here? Did that mean there was no chance of rescue?

The Boss seemed happy with his effect on them. "All right, Andy, you can take the gags off. Then lock 'em in and come with me."

The Boss left, and Andy undid Poppy's gag. She dragged in some sobbing breaths, and Andy, seeming a little unnerved by her crying, said, "Oh, can it, kid! Nobody's hurting you, are they? As soon as your old man coughs up the dough, you'll be home and dry."

"He'll *never* pay you!" Poppy sobbed passionately. "Daddy won't give you a *penny*!"

"You'd just better hope he does," Andy said grimly. "I reckon you can manage for yourself, princess." Emma undid the gag, and he held out his hand for it impassively, and then went away, banging the door behind him. Poppy flung herself into Emma's arms, and Emma let her have her cry out. When the child was calm again, Emma got up and went over to the corner, took the handkerchief out of her pocket and poked it through the hole in the wall. There was a saying about stable doors and horses; but there was just an outside chance that someone might come back. And in any case, there was nothing else she could do.

Gavin wandered round in a fret of anxiety. Something about the house bothered him, but what? It nagged and nagged at him senselessly; like the sound of a baby crying in the distance, it was something he couldn't quite ignore, and yet which he could do nothing about.

The police had their duties to follow, leaning on Billy Metcalf, looking for Andy Luckmeed, trying to prove a recent connection between them and Harry James, searching for any clue as to where the hostages had been moved to — and how. But Gavin, with nothing to do to occupy him, just went over and over the situation in his head, retreading in imagination the bare floorboards of that house, seeing again the dusty rooms, empty but for dead leaves and bits of fallen plaster. The search had been thorough enough to satisfy even him that Poppy and Emma were not there.

But what, he asked himself, was Sparlings for, if it was not where they had taken the victims? Why would James go to the trouble of setting up the house just for himself, while his prisoners were kept somewhere else? Logic had led the searchers to Sparlings, a logic which said the gang needed an isolated place, and a place they knew would be empty. How many more such were there within the area? Why hadn't the police, who had been methodically visiting every isolated house, found it by now?

No, Sparlings must have been meant as the hideout. But if that were so, why would they move the prisoners elsewhere? And when? They could not have done it when the police first arrived: the house had been surrounded, and no one had come out. And if they did it *before* the police arrived – well, why? You were back to *why*? It made no sense.

Yet Harry James had been so utterly confident that they would find nothing; his confidence, and the fruitless search, had convinced Superintendent Moss. But Gavin's mind would not rest. Logic said the prisoners must be in the house; and if that were the case, they must be hidden in some particularly clever way. Yes, Harry James was pleased with himself – pleased with his cleverness. The prisoners were there, but James was sure they would never find them.

The only thing to do, he thought, was to go back and have another look. The police wouldn't do it, of course. They were pursuing their own plan. But there was nothing – except the police themselves – to prevent Gavin from breaking in at night and taking a look around. As soon as he came to the decision, a great calmness came over him. He was going to take action at last; and it was the right thing to do. He knew they were in there somewhere.

When the house was quiet, he got up, dressed in black trousers and a black roll-neck sweater, put on soft-soled black moccasins. He put his Swiss army knife into his pocket, and a pencil torch and a short but very heavy spanner into the other pocket. On a thought he added a plastic card with which to slip any Yale lock he might encounter. Then he went quietly down the back stairs and out into the park. The moon was in its first quarter, but it was a clear night, so there was enough light to see by.

He had moved his car during the day, leaving it near the side gate to the park, which he had left unlocked. He drove as near as he dared to the place, and then left his car and walked the rest. He had the advantage that he knew the ground and he knew where the police were positioned. The officers had made a loose perimeter round the house, but they would be looking for someone to break out, not to break in. And with all his experience of badger-watching and bird-watching, Gavin could move as soundlessly as a cat.

His object was a small window in the side of the house facing onto the back yard. Once you got up to it, it was hidden from view by a jutting-out corner of brickwork, and it gave onto one of the old pantries, the inside door of which was not lockable. As long as it hadn't been nailed up – and he saw no reason why it should have been – he would be able to get into the rest of the house from there.

Nearing the house, he looked up at the sky, and then hunkered down amongst the bushes to wait. There was a swathe of clouds moving across the sky, which in five or ten minutes would obscure the moon. It would then be quite dark. He had only to wait. It was very unlikely that he would be seen – but if he was, what could they do? They couldn't shoot him, or even shout at him. They could only wait for him to come out again – and he didn't mind if they grabbed him after he came out.

The cloud shadow came up; the moon disappeared. In the blackness Gavin rose and ran quickly and silently across the open space and into the shelter of the house wall, and crept along it to the window. There he stood, listening. Everything was silent, inside and out. Good!

There was a board over the window, but it didn't take him long with his knife to prise the nails out of the rotten wood and set the board aside. Behind it the window was totally innocent of glass: many a boy had wriggled in this way, he thought, over the years – he had done so himself. He thanked God that he was slim, and agile: he hoisted himself up, squeezed through, and dropped lightly to the floor in the empty pantry. The pantry door was not nailed up: it yielded to a push, and he opened it a crack, listened, opened it a little further, and finally slipped out into the empty kitchen passage.

There he stopped and listened again. The house was in silence, except for the pounding in his ears of his own heart. He stood still, breathing slowly and deeply until he was calm again; and then, all his senses on the stretch, he began his search.

It was easier than he had thought it would be to eliminate rooms in which they could not be concealed. There were no cellars to the house, but he wondered whether some secret underground room might have been dug out by the villains for the purpose, though he thought it unlikely they could have managed that in the time available, and without attracting attention. However, he concentrated on looking for doors, concealed or new, which might lead to some underground space, or any door to any room which was locked or barred.

He found nothing. At the foot of the stairs he listened again, but the house was in silence. The stairs yawned before him, empty and menacing. He hesitated. His instincts feared a trap. Anything might be up there, waiting for him. As soon as he started up, he would be vulnerable. But then he thought of Emma. Suddenly she came into his mind, and it was like looking at a fragment of video film: he saw her as he had never seen her in life, turning over in bed with a little sigh as she stirred in her sleep. Was it just imagination, or was she here somewhere, had she just turned like that in real life, and in his heightened state of awareness he had somehow seen her do it? He shook the thoughts away. They were needlessly distracting. But they had cured his hesitation: he had come too far now to be put off. He started up, keeping close to the wall where there was less likelihood of the stairs creaking.

On the first floor there were closed doors and open doors leading off the landing. He chose the nearest open door. It was empty of furniture, and dark — darker than anywhere else in the house. He couldn't even see the outline of the window. Very cautiously, he put on his torch, aiming it at the floor. Dusty, naked floorboards. He advanced the beam slowly. No furniture, only bare boards and a cigarette butt trodden out on the floor. Bare white walls. Ah, that was why it was so dark in here — there was no window; only, on the far side, one of those huge, ugly Victorian wardrobes that often get left in houses when people move out because they won't fit in the new house. He remembered this room, now, from his earlier visit with Moss, remembered the wardrobe. They had looked inside it, of course, and found it empty.

Next to it, against the wall, was a rickety kitchen table; and on the floor under the table was something white. A piece of paper? Had it been there before? He couldn't remember. He crossed the room and picked it up. It was a handkerchief, ragged and torn. Was it a clue? Maybe. Maybe. He shoved it into his pocket, and was about to go when the thing that had been bothering him came up clearly into his mind at last. The room had no window. It was too large a room to be a cupboard: it was clearly a bedroom, but it had no window. That was not only odd, inexplicable, but he also knew that he had played in this house when he was a lad, and he didn't remember a windowless bedroom.

He looked at the wardrobe again. He didn't remember that being here when he was a lad, either. There hadn't been any furniture at all. Of course, someone could have moved it in at any time — there may well have been tramps or squatters here over the years — but a large wardrobe was an odd choice of furniture to bother with. He opened the door and glanced in, shining his torch, but it was still empty — not even a scrap of fluff.

Perhaps, he thought, the window was behind the wardrobe. It would be an odd thing to do, to put a wardrobe over the window, but the wall where it stood was the logical place in the room to *have* a window. He walked round the side of it and shone his torch. He didn't know what he had expected to see, but what he did see was that the wardrobe was absolutely flush with the wall, so close that not even a cigarette paper could have been slipped between. In fact, it looked as though it were part of the wall, joined to it like a built-in wardrobe.

Was this it? His heart was racing again, his palms sweating. He wiped them down his trouser legs. In doing so, he dropped the handkerchief, which he had not pushed into his pocket properly: the roughness of its torn surface caught on his fingers. He stooped to pick it up; and then, instead, flattened it out against the floorboards and shone his torch at it.

Through the white material the dark floorboards showed in the shape of frayed and crudely-cut letters, which seemed to shout at him like a shrill imperative – HELP POPPY!

They were here! He took another look at the wall and wardrobe, and understood everything. And now he must get out and get help, though every fibre of him wanted to tear the place apart with his bare hands. But he must do the sensible thing. He must not be caught now, when he had the information that was needed. His nerves were stretched to the limit, his hair was standing on end with the tension and the fear of being caught, and the adrenalin surging into his blood was screaming at him to run as fast as his legs could pump. It was the hardest thing he had ever had to do in his life, to make himself retrace his steps cautiously, quietly, slowly, on tiptoe, and without looking back. If the sound of his heart thudding didn't wake the villains, he thought, nothing would . . .

As soon as he reached the bushes, he was seized ungently by

two enormous pairs of hands. They must have seen him go in after all. Between them, two burly policemen bundled him hastily away from the house to a safe distance where they could bawl him out. He was not sorry for the support, since his own legs seemed to have gone temporarily on strike.

"You bloody idiot!" one of them hissed, so outraged he actually shook him. "What the hell did you think you were doing?"

Gavin had to search around for his voice, and when he found it, it didn't sound terribly like his.

"They're in there," he said. "I know where. I've got the proof."

"I should never have let you near the place," Superintendent Moss grumbled. "That's what comes of letting amateurs in on the game." But he didn't sound really put out about it. He had got his roaring over before Gavin came into his presence; and there was no doubt that Gavin's lunatic prank had advanced matters considerably.

"I realised that you couldn't be expected to break in," Gavin justified himself, "so I thought I'd do it for you. And besides, I know the house; I've been in it a hundred times."

"Well, as it happens, it's turned out all right, but you could have blown the whole thing, you know, and got yourself killed, to say nothing of your sister."

"I'm sure they didn't hear me. They'd have been down to find out what was going on if they'd heard anything."

"I won't ask where you learned your house-breaking skills, but you seem to have been lamentably professional about it," Moss said sternly. "But we must go carefully, now that we know your sister and Miss Ruskin are in there. What we don't want is for a hostage situation to develop, especially if they're armed. So no more unilateral action, all right, Mr Akroyd?"

"I promise you," Gavin said. "I'm no hero, and I wouldn't

do anything to put them in danger. What are you going to do now?"

"Get the armed units in position, and then try and talk them out."

"Please – you will let me come?"

"As long as I can trust you to stay out of the way."

"I promise."

"Right, then you may be useful. I may need you tell me the layout of the house."

And he waved Gavin away to get himself a cup of coffee, while he got on the telephone and started issuing instructions.

Chapter Fourteen

The Boss did not sleep well on a camp-bed. A good measure of Scotch got him off all right, but then he tended to wake after an hour or two and toss and turn the rest of the night, finally dropping off at about six and sleeping heavily until Andy woke him. He was in the tossing and turning stage of this annoying regime when he came suddenly full awake, and lay for a moment staring at the ceiling, frowning. Something had disturbed him, and he had learned during a misspent life not to ignore his instincts.

The dawn chorus was going on outside – was it that which had woken him? No, wait: the dawn chorus was general, but had fallen silent in the immediate vicinity of the house. And, yes, leafing through memory he dredged up the sharp *chack-chack-chack* alarm call of a blackbird: that was what had brought him to consciousness. Now all his senses were prickling. Something was going on out there.

He crawled stiffly out of bed (*never again*, he thought as he threw an evil glance at the thing) and, keeping out of line of sight, made his way to the window. He saw nothing unusual, but he knew all the same that something was happening. And after watching for some time he at last spotted a movement in the bushes, and caught a glimpse of the blue baseball cap with the black-and-white check band which could only belong to a police marksman.

He jumped back from the window and cursed long and fluently. He knew the form, and he knew that Moss would not have been able to turn out an armed unit without convincing evidence that this was the right place. They were on to him, and in a big way. But what had given it away? He was sure Moss had been merely busking when he paid his visit here — though the Boss would have liked to know what brought the copper to this particular address in the first place. But Moss hadn't known that the kid and the girl were here when he first came — the Boss would have staked his reputation on that. Evidently some new information had come his way. It had to be Billy Metcalf, didn't it? The fool had got himself taken up and had given the game away. That must be it. The Boss cursed Metcalf, and indulged a brief dream of what he'd do to him when he got hold of it. That's what came of working with kids. The Boss had never trusted Metcalf, who was a loud-mouthed, flash little sod; but of course he'd had to bring him in after Metcalf tipped him off about the girl.

Well, there was no use crying about it now. He was dressing himself with quick, economical movements, his mind running ahead. The thing now was to get out, while the cops still thought they had the jump on him. He didn't want a shoot-out, particularly not with frustrated police marksmen, who yearned so much for the chance to pull the trigger they made Al Capone's gang look like the Salvation Army. Once it got to a siege, it was only a matter of time before you gave up or got shot, and the Boss had no intention of doing either. He was going to get away with the kid, and live to collect the loot. If necessary he'd shoot Andy and the other female: they were expendable. If they slowed him down, they were out, he thought, slipping his gun into the waistband of his trousers, and went to wake Andy.

"Come on you, get up, get some clothes on," he said, shaking him roughly.

"Wha? Whazza marra? Whassup?" Andy mumbled thickly, ungluing his eyes with difficulty. He was a revolting sight, the Boss thought dispassionately. God help anyone who had to rely on trash like this.

"Shut your mouth! The rozzers are outside. Billy must have blown us. Come on, get up! We've got to make a run for it."

Gavin was as tense as an overstrung violin as he waited with Superintendent Moss while the various police officers got themselves into position. They were highly-trained professionals, and they moved quietly, but there were so many of them, Gavin could not believe that the criminals inside hadn't been alerted. But the house remained quiet, and no faces showed at the windows.

Moss was checking the various units in on the radio link. Gavin thought about Poppy and Emma, and wondered if they were all right. Was Emma awake and wondering if she was going to be rescued? He imagined how frightened she must have been – probably still was, not knowing what was going to happen to her and Poppy. He tried to send her a thought wave: *Not long now. We're coming. Hold on.*

At last Superintendent Moss nudged Gavin and beckoned. "Come with me," he whispered.

"Is everyone in place?" Gavin asked.

"Nearly. I want you to come with me round the back and let me know any places you think they might make a break for it, any places we need to cover."

"OK."

"The place you broke in, for instance," Moss added with grim humour.

"Right. And what happens then? When everyone's in place?"

"We talk 'em out. There's a regular procedure for this sort of thing."

Gavin nodded. He'd seen it on the news and on films often enough. But in television dramas it never went right; someone always got killed. His mouth dry, he fell in behind Moss and they began to make their way round the house.

173

They had only gone half-way when there was a commotion from the back of the house: shouts, and a burst of gunfire. Moss's radio suddenly crackled into life. He clamped it to his ear.

"Damn it, they've made a run for it!" he shouted, breaking into a run. "Two of 'em, and the girls. Might be more still inside." And he shouted orders into the radio, for half the squad to close the circle round the house while the others pursued the fugitives.

The next few minutes seemed to Gavin a nightmare confusion of running and shouting. No one seemed to notice him. He simply stuck to the Superintendent, hoping no one would shoot him or turn him back. The man Harry James and another crook, with the hostages, had made a dash for it out of the back, shooting and wounding Simpson, who was just getting into position and had been in their way. Now they were running into the woods behind the house.

Alone, either of them could have got clean away, but the hostages were slowing them down. The Boss weighed the chances as they ran. He couldn't yet bring himself to abandon his scheme, his last hope for the Big Score; and besides, the police wouldn't fire on him while he had the kid as a shield. He jerked her along, and she stumbled again and almost tripped him. The wood was petering out up ahead, but there were too many people on their tails for them to run anywhere but straight on, up the slight slope and out of cover.

"Boss, let's dump 'em," Andy pleaded, panting. "We can make it on our own." He had charge of Emma, whose arms were once more tied. Every time she stumbled over her long dressing-gown, he hauled her upright by main force, which was exhausting to him and agonising to her.

"Don't be a fool," the Boss snapped. "D'you want to get shot? Without these two, we're sitting ducks." Poppy was white-faced, dazed, staggering like a zombie as he hauled at her arm; she'd have him down any minute. He stopped, grabbed her round the waist and hoisted her over his shoulder like a sack. But though small, she was a solid little kid, and he was not a fit man. His lungs laboured and his nerves screamed as he tried to keep his feet on the uneven, tussocky ground, hearing the police crashing through the undergrowth behind them like hunting dogs.

"'Sno use!" Andy gasped behind him. "We can't make it!"

The Boss knew he was right. Like flushed game they had been driven out of the trees and into the open, and running uphill they were losing ground. And there was nothing in front of them but more of the same, open country, no cover, nowhere to hide, no chance of stealing a car. It was over. The Boss saw his golden vision of comfortable retirement in the sun dissolve into the prospect a long gaol sentence – the discomfort, the smells, the squalor, the hopelessness. It was a last stand now, or nothing.

He stopped and turned in his tracks, swinging Poppy down from his shoulder onto her feet, and dragging her round in front of him, holding her round the throat with one arm while he drew his gun and thumbed off the safety. Andy, seeing the action, did likewise, taking stand beside him with Emma as his shield.

"Stand still!" the Boss shouted. "Stay where you are!"

The command was hardly needed. The police stopped as soon as they saw what was happening. They were a few yards off. Superintendent Moss, with Gavin still at his elbow, came through to the front of the line. The Boss waved his pistol to make sure they had seen it. "That's right, Mossy. Don't come any closer or the kid gets it," he said, putting the muzzle of the pistol against Poppy's right temple. Everyone froze.

Poppy drooped in the Boss's grip, looking dazed, as if she had only half an idea what was happening; but when her drifting gaze found Gavin, she stiffened and cried out "Gavin!" in a tone of desperate appeal. At the sound of her voice Gavin's body jerked forward in automatic response, but the Boss made a savage gesture with the pistol and snarled, "You want some? You first, then the kid! I'm warning you! Moss, keep your dogs back. I'm not kidding."

Moss laid a hard hand on Gavin's arm, but Gavin had already stopped himself. He stared at the two men in front of him with horrified eyes. He couldn't believe this was happening.

"All right, Harry, take it easy," Moss said. He sounded amazingly calm, almost conversational, but Gavin beside him could feel the Superintendent's body vibrating with tension. "Why don't you do yourself a favour? You know it's all over. There's nowhere else to go. Don't make it worse for yourself."

"You make me laugh," the Boss sneered. "I'm holding all the aces, Mossy, so don't kid yourself."

Moss didn't seem even to have heard him. "Listen," he went on, "if you chuck it up now and come quietly, I'll put in a good word for you. I'll do what I can to talk your sentence down. But if you make me take you, by God you'll be sorry. What about it?"

"Go—yourself!" snarled the Boss, with a violent obscenity that made Gavin flinch.

Moss had been trying to inch forward as he spoke, but he saw James's finger shiver on the trigger, and realised he was too far gone to be reasoned with. He turned his attention instead to the younger man.

"What about you, son? Are you going to be sensible? Come on, Andy, we know all about you. You can't get away, you're going down one way or another, but you don't want to do longer than you have to, do you? Chuck it up now, and do yourself a favour. Don't let old Gentleman Jim talk you into a twenty-stretch. Let him do his own time."

Andy licked his lips uncertainly, and glanced at the Boss.

"He's right, Boss," he said. "We've had it. Let's chuck it up. We don't want anyone to get hurt—"

"*Shut up*! You snivelling little rat, shut your face!" the Boss yelled. "You try it and I'll shoot you first!"

"But Boss—"

In that instant, when the Boss's attention was distracted, Gavin caught Emma's eye. In the extraordinary tension of the moment, understanding flowed between them like a surge of electricity. Gavin felt the hair rise on his scalp. It was as if, just for that split second, each knew exactly what the other was thinking.

Andy's grip on Emma had slackened as his attention was focused on the Boss. It was enough for her. As she and Gavin exchanged that strange knowledge, she jabbed backwards with her elbows with all her strength, throwing her weight with them. Andy grunted with pain, and staggered, thrown off balance; Emma wrenched herself free, and made a break for it, running away from the group, sideways, away from the Boss.

Everything happened in a second. Andy staggered, the Boss thrust Poppy away from him as he took aim at Emma, and Gavin flung himself in one springing leap at the Boss's gun-arm.

Gavin's hands closed over the Boss's wrist. He felt the weight of the gun in the man's hand. He thrust the arm away from him, trying to push it upwards; and as the gun went off he felt the violent concussion a split second before he heard the explosion.

Gavin had been quick enough to spoil the Boss's aim, but not quick enough to prevent him firing. While the shot was still ringing on the quiet morning air, the rest of the police piled in, snatching Poppy away and overpowering both men. It was all over in the blinking of an eye; but to Gavin it seemed as though time had stopped, and he was frozen into immobility, staring at the crumpled figure of Emma, lying a few yards away, face down in the tussocky grass.

177

It was months before he managed to rid his memory of the image, and stop replaying in his dreams the moment when the shot rang out and she fell, and lay still, face down as she had fallen, in that terrible silence. He had known then that she was dead, that he had killed her, and his heart had died too in that moment.

He and another policeman reached her simultaneously. They could not have taken a second, for the pigeons were still rattling up from the trees, disturbed by the shot. Four eager hands turned her over; and then her eyes opened and she looked up at Gavin, and he felt sick with relief. "Emma," he said, and it was like a prayer, like thanksgiving.

"My leg," she whispered.

"She couldn't save herself," the policeman said, "because of her hands being tied." He was examining the wound. "I don't think it's too bad. Looks as if it's gone through the fleshy part. Bit of a mess," he added in a lower voice to Gavin, "but as long as the bone's not broken—"

"It hurts," Emma moaned.

"Don't worry, love, we'll get an ambulance to you right away," the policeman said, standing up; and to Gavin, "Stay with her, all right?"

Gavin didn't even hear him. He was busy working on the knot in the rope that tied her arms; then he remembered his knife, and got on quicker. He felt sick again at the sight of the ragged wounds on her wrists. "Oh Emma," he moaned, "what did they do to you?"

She looked up at him imploringly; he read her eyes and took her into his arms, holding her close against him. She shivered, feeling the terror of the past week begin to drain from her at last into the strength of his body. And then there were hurrying feet and a small, desperate voice crying, "*Gavin!*" and Poppy flung herself on them. Gavin opened up one arm and took her in too, and hugged them both tightly.

178

"I'll never let either of you out of my sight, ever again," he said. He held them tighter, and heard himself make a strange noise, like a sob, or a laugh of relief – perhaps both.

"Ambulance is on its way," came Superintendent Moss's voice from behind him. "And one of the lads is bringing up a first aid kit from one of the cars, see if we can dress that until it comes."

Gavin laid Emma back down on the grass, and looked up at the Superintendent. "Thank you for getting them back," he said, his whole heart in his voice.

"Couldn't have done it without you," Moss said kindly. "You've been a bloody nuisance, but you've been a great help too. And that was a brave thing you did, Miss Ruskin. Foolhardy, but brave."

"She's been brave all the time," Poppy said, garrulous with the relief and excitement of their rescue. "She's been so brave and clever you wouldn't believe! And those two men, I hope they go to prison for ever and ever! Poor Emma, does it hurt a lot? I'm so sorry to make all this trouble for you."

Emma tried to speak, to reassure her, but she was greying out with the pain. Gavin saw, and took hold of her hand, squeezing it hard. "Hold on to me," he said softly. "Not long now."

It seemed an eternity, the wait for the ambulance; but after a while Emma seemed to grow detached from it, so that she *knew* she was in pain rather than *felt* it. The rough grass under her, the open sky above her; the warmth of the sun on her face and the sound of birds and distant voices; all these drifted in and out of her consciousness as she floated a little out of her body. But Gavin's hand holding hers – the warmth and hardness of it, the shape of the palm and the impress of every finger – that was real. It was the point of contact which kept her tethered to the earth, and stopped her letting go and floating right away like a big, weightless, pain-filled balloon.

*   *   *

179

It wasn't until the afternoon that the hospital allowed the police in to take a preliminary statement; and even then, Emma was so drowsy with painkillers and shock that they did not stay long. Just a few points, they said, and they'd leave her to sleep. They could come back the next day for a more detailed statement.

Moss himself called in the next morning, to thank her again, and see how she was getting on.

"It hurts," she said briefly. She felt very low and rather tearful, which the nursing staff said was reaction to the fear and suspense of the past week. "What will happen to the Boss and Andy?"

"Twenty years, I should think," Moss said tersely. "Andy Luckmeed might get less, given that Harry James was the brains behind it; but neither of them will be seeing the light of day again for a long, long time."

It took hours to take her statement; she needed frequent breaks. The policemen went out obediently when the medical staff made their rounds, and again when the nurses came to take her temperature and give her painkillers. She bore it all stoically. She wanted them to have every detail that might put the two men away for a good, long time.

In the afternoon there was a very embarrassing visit from Mr Akroyd. He tiptoed in almost camouflaged with a vast bouquet of roses; and seeing she was awake, stood at the foot of the bed and looked at her, giving the impression that if he had been a cap-wearer, he would have been twisting it round and round in his hands.

"I want to thank you, Miss Ruskin," he said, "but I can't think of any words that would be enough. You saved my little girl. What can I say? Anything you want, anything at all, just name it – it's yours."

"You don't have to thank me," Emma said awkwardly.

"But I do," Mr Akroyd went on; and a surprising blush coloured his face. "And I have to apologise to you. When all this came out – well, the police said it must have been an inside job, someone who knew the ropes, you see. And, not to beat about the bush, I thought it was you. You'd only been with us a few weeks. It seemed obvious that it must be you. Well, I was wrong, I admit it. I feel as bad as can be that it even crossed my mind. I hope you can forgive me."

"It's all right," Emma said. "It doesn't matter."

"It does matter." Mr Akroyd was not used to being contradicted. "It seems from what Superintendent Moss says that you've acted throughout the whole business with courage and resourcefulness, and that if it wasn't for you they'd never have found you both, or got you away from the kidnappers. It was all down to your guts and initiative that we got Poppy back. So whatever you want by way of a reward, it's all right with me. The sky's the limit – and I won't take no for an answer, so just think on! You can let me know what you've decided when you come home."

Emma was feeling very tired and the painkillers were wearing off again, and Mr Akroyd's belligerent determination to see himself in her debt made her feel tearful. She felt he wanted to pay her off, so that he needn't be under obligation to her, needn't think about her any more. And to call Long Hempdon 'home'! It was not her home, and never could be. She was glad when a nurse came in and chased him away.

That evening she had the visit she'd been waiting for. Gavin came in, weighted down with flowers, gifts, messages and cards.

"Hullo, how are you feeling?" he said. He put the whole armful down on the floor so that he could lean over and kiss her cheek. "You look tired. How's the leg?"

"Hurts like hell," she said. She was glad she didn't need to be polite about it, not to him.

He frowned and picked up her hand and kissed her bandaged wrist. "I don't know how we can ever repay you."

"Oh, don't you start," she said wearily. "I had your

father in earlier, threatening me with a reward, like a belligerent Father Christmas. I can't accept anything, you must know that."

Gavin smiled. "I'll talk to him, try and head him off. What did they say about your leg?"

"The doctor said the bullet passed right through the calf, which is the good news. If it had hit bone, I'd have been in a terrible mess. As it is, he says it will heal eventually, though I may be left with some permanent muscle damage."

Gavin looked stricken. "Oh Emma, what can I say? All this for our little girl!"

"How is she? How is Poppy?" Emma asked, knowing she'd get the truth from him. "I haven't seen her since the arrest."

"She's really wonderful. I can't believe how she's bounced back. She's so full of talk and self-confidence, you'd think she'd been on some kind of adventure holiday, rather than an ordeal like that. The only thing is—" he bit his lip. "She thinks you might blame her for what's happened to you."

"That's silly!"

"She thinks you won't come back. That's what's worrying Dad, as well. I know it must have been a dreadful experience for you, but I promised them both that I would ask you." He looked at her with a veiled, watchful expression. "When you're well, will you come back and teach her again?"

Emma looked at him, her heart a cold lump in her chest. In the woods he had held her close, and she had seen love and concern in his face; now he was wary, detached, non-committal. She was just an employee to him after all; she had been mistaken.

"No," she said, "I won't. I love Poppy dearly, as if she was my own sister – almost as if she was my daughter – but it isn't right. She needs to go to school and be with other children her own age, not to be shut up in that house all day with an adult. In the right school, she'll flourish – and I say this though it will make me very sad

182

never to see her again, so you know how strongly I feel about it."

"Good," Gavin said, his face clearing. "I'm glad you feel like that, for two reasons. The first is that I have a plan for Poppy which I'm hoping to persuade my parents to agree to, and having your approval will make it easier. I want to enrol her in a school in London that I know of – the child of a friend of mine goes there, and he recommended it. I'm going to get a flat near by, so that she can be a day pupil and live with me during the week. And she can go home to Long Hempdon for weekends and holidays. What do you think?"

"I think it sounds pretty good." Emma was surprised. Mrs Grainger had said he was like a father to Poppy, but this seemed quite a sacrifice on his part. She wondered whether he would manage to look after a little girl all on his own. But of course, being rich he could afford a housekeeper, or whatever was needed. "How will that fit in with your work?" she asked.

"I've been offered a management job with a firm outside the group. It's based in London, and I'd like to take it for a couple of years, to get some experience before I step into the family business."

"Well, that seems to have worked out nicely, doesn't it," she said. And then, "You said there were two reasons. What's the second?"

Gavin looked at her almost timidly. He picked up her hand and stroked it. "You said that you'd be sorry never to see Poppy again. How would you like to really be her sister?" She stared at him. "I'm not making much of a job of this, am I?" he said with a rueful smile. "What I'm trying to say is that I love you, Emma. Will you marry me?"

"Marry you?" she whispered blankly.

"Oh my God, is it such a terrible prospect? Which of us is it you don't want to live with – me or Poppy? Tell me the truth – I can take it." He lifted her hand and put it to his cheek. "Look at me, clowning to cover up my nerves. Emma, put me out of my misery! Was I mistaken? I thought you cared for me."

"I do," she said suddenly, her poor overloaded brain catching up with her tongue at last. "I do – but – but do you really love me?"

"Madly. Entirely. Will you marry me?"

"Yes," she said.

"Yes?"

"Yes! Kiss me, you idiot!"

He didn't need asking twice. He kissed her long and thoroughly, and when he let her go, she only sighed and smiled at him. "I've waited so long for that," she murmured.

"Me too," he said. "D'you mind if I do it again?"

He came to visit her every day, and spent as much time with her as he could. Her leg was going to be a long time mending; it was lucky they had plenty to talk about. They told each other their side of events; Gavin told her, gravely, about Zara's involvement. She was shocked, but, on later reflection, not terribly surprised. Zara was being sent abroad for six months, to a Swiss academy to learn cordon bleu cookery. It was what Society people did with difficult girls, she learned.

She had other visitors too. Her parents came, in a state of delayed panic; Poppy and Mrs Henderson both came; Lady Susan almost did – she was moved enough to send a message of thanks and some grapes. The police came and reporters came – the hospital wasn't too pleased about that. And there were heaps of letters, cards and flowers, many of them from complete strangers.

"You're quite famous in a quiet sort of way," Gavin said.

"This is quiet?" she protested.

"You know what I mean. You're a heroine. Here, I promised to see you got this one." He distracted her with a large card, signed by her former flat-mates. "They were worried sick – saw the arrest in the papers. They want to know if they can come and visit you at the weekend."

"Of course! I'd love to see them. I do miss them. Have you spoken to them, then?"

"I called in yesterday when I was up in town."

"I suppose they were all over you? You made a big impression there, you know."

"They're nice. And I envied you so much, living like that."

"So tell me," Emma said, getting to a question she had long wanted to ask, "how come you were so affable and easy-going with them the first time you met them, and with me you were stiff and formal and practically hostile."

"I wasn't in love with them."

"Don't tease – I want to know."

"It's true – I fell in love with you almost the moment I met you."

"But you were so cold and aloof with me, I thought you despised me."

"It wasn't all my fault, you know. You were very brittle and uncompromising. You picked on me all the time. I thought you despised me."

She grinned. "So that's what you liked about me!"

"I'd never met anyone like you – you were so bull-headed and determined."

"How feminine you make me sound!"

"And when I found you loved Poppy, I loved you even more. And then you disappeared and I thought, if I should lose you—" He stopped. "I don't ever want to go through anything like that again."

They were silent, and he saw that he had made her relive it, and was sorry. To lighten the mood he said, "Would you mind living in the house in Mayfair for a short time after we're married? Just until we get a flat?"

"No, I suppose not. Why?"

185

He grinned. "I promised the girls we'd have them to dinner there."

"You like them that much?" she laughed.

"I like them so much, I think they ought to be your bridesmaids, along with Poppy, of course – and Zara if you can stand her."

"Five bridesmaids trooping along behind a limping bride? It'd have the congregation in stitches," Emma said. "Are you sure we have to have a big wedding?"

"I'm afraid so. My stepmother and all her friends will expect it. Penalty of being rich: you can't just please yourself."

"Oh well, I suppose I can survive it," she said, and looked up at him with a smile which said she could survive anything as long as he was there with her. Then she laughed. "I've just thought of something."

"What?"

"If I marry a millionaire's son and heir—"

"Yes?"

"How will Suzanne ever be able to forgive me?"

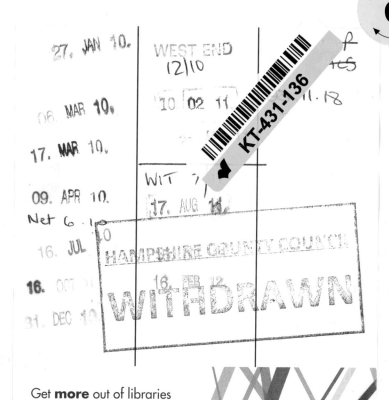

Get **more** out of libraries

Please return or renew this item by the last date shown.
You can renew online at www.hants.gov.uk/library
Or by phoning 0845 603 5631

🏰 Hampshire
County Council

FINE JUST THE WAY IT IS

FINE JUST THE WAY IT IS

Annie Proulx

CHIVERS

British Library Cataloguing in Publication Data available

This Large Print edition published by BBC Audiobooks Ltd, Bath, 2009.
Published by arrangement with HarperCollins Publishers .

U.K. Hardcover ISBN 978 1 408 42165 9
U.K. Softcover ISBN 978 1 408 4 2166 6

Printed and bound in Great Britain by
CPI Antony Rowe, Chippenham, Wiltshire

For Muffy & Geoff
Jon & Gail
Gillis
Morgan

Contents

Contents

On the surface, everything was lovely, but when you got into the inside circle you soon found out that the lines of demarcation were plainly marked.

—John Clay, *My Life on the Range*

Family Man

The Mellowhorn Home was a rambling one-story log building identifying itself as western—the furniture upholstered in fabrics with geometric 'Indian' designs, lampshades sporting buckskin fringe. On the walls hung Mr. Mellowhorn's mounted mule deer heads and a two-man crosscut saw.

It was the time of year when Berenice Pann became conscious of the earth's dark turning, not a good time, she thought, to be starting a job, especially one as depressing as caring for elderly ranch widows. But she took what she could get. There were not many men in the Mellowhorn Retirement Home, and those few were so set upon by the women that Berenice pitied them. She had believed the sex drive faded in the elderly, but these crones vied for the favors of palsied men with beef jerky arms. The men could take their pick of shapeless housecoats and flowery skeletons.

Three deceased and stuffed Mellowhorn dogs stood in strategic guard positions—near the front door, at the foot of the stairs, and beside the rustic bar made from old fence posts. Small signs, the product of the pyrographer's art, preserved their names: Joker, Bugs and Henry. At least, thought Berenice, patting Henry's head, the Home had a view of the enclosing mountains. It had rained all day and now, in the stiffening gloom, tufts of bunchgrass showed up like bleached hair. Down along an old irrigation ditch willows made a ragged line of somber maroon, and the stock pond at the bottom of the hill was as flat as zinc. She went to another window to look at coming weather. In the northwest a wedge of sky, milk-white and chill, herded the rain before it. An old man sat at the community room window staring out at the grey autumn. Berenice knew his name, knew all their names; Ray Forkenbrock.

'Get you something, Mr. Forkenbrock?' She made a point of prefacing the names of residents with the appropriate honorifics, something the rest of the staff did not do, slinging around first names as though they'd all grown up together. Deb Slaver was familiar to a fault, chumming up with 'Sammy,' and 'Rita' and 'Delia,' punctuated with 'Hon,' 'Sweetie' and 'Babes.'

'Yeah,' he said. He spoke with long pauses between sentences, a slow unfurling of words that made Berenice want to jump in with word suggestions.

'Get me the hell out a here,' he said.

'Get me a horse,' he said.

'Get me seventy year back a ways,' said Mr. Forkenbrock.

'I can't do that, but I can get you a nice cup of tea. And it'll be Social Hour in ten minutes,' she said.

She couldn't quite meet his stare. He was something to look at, despite an ordinary face with infolded lips, a scrawny neck. It was the eyes. They were very large and wide open and of the palest, palest blue, the color of ice chipped with a pick, faint blue with crystalline rays. In photographs they appeared white like the eyes of Roman statues, saved from that blind stare only by the black dots of pupils. When he looked at you, thought Berenice, you could not understand a word he said for being fixed by those strange white eyes. She did not like him but pretended she did. Women had to pretend to like men and to admire the things they liked. Her own sister had married a man who was interested in rocks and now she had to drag around deserts and steep mountains with him.

*   *   *

At Social Hour the residents could have drinks and crackers smeared with cheese paste from the Super Wal-Mart where Cook shopped. They were all lushes, homing in on the whiskey bottle. Chauncey Mellowhorn, who had built the Mellowhorn Retirement Home and set all policy, believed that the last feeble years should be enjoyed, and promoted smoking, drinking, lascivious television programs and plenty of cheap food. Neither teetotalers nor

3

bible thumpers signed up for the Mellowhorn Retirement Home.

Ray Forkenbrock said nothing. Berenice thought he looked sad and she wanted to cheer him up in some way.

'What did you used to do, Mr. Forkenbrock? Were you a rancher?'

The old man glared up at her. 'No,' he said. 'I wasn't no god-damn rancher. I was a hand,' he said.

'I worked for them sonsabitches. Cowboyed, ran wild horses, rodeoed, worked in the oil patch, sheared sheep, drove trucks, did whatever,' he said. 'Ended up broke.

'Now my granddaughter's husband pays the bills that keep me here in this nest of old women,' he said. He often wished he had died out in the weather, alone and no trouble to anyone.

Berenice continued, making her voice cheery. 'I had a lot a different jobs too since I graduated high school,' she said. 'Waitress, day care, housecleaning, Seven-Eleven store clerk, like that.' She was engaged to Chad Grills; they were to be married in the spring and she planned to keep working only for a little while to supplement Chad's paycheck from Red Bank Power. But before the old man could say anything more Deb Slaver came pushing in, carrying a glass. Berenice could smell the dark whiskey. Deb's vigorous voice pumped out of her ample chest in jets.

4

'Here you go, honey-boy! A nice little drinkie for Ray!' she said. 'Turn around from that dark old winder and have some fun!' She said, 'Don't you want a watch *Cops* with Powder Face?' (Powder Face was Deb's nickname for a painted harridan with hazelnut knuckles and a set of tawny teeth.) 'Or is it just one a them days when you want a look out the winder and feel blue? Think of some troubles? You retired folks don't know what trouble is, just setting here having a nice glass of whiskey and watching teevee,' she said.

She punched the pillows on the settee. 'We're the ones with troubles—bills, cheating husbands, sassy kids, tired feet,' she said. 'Trying to scrape up the money for winter tires! My husband says the witch with the green teeth is plaguing us,' she said. 'Come on, I'll set with you and Powder Face awhile,' and she pulled Mr. Forkenbrock by his sweater, threw him onto the settee and sat beside him.

Berenice left the room and went to help in the kitchen, where the cook was smacking out turkey patties. A radio on the windowsill murmured.

'Looks like it is clearing up,' Berenice said. She was a little afraid of the cook.

'Oh good, you're here. Get them French fry packages out of the freezer,' she said. 'Thought I was going to have to do ever-thing myself. Deb was supposed to help, but she rather tangle up with them old boys. She hopes

5

they'll put her in their will. Some of them's got a little property or a mineral-rights check coming in,' she said. 'You ever meet her husband, Duck Slaver?' Now she was grating a cabbage into a stainless steel bowl.

Berenice knew only that Duck Slaver drove a tow truck for Ricochet Towing. The radio suddenly caught the cook's attention and she turned up the volume, hearing that it would be cloudy the next day with gradual clearing, the following day high winds and snow showers.

'We ought to be grateful for the rain in this drought. Know what Bench says?' Bench was the UPS driver, the source of Cook's information on everything from road conditions to family squabbles.

'No.'

'Says we are in the beginning of turning into a desert. It's all going to blow away,' she said.

When Berenice went to announce dinner—turkey patties, French fries (Mr. Mellowhorn still called them 'freedom fries') with turkey patty gravy, cranberry relish, creamed corn and homemade rolls—she saw that Deb had worked Mr. Forkenbrock into the corner of the settee, and Powder Face was in the chair with the bad leg watching cops squash the faces of black men onto sidewalks. Mr. Forkenbrock was staring at the dark window, the coursing raindrops catching the blue television flicker. He gave off an aura of separateness. Deb and Powder Face might

6

have been two more of Mellowhorn's stuffed dogs.

After dinner, on her way back to the kitchen to help the cook clean up, Berenice opened the door for a breath of fresh air. The eastern half of the sky was starry, the west a slab of basalt.

*   *   *

In the early morning darkness the rain began again. He did not know but would have understood the poet's line 'I wake and feel the fell of dark, not day.' Nothing in nature seemed more malign to Ray Forkenbrock than this invisible crawl of weather, the blunt-nosed cloud advancing under the lid of darkness. As the dim morning emerged, like a photograph in developing solution, the sound of the rain sharpened. That's sleet, he thought, remembering a long October ride in such weather when he was young, his denim jacket soaked through and sparkling with ice, remembered meeting up with that old horse catcher who lived out in the desert, must have been in his eighties, out there in the rattling precip limping along, heading for the nearest ranch bunkhouse, he said, to get out of the weather.

'That'd be Flying A,' said Ray, squinting against the slanting ice.

'Ain't that Hawkins's place?'

7

'Naw. Hawkins sold out couple years ago. A fella named Fox owns it now,' he said.

'Hell, I lose touch out here. Had a pretty good shack up until day before yesterday,' the horse catcher said between clicking teeth and went on to tell that his place had burned down and he'd slept out in the sage for two nights but now his bedroll was soaked and he was out of food. Ray felt bad for him and at the same time wanted to get away. It seemed awkward to be mounted while the man was afoot, but then he always had that same uncomfortable, guilty itch when he rode past a pedestrian. Was it his fault the old man didn't have a horse? If he was any good at horse catching he should have had a hundred of them. He foraged through his pockets and found three or four stale peanuts mixed with lint.

'It ain't much but it's all I got,' he said, holding them out.

The old boy had never made it to the Flying A. He was discovered days later sitting with his back against a rock. Ray remembered the uncomfortable feeling he'd had exchanging a few words with him, thinking how old he was. Now he was the same age, and he had reached the Flying A—the warmth and dry shelter of the Mellowhorn Home. But the old horse catcher's death, braced against a rock, seemed more honorable.

It was six-thirty and there was nothing to get up for, but he put on his jeans and shirt, added

8

an old man's sweater as the dining room could be chilly in the morning before the heat got going, left his boots in the closet and shuffled down the hall in red felt slippers, too soft to deliver a kick to stuffed Bugs with the googly eyes at the foot of the stairs. The slippers were a gift from his only granddaughter, Beth, married to Kevin Bead. Beth was important to him. He had made up his mind to tell her the ugly family secret. He would not leave his descendants to grapple with shameful uncertainties. He was going to clear the air. Beth was coming on Saturday afternoon with her tape recorder to help him get it said. During the week she would type it into her computer and bring him the crisp printed pages. He might have been nothing more than a ranch hand in his life, but he knew a few things.

*   *   *

Beth was dark-haired with very red cheeks that looked freshly slapped. It was the Irish in her he supposed. She bit her finger-nails, an unsightly habit in a grown woman. Her husband, Kevin, worked in the loan department of the High Plains Bank. He complained that his job was stupid, tossing money and credit cards to people who could never pay up.

'Used to be to get a card you had to work

9

hard and have good credit. Now the worse your credit the easier it is to get a dozen of them,' he said to his wife's grandfather. Ray, who had never had a credit card, couldn't follow the barrage of expository information that followed about changing bank rules, debt. These information sessions always ended with Kevin sighing and saying in a dark tone that the day was coming.

Ray Forkenbrock guessed Beth would use the computer at the real estate office where she worked to transcribe his words.

'Oh no, Grandpa, we've got a computer and printer at home. Rosalyn wouldn't like for me to do it in the office,' she said. Rosalyn was her boss, a woman Ray had never seen but felt he knew well because Beth talked often about her. She was very, very fat and had financial trouble. Scam artists several times stole her identity. Every few months she spent hours filling out fraud affidavits. And, said Beth, she wore XXXL blue jeans and a belt with a silver buckle as big as a pie tin that she had won at a bingo game.

Ray snorted. 'A buckle used to mean something,' he said. 'A rodeo buckle, best part of the prize. The money was nothing in them days,' he said. 'We didn't care about the money. We cared about the buckle,' he said, 'and now fat gals win them at bingo games?' He twisted his head around and looked at the closet door. Beth knew he must have a belt with a rodeo buckle in there.

'Do you watch the National Finals on television?' she said. 'Or the bull-riding championship?'

'Hell, no,' he said. 'The old hens here wouldn't put up with it. They got that teevee lined out from dawn to midnight— crime, that reality shit, fashion and python shows, dog and cat programs. Watch rodeo? Not a chance,' he said.

He glared at the empty hall beyond the open door. 'You wouldn't never guess the most of them lived on ranches all their life,' he added sourly.

*   *   *

Beth spoke to Mr. Mellowhorn and said she thought her grandfather could at least watch the National Finals or the PBR rodeos considering what they were paying for his keep. Mr. Mellowhorn agreed.

'But I like to keep out of residents' television choices, you know, democracy rules at the Mellowhorn Home, and if your grandfather wants to watch rodeo all he has to do is persuade a majority of the inhabitants to sign a petition and—'

'Do you have any objection if my husband and I get him a television set for his room?'

'Well, no, of course not, but I should just mention that the less fortunate residents might

11

see him as privileged, even a little high-hat if he holes up in his room and watches rodeo instead of joining the community choice—'

'Fine,' said Beth, cutting past the social tyranny of the Mellowhorn Home. 'That's what we'll do, then. Get him a snooty, high-hat television. Family counts with me and Kevin,' she said. 'I don't suppose you have a satellite hookup, do you?' she asked.

'Well, no. We've discussed it, but—maybe next year—'

She brought Ray a small television set with a DVD player and three or four discs of recent years' rodeo events. That got him going.

'Christ, I remember when the finals was in Oklahoma City, not goddamn Las Vegas,' he said. 'Of course bull riding has pushed out all the other events now, good-bye saddle bronc and bareback. I was there when Freckles Brown rode Tornado in 1962,' he said. 'Forty-six year old, and the ones they got now bull riding are children! Make a million dollars. It's all show business now,' he said. 'The old boys was a rough crew. Heavy drinkers, most of them. You want to know what pain is, try bull riding with a bad hangover.'

'So I guess you did a lot of rodeo riding when you were young?'

'No, not a lot, but enough to get broke up some. And earned a buckle,' he said. 'You heal fast when you're young, but the broke places sort of come back to life when you are old. I

12

busted my left leg in three places. Hurts now when it rains,' he said.

'How come you cowboyed for a living, Grandpa Ray? Your daddy wasn't a rancher or a cowboy, was he?' She turned the volume knob down. The riders came out of a chute, again and again, monotonously, all apparently wearing the same dirty hat.

'Hell no, he wasn't. He was a coal miner. Rove Forkenbrock,' he said. 'My mother's name was Alice Grand Forkenbrock. Dad worked in the Union Pacific coal mines. Something happened to him and he quit. Moved into running errands for different outfits, Texaco, California Petroleum, big outfits.

'Anyway, don't exactly know what the old man did. Drove a dusty old Model T. He'd get fired and then he had to scratch around for another job. Even though he drank—that's what got him fired usually—he always seemed to get another job pretty quick.' He swallowed a little whiskey.

'Anymore I wouldn't go near the mines. I liked horses almost as much as I liked arithmetic, liked the cow business, so after I graduated eighth grade and Dad said better forget high school, things were tough and I had to find work,' he said. 'At the time I didn't mind. What my dad said I generally didn't fuss over. I respected him. I respected and honored my father. I believed him to be a good and fair

13

man.' He thought, unaccountably, of weeds.

'I tried for a job and got took on at Bledsoe's Double B,' he said. 'The bunkhouse life. The Bledsoes more or less raised me to voting age. At that point I sure didn't want nothing to do with my family,' he said and fell into an old man's reverie. Weeds, weeds and wildness.

Beth was quiet for a few minutes, then chatted about her boys. Syl had acted the part of an eagle in a school play and what a job, making the costume! Just before she left she said offhandedly, 'You know, I want my boys to know about their great-granddad. What do you think if I bring my recorder and get it on tape and then type it up? It would be like a book of your life— something for the future generations of the family to read and know about.'

He laughed in derision.

'Some of it ain't so nice to know. Every family got its dirty laundry and we got ours.' But after a week of thinking about it, of wondering why he'd kept it bottled up for so long, he told Beth to bring on her machine.

*   *   *

They sat in his little room with the door closed.

' "Antisocial," they'll say. Everybody else sits with the door open hollering at each other's

14

folks as if they was all related somehow. A regional family, they call it here. I like my privacy.'

She put a glass of whiskey, another of water and the tape recorder, smaller than a pack of cigarettes, on the table near his elbow and said, 'It's on, Grandpa. Tell me how it was growing up in the old days. Just talk any time you are ready.'

He cleared his throat and began slowly, watching the spiky volume meter jump. 'I'm eighty-four years old and most of them involved in the early days has gone on before, so it don't make much difference what I tell.' He took a nervous swallow of the whiskey and nodded.

'I was fourteen year old in nineteen and thirty-three and there wasn't a nickel in the world.' The silence of that time before traffic and leaf blowers and the boisterous shouting of television was embedded in his character, and he spoke little, finding it hard to drag out the story. The noiselessness of his youth except for the natural sound of wind, hoofbeats, the snap of the old house logs splitting in winter cold, wild herons crying their way downriver was forever lost. How silent men and women had been in those times, trusting to observational powers. There had been days when a few little mustache clouds moved, and he could imagine them making no more sound than dragging a feather across a wire. The

15

wind got them and the sky was alone.

'When I was a kid we lived hard, let me tell you. Coalie Town, about eight miles from Superior. It's all gone now,' he said. 'Three-room shack, no insulation, kids always sick. My baby sister Goldie died of meningitis in that shack,' he said.

Now he was warming up to his sorry tale. 'No water. A truck used to come every week and fill up a couple barrels we had. Mama paid a quarter a barrel. No indoor plumbing. People make jokes about it now but it was miserable to go out there to that outhouse on a bitter morning with the wind screaming up the hole. Christ,' he said. He was silent for so long Beth backed up the tape and pressed the pause button on the recorder. He lit a cigarette, sighed, abruptly started talking again. Beth lost a sentence or two before she got the recorder restarted.

'People thought they was doing all right if they was alive. You can learn to eat dust instead of bread, my mother said many a time. She had a lot a old sayings. Is that thing on?' he said.

'Yes, Grandpa,' she said. 'It is on. Just talk.'

'Bacon,' he said. 'She'd say if bacon curls in the pan the hog was butchered wrong side of the moon. We didn't see bacon very often and it could of done corkscrews in the pan, would have been okay with us long as we could eat it,' he said.

16

'There was a whole bunch a shacks out there near the mines. They called it Coalie Town. Lot of foreigners.

'As I come up,' he said, 'I got a pretty good education in fighting, screwing—pardon my French—and more fighting. Every problem was solved with a fight. I remember all them people. Pattersons, Bob Hokker, the Grainblewer twins, Alex Sugar, Forrie Wintka, Harry and Joe Dolan . . . We had a lot of fun. Kids always have fun,' he said.

'They sure do,' said Beth.

'Kids don't get all sour thinking about the indoor toilets they don't have, or moaning because there ain't no fresh butter. For us everthing was fine the way it was. I had a happy childhood. When we got bigger there was certain girls. Forrie Wintka. Really good looking, long black hair and black eyes,' he said, looking to see if he had shocked her.

'She finally married old man Dolan after his wife died. The Dolan boys was something else. They hated each other, fought, really had bad fights, slugged each other with boards with nails in the end, heaved rocks.'

Beth tried to shift him to a description of his own family, but he went on about the Dolans.

'I'm pretty set in my ways,' he said. She nodded.

'One time Joe knocked Harry out, kicked him into the Platte. He could of drowned, probably would of but Dave Arthur was riding along the river, seen this bundle of rags snarled up in a cottonwood sweeper—it had fell in the river and caught up all sorts of river trash. He thought maybe some clothes. Went to see and pulled Harry out,' he said.

'Harry was about three-quarters dead, never was right after that, neither. But right enough to know that his own brother had meant to kill him. Joe couldn't never tell if Harry was going to be around the next corner with a chunk of wood or a gun.' There was a long pause after the word 'gun.'

'Nervous wreck,' he said. He watched the tape revolve for long seconds.

'Dutchy Green was my best friend in grade school. He was killed when he was twenty-five, twenty-six, shooting at some of them old Indian rock carvings. The ricochet got him through the right temple,' he said.

He took a swallow of whiskey. 'Yep, our family. There was my mother. She was tempery, too much to do and no money to do it. Me, the oldest. There was a big brother, Sonny, but he drowned in an irrigation ditch before I come along,' he said.

'Weren't there girls in the family?' asked Beth. Not content with two sons, she craved a daughter. .

*　　*　　*

'My sisters, Irene and Daisy. Irene lives in
18

Greybull and Daisy is still alive out in California. And I mentioned, the baby Goldie died when I was around six or seven. The youngest survivor was Roger. Mama's last baby. He went the wrong way. Did time for robbing,' he said. 'No idea what happened to him.' Under the weeds, damned and dark.

Abruptly he veered away from the burglar brother. 'You got to understand that I loved my dad. We all did. Him and Mother was always kissing and hugging and laughing when he was home. He was a wonderful man with kids, always a big smile and a hug, remembered all your interests, lots of times brought home special little presents. I still got every one he give me.' His voice trembled like that of the old horse catcher in the antique sleet.

'Remembering this stuff makes me tired. I guess I better stop,' he said. 'Anymore two new people come in today and the new ones always makes me damn tired.'

'Women or men?' asked Beth, relieved to turn the recorder off as she could see her only tape was on short time. She remembered now she had recorded the junior choir practice.

'Don't know,' he said. 'Find out at supper.'

'I'll come next week. I think what you are saying is important for this family.' She kissed his dry old man's forehead, brown age spots.

'Just wait,' he said.

After she left he started talking again as if the tape were still running. 'He died age forty-seven. I thought that was real old. Why didn't he jump?' he said.

Berenice Pann, bearing a still-warm chocolate cupcake, paused outside his door when she heard his voice. She had seen Beth leave a few minutes earlier. Maybe she had forgotten something and come back. Berenice heard something like a strangled sob from Mr. Forkenbrock. 'God, it was lousy,' he said. 'So we could work. Hell, I liked school. No chance when you start work at thirteen,' he said. 'Wasn't for the Bledsoes I'd ended up a bum,' he said to himself. 'Or worse.'

Berenice Pann's boyfriend, Chad Grills, was the great-grandson of the old Bledsoes. They were still on the ranch where Ray Forkenbrock had worked in his early days, both of them over the century mark. Berenice became an avid eavesdropper, feeling that in a way she was related to Mr. Forkenbrock through the Bledsoes. She owed it to herself and Chad to hear as much as she could about the Bledsoes, good or bad. Inside the room there was silence, then the door flung open.

'Uh!' cried Berenice, the cupcake sliding on its saucer. 'I was just bringing you this—'

'That so?' said Mr. Forkenbrock. He took the cupcake from the saucer and instead of

20

taking a sample bite crammed the whole thing into his mouth, paper cup and all. The paper massed behind his dentures.

*   *   *

At the Social Hour, Mr. Mellowhorn arrived to introduce the new 'guests.' Church Bollinger was a younger man, barely sixty-five, but Ray could tell he was a real slacker. He'd obviously come into the Home because he couldn't get up the gumption to make his own bed or wash his dishes. The other one, Mrs. Terry Taylor, was around his age, early eighties despite the dyed red hair and carmine fingernails. She seemed soft and sagging, somehow like a candle standing in the sun. She kept looking at Ray. Her eyes were khaki-colored, the lashes sparse and short, her thin old lips greased up with enough lipstick to leave red on her buttered roll. Finally he could take her staring no longer.

'Got a question?' he said.

'Are you Ray Forkenknife?' she said.

'Forkenbrock,' he said, startled.

'Oh, right. Forkenbrock. You don't remember me? Theresa Worley? From Coalie Town? Me and you went to school together except you was a couple grades ahead.'

But he did not remember her.

*   *   *

The next morning, fork poised over the poached egg reclining like a houri on a bed of soggy toast, he glanced up to meet her intense gaze. Her red-slick lips parted to show ocher teeth that were certainly her own, for no dentist would make dentures that looked as though they had been dredged from a sewage pit.

'Don't you remember Mrs. Wilson?' she said. 'The teacher that got froze in a blizzard looking for her cat? The Skeltcher kids that got killed when they fell in a old mine shaft?'

He did remember something about a schoolteacher frozen in a June blizzard but thought it had happened somewhere else, down around Cold Mountain. As for the Skeltcher kids, he denied them and shook his head.

*   *   *

On Saturday Beth came again, and again set out the glass of water, the glass of whiskey and the tape recorder. He had been thinking what he wanted to say. It was clear enough in his head, but putting it into words was difficult. The whole thing had been so subtle and painful it was impossible to present it without sounding like a fool. And Mrs. Terry Taylor, a.k.a. Theresa Worley, had sidelined him. He strove to remember the frozen teacher, the

22

Skeltcher kids in the mine shaft, how Mr. Baker had shot Mr. Dennison over a bushel of potatoes and a dozen other tragedies she had laid out as mnemonic bait. He remembered very different events. He remembered walking to the top of Irish Hill with Dutchy Green to meet Forrie Wintka, who was going to show them her private parts in exchange for a nickel each. It was late autumn, the cottonwoods leafless along the grim trickle of Coal Creek, warm weather holding. They could see Forrie Wintka toiling up from the shacks below. Dutchy said it would be easy, not only would she show them, they could do it to her, even her brother did it to her.

Dutchy whispered as though she could hear them. 'Even her stepfather. He got killed by a mountain line last year.'

And now, seventy-one years later, it hit him. Her father had been Worley, Wintka was the stepfather who had carried the mail horseback and in Snakeroot Canyon had been dragged into the rocks by a lion. The first female he had ever plowed, a coal-town slut, was sharing final days with him at the Mellowhorn Home.

'Beth,' he said to his granddaughter. 'I can't talk about nothing today. There's some stuff come to mind just now that I got to think my way through. The new woman who come here last week. I knew her and it wasn't under the best circumstances,' he said. That was the trouble with Wyoming; everything you ever did

23

or said kept pace with you right to the end. The regional family again.

*   *   *

Mr. Mellowhorn started a series of overnight outings he dubbed 'Weekend Adventures.' The first one had been to the Medicine Wheel up in the Big Horns. Mrs. Wallace Kimes had fallen and scraped her knees on the crushed stone in the parking lot. Then came the dude ranch weekend where the Mellowhorn group found itself sharing the premises with seven elk hunters from Colorado, most of them drunk and disorderly and given over to senseless laughter topping 110 decibels. Powder Face laughed senselessly with them. The third trip was more ambitious; a five-day excursion to the Grand Canyon where no one at the Mellowhorn Home had ever been. Twelve people signed up despite the hefty fee to pay for lodging and transportation.

'You only live once!' cried Powder Face.

The group included newcomer Church Bollinger and Forrie Wintka, a.k.a. Theresa Worley, a.k.a. Terry Dolan and, finally, as Terry Taylor. Forrie and Bollinger sat together in the van, had drinks together in the bar of El Tovar, ate dinner at a table for two and planned a trail-ride expedition for the next morning. But before the mule train left, Forrie asked Bollinger to take some photographs she

Stubbington Library 1
RENEW ONLINE at www.hants.gov.uk/library or
phone 0300 555 1387

LOVE YOUR LIBRARY

Customer ID: ******1555

Items borrowed today

Title: Fine just the way it is
ID: C014589322
Due: 15 October 2022

Total items: 1
Account balance: £0.00
17/09/2022 11:51
Items borrowed: 1
Overdue items: 0
Reservations: 0
Reservations for collection: 0

Download the Spydus Mobile App to control your
loans and reservations from your smartphone.
Thank you for using the Library.

could send to her granddaughters. She stood on the parapet with the famous view behind her. She posed with one hand holding her floppy new straw hat purchased in the hotel gift shop. She took off the hat and turned, shading her eyes with her hand, and pretended to be peering into the depths like a stage character of yore. She clowned, pretending she was unsteady and losing her balance. There was a stifled 'Oh!' and she disappeared. A park ranger rushed to the parapet and saw her on the slope ten feet below, clutching at a small plant. Her hat lay to one side. Even as he climbed over the parapet and reached for her, the plant trembled and loosened. Forrie dug her fingers into the gravel as she began to slide toward the edge. The ranger thrust his foot toward her, shouting for her to grab on. But his saving kick connected with Forrie's hand. She shot down the slope as one on a waterslide, leaving ten deep grooves to mark her trail, then, in a last desperate effort, reached for and almost seized her new straw hat.

The subdued group returned to Wyoming the next day. Again and again they told each other that she had not even cried out as she fell, something they believed denoted strong character.

*　　　*　　　*

Ray Forkenbrock resumed his memoir the next weekend. Berenice waited a few minutes after Beth arrived before taking up a listening post outside the room. Mr. Forkenbrock had a monotonous but loud voice, and she could hear every word.

'So, things was better for the family after he got the jobs driving machine parts around to the oil rigs,' he said. 'The money was pretty good and he joined some one of them fraternal organizations, the Pathfinders. And they had a ladies' auxiliary, which my mother got into; they called it "The Ladies," like it was a rest-room or something. They both got real caught up in Pathfinders, the ceremonies, the lodge, the good deeds and oaths of allegiance to whatever.

'Mother was always baking something for them,' he said. 'And there was kid stuff for us, fishing derbies and picnics and sack races. It was like Boy Scouts, or so they said. Boy Scouts with a ranch twist, because there was always some class in hack-amore braiding or raising a calf. Sort of a kind of a mix of Scouts and 4-H which we did not belong to.'

Berenice found this all rather boring. When would he say something about the Bledsoes? She saw Deb Slaver at the far end of the hall coming out of Mr. Harrell's room with a tray of bandages. Mr. Harrell had a sore on his shin that wouldn't heal and the dressing had to be changed twice a day.

'Now don't you pick at it, you bad boy!'
yelled Deb, disappearing around the corner.

'Anyway, Mother was probably more into it
than Dad. She liked company and hadn't had
much luck with neighbors there in Coalie
Town. The Ladies got up a program of history
tours to various massacre sites and old logging
flumes. Mother loved those trips. She had a
little taste for what had happened in the long
ago. She'd come home all excited and carrying
a pretty rock. She had about a dozen rocks
from those trips when she died,' he said.

In the hall Berenice thought of her sister
toiling up rocky slopes, trying to please her
rock hound husband, carrying his canvas sack
of stones.

'The first hint I got that there was
something peculiar in our family tree was
when she come home from a visit to Farson. I
do not know what they were doing there, and
she said that the Farson Auxiliary had served
them lunch—potato salad and hot dogs,' he
said.

'One of the Farson ladies said she knew a
Forkenbrock down in Dixon. She thought he
had a ranch in the Snake River valley. Well,
my ears perked up when I heard "ranch,"' he
said.

'And Forkenbrock ain't that common of a
name. So I asked Mother if they were Dad's
relatives,' he said. 'I would of liked it if we had
ranch kin. I was already thinking about getting

into cowboy ways. She said no, that Dad was an orphan, that it was just a coincidence. So she said.'

*   *   *

At dinner that night, once Forrie Wintka's dramatic demise had been hashed through again, Church Bollinger began to describe his travels through the Canadian Rockies.

'What we'd do is fly, then rent a car instead of driving. Those interstates will kill you. The wife enjoyed staying at nice hotels. So we flew to San Francisco and decided to drive down the coast. We stopped in Hollywood. Figured we'd see what Hollywood was all about. They had these big concrete columns. Time came to leave, I got in and backed up and crunch, couldn't get out. I finally got out but I had a bad scratched door on the rental car. Well, I bought some paint and I painted it and you could never tell. I drove to San Diego. Waited for a letter from the rental outfit but it never came. Another time I rented a car there was a crack in the windshield. I says, "Is this a safety problem?" The guy looks at me and says "No." I drive off and it never *was* a problem. We did the same thing when we went to Europe. In Spain we went to the bullfights. We left after two. I wanted to experience that.'

'But are they wounded?' asked Powder Face.

Mr. Bollinger, thinking of rental cars, did not reply.

*   *   *

When Berenice told Chad Grills about old Mr. Forkenbrock who used to work for his grandparents, he was interested and said he would talk to them about it next time he went out to the ranch. He said he hoped Berenice liked ranch life because he was in line to inherit the place. He told Berenice to find out all she could about Forkenbrock's working days. Some of those cagey old boys managed to get themselves situated to put a claim on a ranch through trumped-up charges of unpaid back wages. Whenever Beth came with her tape recorder, Berenice found something to do in the hall outside Ray Forkenbrock's room, listening, expecting him to tell about the nice ranch he secretly owned. She didn't know what Chad would do.

*   *   *

Ray said, 'I think when she heard about the Dixon Forkenbrocks, Mother had a little feeling that something wasn't right because she wrote back to the Farson lady thanking her for the nice lunch. I think she wanted to strike up a friendship so she could find out more about the Dixon people, but, far as I know, that

29

didn't happen. It stuck in my mind that we wasn't the only Forkenbrock family.' Beth was glad he didn't pause so often now that he was into the story, letting his life unreel.

'The last day of school was a trip and a big picnic. The whole outfit usually went on the picnic, since learning academies of the day was small and scattered. When I was twelve the seventh grade had only three kids—me, one of my sisters who skipped a grade and Dutchy Green. We was excited when we found out the trip was to the old Butch Cassidy outlaw cabin down near the Colorado border. Mrs. Ratus, the teacher, got the map of Wyoming hung up and showed us where it was. I seen the word "Dixon" down near the bottom of the map. Dixon! That's where the mystery Forkenbrocks lived. Dutchy was my best friend and I told him all about it and we tried to figure a way to get the bus to stop in Dixon. Maybe there'd be a sign for the Forkenbrock Ranch,' he said.

'As it turned out,' he said, 'we stopped in Dixon anyways because there was something wrong with the bus.

'There was a pretty good service station in Dixon that had been an old blacksmith shop. The forge was still there and the big bellows, which us boys took turns working, pretending we had a horse in the stall. I asked the mechanic who was fixing the bus if he knew of any Forkenbrocks in town and he said he

30

heard of them but didn't know them. He said he had just moved down from Essex. Dutchy and me played blacksmith some more but we never got to Butch Cassidy's cabin because they couldn't fix the bus and another one had to come take us back. We ate the picnic on the bus on the way home. After that I kind of forgot about the Dixon Forkenbrocks,' he said. He was beginning to slow down again.

'I didn't think about it until Dad died in an automobile accident on old route 30,' he said.

'He was taking a shortcut, driving on the railroad ties, and a train come along,' he said.

He said, 'I'd been working for the Bledsoes for a year and hadn't been home.'

At the mention of the Bledsoes, Berenice, out in the hallway, snapped her head up.

'Mr. Bledsoe drove me back so I could attend the funeral. They had it in Rawlins and the Pathfinders had took care of everything,' he said.

Beth looked puzzled. 'Pathfinders?'

'That organization they belonged to. Pathfinders. All we had to do with it was show up. Which we done. Preacher, casket, flowers, Pathfinder flags and mottoes, grave plot, headstone—all fixed up by the Pathfinders.' He coughed and took a sip of whiskey, thinking of cemetery weeds and beyond the headstones the yellow wild pastures.

Berenice couldn't listen anymore because the chime for Cook's Treats rang. It was part

31

of her job to bring the sweets to the residents, the high point in their day trumped only by the alcoholic Social Hour. Cook was sliding triangles of hot apple pie onto plates.

'You hear about Deb's husband? Had a heart attack while he was hitching the tow bar to some tourist. He's in the hospital. It's pretty serious, touch and go. So we won't be seeing Deb for a little while. Maybe ever. I bet she's got a million insurance on him. If he dies and Deb gets a pile a money, I'm going to take out a policy on my old man.'

When Berenice carried out the tray of pie, Mr. Forkenbrock's door stood open and Beth was gone.

*   *   *

Sundays Berenice and Chad Grills drove out on the back roads in Chad's almost-new truck. Going for a ride was their kind of date. The dust was bad, churned up by the fast-moving energy company trucks. Chad got lost because of all the new, unmarked roads the companies had put in. Time after time they turned onto a good road only to end up at a dead-end compression station or well pad. Getting lost where you had been born, brought up and never left was embarrassing, and Chad cursed the gas outfits. Finally he took a sight line on Doty Peak and steered toward it, picking the bad roads as the true way. Always his mind

32

seized on a mountain. In a flinty section they had a flat tire. They came out at last near the ghost town of Dad. Chad said it hadn't been a good ride and she had to agree, though it hadn't been the worst.

Deb Slaver did not come in all the next week, and the extra work fell on Berenice. She hated changing Mr. Harrell's bandage and skipped the chore several times. She was glad when on Wednesday, Doc Nelson's visit day, he said Mr. Harrell had to go into the hospital. On Saturday, Beth's day to visit Mr. Forkenbrock, Berenice got through her chores in a hurry so she could lean on a dust mop outside the door and listen. Impossible to know what he'd say next with all the side stories about his mother's garden, long-ago horses, old friends. He hardly ever mentioned the Bledsoes who had been so good to him.

*   *   *

'Grandpa,' said Beth. 'You look tired. Not sleeping enough? What time do you go to bed?' She handed him the printout of his discourse.

'My age you don't need sleep so much as a rest. Permanent rest. I feel fine,' he said. 'This looks pretty good—reads easy as a book.' He was pleased. 'Where did we leave off,' he said, turning the pages.

'Your dad's funeral,' said Beth.

33

'Oh boy,' he said. 'That was the day I think Mother begin to put two and two together. I sort of got it, at least I got it that something ugly had happened, but I didn't really understand until years later. I loved my dad so I didn't want to understand. I still got a little Buck knife he give me and I wouldn't part with it for anything in this world,' he said.

There was a pause while he got up to look for the knife, found it, showed it to Beth and carefully put it away in his top drawer.

'So there we all were, filing out of the church on our way to the cars that take us to the graveyard, me holding Mother's arm, when some lady calls out, 'Mrs. Forkenbrock! Oh, Mrs. Forkenbrock!' Mother turns around and we see this big fat lady in black with a wilted lilac pinned on her coat heading for us,' he said.

'But she sails right past, goes over to a thin, homely woman with a boy around my age and offers her condolences. And then she says, looking at the kid, "Oh, Ray, you'll have to be the man of the house now and help your mother every way you can,"' he said. He paused to pour into the whiskey glass.

'I want you to think about that, Beth,' he said. 'You are so strong on family ties. I want you to imagine that you are at your father's funeral with your mother and sisters and somebody calls your mother, then walks right over to another person. And that other person has a kid with her and that kid has your name. I was—all I could think was that they had to be the Dixon Forkenbrocks and that they was related to us after all. Mother didn't say a word, but I could feel her arm jerk,' he said. He illustrated this by jerking his own elbow.

'At the cemetery I went over to the kid with my name and asked him if they lived in Dixon and if they had a ranch and was they related to my father who we was burying. He gives me a look and says they don't have a ranch, they don't live in Dixon but in LaBarge, and that it is *his* father we are burying. I was so mixed up at this point that I just said "You're crazy!" and went back to Mother's side. She never mentioned the incident and finally we went home and got along like usual although with damn little money. Mother got work cooking at the Sump ranch. It was only when she died in 1975 that I put the pieces together,' he said. 'All the pieces.'

*   *   *

On Sunday Berenice and Chad went for their weekly ride. Berenice brought her new digital camera. For some reason Chad insisted on going back to the tangle of energy roads, and it was almost the same as before—a spiderweb of wrong-turn gravel roads without signs. Far ahead of them they could see trucks at the side of the road. There was a deep ditch with black

35

pipe in it big enough for a dog to stroll through. They came around a corner and men were feeding a section of pipe into a massive machine that welded the sections together. Berenice thought the machine was interesting and put her camera up. Behind the machine a truck idled, a grubby kid in dark glasses behind the wheel. Thirty feet away another man was filling in the ditch with a backhoe. Chad put his window down, grinned and, in an easy voice, asked the kid how the machine worked.

The kid looked at Berenice's camera. 'What the fuck do you care?' he said. 'What are you doin out here anyway?'

'County road,' said Chad, flaring up, 'and I live in this county. I was born here. I got more rights to be on this road than you do.'

The kid gave a nasty laugh. 'Hey, I don't care if you was born on top of a flagpole, you got *no* rights interferin with this work and takin pictures.'

'Interfering?' But before he could say any more the man inside the pipe machine got out and the two who had been handling the pipe walked over. The backhoe driver jumped down. They all looked salty and in good shape. 'Hell,' said Chad, 'we're just out for a Sunday ride. Didn't expect to see anybody working on Sunday. Thought it was just us ranch types got to do that. Have a good day,' and he trod on the accelerator, peeling out in a burst of dust. Gravel pinged the undercarriage.

Berenice started to say 'What was *that* all about?' but Chad snapped 'Shut up' and drove too fast until they got to the black-top and then he floored it, looking in the rearview all the way. They didn't speak until they were back at Berenice's. Chad got out and walked around the truck, looking it over.

'Chad, how come you to let them throw off on you like that?' said Berenice.

'Berenice,' he said carefully, 'I guess that you didn't see one a them guys had a .44 on him and he was taking it out of the holster. It is not a good idea to have a fight on the edge of a ditch with five roustabouts in a remote area. Loser goes in the ditch and the backhoe guy puts in five more minutes of work. Take a look at this,' he said, and he pulled her around to the back of the truck. There was a hole in the tailgate.

'That's Buddy's .44 done that,' he said. 'Good thing the road was rough. I could be dead and you could still be out there entertaining them.' Berenice shuddered. 'Probably,' said Chad, 'they thought we were some kind of environmentalists. That camera of yours. Leave it home next time.'

Right then Berenice began to cool toward Chad. He seemed less manly. And she would take her camera wherever she wanted..

*   *   *

On Monday Berenice was in the kitchen looking for the ice cream freezer which hadn't been used for two years. Mr. Mellowhorn had just come back from Jackson with a recipe for apple pie ice cream and he was anxious for everyone to share his delight. As she fumbled in the dark cupboard Deb Slaver banged in, bumping the cupboard door.

'Ow!' said Berenice.

'Serves you right,' snarled Deb, sweeping out again. There was a sound in the hall as of someone kicking a stuffed dog.

'She's pretty mad,' said Cook. 'Duck didn't die so she don't get the million-dollar insurance, but even worse, he's going to need dedicated care for the rest of his life—hand and foot waiting on, nice smooth pillows. She's got to take care of him forever. I don't know if she'll keep working and try to get an aide to come in or what. Or maybe Mr. Mellowhorn will let him stay here. Then we'll *all* get to wait on him hand and foot.'

*　　　*　　　*

Saturday came, and out of habit, because she had broken up with Chad and no longer really cared about the Bledsoes or their ranch, Berenice hung around in the hall outside Mr. Forkenbrock's room. Beth had brought him a dish of chocolate pudding. He said it was good but not as good as whiskey and she poured out his usual glass.

'So,' said Beth. 'At the funeral you met the other Forkenbrocks but they didn't live in Dixon anymore?'

'No. No, no,' he said. 'You ain't heard a thing. The ones at the funeral were *not* the Dixon Forkenbrocks. They was the LaBarge Forkenbrocks. There was another set in Dixon. When Mother died, me and my sisters had a go through her stuff and sort it all out,' he said.

'I'm sorry,' said Beth. 'I guess I misunderstood.'

'She had collected all Dad's obituaries she could find. She never said a word to us. Kept them in a big envelope marked "Our Family." I never knew if she meant that sarcastic or not. The usual stuff about how he was born in Nebraska, worked for Union Pacific, then for Ohio Oil and this company and that, how he was a loyal Pathfinder. One said he was survived by Lottie Forkenbrock and six children in Chadron, Nebraska. The boy was named Ray. Another said his grieving family lived in Dixon, Wyoming, and included his wife Sarah-Louise and two sons, Ray and Roger. Then there was one from the Casper *Star* said he was a well-known Pathfinder survived by wife Alice, sons Ray and Roger, daughters Irene and Daisy. That was us. The last one said his wife was Nancy up in LaBarge and the kids were Daisy, Ray and Irene. That

39

was four sets. What he done, see, was give all the kids the same names so he wouldn't get mixed up and say "Fred" when it was Ray.'

He was breathless, his voice high and tremulous. 'How my mother felt about this surprise he give her I never knew because she didn't say a word,' he said.

He swallowed his whiskey in a gulp and coughed violently, ending with a retching sound. He mopped tears from his eyes. 'My sisters bawled their eyes out when they read those death notices and they cursed him, but when they went back home they never said anything,' he said. 'Everybody, the ones in LaBarge and Dixon and Chadron and god knows where else kept real quiet. He got away with it. Until now. I think I'll have another whiskey. All this talking kind of dries my throat,' he said, and he got the bottle himself.

'Well,' said Beth, trying to make amends for misunderstanding, 'at least we've got this extended family now. It's exciting finding out about all the cousins.'

'Beth, they are not cousins. Think about it,' he said. He had thought she was smart. She wasn't.

'Honestly, I think it's cool. We could all get together for Thanksgiving. Or Fourth of July.'

Ray Forkenbrock's shoulders sagged. Time was swinging down like a tire on the end of a rope, slowing, letting the old cat die.

'Grandfather,' said Beth gently. 'You have

to learn to love your relatives.'

He said nothing, and then, 'I loved my father.

'That's the only one I loved,' he said, knowing it was hopeless, that she was not smart and she didn't understand any of what he'd said, that the book he thought he was dictating would be regarded as an old man's senile rubbish. Unbidden, as wind shear hurls a plane down, the memory of the old betrayal broke the prison of his rage and he damned them all, pushed the tape recorder away and told Beth she had better go back home to her husband.

* * *

'It's ridiculous,' Beth said to Kevin. 'He got all worked up about his father who died back in the 1930s. You'd think there would have been closure by now.'

'You'd think,' said Kevin, his face seeming to twitch in the alternating dim and dazzle of the television set.

I've Always Loved This Place

Duane Fork, the Devil's demon secretary, rushed around readying the suite of offices. He sprinkled grit and dust on the desktops, gravel on the floor, pulled closed the heavy red velvet drapes and sprayed the room with Eau de Fumier. Precisely on the dot of midnight he heard the familiar hoof steps coming down the hallway and drew up to attention.

'Good morning, sir,' said Duane obsequiously.

'*Merde,*' grunted the Devil, looking around with a peevish eye. 'This place is— unspeakable.' He had just come back from the Whole World Design & Garden show in Milan, where he posed as an avant-garden-furniture designer who worked in crushed white paper. 'If it gets rain-spotted and grimy, who cares? Just kick it into the barbecue and burn it up,' he advised. But all the while his guts were twisting with jealous desire as he looked at plastic poolside sofas, walkways beneath pleached tree boughs, tropical palm gardens, rock grottoes and cantilevered decks. On the way back to Hell he leafed through half a dozen design glossies, filled out the subscription blank for *Dwell* and thought briefly of starting a rival publication to be called *Dwell in Hell*. Studying the magazines, he understood that his need was more for landscaping, riverside parks and monuments than for architectural design.

'Nothing has been done with this damn place for aeons. It's old-fashioned, it's passé, people yawn when they think of Hell. Slimy rocks and gloomy forests do not have the negative frisson of yesteryear—there are environmentalists now who love such features. We need to keep up with the times. Modernize. Expand and enlarge. We've *got* to enlarge now that our Climate Rehab Program is working—deserts, melting glaciers, inundations. We're starting to look frumpy in comparison. And, Duane, all signs in the Human Abode point to a major religious war on the way; if we don't get ready for an influx we'll have a vexing problem.'

On the way home from the design show he had also read a japish piece in a screed that called itself *The Onion* pretending to report on the addition of a tenth circle to accommodate an increasing number of Total Bastards, most of them American businessmen. The Devil had smiled. A tenth circle was not a bad idea, but Hell's coming population increase would demand much more than providing quarters for tobacco lobbyists and corporate executives. In the long run there was probably no need to build an extension; since nearly all humans were inevitably damned, a simple inversion would do, much like turning a length of intestine inside out and using it as a sausage casing. The earth itself, with no labor on his part, would become Hell Plus. In the meantime he intended to upgrade the current facilities.

'Today, Duane, we are going to tour the property and see where we can make improvements. I want you to bring your notebook. *Andiamo!'* They set out on a red golf cart, the Devil wearing only his shooting jacket, Duane, an eyeshade.

On the way the Devil tossed out infomercial nuggets he had absorbed from his study of the magazines. 'It's not so much that we want to tear things down and start over with restructuring, bulldozers, topsoil and fill and imported rocks. What we want is to see the potential in what's already here and work with that. The basic bones of the place are good. We know that. We'll use a construction outfit that has worked in Iraq—Rout & Massacre sounds like our kind of company. Give them a call and get an idea of their fees. If they are too high we'll forcibly transfer them here and make them a local company.'

At the main gate the Devil rolled his eyes.

'Got to keep the sign,' he said. 'You can't really improve on that last line, "ABANDON HOPE, ALL YE WHO ENTER HERE!" But the gate is boring. Without the sign it's just another Romanesque stone gate. But if we replace it with something modern like the St.

Louis arch and an electric fall—'

Duane Fork's furrowed brow and wry face indicated confusion. 'What's the matter?' asked the Devil. 'You prefer pepper spray?'

'Oh no! I guess I just don't know what an electric fall is.'

'Heard of a waterfall, haven't you?'

'Yessir.'

'An electric fall is the same thing, but with electricity, not water. Of course we could mix them—that make you happy?'

'I'm happy with whatever you want to do, sir.'

'Good. Make a note. Entrance Gate—St. Louis arch with electrified waterfall.'

At the river the Devil cracked a few jokes with Charon but had no suggestions for enhancing the crossing process after the old man snarled 'Fine just the way it is.' Charon's hot-coal eyes winked spasmodically. He smote five or six naked wretches with his oar and said, 'You remember to pick up my eyedrops?'

'Damn!' said the Devil. 'I forgot again! Next time for sure. Try sticking your head in the river.' He floored it and they drove away from the riverbank, whizzed through the suburb of Limbo.

'Bor-ring,' said the Devil, glancing at the writers and poets standing around the film producers, the scribblers holding manuscripts and talking up their ideas.

At the second circle, the source of the dark-

45

and-stormy-night literary genre and a warehouse for marital cheaters, the Devil bawled, 'Close the wind vent, Minos, it's wrecking my coif.' As they drove he switched on the golf cart's headlight and recognized a few of the adulterous spirits maledict. 'How they hangin, baby?' he said, slapping Paris on the rump. Duane Fork dared to lick Cleopatra's left breast. Ideas for reshaping this corner of Hell did not come; it was cast in stone that adulterers would puke and heave in permanent nausea; it would be a waste of time to design anything more than the concrete gutters already in situ.

It was not until the third circle that the Devil came alive with inventive eagerness. Cold rain and sleet hammered down on soil the consistency of a decayed sponge. Figures writhed in the mud. The Devil paused to hear some of the latest gossip which came in a hundred languages. The hoarse, desperate howling of Cerberus echoed from the black cliffs.

'Bad boy! Bad boy!' shouted the Devil encouragingly as he tossed the creature a handful of meatballs. Multiple heads snapped at the flying treats, none escaping the triple throat. Cerberus barked out thanks and a bit of news.

'Did you know that about Sarkozy?'

'No sir,' said Duane, taking a note.

'We can do something here,' said the Devil.

'What we need are all those things that made New Orleans so great—slippery car tops, floating boards with protruding nails, a lot of sewage in the water, conflicting orders. Or maybe a tsunami once in a while. The place seems made for a classy tsunami. And I would like a heavy miasma to hang over everything. This ground fog is almost worthless.' He looked at the Stygian rock slopes streaming with black water. 'Hell, the view alone is worth billions. Breathtaking. I've always loved this place.'

The golf cart lurched through the mire. They skirted the great marsh that prefaced the river Styx, but the sounds of the damned choking on silty mud carried through the humid atmosphere like hundreds of hogs at the trough. On the far shore they could see an unbelievably steep mountain and on its peak the city of Dis outlined against a fiery sky. At the boat landing the Devil whistled shrilly, and in the distance they saw the boatman Phlegyas poling toward them.

'You know, this is really Charon's job, but I put him on the Acheron because he's got a maître d' personality—ushers in the newcomers with style. And Phlegyas is good enough at what he does.' The powerful boatman lifted the golf cart into the vessel and they set out across black water crowded with floundering swimmers whose numbers impeded the boat's progress.

'Take a note, Duane. We want to put two or three hundred saltwater crocs in here. Order them from Australia. Double our fly-gnat-mosquito-chigger package order.'

Once landed at the base of the mountain, the Devil made a frame with his fingers and held it up against various vistas. He kept coming back to the city at the top.

'Location, location,' he murmured. 'And we've been wasting it all this time. It is the ideal end point for the Tour de France. Pro cyclists have earned a place in Hell. It is twice the size of any Alp.' They set off up the steep slope, swerving around the boulders on the path.

'Just what I thought. Soft and easy. Let's take a page from the Paris-Roubaix race, erroneously called "the Hell of the North." Let's get some coarse and broken cobbles on the steepest stretches here. I want those guardrails removed from the abyss, and plenty of flints and Clovis points protruding from the final five kilometers. Varied weather will help; sleet storms, parching heat, black ice on the cobbles, hurricane force crosswinds and a few thousand clones of that German so-called Devil guy who dresses up in a smelly red union suit and runs around with a cardboard pitchfork, the jerk. He's been looking at too many old woodcuts and I've got a place for him some sweet day. Every rider will be on drugs and some will go down frothing at the lips like Simpson on Mount Ventoux in nineteen sixty-whatever. And let's have screaming crowds who throw buckets of filth and fine dust, handfuls of carpet tacks, who squirt olive oil and then piss on the riders. Water bottles filled with kerosene or alkali water. Riders have to fix their own bikes and carry spare tires around their necks. If they fall off and break an arm or leg no one can help them. More dogs on the course. And rattlesnakes. Let's see—how about an obligatory enema in the starting gate and EPO breaks every thirty minutes? As for the UCI—' He whispered in the demon's ear.

'*Chapeau!*' cried Duane Fork.

At the city of Dis the Devil told the enraged and tormented inhabitants to get ready for big-time bicycle racing. Gliding down through the next circles the Devil decided on a number of presidential suites modeled on Japanese hotel cubicles and Wal-Mart men's rooms, added a slaughterhouse nightclub and made the decision that after a newcomer passed through the gate and was discharged by Charon into the main Welcome to Hell foyer he or she would find combined features of the world's worst air terminals, Hongqiao in Shanghai the ideal, complete with petty officials, sadomasochistic staffers, consecutive security checks of increasing harshness, rapidly fluctuating gate changes and departure times and, finally, a twenty-seven-hour trip in an antiquated and overcrowded bucket flying through typhoons while rivets popped against the fuselage.

On the climb up to Dis the Devil had noticed a cluster of scorched bowlegged men lollygagging near a boiling water hole. This area was posted as a reserve for Italian Renaissance politicians. Trespassing was forbidden.

'I'll be damned,' he said. 'That's Butch Cassidy and some of his old gang. Cheeky bastards. Let's plan something good for all the old rustlers and cowboys who have made it over the winding trail. I think we'll give them a taste of their own medicine. Let's get the Four Horsemen and some of our assistant imp riders and start herding those cowboys into bunches, cutting them out and moving them into pens. We'll rope and throw them, castrate, vaccinate and brand them with my big Pitchfork iron. Oh, there'll be plenty of dust and bawling and pleas. They'll try to break away. They will screech and gibber. In the end we'll turn them in to a sand pasture full of cheatgrass, goat-heads, cockleburs and ticks. They can ride the bicycles discarded by the tour racers and listen to Slim Whitman doing "Indian Love Call" over the loudspeaker.'

'Ranchers, too?' asked Duane Fork.

'Nah. Nothing here would bother *them.*' He thought a moment and then said, 'Wait! Better yet, give the ranchers herds of irritable

50

minotaurs. And headstrong centaurs for mounts. Which reminds me, order one roasted for my dinner.'

'Which, minotaur, centaur or ranchaur?'

'Whatever's easiest. Medium rare.'

As they drew abreast of the loungers the Devil called, 'Hey, Butch, fucked any mules lately? Ha ha ha ha. Shake that wooden leg.'

Annoyed by the polyglot babbling of Dis, the Devil decided to standardize. 'I think we'll make the Khoisan language of the Bushmen the official language of Hell,' he said in a fluent stipple of dental, palatal, alveolar, lateral and bilabial clicks. Duane Fork whooshed agreement.

'Your accent is getting better, Duane, but it is still not crisp enough.' The Devil looked around at the mud and black tronawater fountains. 'I don't see any nettles or leafy spurge or millefoil or crabgrass or water hyacinth. Let's get a few of those USDA hacks to work—get some devil's club in here.'

The Devil's thoughts kept turning back to bicycle racers and he called the guard tower and ordered all the Junior Satan Scouts who patrolled the approach to the city to helpfully point racers toward projecting street furniture, pylons, potholes and drop-offs. Now that he was tuned in to something he was mentally calling 'Sports of Hell,' the ideas flew like lekking mayflies. Duane Fork's pencil ripped across the pages, skidding at the end of each

51

line. Soccer alone sprouted eleven hundred improvements, and from soccer it was an easy leap to cricket and caber tossing and on to special arrangements for rental chefs, insecticide manufacturers, world leaders, snowplow drivers.

'Construction workers!' the Devil shouted. 'Their hard hats will melt, their scaffolds collapse unceasingly. Ice cream truck vendors? A hot coal in each scoop of vanilla. Goat turds in the chocolate—I'll make them myself.' He seized two fire cones from the roadside dispenser for refreshment. Then a glimpse of roasting moneylenders in the distance made him think of banks and loans, bills and taxes.

'Canada Revenue! We'll let them play hockey, their national sport, down on Circle Nine's ice.'

'Wouldn't the IRS be better? More infamous?'

'Duane, the IRS is a babe in the woods compared to Canada Revenue. There is no agency on earth as contumacious, bureaucratized, power-obsessed, backhanded, gouging, red-taped, cavernous and carnivorous as Canada Revenue.'

'But if hockey is their national sport, won't they take pleasure in playing it?'

'I think not. The blades will be inside the skates. And those blades will be warm.'

But the idea of a tenth circle haunted him. He might do it. It would have to be something utterly unexpected, a stunning surprise, a coup. As he steered the golf cart it came to him—an art museum. Not just a collection of works earthly museum directors wished to consign to Hell but depictions of himself through the millennia in every guise from monstrous yellow-eyed goats to satin-winged bats, the fabulous compartments of the Nether Regions and, of course, a catalog of human vices and evils, of plummeting sinners.

His ideas tumbled out. In one of the museum's galleries he would set up the Musical Inferno which Hieronymus Bosch had painted so cleverly. He would have all of Goya's witches and his stinking hordes, toothless, pierced, howling, wracked and terrified. He would have every piece of Satanic art even though many showed him as humbled by upward-gazing saints; he always had the last laugh there. Venusti showed a fatuous Saint Bernard holding him chained, but a moment later the chain had melted. The painter had not dared to show that. Michael Pacher had given him a fabulous frog-green skin, but the deer antlers and the buttocks-face were overdone. Gerard David's portrait was finer. A special room for Gustave Doré, whose inventiveness he cherished. Very pleasant as well were the many harvest pictures where he tossed damned souls into his fireproof gunnysack. He would crowd the museum with all the Last Judgments, the damned dropping into the inferno like ripe figs from a tree. Signorelli—he couldn't understand how Signorelli had known to give his demons green and grey and violet skins—a lucky guess perhaps. And surely one of Signorelli's demons was Duane Fork biting at a man's head? He might ask the painter—if he could find him. They had to start compiling a database of the damned and their particular niches; it was impossible to find anyone in Hell.

Still on the idea of the art museum, he planned a solitary room with no other paintings where he thought he would hang William Blake's *Satan Instigating the Rebel Angels,* which showed him as the most beautiful angel of all, more handsome than any Greek god, before the rebellion failed and he was cast down and out. But thinking of that time made him morose and he decided to eschew the Blake; he'd have Rubens instead and Tiepolo. As he made his mental list of the paintings and sculptures he intended to gather, he realized what a terrific labor it would be to pry them away from the Prado, the Duomo, the Louvre, the Beaux-Arts, various art institutes and bibliothèques, private collections and monasteries, cathedrals and churches. The plan abruptly crashed. Well, well, there was the rub; he was not going into any monasteries or churches. And there the renovation plans stopped. His one-track mind could not get past the monasteries, cathedrals and churches.

He ought to have plucked some professional art thieves from their fiery labors and sent them up to do the job, but the story says nothing about that.

Them Old Cowboy Songs

There is a belief that pioneers came into the country, homesteaded, lived tough, raised a shoeless brood and founded ranch dynasties. Some did. But many more had short runs and were quickly forgotten.

ARCHIE & ROSE, 1885

Archie and Rose McLaverty staked out a homestead where the Little Weed comes rattling down from the Sierra Madre, water named not for miniature and obnoxious flora but for P. H. Weed, a gold seeker who had starved near its source. Archie had a face as smooth as a skinned aspen, his lips barely incised on the surface as though scratched in with a knife. All his natural decoration was in his red cheeks and the springy waves of auburn hair that seemed charged with voltage. He usually lied about his age to anyone who asked—he was not twenty-one but sixteen. The first summer they lived in a tent while Archie worked on a small cabin. It took him a month of rounding up stray cows for Bunk Peck before he could afford two glass windows. The cabin was snug, built with eight-foot squared-off logs tenoned on the ends and dropped into mortised uprights, a size Archie could handle with a little help from their only neighbor, Tom Ackler, a leathery prospector with a summer shack up on the mountain. They chinked the cabin with heavy yellow clay. One day Archie dragged a huge flat stone to the house for their doorstep. It was pleasant to sit in the cool of the evening with their feet on the great stone and watch the deer come down to drink and, just before darkness, to see the herons flying upstream, their color matching the sky so closely they might have been eyes of wind. Archie dug into the side of the hill and built a stout meat house, sawed wood while Rose split kindling until they had four cords stacked high against the cabin, almost to the eaves, the pile immediately tenanted by a weasel.

'He'll keep the mice down,' said Rose.

'Yeah, if the bastard don't bite somebody,' said Archie, flexing his right forefinger. 'And you'll wear them windows out, warshin em so much,' but he liked the way the south glass caught Barrel Mountain in its frame. A faint brogue flavored his sentences, for he had been conceived in Ireland, born in 1868 in Dakota Territory of parents arrived from Bantry Bay, his father to spike ties for the Union Pacific Railroad. His mother's death from cholera when he was seven was followed a few weeks later by that of his father, who had whole-hog guzzled an entire bottle of strychnine-laced patent medicine guaranteed to ward off cholera and measles if taken in teaspoon quantities. Before his mother died she had taught him dozens of old songs and the rudiments of music structure by painting a plank with black and white piano keys, sitting him before it and encouraging him to touch the keys with the correct fingers. She sang the single notes he touched in her tone-pure voice. The family wipeout removed the Irish influence. Mrs. Sarah Peck, a warmhearted Missouri Methodist widow, raised the young orphan to the great resentment of her son, Bunk.

*   *   *

A parade of saddle bums drifted through the Peck bunkhouse and from an early age Archie listened to the songs they sang. He was a quick study for a tune, had a memory for rhymes, verses and intonations. When Mrs. Peck went to the land of no breakfast forever, caught in a grass conflagration she started while singeing slaughtered chickens, Archie was fourteen and Bunk in his early twenties. Without Mrs. Peck as buffer, the relationship became one of hired hand and boss. There had never been any sense of kinship, fictive or otherwise, between them. Especially did Bunk Peck burn over the hundred dollars his mother left Archie in her will.

Everyone in the sparsely settled country was

58

noted for some salty dog quirk or talent. Chay Sump had a way with the Utes, and it was to him people went when they needed fine tanned hides. Lightning Willy, after incessant practice, shot both pistol and carbine accurately from the waist, seemingly without aiming. Bible Bob possessed a nose for gold on the strength of his discovery of promising color high on the slope of Singlebit Peak. And Archie McLaverty had a singing voice that once heard was never forgotten. It was a straight, hard voice, the words falling out halfway between a shout and a song. Sad and flat and without ornamentation, it expressed things felt but unsayable. He sang plain and square-cut, 'Brandy's brandy, any way you mix it, a Texian's a Texian any way you fix it,' and the listeners laughed at the droll way he rolled out 'fix it,' the words surely meaning castration. And when he moved into 'The Old North Trail,' laconic and a little hoarse, people got set for half an hour of the true history they all knew as he made his way through countless verses. He could sing every song—'Go Long Blue Dog,' and 'When the Green Grass Comes,' 'Don't Pull off My Boots,' and 'Two Quarts of Whiskey,' and at all-male roundup nights he had endless verses of 'The Stinkin Cow,' 'The Buckskin Shirt' and 'Cousin Harry.' He courted Rose singing 'never marry no good-for-nothin boy,' the boy understood to be himself, the 'good-for-nothin' a disclaimer. Later, with winks and innuendo, he sang, 'Little girl, for safety you better get branded . . .'

Archie, advised by an ex-homesteader working for Bunk Peck, used his inheritance from Mrs. Peck to buy eighty acres of private land. It would have cost nothing if they had filed for a homestead twice that size on public land, or eight times larger on desert land, but Archie feared the government would discover he was a minor, nor did he want a five-year burden of obligatory cultivation and irrigation. Since he had never expected anything from Mrs. Peck, buying the land with the surprise legacy seemed like getting it for free. And it was immediately theirs with no strings attached. Archie, thrilled to be a landowner, told Rose he had to sing the metes and bounds. He started on the southwest corner and headed east. It was something he reckoned had to be done. Rose walked along with him at the beginning and even tried to sing with him but got out of breath from walking so fast and singing at the same time. Nor did she know the words to many of his songs. Archie kept going. It took him hours. Late in the afternoon he was on the west line, drawing near and still singing though his voice was raspy, 'an we'll go downtown, an we'll buy some shirts . . .,' and slouching down the slope the last hundred feet in the evening dusk so worn of voice she could hardly hear him breathily half-chant 'never had a nickel and I don't give a shit.'

*   *   *

There is no happiness like that of a young couple in a little house they have built themselves in a place of beauty and solitude. Archie had hammered together a table with sapling legs and two benches. At the evening meal, their faces lit by the yellow shine of the coal oil lamp whose light threw wild shadows on the ceiling, their world seemed in order until moths flew at the lamp and finally thrashed themselves to sticky death on the plates.

Rose was not pretty, but warmhearted and quick to laugh. She had grown up at the Jackrabbit stage station, the daughter of kettle-bellied Sundown Mealor, who dreamed of plunging steeds but because of his bottle habit drove a freight wagon. The station was on a north-south trail connecting hardscrabble ranches with the blowout railroad town of Rawlins after the Union Pacific line went through. Rose's mother was grey with some wasting disease that kept her to her bed, sinking slowly out of life. She wept over Rose's early marriage but gave her a family treasure, a large silver spoon that had come across the Atlantic.

The stationmaster was the politically

minded Robert F. Dorgan, affable and jowly, yearning to be appointed to a position of importance and seeing the station as a brief stop not only for freight wagons but for himself. His second wife, Flora, stepmother to his daughter, Queeda, went to Denver every winter with Queeda, and so they became authorities on fashion and style. They were as close as a natural mother and daughter. In Denver, Mrs. Dorgan sought out important people who could help her husband climb to success. Many political men spent the winter in Denver, and one of them, Rufus Clatter, with connections to Washington, hinted there was a chance for Dorgan to be appointed as territorial surveyor.

'I'm sure he knows a good deal about surveying,' he said with a wink.

'Considerable,' she said, thinking that Dorgan could find some stripling surveyor to do the work for a few dollars.

'I'll see what I can do,' said Clatter, pressing heavily against her thigh, but tensed to step back if she took offense. She allowed him a few seconds, smiled and turned away.

'Should such an appointment come to pass, you will find me grateful.'

In the spring, back at the station, where her rings and metallic dress trim cast a golden aura, she bossed the local gossip saying that Archie Laverty had ruined Rose, precipitating their youthful marriage, Rose barely fourteen, but what could you expect from a girl with a drunkard father, an uncontrolled girl who'd had the run of the station, sassing rough drivers and exchanging low repartee with bumpkin cowhands, among them Archie Laverty, a lowlife who sang vulgar songs. She whisked her hands together as though ridding them of filth.

The other inhabitant of the station was an old bachelor—the country was rich in bachelors—Harp Daft, the telegraph key operator. His face and neck formed a visor of scars, moles, wens, boils and acne. One leg was shorter than the other and his voice twanged with catarrh. His window faced the Dorgan house, and a black circle which Rose knew to be a telescope sometimes showed in it.

Rose both admired and despised Queeda Dorgan. She greedily took in every detail of the beautiful dresses, the fire opal brooch, satin shoes and saucy hats so exquisitely out of place at the dusty station, but she knew that Miss Dainty had to wash out her bloody menstrual rags like every woman, although she tried to hide them by hanging them on the line at night or inside pillow slips. Beneath the silk skirts she too had to put up with sopping pads torn from old sheets, the crusted edges chafing her thighs and pulling at the pubic hairs. At those times of the month the animal smell seeped through Queeda's perfumed defenses. Rose saw Mrs. Dorgan as an iron-boned two-faced enemy, the public sweetness offset by private coarseness. She had seen the woman spit on the ground like a drover, had seen her scratch her crotch on the corner of the table when she thought no one was looking. In her belief that she was a superior creature, Mrs. Dorgan never spoke to the Mealors or to the despicable bachelor pawing his telegraph key, or, as he said, seeking out constellations.

*　　*　　*

Every morning in the little cabin Rose braided her straight brown hair, dabbed it with drops of lilac water from the blue bottle Archie had presented her on the day of their wedding and wound it around her head in a coronet, the way Queeda Dorgan bound up her hair. At night she let it fall loose, releasing the fragrance. She did not want to become like a homestead woman, skunky armpits and greasy hair yanked into a bun. Archie had crimpy auburn locks, and she hoped that their children would get those waves and his red-cheeked handsome face. She trimmed his hair with a pair of embroidery scissors dropped in the dust by some stagecoach lady passenger at the station years before, the silver handles in the shape of bent-necked cranes. But it was hard, keeping clean. Queeda Dorgan, for example, had little to do at the station but primp and wash and flounce, but Rose, in her cabin, lifted heavy kettles, split kindling, baked bread, scrubbed pots and hacked the stone-filled ground for a garden, hauled water when Archie was not there. They were lucky their first winter that the river did not freeze. Her personal wash and the dishes and floor took four daily buckets of water lugged up from the Little Weed, each trip disturbing the ducks who favored the nearby setback for their business meetings. She tried to keep Archie clean as well. He rode in from days of chasing Peck's cows or running wild horses on the desert, stubbled face, mosquito-bitten neck and grimed hands, cut, cracked nails and stinking feet. She pulled off his boots and washed his feet in the enamel dishpan, patting them dry with a clean feed sack towel.

'If you had stockins, it wouldn't be so bad,' she said. 'If I could get me some knittin needles and yarn I could make stockins.'

'Mrs. Peck made some. Once. Took about a hour before they was holed. No point to it and they clamber around in your boots. Hell with stockins.'

Supper was venison hash or a platter of fried sage hen she had shot, rose-hip jelly and fresh bread, but not beans, which Archie said had been and still were the main provender at Peck's. Occasionally neighbor Tom Ackler rode down for supper, sometimes with his yellow cat, Gold Dust, riding behind him on the saddle. While Tom talked, Gold Dust set to work to claw the weasel out of the woodpile. Rose liked the black-eyed, balding prospector and asked him about the gold earring in his left ear.

'Used a sail the world, girlie. That's my port ear and that ring tells them as knows that I been east round Cape Horn. And if you been east, you been west, first. Been all over the world.' He had a rich collection of stories of storms, violent williwaws and southerly busters, of waterspouts and whales leaping like trout, icebergs and doldrums and enmeshing seaweed, of wild times in distant ports.

'How come you to leave the sailor-boy life?' asked Rose.

'No way to get rich, girlie. And this fella wanted a snug harbor after the pitchin deck.'

Archie asked about maritime songs, and the next visit Tom Ackler brought his concertina with him and for hours sea chanteys and sailors' verses filled the cabin, Archie asking for a repeat of some and often chiming in after a single hearing.

> They say old man your horse will die.
> And they say so, and they hope so.
> O poor old man your horse will die.
> O poor old man.

Rose was an eager lover when Archie called 'put your ass up like a whippoorwill,' and an expert at shifting his occasional glum moods

66

into pleased laughter. She seemed unaware that she lived in a time when love killed women. One summer evening, their bed spread on the floor among the chips and splinters in the half-finished cabin, they fell to kissing. Rose, in some kind of transport began to bite her kisses, lickings and sharp nips along his neck, his shoulder, in the musky crevice between his arm and torso, his nipples until she felt him shaking and looked up to see his eyes closed, tears in his lashes, face contorted in a grimace.

'Oh Archie, I didn't mean to hurt, Archie—'

'You did not,' he groaned. 'It's. I ain't never been. Loved. I just can't hardly *stand it*—' and he began to blubber 'feel like I been shot,' pulling her into his arms, rolling half over so that the salty tears and his saliva wet her embroidered waist shirt, calling her his little birdeen, and at that moment she would have walked into a furnace for him.

On the days he was away she would hack at the garden or take his old needle gun and hunt sage grouse. She shot a hawk that was after her three laying hens, plucked and cleaned it and threw it in the soup pot with a handful of wild onions and some pepper. Another day she had gathered two quarts of wild strawberries, her fingers stained deep red that would not wash away.

'Look like you killed and skinned a griz bear by hand,' he said. 'It could be a bear might

come down for his berries, so don't you go
pickin no more.'

*   *   *

The second winter came on and Bunk Peck
laid off all the men, including Archie.
Cowhands rode the circuit, moving from ranch
to ranch, doing odd jobs in return for a place
in the bunkhouse and three squares. Down on
the Little Weed, Archie and Rose were ready
for the cold. He had waited for good tracking
snow and shot two elk and two deer in
November when the weather chilled, swapping
a share of the meat to Tom Ackler for his help,
for it could take a lone man several days to
pack a big elk out, with bears, lions and
wolves, coyotes, ravens and eagles gorging as
much of the unattended carcass as they could.
One rough acre was cleared where Archie
planned to sow Turkey Red wheat. The meat
house was full. They had a barrel of flour and
enough baking powder and sugar for the city
of Chicago. Some mornings the wind stirred
the snow into a scrim that bleached the
mountains and made opaline dawn skies. Once
the sun below the horizon threw savage red
onto the bottom of the cloud that hung over
Barrel Mountain and Archie glanced up, saw
Rose in the doorway burning an unearthly
color in the lurid glow.

By spring both of them were tired of elk and venison, tired of bumping into each other in the little cabin. Rose was pregnant. Her vitality seemed to have ebbed away, her good humor with it. Archie carried her water buckets from the river and swore he would dig a well the coming summer. It was hot in the cabin, the April sun like a furnace door ajar.

'You better get somebody knows about well diggin,' she said sourly, slapping the bowls on the table for the everlasting elk stew, nothing more than meat, water and salt simmered to chewability, then reheated for days. 'Remember how Mr. Town got killed when his well caved in and him in it?'

'A well can damn cave in and *I* won't be in it,' he said. 'I got in mind not diggin a deep killin well, but clearin out that little seep east a the meat house. Could make a good spring and I'd build a springhouse, put some shelves, and maybe git a cow. Butter and cream cow. Hell, I'm goin a dig out that spring today.' He was short but muscular, and his shoulders had broadened, his chest filled out with the work. He started to sing 'got to bring along my shovel if I got a dig a spring,' ending with one of Tom's yo-heave-hos, but his jokey song did not soothe her irritation. An older woman would have seen that although they were little

69

more than children, they were shifting out of days of clutching love and into the long haul of married life.

'Cows cost money, specially butter and cream cows. We ain't got enough for a butter dish even. And I'd need a churn. Long as we are dreamin, might as well dream a pig, too, give the skim and have the pork in the fall. Sick a deer meat. It's too bad you spent all your money on this land. Should a saved some out.'

'Still think it was the right way to do, but we sure need some chink. I'm ridin to talk with Bunk in a few days, see can I get hired on again.' He pulled on his dirty digging pants still spattered with mud from the three-day job of the privy pit. 'Don't git me no dinner. I'll dig until noon and come in for coffee. We got coffee yet?'

Bunk Peck took pleasure in saying there was no job for him. Nor was there anything at the other ranches. Eight or ten Texas cowhands left over from last fall's Montana drive had stayed in the country and taken all the work.

He tried to make a joke out of it for Rose, but the way he breathed through his teeth showed it wasn't funny. After a few minutes she said in a low voice, 'At the station they used a say they pay a hunderd a month up in Butte.'

'Missus McLaverty, I wouldn't work in no mine. You married you a cowboy.' And he

70

sang 'I'm just a lonesome cowboy who loves a gal named Rose, I don't care if my hat gets wet or if I freeze my toes, but I won't work no copper mine, so put that up your nose.' He picked a piece of turnip from the frying pan on the stove and ate it. 'I'll ride over Cheyenne way an see what I can find. There's some big ranches over there and they probly need hands. Stop by Tom's place on my way and ask him to look in on you.'

The next day he went on the drift. We need the chink, she thought, don't we?

*   *   *

Despite the strong April sun there was still deep snow under the lodgepoles and in north hollows around Tom Ackler's cabin; the place had a deserted feeling to it, something more than if Tom had gone off for the day. His cat, Gold Dust, came purring up onto the steps but when Archie tried to pet her, tore his hand and with flattened ears raced into the pines. Inside the cabin he found the stub of a pencil and wrote a note on the edge of an old newspaper, left it on the table.

> Tom I looking for werk arond Shyanne.
> Check on Rose now & than, ok?
>   Arch McLaverty

*   *   *

In a saloon on a Cheyenne street packed with whiskey mills and gambling snaps he heard that a rancher up on Rawhide Creek was looking for spring roundup hands. The whiskey bottles glittered as the swinging doors let in planks of light—Kellogg's Old Bourbon, Squirrel, McBryan's, G. G. Booz, Day Dream and a few sharp-cornered gin bottles. He bought the man a drink. The thing was, said his informant, a big-mustached smiler showing rotten nutcrackers, putting on the sideboards by wrapping his thumb and forefinger around the shot glass to gain another inch of fullness, that although Karok paid well and he didn't hardly lay off men in the fall, he would not hire a married man, claiming they had the bad habit of running off home to see wife and kiddies while Karok's cows fell in mud holes, were victimized by mountain lions and rustlers, drifted down the draw and suffered the hundred other ills that could befall untended cattle. The bartender, half-listening, sucked a draught of Wheatley's Spanish Pain Destroyer from a small bottle near the cash register.

'Stomach,' he said to no one, belching.

Big Mustache knocked back his brimming shot of Squirrel and went on. 'He's a foreigner from back east, and the only thing counts to him is cows. He learned that fast when he come here back in the early days, cows is the only thing. Grub's pretty poor, too. There ain't no chicken in the chicken soup.'

'Yeah, and no horse in the horseradish,' said Archie who'd heard all the feeble bunkhouse jokes.

'Huh. Well, he rubs some the wrong way. Most a them quit. What I done. Some law dog come out there once with his hand hoverin over his shooter and I could see he was itchin to dabble in gore. I felt like it was a awful good place a put behind me. But there's a few like Karok's ways. Maybe you are one a them. Men rides for him gets plenty practice night ropin. See, his herd grows like a son of a bitch if you take my meanin. But I'll give you some advice: one a these days there'll be some trouble there. That's how come that law was nosin round.'

Archie rode up through country as yellow and flat as an old newspaper and went to see Karok. There was a big sign on the gate: NO MaRIED MeN. When the dour rancher asked him, Archie lied himself single, said that he had to fetch his gear, would be back in six days.

'Five,' said the kingpin, looking at him suspiciously. 'Other fellas look for work they carry their fixins. They don't have to go home and git it.'

Archie worked up some story about visiting Cheyenne and not knowing he'd been laid off until one of the old outfit's boys showed up

73

and said they were all on the bum and, said Archie, he had come straight to Karok when he heard there might be a job.

'Yeah? Get goin, then. Roundup started two days ago.'

*   *   *

Back on the Little Weed with Rose, he half-explained the situation, said she would not be able to send him letters or messages until he worked something out, said he had to get back to Karok's outfit fast and would be gone for months and that she had better get her mother to come down from the station and stay, to help with the baby expected in late September.

'She can't stand a make that trip. You know how sick she is. Won't you come back for the baby?' Even in the few days he had been gone he seemed changed. She touched him and sat very close, waiting for the familiar oneness to lock them together.

'If I can git loose I will. But this is a real good job, good money, fifty-five a month, almost twict what Bunk Peck pays and I'm goin a save ever nickel. And if she can't come down, you better go up there, be around womenfolk. Maybe I can git Tom to bring you up, say in July or August? Or sooner?' He was fidgety, as though he wanted to leave that minute. 'He been around? His place was closed up when I stopped there before. I'll stop again on my

74

way.'

Rose said that if she had to go to the station early September was soon enough. She did not want to be where she would have to tend her sick mother and put up with her drunk father, to see the telegraph man's face like an eroded cliff, to suffer Mrs. Dorgan's supercilious comments about 'some people' directed at Queeda but meant for Rose to hear, did not want to show rough and distended beside Queeda's fine dresses and slenderness, to appear abandoned, without the husband they had prophesied would skedaddle. September was five months away and she would worry about it when it came. Together they added up what a year's pay might come to working for Karok.

'If you save everthing it will be six hundred fifty dollars. We'll be rich, won't we?' she asked in a mournful tone he chose not to notice.

He spoke enthusiastically. 'And that's not countin what I maybe can pick up in wolf bounties. Possible another hunderd. Enough to git us started. I'm thinkin horses, raise horses. Folks always need horses. I'll quit this feller's ranch after a year an git back here.'

'How do I get news to you—about the baby?'

'I don't know yet. But I'll work somethin out. You know what? I feel like I need my hair combed some. You want a comb my hair?'

'Yes,' she said, and laughed just when he'd thought she was going to cry. But for the first time she recognized that they were not two cleaving halves of one person but two separate people, and that because he was a man he could leave any time he wanted, and because she was a woman she could not. The cabin reeked of desertion and betrayal.

ARCHIE & SINK

Men raised from infancy with horses could identify salient differences with a glance, but some had a keener talent for understanding equine temperament than others. Sink Gartrell was one of those, the polar opposite of Montana bronc-buster Wally Finch, who used a secret ghost cord and made unrideable outlaws of the horses he was breaking. Sink gave off a hard air of competence. On roundup the elegant Brit remittance man Morton Frewen had once noticed him handling a nervous cloud-watcher horse and remarked that the rider had 'divine hands.' The adjective set the cowhands guffawing and imitating Frewen's stuffed-nose accent for a few days, but ridicule slid off Sink Gartrell like water off a river rock.

Sink thought the new kid might make a top hand with horses if he got over being a show-off. The second or third morning after he joined the roundup Archie had wakened early, sat up in his bedroll while cookie Hel was stoking his fire, and let loose a getting-up holler decorated with some rattlesnake yodels, startling old Hel, who dropped the coffeepot in the fire, and earning curses from the scattered bedrolls. The black smell of scorched coffee knocked the day over on the wrong side. Foreman Alonzo Lago, who had barely noticed him before, stared hard at the curly-haired new hand who'd made all the noise. Sink noticed him looking.

Later Sink took the kid aside and put the boo on him, told him the facts of life, said that old Lon would bull him good if ever he agreed to get into a bedroll with him, said that the leathery old foreman was well known for bareback riding of new young hires. Archie, who'd seen it all at Peck's bunkhouse, gave him a look as though he suspected Sink of the same base design, said he could take care of himself and that if anyone tried anything on him he'd clean his plow good. He moved off. When Sink came in from watch at the past-midnight hour, he walked past the foreman's bedroll but there was only a solitary head sticking out from under the tarpaulin; the kid was somewhere far away in the sage with the coyotes. Just the same, thought Sink, he would watch Lon the next time he got into the red disturbance and starting spouting that damn poem about Italian music in Dakota, for the top screw was a sure-enough twister.

For Archie the work was the usual ranch hand's luck—hard, dirty, long and dull. There was no time for anything but saddle up, ride, rope, cut, herd, unsaddle, eat, sleep and do it again. On the clear, dry nights coyote voices seemed to emanate from single points in straight lines, the calls crisscrossing like taut wires. When cloud cover moved in, the howls spread out in a different geometry, overlapping like concentric circles from a handful of pebbles thrown into water. But most often the wind surging over the plain sanded the cries into a kind of coyote dust fractioned into particles of sound. He longed to be back on his own sweet place fencing his horse pastures, happy with Rose. He thought about the coming child, imagined a boy half-grown and helping him build wild horse traps in the desert, capturing the mustangs. He could not quite conjure up a baby.

As the late summer folded Sink saw that Archie sat straight up in the saddle, was quiet and even-tempered, good with horses. The kid was one of the kind horses liked, calm and steady. No more morning hollers and the only songs he sang were after supper when somebody else started one, where his voice was appreciated but never mentioned. He kept to himself pretty much, often staring into the distance, but every man had something of value beyond the horizon. Despite his ease with horses he'd been bucked off an oily bronc ruined beyond redemption by Wally Finch, and instinctively putting out one hand to break his fall, snapped his wrist, spent weeks with his arm strapped to his body, rode and did everything else one-handed. Foreman Alonzo Lago fired Wally Finch, refused to pay him for ruined horses, even if they were mustangs from the wild herds, sent him walking north to Montana.

'Kid, there's a way you fall so's you don't get hurt,' said Sink. 'Fold your arms, see, get one shoulder up and your head down. You give a little twist while you're fallin so's you hit the ground with your shoulder and you just roll right on over and onto your feet.' He didn't know why he was telling him this and grouched up. 'Hell, figure it out yourself.'

ROSE & THE COYOTES

July was hot, the air vibrating, the dry land like a scraped sheep hoof. The sun drew the color from everything and the Little Weed trickled through dull stones. In a month even that trickle would be dried by the hot river rocks, the grass parched white and preachers praying for rain. Rose could not sleep in the cabin, which was as hot as the inside of a black hatbox. Once she carried her pillow to the big stone doorstep and lay on its chill until mosquitoes drove her back inside.

She woke one morning exhausted and

sweaty and went down to the Little Weed hoping for night-cooled water. There was a dark cloud to the south and she was glad to hear the distant rumble of thunder. In anticipation she set out the big kettle and two buckets to catch rainwater. The advance wind came in, thrashing tree branches and ripping leaves. The grass went sidewise. Lightning danced on the crest of Barrel Mountain, and then a burst of hail swallowed up the landscape in a chattering, roaring sweep. She ran inside and watched the ice pellets flail the river rocks and slowly give way to thrumming rain. The rocks disappeared in the foam of rising water. Almost as quickly as it had started the rain stopped, a few last hailstones fell and against the moving cloud the arc of a double rainbow promised everything. Her buckets were full of sweet water and floating hailstones. She stripped and poured dippers of goose-bump water over her head again and again until one bucket was nearly empty and she was shaking. The air was as cool and fresh as September, the heat broken. Around midnight the rain began again, slow and steady. Half awake she could hear it dripping on the stone doorstep.

The next morning it was cold and sleety and her back ached; she wished for the heat of summer to return. She staggered when she walked and it didn't seem worthwhile to make coffee. She drank water and stared at the icy

80

spicules sliding down the window glass. Around midmorning the backache increased, working itself into a slow rhythm. It dawned on her very slowly that the baby was not waiting for September. By afternoon the backache was an encircling python and she could do nothing but pant and whimper, the steady rattle of rain dampening her moaning call for succor. She wriggled out of her heavy dress and put on her oldest nightgown. The pain increased to waves of cramping agony that left her gasping for breath, on and on, the day fading into night, the rain torn away by wind, the dark choking hours eternal. Another dawn came sticky with the return of heat and still her raw loins could not deliver the child. On the fourth afternoon, voiceless from calling for Archie, her mother, Tom Ackler, Tom Ackler's cat, from screaming imprecations at all of them, at god, any god, then at the river ducks and the weasel, to any entity that might hear, the python relaxed its grip and slid off the bloody bed, leaving her spiraling down in plum-colored mist.

It seemed late afternoon. She was glued to the bed and at the slightest movement felt a hot surge that she knew was blood. She got up on her elbows and saw the clotted child, stiff and grey, the barley-rope cord and the afterbirth. She did not weep but, filled with an ancient rage, got away from the tiny corpse, knelt on the floor ignoring the hot blood

81

seeping from her and rolled the infant up in the stiffening sheet. It was a bulky mass, and she felt the loss of the sheet as another tragedy. When she tried to stand the blood poured, but she was driven to bury the child, to end the horror of the event. She crept to the cupboard, got a dish towel and rewrapped him in a smaller bundle. Her hand closed on the silver spoon, her mother's wedding present, and she thrust it into the placket neck of her nightgown, the cool metal like balm.

Clenching the knot of the dish towel in her teeth, she crawled out the door and toward the sandy soil near the river, where, still on hands and knees, still spouting blood, she dug a shallow hole with the silver spoon and laid the child in it, heaping it with sand and piling on whatever river stones were within reach. It took more than an hour to follow her blood trail back to the cabin, the twilight deep by the time she reached the doorstep.

The bloody sheet lay bunched on the floor and the bare mattress showed a black stain like the map of South America. She lay on the floor, for the bed was miles away, a cliff only birds could reach. Everything seemed to swell and shrink, the twitching bed leg, a dank clout swooning over the edge of the dishpan, the wall itself bulging forward, the chair flying viciously—all pulsing with the rhythm of her hot pumping blood. Barrel Mountain, bringing darkness, squashed its bulk against the window and owls crashed through, wings like iron bars. Struggling through the syrup of subconsciousness in the last hour she heard the coyotes outside and knew what they were doing.

* * *

As the September nights cooled, Archie got nervous, went into town as often as he could, called at the post office, but no one saw him come out with any letters or packages. Alonzo Lago sent Sink and Archie to check some distant draws ostensibly for old renegade cows too wily or a few mavericks too young to be caught in any roundup.

'What's eatin you?' said Sink as they rode out, but the kid shook his head. Half an hour later he opened his mouth as if he were going to say something, looked away from Sink and gave a half shrug.

'Got somethin you want a say,' said Sink. 'Chrissake say it. I got my head on backwards or what? You didn't know we was goin a smudge brands? Goin a get all holy about it, are you?'

Archie looked around.

'I'm married,' he said. 'She is havin a baby. Pretty soon.'

'Well, I'm damned. How old are you?'

'Seventeen. Old enough to do what's got a be did. Anyway, how old are *you?*'

'Thirty-two. Old enough a be your daddy.'
There was a half-hour silence, then Sink
started again. 'You know old Karok don't keep
married fellers. Finds out, he'll fire you.'

'He ain't goin a find out from me. And it's
more money than I can git on the Little Weed.
But I got a find a way Rose can let me know.
About things.'

'Well, I ain't no wet nurse.'

'I know that.'

'Long as you know it.' Damn fool kid, he
thought, his life already too complicated to
live, and said aloud, 'Me, I wouldn't never git
hitched to no fell-on-a-hatchet female.'

The next week half the crew went in to town
and Archie spent an hour on the bench outside
the post office writing on some brown
wrapping paper, addressed the tortured
missive to Rose at the stage station where he
believed her to be. What about the baby, he
wrote. Is he born? But inside the post office
the walleyed clerk with fingernails like yellow
chisels told him the postage had gone up.

'First time in a hunderd year. Cost you two
cents a send a letter now,' he smirked with
satisfaction. Archie, who had only one cent,
tore up his letter and threw the pieces in the
street. The wind dealt them to the prairie, its
chill promising a tight-clenched winter.

*   *   *

84

Rose's parents, the Mealors, moved to Omaha in November seeking a cure for Mrs. Mealor's declining health.

'You think you can stay sober long enough to ride down and let Rosie and Archie know we are going?' the sick woman whispered to Sundown.

'Why I am goin right now soon as I find my other boot. Just you don't worry, I got it covered.'

A full bottle of whiskey took him as far as the river crossing. Dazedly drunk, he rode to the little cabin on the river but found the place silent, the door closed. Swaying, feeling the landscape slide around, he called out three or four times but was unable to get off his horse and knew well enough that if he did he could never get back on.

'G'up! Home!' he said to Old Slope and the horse turned around.

'They're not there,' he reported to his wife. 'Not there.'

'Where could they be? Did you put a note on the table?'

'Didn't think of it. Anyway, not there.'

'I'll write her from Omaha,' she whispered.

Within a week of their departure a replacement freighter arrived, Buck Roy, his heavyset wife and a raft of children. The Mealors, who had failed even to be buried in the stage station's cemetery, were forgotten.

There were no cattle as bad as Karok's to stray, and ranchers said it was a curious thing the way his cows turned up in distant locations. December was miserable, one storm after another bouncing in like a handful of hurled poker chips, and January turned cold enough to freeze flying birds dead. Foreman Alonzo Lago sent Archie out alone to gather any bovine wanderers he could find in a certain washout area, swampy in June, but now hundreds of deep holes and snaky little streams smoothly covered with snow.

'Keep your eyes peeled for any Wing-Cross leather-pounders. Better take some sticks and a cinch ring.' So Archie knew he was looking for Wing-Cross cows to doctor their brands. But the Wing-Cross had its own little ways with brand reworkings, so he guessed it was more or less an even exchange.

The horse did not want to go into the swamp maze. It was one of the warm days between storms and the snow was soft. Archie dismounted and led his horse, keeping to the edge of the bog, waded through wet snow for hours. The exercise sweated him up. Only two cows allowed themselves to be driven out into the open, the others scattering far back into the coyote willows behind the swamp. In the murky, half-frozen world of stream slop and trampled stems there was no way a man alone could fix brands. He watched the cows circle around to the backcountry. The wind dived, pulling cold air with it. The weather was changing. When he reached the bunkhouse four hours after dark, the thermometer had fallen to zero. His boots were frozen, and, chilled to the liver, he fell asleep without eating or undressing beyond his boots.

'Git back and git them cows,' hissed Alonzo Lago two hours later, leaning over his face. 'Git up and on it. Rat now! Mr. Karok wants them cows.'

'Goddamn short nights on this goddamn ranch,' muttered Archie, pulling on his wet boots.

Back in the swamp it was just coming light, like grey polish on the cold world, the air so still Archie could see the tiny breath cloud of a finch on a willow twig. Beneath the hardened crust the snow was wallowy. His fresh horse was Poco, who did not know swamps. Poco blundered along, stumbled in an invisible sinkhole and took Archie deep with him. The snow shot down his neck, up his sleeves, into his boots, filled eyes, ears, nose, matted his hair. Poco, in getting up, rammed his hat deep into the bog. The snow in contact with his body heat melted, and as he climbed back into the saddle the wind that accompanied the pale sunlight froze his clothes. Somehow he managed to push eight Wing-Cross strays out of the swamp and back toward the high

87

ground, but his matches would not light and while he struggled to make a fire the cows scattered. He could barely move and when he got back to the bunkhouse he was frozen into the saddle and had to be pried off the horse by two men. He heard cloth rip.

Sink thought the kid had plenty of sand, and muttering that he wasn't no wet nurse, pulled off the icy boots, unbuttoned coat and shirt, half-hauled him stumbling to his bunk and brought two hot rocks from under the stove to warm him up. John Tank, a Texas drifter, said he had an extra pair of overalls Archie could have—old and mended but still with some wear in them.

'Hell, better'n ridin around bare-ass in January.'

But the next morning when Archie tried to get up he was overcome by dizziness. Boiling heat surged through him, his cheeks flamed red, his hands burned with high fever and he had a dry, constant cough. His head ached, the bunkhouse slopped back and forth as if on rockers. He could not stand, and he breathed with a sound like a blacksmith's bellows.

Sink looked at him and thought, pneumonia. 'You look pretty bad. I'll go see what Karok says.'

When he came back half an hour later Archie was burning.

'Karok says to git you out a here, but the bastard won't let me take the wagon. He says he's got a cancer in his leg and he needs that wagon for hisself to have the doc at the fort cut it out. Lon's fixin up a kind a travois. His ma had some Indan kin so he knows how to fix it. Sometimes he ain't so bad. We'll git you down to Cheyenne and you can ride the train a where your mother is, your folks, Rawlins, whatever. Karok says. And he says you are fired. I had a tell him you was married so he would let you loose. He was all set a have you die in the bunkhouse. We'll get a doc, beat this down. It's only pneumony. I had it twice.'

Archie tried to say his mother was long gone and that he needed to get to Rose down on the Little Weed, tried to say that it was sixty-odd miles from Rawlins to their cabin, but he couldn't get out a word because of the wheezing, breath-sucking cough. Sink shook his head, got some biscuits and bacon from the cook.

Foreman Alonzo had trimmed out two long poles and laced a steer hide to them in a kind of sling arrangement. Sink wrapped the legs of a horse named Preacher in burlap to keep the crust from cutting them, lashed the travois poles to his saddle, a tricky business to get the balance right. The small ends projected beyond the horse's ears, but the foreman said that was to accommodate wear on the drag-ends. They rolled Archie and his bedroll in a buffalo robe and Sink began to drag him to Cheyenne, a hundred miles south. With the wagon it would have been easy. Sink thought the travois was not as good a contraption as Indians claimed. The wind, which had dropped a little overnight, came up, pushing a lofty bank of cloud. After four hours they had covered nine miles. The snow began, increasing in intensity until they were traveling blind.

'Kid, I can't see nothin,' called Sink. He stopped and dismounted, went to Archie. The earlier snow had melted as fast as it touched that red, feverish face, but gradually, just a fraction of an inch above the surface of the hot flesh, a mask of ice now formed a grey glaze. Sink thought the mask could become the true visage.

'Better hole up. There's a line shack somewheres around here could we find it. I was there all summer couple years back. Down a little from the top of a hogback.'

The horse, Preacher, had also spent that summer at the line camp and he went straight to it now. It was on the lee side of the hogback, a little below the crest. The wind had dumped an immense amount of snow on the tiny cabin, but Sink found the door to the lean-to entryway, and that would do to shelter the horse. A shovel with a broken handle leaned against the side of the single stall. Inside the cabin there was a table and backless chair, a plank bunk about twenty inches wide. The stove was heaped with snow, and the stovepipe lay on the floor. Sink recognized the chipped enamel plate and cup on the table.

He wrestled Archie inside and got him and the buffalo robe onto the plank bunk, then put the stovepipe together and jammed it up through the roof hole. Neither inside nor in the entryway could he see any chunk wood, but he remembered where the old chip pile had been and, using the broken shovel, scraped up enough snow-welded chips to get the fire going. While the chips were steaming and sizzling in the stove, he unsaddled Preacher, removed the gunnysacks from his legs and rubbed the horse down. He checked the lean-to's shallow loft hoping for hay, but there was nothing.

'Goddamn,' he said and tore some of the loft floorboards loose to burn in the stove. Back outside he dug through the snow with the broken shovel until he hit ground, got out his knife and sawed off the sun-cured grass until he had two or three hatfuls.

'Best I can do, Preacher,' he said, tossing it down for the horse.

It was almost warm inside the shack. From his saddlebag he took a small handful of the coffee beans he always carried. The old coffee grinder was still on the wall but a mouse had built a nest in it, and he had no way to unbolt the machine to clean it out. Unwilling to drink boiled mouse shit, he crushed the beans on the table with the flat of his knife. He looked around for the coffeepot that belonged to the cabin but did not see it. There was a five-gallon coal oil tin near the bunk. He sniffed at it, but could detect no noisome odors, packed it with snow and put it on the stove to melt. It was while he was scraping up snow outside that the edge of the coal oil can hit the coffeepot, which, for some unfathomable reason, had been tossed into the front yard. That too he packed with snow. It looked to him as though the last occupant of the shack had been someone with a grudge, showing his hatred of Karok by throwing coffeepots and burning all the wood. Maybe a Wing-Cross rider.

The coffee was hot and black but when he brought the cup to Archie the kid swallowed one mouthful, then coughed and finally puked it up. Sink drank the rest himself and ate one of the biscuits.

It was a bad night. The bunk was too narrow and the kid so hot and twitchy that Sink swooned in and out of forty-wink snaps of sleep, finally got up and slept in the chair with his head on the table. A serious blizzard and fatal cold began to slide down from the Canadian plains that night, and when it broke twelve days later the herds were decimated, cows packed ten deep against barbwire fences, pronghorn congealed into statues, trains stalled for three weeks by forty-foot drifts and two cowpunchers in a line shack frozen together in a buffalo robe.

It was May before Tom Ackler rode up from Taos where he had spent the fall and winter. Despite the beating sunshine the snow was still deep around his cabin. Patches of bare ground showed bright green with a host of thrusting thistles. He wondered if Gold Dust had made it through. He could see no cat tracks. He lit a fire using an old newspaper on the table, and just before the flame swallowed it, glimpsed a few penciled words and the signature 'Arch McLaverty.'

'Lost whatever it was. I'll go down tomorrow and see how they are doin'.' And he unpacked his saddlebags, wrestled his blankets out of the sack hanging from a rafter where they were safe from mice.

In the morning Gold Dust pranced out of the trees, her coat thick. Tom let her in, threw her a choice piece of bacon.

'Look like you kept pretty good,' he said. But the cat sniffed at the bacon, went to the door and, when he opened it, returned to the woods. 'Probly shacked up with a bobcat,' he said, 'got the taste for wild meat.' Around noon he saddled the horse and headed for the McLaverty cabin.

No smoke rose from the chimney. A slope of snow lay against the woodpile. He noticed that very little wood had been burned. The weasel's tracks were everywhere, and right up into the eaves. Clear enough the weasel had gotten inside. 'Damn sight more comfortable than a woodpile.' As he squinted at the tracks the weasel suddenly squirted out of a hole in the eaves and looked at him. It was whiter than the rotting snow, and its black-tipped tail twitched. It was the largest, handsomest weasel he had ever seen, shining eyes and a lustrous coat. He thought of his cat and it came to him that wild creatures managed well through the winter. He wondered if Gold Dust could breed with a bobcat and recalled then that Rose had been expecting. 'Must be they went to the station.' But he opened the door and looked inside, calling 'Rose? Archie?' What he found sent him galloping for the stage station.

*　　*　　*

At the station everything was in an uproar, all of them standing in the dusty road in front of the Dorgans' house, Mrs. Dorgan crying, Queeda with her mouth agape and Robert F. Dorgan shouting at his wife, accusing her of betraying him with a human wreck. They paid little attention to Tom Ackler when he slid in on his lathered horse calling that Rose McLaverty was raped and murdered and mutilated by Utes, sometime in the winter, god knew when. Only Mrs. Buck Roy, the new freighter's wife, who was terrified of Indians,

94

gave him much attention. The Dorgans continued to scream at each other. The more urgent event to them was the suicide that morning of the old bachelor telegraph operator who had swallowed lye after weeks of scribbling a four-hundred-page letter addressed to Robert Dorgan and outlining his hopeless adoration of Mrs. Dorgan, the wadded pages fulsomely riddled with references to 'ivory thighs,' 'the Adam and Eve dance,' 'her secret slit' and the like. What Tom Ackler had thought was an old saddle and a pile of grain sacks on the porch was the corpse.

'Where there's smoke there's fire!' bellowed Robert F. Dorgan. 'I took you out a that Omaha cathouse and made you a decent woman, give you everthing and here's how you reward me, you drippin bitch! How many times you snuck over there? How many times you took his warty old cock?'

'I never! I didn't! That filthy old brute,' sobbed Mrs. Dorgan, suffused with rage that the vile man had fastened his attentions on her, had dared to write down his lascivious thoughts as real events, putting in the details of her pink-threaded camisole, the red mole on her left buttock, and, finally, vomiting black blood all over the telegraph shack and the front porch of the Dorgans' house where he had dragged himself to die, the four-hundred-page bundle of lies stuffed in his shirt. For years she had struggled to make herself into a

95

genteel specimen of womanhood, grateful that
Robert F. Dorgan had saved her from
economic sexuality and determined to erase
that past. Now, if Dorgan forced her away, she
would have to go back on the game, for she
could think of no other way to make a living.
And maybe Queeda, too, whom she'd brought
up as a lady! Her sense of personal worth
faltered, then flared up as if doused with
kerosene.

'Why you dirty old rum-neck,' she said in a
hoarse voice, 'what gives you the idea that you
got a right to a beautiful wife and daughter?
What gives you the idea we would stay with
you? Look at you—you want a be the territory
surveyor, but without me and Queeda to talk
up the important political men you couldn't
catch a cold.'

Dorgan knew it was true and gnawed at his
untrimmed mustache. He turned and
melodramatically strode into his house,
slamming the door so hard the report killed
mice. Mrs. Dorgan had won and she followed
him in for a reconciliation.

Tom Ackler looked at Queeda who was
tracing an arc in the dirt with the toe of her
kid-leather boot. They heard the rattle of a
stove lid inside the house—Mrs. Dorgan
making up a fire to warm the parlor and
bedroom.

'Rose McLaverty—' he said, but Queeda
shrugged. A tongue of wind lapped the dust,

creating a miniature whirl as perfect in shape as any tornado snaking down from black clouds that caught up straws, horsehairs, minute mica fragments and a feather. The dust devil collapsed and died. Queeda turned away, walked around the shaded back of the Dorgan house. Tom Ackler stood holding the reins, then remounted and started back, the horse moving in a kind of equine stroll.

On the way he thought of the whiskey in his cupboard, then of Rose and decided he would get drunk that night and bury her the next day. It was the best he could do for her. He thought too that perhaps it hadn't been Utes who killed her but her young husband, berserk and raving, and now fled to distant ports. He remembered the burned newspaper with Archie's message consumed before it could be read and thought it unlikely if Archie had killed his young wife in a frenzy, that he would stop by a neighbor's place and leave a signed note. Unless maybe it was a confession. There was no way to know what had happened. The more he thought about Archie the more he remembered the clear, hard voice and the singing. He thought about Gold Dust's rampant vigor and rich fur, about the sleek weasel at the McLaverty cabin. Some lived and some died, and that's how it was.

He buried Rose in front of the cabin and for a tombstone wrestled the big sandstone rock Archie had hauled in for a doorstep upright.

He wanted to chisel her name but put it off until the snows started. It was too late then, time for him to head for Taos.

The following spring as he rode past their cabin he saw that frost heaves had tipped the stone over and that the ridgepole of the roof had broken under a heavy weight of snow. He rode on, singing 'when the green grass comes, and the wild rose blooms,' one of Archie's songs, wondering if Gold Dust had made it through again.

The Sagebrush Kid

For George Jones

Those who think the Bermuda Triangle disappearances of planes, boats, long-distance swimmers and floating beach balls a unique phenomenon do not know of the inexplicable vanishings along the Red Desert section of Ben Holladay's stagecoach route in the days when Wyoming was a territory.

Historians have it that just after the Civil War Holladay petitioned the U.S. Postal Service, major source of the stage line's income, to let him shift the route fifty miles south to the Overland Trail. He claimed that the northern California-Oregon-Mormon Trail had recently come to feature ferocious and unstoppable Indian attacks that endangered the lives of drivers, passengers, telegraph operators at the stage stops, smiths, hostlers and cooks at the swing stations, even the horses and the expensive red and black Concord coaches (though most of them were actually Red Rupert mud wagons). Along with smoking letters outlining murderous Indian attacks he sent Washington detailed lists of goods and equipment damaged or lost—a Sharp's rifle, flour, horses, harness, doors, fifteen tons of hay, oxen, mules, bulls, grain burned, corn stolen, furniture abused, the station itself along with barn, sheds, telegraph office burned, crockery smashed, windows ditto. No matter that the rifle had been left propped against a privy, had been knocked to the ground by the wind and buried in sand before the owner exited the structure, or that the dishes had disintegrated in a whoop-up shooting contest, or that the stagecoach damage resulted from shivering passengers building a fire inside the stage with the bundles of government documents the coach carried. He knew his bureaucracy. The Washington post office officials, alarmed at the bloodcurdling news, agreed to the route change, saving the Stagecoach King a great deal of money, important at that time while he, privy to insider information, laid his plans to sell the stage line the moment the Union Pacific gathered enough shovels and Irishmen to start construction on the transcontinental railroad.

Yet the Indian attack Holladay so gruesomely described was nothing more than a failed Sioux war party, the battle ruined when only one side turned up. The annoyed Indians, to reap something from the trip, gathered up a coil of copper wire lying on the ground under a telegraph pole where it had been left by a wire stringer eager to get to the saloon. They carted it back to camp, fashioned it into bracelets and necklaces. After a few days of wearing the bijoux, most of the war party broke out in severe rashes, an affliction that persisted until a medicine man, R. Singh, whose presence among the Sioux cannot be detailed here, divined the evil nature of the talking wire and caused the remainder of the coil and all the bracelets and earbobs to be buried. Shortly thereafter, but in no apparent way connected to the route change or the copper wire incident, travelers began to disappear in the vicinity of the Sandy Skull station.

The stationmaster at Sandy Skull was Bill Fur, assisted by his wife, Mizpah. In a shack to one side a telegraph operator banged his message key. The Furs had been married seven years but had no children, a situation in those fecund days that caused them both grief. Mizpah was a little cracked on the subject and traded one of Bill's good shirts to a passing emigrant wagon for a baby pig, which she dressed in swaddling clothes and fed from a nipple-fitted bottle that had once contained Wilfee's Equine Liniment & Spanish Pain Destroyer but now held milk from the Furs' unhappy cow—an object of attention from range bulls, rustlers and roundup cowboys, who spent much of her time hiding in a nearby cave. The piglet one day tripped over the hem of the swaddling dress and was carried off by a golden eagle. Mrs. Fur, bereft, traded another of her husband's shirts to a passing emigrant wagon for a chicken. She did not make the swaddling gown mistake twice, but fitted the chicken with a light leather jerkin and a tiny bonnet. The bonnet acted as blinders and the unfortunate poult never saw the coyote that seized her within the hour.

Mizpah Fur, heartbroken and suffering from loneliness, next fixed her attention on an inanimate clump of sagebrush that at twilight took on the appearance of a child reaching upward as if piteously begging to be lifted from the ground. This sagebrush became the lonely woman's passion. It seemed to her to have an enchanting fragrance reminiscent of pine forests and lemon zest. She surreptitiously brought it a daily dipper of water (mixed with milk) and took pleasure in its growth response, ignoring the fine cactus needles that pierced her worn moccasins with every trip to the beloved *Atriplex*. At first her husband watched from afar, muttering sarcastically, then himself succumbed to the illusion, pulling up all grass and encroaching plants that might steal sustenance from the favored herb. Mizpah tied a red sash around the sagebrush's middle. It seemed more than ever a child stretching its arms up, even when the sun leached the wind-fringed sash to pink and then dirty white.

Time passed, and the sagebrush, nurtured and cosseted as neither piglet nor chicken nor few human infants had ever been— for Mizpah had taken to mixing gravy and meat juice with its water—grew tremendously. At twilight it now looked like a big man hoisting his hands into the air at the command to stick em up. It sparkled festively in winter snow. Travelers noted it as the biggest sagebrush in the lonely stretch of desert between Medicine Bow and Sandy Skull station. It became a landmark for deserting soldiers. Bill Fur, clutching the handle of a potato hoe, hit on the right name when he announced that he guessed he would go out and clear cactus away from the vicinity of their Sagebrush Kid.

About the time that Bill Fur planed a smooth path to and around the Sagebrush Kid, range horses became scarce in the vicinity of the station. The Furs and local ranchers had always been able to gather wild mustangs, and through a few sessions with steel bolts tied to their forelocks, well-planned beatings with a two-by-four and merciless first rides by some youthful buster whose spine hadn't yet been compressed into a solid rod, the horses were deemed ready-broke to haul stagecoaches or carry riders. Now the mustangs seemed to have moved to some other range. Bill Fur blamed it on the drought which had been bad.

'Found a water hole somewheres else,' he said.

A party of emigrants camped overnight near the station, and at dawn the captain pounded on the Furs' door demanding to know where their oxen were.

'Want a git started,' he said, a man almost invisible under a flop-rimmed hat, cracked spectacles, full beard and a mustache the size of a dead squirrel. His hand was deep in his coat pocket, a bad sign, thought Bill Fur who had seen a few coat-pocket corpses.

'I ain't seen your oxes,' he said. 'This here's a horse-change station,' and he pointed to the corral where two dozen broom-tails stood soaking up the early sun. 'We don't have no truck with oxes.'

'Them was fine spotted oxen, all six matched,' said the captain in a dangerous, low voice.

Bill Fur, curious now, walked with the bearded man to the place the oxen had been turned out the night before. Hoofprints showed where the animals had ranged around eating the sparse bunchgrass. They cast wide and far but could not pick up the oxen trail as the powdery dust changed to bare rock that took no tracks. Later that week the disgruntled emigrant party was forced to buy a mixed lot of oxen from the sutler at Fort Halleck, a businessman who made a practice of buying up worn-out stock for a song, nursing them back to health and then selling them for an opera to those in need.

'Indans probly got your beasts,' said the sutler. 'They'll bresh out the tracks with a sage branch so's you'd never know but that they growed wings and flapped south.'

The telegraph operator at the station made a point of keeping the Sabbath. After his dinner of sage grouse with rose-haw jelly, he strolled out for an afternoon constitutional and never returned to his key. This was serious, and by Wednesday Bill Fur had had to ride into Rawlins and ask for a replacement for 'the bible-thumpin, damn old goggle-eyed snappin turtle who run off.' The replacement, plucked from a Front Street saloon, was a tough drunk who lit his morning fires with pages from the former operator's bible and ate one pronghorn a week, scorching the meat in a never-washed skillet.

'Leave me have them bones,' said Mizpah, who had taken to burying meat scraps and gnawed ribs in the soil near the Sagebrush Kid.

'Help yourself,' he said, scraping gristle and hocks onto the newspaper that served as his tablecloth and rolling it up. 'Goin a make soup stock, eh?'

Two soldiers from Fort Halleck dined with the Furs and at nightfall slept out in the sagebrush. In the morning their empty bedrolls, partly drifted with fine sand, lay flat, the men's saddles at the heads for pillows, their horse tack looped on the sage. The soldiers themselves were gone, apparently deserters who had taken leave bareback. The wind had erased all signs of their passage. Mizpah Fur made use of the bedrolls, converting them into stylish quilts by appliquéing a pleasing pattern of black stripes and yellow circles onto the coarse fabric.

It may have been a trick of the light or the poor quality window glass, as wavery and distorting as tears, but Mizpah, sloshing her dishrag over the plates and gazing out, thought she saw the sagebrush's arms not raised up but akimbo, as though holding a water divining rod. Worried that some rambunctious buck trying his antlers had broken the branches, she stepped to the door to get a clear look. The arms were upright again and tossing in the wind.

Dr. Frill of Rawlins, on a solitary hunting trip, paused long enough to share a glass of bourbon and the latest town news with Mr. Fur. A week later a group of the doctor's scowling friends rode out inquiring of the medico's whereabouts. Word was getting around that the Sandy Skull station was not the best place to spend the night, and suspicion was gathering around Bill and Mizpah Fur. It would not be the first time a stationmaster had taken advantage of a remote posting. The Furs were watched for signs of opulence. Nothing of Dr. Frill was ever found, although a hat, stuck in the mud of a playa three miles east, might have been his.

A small group of Sioux, including R. Singh, on their way to the Fort Halleck sutler's store to swap hides for tobacco, hung around for an hour one late afternoon asking for coffee and bread which Mizpah supplied. In the early evening as the dusk thickened they resumed their journey. Only Singh made it to the fort, but the shaken Calcutta native could summon neither Sioux nor American nor his native tongue to his lips. He bought two twists of tobacco and through the fluid expression of sign language tagged a spot with a Mormon freight group headed for Salt Lake City.

A dozen outlaws rode past Sandy Skull station on their way to Powder Springs for a big gang hooraw to feature a turkey pull, fried turkey and pies of various flavors as well as the usual floozy contingent and uncountable bottles of Young Possum and other liquids pleasing to men who rode hard and fast on dusty trails. They amused themselves with target practice on the big sagebrush, trying to shoot off its waving arms. Five of them never got past Sandy Skull station. When the Furs, who had been away for the day visiting the Clug ranch, came home they saw the Sagebrush Kid maimed, only one arm, but that still bravely raised as though hailing them. The telegraph operator came out of his shack and said that the outlaws had done the deed and that he had chosen not to confront them, but to bide his time and get revenge later, for he too had developed a proprietorial interest in the Sagebrush Kid. Around that time he put in a request for a transfer to Denver or San Francisco.

Everything changed when the Union Pacific Railroad pushed through, killing off the stagecoach business. Most of the stage station structures disappeared, carted away bodily by ranchers needing outbuildings. Bill and Mizpah Fur were forced to abandon the Sandy Skull station. After tearful farewells to the Sagebrush Kid they moved to Montana, adopted orphan cowboys and ran a boardinghouse.

*　　　*　　　*

The decades passed and the Sagebrush Kid continued to grow, though slowly. The old stage road filled in with drift sand and greasewood. A generation later a section of the coast-to-coast Lincoln Highway rolled past. An occasional motorist, mistaking the Sagebrush Kid for a distant shade tree, sometimes approached, swinging a picnic basket. Eventually an interstate highway swallowed the old road and truckers used the towering Sagebrush Kid in the distance as a marker to tell them they were halfway across the state. Although its foliage remained luxuriant and its size enormous, the Kid seemed to stop growing during the interstate era.

Mineral booms and busts surged through Wyoming without affecting the extraordinary shrub in its remote location of difficult access until BelAmerCan Energy, a multinational methane extraction company, found promising indications of gas in the area, applied for and got permits and began drilling. The promise was realized. They were above a vast deposit of coal gas. Workers from out of state rushed to the bonanza. A pipeline had to go in and more workers came. The housing shortage forced men to sleep four to a bed in shifts at the dingy motels forty miles north.

To ease the housing difficulties, the company built a man-camp out in the sagebrush. The entrance road ran close to the Sagebrush Kid. Despite the Kid's size, because it was just a sagebrush, it went unnoticed. There were millions of sagebrush plants— some large, some small. Beside it was a convenient pull-out. The man-camp was a large gaunt building that seemed to erupt from the sand. The cubicles and communal shower rooms, stairs, the beds, the few doors were metal. A spartan kitchen staffed by Mrs. Quirt, the elderly wife of a retired rancher, specialized in bacon, fried eggs, boiled potatoes, store-bought bread and jam and occasionally a stewed chicken. The boss believed the dreary sagebrush steppe and the monotonous diet were responsible for wholesale worker desertion. The head office let him hire a new cook, an ex-driller with a meth habit whose cuisine revolved around canned beans and pickles.

After three weeks Mrs. Quirt was reinstated, presented with a cookbook and a request to try something new. It was a disastrous order. She lit on complex recipes for boeuf bourguignonne, parsnip gnocchi, bananas stuffed with shallots, kale meatballs with veal ice cream. When the necessary ingredients were lacking she did what she had always done on the ranch—substituted what was on hand, as bacon, jam, eggs. After a strange repast featuring canned clams, strawberry Jell-O and stale bread, many men went outside to heave it up in the sage. Not all of them came back and it was generally believed they had hiked forty miles to the hot-bed motel town.

The head office, seeing production, income and profits slump because they could not keep workers on, hired a cook who had worked for an Italian restaurant. The food improved dramatically, but there was still an exodus. The cook ordered exotic ingredients that were delivered by a huge Speedy Food truck. After the driver delivered the cases of sauce and mushrooms, he parked in the shade of the big sagebrush to eat his noontime bologna sandwich, read a chapter of *Ambush on the Pecos Trail* and take a short nap. Three drillers coming in from the day shift noticed the truck idling in the shade. They noticed it again the next morning on the way to the rig. A refrigerator truck, it was still running. A call came three days later from the company asking if their driver had been there. The news that the truck was still in the sagebrush brought state troopers. After noticing spots of blood on the seat and signs of a struggle (a dusty boot print on the inside of the windshield), they began stringing crime-scene tape around the truck and the sagebrush.

'Kellogg, get done with the tape and get out here,' called a sergeant to the laggard trooper behind the sagebrush. The thick branches and foliage hid him from view and the tape trailed limply on the ground. Kellogg did not answer. The sergeant walked around to the back of the sagebrush. There was no one there.

'Goddamn it, Kellogg, quit horsin around.' He ran to the front of the truck, bent and looked beneath it. He straightened, shaded his eyes and squinted into the shimmering heat. The other two troopers, Bridle and Gloat, stood slack-jawed near their patrol car.

'You see where Kellogg went?'

'Maybe back up to the man-camp? Make a phone call or whatever?'

But Kellogg was not at the man-camp, had not been there. 'Where the hell did he go? *Kellogg!!!*'

Again they all searched the area around the truck, working out farther into the sage, then back toward the truck again. Once more Bridle checked beneath the truck, and this time he saw something lying against the back

111

inner tire. He pulled it out.

'Sergeant Sparkler, I found this.' He held out a tiny scrap of torn fabric that perfectly matched his own brown uniform. 'I didn't see it before because it's the same color as the dirt.' Something brushed the back of his neck and he jumped, slapping it away.

'Damn big sagebrush,' he said, looking at it. Deep in the branches he saw a tiny gleam and the letters 'OGG.'

'Jim, his nameplate's in there!' Sparkler and Gloat came in close, peering into the shadowy interior of the gnarled sagebrush giant. Sergeant Sparkler reached for the metal name tag.

*　　　*　　　*

The botanist sprayed insect repellent on his ears, neck and hair. The little black mosquitoes fountained up as he walked toward the tall sagebrush in the distance. It looked as large as a tree and towered over the ocean of lesser sage. Beyond it the abandoned man-camp shimmered in the heat, its window frames warped and crooked. His heart rate increased. Years before he had scoffed at the efforts of botanical explorers searching for the tallest coast red-wood, or the tallest tree in the New Guinea jungle, but at the same time he began looking at sagebrush with the idea of privately tagging the tallest. He had measured

112

some huge specimens of basin big sagebrush near the Killpecker dunes and recorded their heights in the same kind of little black notebook used by Ernest Hemingway and Bruce Chatwin. The tallest reached seven feet six inches. The monster before him certainly beat that by at least a foot.

As he came closer he saw that the ground around it was clear of other plants. He had only a six-foot folding rule in his backpack, and as he held it up against the huge plant it extended less than half its height. He marked the six-foot level with his eye. He had to move in close to get the next measurement.

'I'm guessing thirteen feet,' he said to the folding rule, placing one hand on a muscular and strangely warm branch.

* * *

The Sagebrush Kid stands out there still. There are no gas pads, no compression stations near it. No road leads to it. Birds do not sit on its branches. The man-camp, like the old stage station, has disappeared. At sunset the great sagebrush holds its arms up against the red sky. Anyone looking in the right direction can see it.

The Great Divide

1920

The black secondhand Essex rattled and throbbed along the frozen dirt road. The sky drooped over the undulating prairie like unrolled bolts of dirty wool, and even inside the car they could smell the coming snow. There was no heater, and Helen, a young woman with walnut-colored hair, was wrapped from her shoulders down in an old-fashioned buffalo robe, the fur worn to the hide in places. At a small cairn of stones her husband, Hi Alcorn, turned left onto a faint track.

'Close now,' he said. 'Maybe two miles.'

'If that storm don't beat us there,' she answered in her breathy voice.

'We're okay,' he said. 'We're A-okay. Headin for our own place. Year from now drivin up we'll be able to see the lighted windows.'

Hi's feet worked the pedals, and she saw that the laces of his old worn oxfords were knotted with bits of string. An impasto of yellow mud which had ossified to stucco and then rubbed back into dust on the Essex's floorboards discolored the shoes.

'I don't see any houses,' she said. 'It's not like what we heard from Mr. Bewley. He said it would be almost a town by now.'

'Not yet. I guess this next year we will all build. The ones of us that come late.'

There were two sides to the colony, the east side already settled, the west side, where they had bought a homestead, still unformed.

Hi coughed a little from the dust and went on. 'Mr. and Mrs. Wash, like us just startin out, and two brothers, Ned and Charlie Volin. They'll be buildin. The Washes was at the picnic.' Abruptly he jerked the wheels to the right where a wooden stake, its top painted white, leaned. Fence posts without wire lined toward the west.

'Was Mrs. Wash the one with the strawberry mark on her chin?'

'I guess that was her. I remember something was wrong about her face. Okay, this's it. Southeast corner. We're on our place. Recognize it?'

They had gone out in May, right after their wedding, looking at homestead sites with Mr. Antip Bewley. They bought the land and had returned in the late summer, at Mr. Bewley's invitation, for the Great Divide picnic. By then they were living in a boarding-house in Craig. Helen made a few dollars a week helping Mrs. Ruffs change the sheets and cook for the boarders. Mrs. Ruffs was a widow who had carried on her husband's freighting business after he died, but found the care of six horses and their heavy harness too much for her. She sold the business, team and wagons, bought a sizable house in Craig and hung out her sign— RUFFS BED & BOARD. Helen hated the job as all the furniture and the spaces behind the wallpaper were infested with bedbugs. They had a peculiar smell, like old beef fat. Hi, of course, had been out to the property many times, measuring, deciding where the house and barn should go, marking his corners and setting fence posts. One man could set posts well enough, but it took two or three to string the wire.

*   *   *

She would not forget the first sight of Mr. Antip Bewley, huge, towering above Hi. His hands were the size of hay forks. His head, hair and skin the color of raw wood, was shaped as though someone had taken a rectangular chunk of twelve-by-twelve and sanded off the corners, leaving a smooth jawline without disguising the blockiness of the shape. The face was indented by two furrowed cheek dimples. But it was when Bewley smiled that the landscape lit up as though a crackle of lightning had traversed it, for his four front teeth, top and bottom, were solid gold, pure as wedding rings.

'Call me Ant,' he had said, pumping Hi's hand, then bending over Helen's rough farm-girl paw as though to kiss it or the air above it, in courtly but ironic mockery. They all rode in Mr. Bewley's touring car.

Hi, who subscribed to *The Great Divide,* already knew something about Bewley. He had been reading Bewley's stories championing homestead settlements of public land in defiance of the big cattlemen—'range hogs,' he called them. On the way out to the platted sites, the big man talked enthusiastically about converting empty rangeland to happy homesteads that would give 'the little people' a chance. Helen, sitting between the two men, was conscious of the body heat each gave off. She made up her mind to sit in the back on the return.

Mr. Bewley talked about growing up in Oklahoma, about his career as a prizefighter, as a lawyer, as a prospector in Alaska and how he had returned to Oklahoma out of love for his wife, and he said this with the same courtly irony as when he had bent over Helen's hand, nudging her with his thigh as though in complicity. She shifted slightly toward Hi.

He told them how he had come to Denver to write for *The Great Divide.* He knew and admired Mr. Bonfils, one of the owners of *The Denver Post,* a powerful friend of 'the little people.' Helen wished he would not refer to the little people so often. She felt it diminished them, for she and Hi were undoubtedly classed among the lowly peasants. It also seemed unfair to Helen that ordinary men—Hi, for

117

example—had great trouble finding an occupation, while Mr. Antip Bewley had enjoyed so many and cast them all to one side.

They spent the day driving from one homestead site to another, horned larks running before them on the roads, flying up only at the last moment. They walked over acres of level ground that seemed much the same to Helen. Around three o'clock they stopped and rested in the shade of the car. Bewley took a dripping basket from the back. Inside were three apples, chunks of melting ice, six bottles of beer and two of sarsaparilla. Bewley and Hi each drank two beers. Helen walked to a draw out of sight of the car to relieve herself, and as she started back she saw the two men were doing the same, standing side by side, separated by a polite distance of eight or ten feet.

'I'll tell you what,' said Antip Bewley, speaking to Hi in a confidential tone as though beer and urination had moved them to another level of intimacy, 'there's a kind a special site I been saving for some special people, and I think you are the ones. It's got a real valuable feature. Wait'll you see it.'

Helen thought the site looked very much the same as the others and stayed in the car, but Bewley led Hi to a small draw where the vegetation appeared different. Birds flew up as they approached it, and the hoofprints of wild horses showed on the damp soil.

'There,' said Bewley. 'What do you think of *that?*'

That was a wet seep at the head of the little draw, hardly more than a slanting crease in the otherwise level ground. 'Nice little spring. Never goes dry. Dig it out, put in a springhouse and you're set for life.'

Right then, Helen, watching from the car, saw that Hi decided this was their place. He tossed his head a little as he always did when he had made up his mind about something.

*   *   *

'Didn't you say we was going to have trees?' Her voice was so light she seemed to have inhaled a ribbon of cloud and to float out her words on its gauzy remnants. But her face was pinched and yellow and she kept her hands under the buffalo robe. He thought she had taken on a Chinese look.

'You saw the place last spring. Did you think trees was goin a grow up by now? We got to plant them. I'll plant them. By the gods, first thing I do soon as the ground thaws, I'll get out here with a load of lumber and some trees and rosebushes. That suit you?' There was in his voice some asperity, as though she had asked for a cobblestone drive and a perpetual fountain.

She nodded, wanting to preserve the peace of the day.

119

His voice mellowed. 'All right, then. Come on, get out and I'll show you the best part.'

Slowly, for her joints were half-frozen, Helen got out of the car, slapping dust from her sleeves, and walked into the sharp air. She was very cold and she wished she had worn her brown merino wool skirt. She followed Hi's striding legs, both of them hurrying now because the first few flakes of snow were gliding down. Last spring the land had been rich green starred with wildflowers, for Antip Bewley had shrewdly showed them around when the season was most promising. When, in late summer, they came for the picnic, they had stayed on the east side. The landscape there was sere, the grass a dry brown color like a coffee stain, and she was glad they were to live on the flowery west side. Now it resembled a wasteland.

'Cold!' she gasped, fumbling with the neck button of her light jacket and wishing she had brought a woolen scarf, wishing she had a heavy duster or an overcoat.

'Take a look at this,' Hi cried in a joyful voice, spreading his arms wide to encompass the two acres he had plowed and disked with the hired help of a Craig farmer. 'Just a second disking in the spring and we'll plant. And how about this?' He pointed to the springhouse he had built a few weeks before. He had cleared out the muddy spring, surrounded it with a cedar box, covered the bottom with clean river gravel and water-smoothed stones, then built a small structure to protect it from range horses, livestock and silt-laden wind. He opened the small door and she could see the black water reflect the square of light that had fallen on it.

She grimaced, and he caught the expression. 'What's the matter with it,' he said.

'Nothing! It's swell! It's just that the baby kicked,' and she put her hand on her belly as actresses did when they wanted to indicate that they were pregnant.

'Well,' he said. 'That's fine. Isn't it? Isn't it, honey?'

'Yes.'

'That's fine, new land, new springhouse, new big house coming, one baby coming. And we'll name him Joe. Joe is a good name for a boy.'

'Yes. Or Jim or Frank.' This was old ground. She knew his horror of burdensome names, for the three Alcorn brothers, Hiawatha, Hamilcar and Seneca, had suffered, and their names had been abbreviated to Hi, Ham and Sen by the end of each boy's respective first day in school. Helen teased him sometimes, chanting in a low voice such as she thought an Indian reciter would use ⌐

By the shores of Gitche Gumee,
By the shining Big-Sea-Water,
Stood the wigwam of Nokomis,
Wherein dwelt young Hiawatha . . .

121

'That's not how it goes,' he said in a tight voice, for he did not stand teasing, and he took up a tin cup fastened to the cedar spring casing by a strip of rawhide, dipped it full, handed it, dripping, to her.

'You did a lot of work,' she said to mollify him.

'You tell em, kid.'

She drank the ice-cold water, pure and sweet and with the faintest taste of cedar, and thought, This is our water, *my* water, for her father had given them one hundred dollars toward the place. The war years had been good for farmers. Corn had gone to two dollars a bushel and it seemed wheat prices would keep rising. The money had helped, for every homestead family, Mr. Bewley said, should have two thousand dollars, six cows, three horses. Hi explained to her on the way to the picnic when the established settlers showed off their squash and corn, that the Great Divide Colony was not a setup for people who were flat busted. It was more for people who had a little something and wanted to get back to the land.

Later, in the pushing crowd, he said 'all these people'—waving in the direction of the crowd watching the bathing beauty contest—'have some money, so the colony is a surefire success.' Helen and Hi had only six hundred dollars and one cow, but Hi was confident they'd make up for it within five years. He had managed to buy three horses, all of them cheap and half-wild as they were fresh off the Red Desert to the northwest.

'I'll have them gentled down pretty quick,' he said. But he was not good with horses and after a few months he sold them, using the money for a down payment on a tractor. He was going to plant corn and wheat.

'Pay the tractor off with what we make on the crops,' he'd said.

Now, standing shirtsleeved in the freezing autumn wind he remarked, 'Quite a few houses already over on the east side. If it wasn't set for snow we could run over there. You could see.' He looked at the churning clouds and the sparse flakes whirling down. She shuddered, said nothing.

'Better idea, hustle back to Craig and get warm. We'll hop right in the bed and get warm.' He rapidly raised and lowered his eyebrows communicating a coarse intention. This eyebrow wriggling was something she thought nastily comic.

*   *   *

Both of them came from Tabletop, Iowa. Hi's father was a strong-minded farmer, and her own parents, Rolfe and Netitia Short, owned a small dairy farm. She was the middle child of nine. Her brothers were dairy farmers as well, and Helen, who had developed a dislike of milk cows and their endless care, had married, in part, to escape cows. She had married, too, to escape the household's obsession with bird eggs. Every surface of the house bore blown bird eggs which Rolfe Short and his sons collected. They often took long trips to distant places to gather more eggs. Her father's climbing paraphernalia hung from hooks in the milk room, and even there, among the dust and hen feathers, wild bird eggs rolled in small arcs whenever the door opened. Three of her brothers collected eggs as well, and at the dinner table there was no end to the talk of tree-climbing adventures and perilous forays onto cliffs to seize coveted clutches.

The trip back to Craig was terrifying, the storm suddenly upon them, Hi cursing as he wrestled the car along the slippery ruts, losing the track in the flying snow. It took them five hours to cover twenty-two miles and Helen thought it a miracle they had survived. Hi was white and exhausted but he said the Essex was a peach of a car.

*   *   *

She had met Hi, then only a few months home from the Great War, at the funeral of her older brother, Ned. It was a sultry day, unrelieved by breeze or cloud cover. The mourners cooled themselves with little round fans bearing the name of the undertaker, Farrow's Funerals.

Hi's brother Sen had been a friend of Ned's and with him on the ill-fated egg-collecting trip. Ned had climbed a hollow tree stub in a black-water swamp to get the egg of a great blue heron while Sen waited in the boat below, and as Ned came even with the nest, the violent bird, defending her egg, had pierced his eye and brain with her beak.

The first thing Hi said to Helen as they walked away from the fresh grave in the sweating company of the mourners was 'If they piled up all the birds' eggs in the world in front a me I would turn the other way.' That put it flat. Her mother overheard the remark and took it as oblique blame for their son's death. From that moment she disliked Hi.

Hi was nine years older than Helen. In the war he had suffered a whiff of gas and a wound in his right thigh. He came home with a limp, brusquely unwilling to farm with his father and brothers. The family did not know what to make of him, and his father sang in a sarcastic voice the new song that every farmer knew—'How you gonna keep em down on the farm, after they seen Paree?'

But of course he had not gone to Paris.

'I wouldn't give them the satisfaction,' he said, as though his refusal to visit the City of Light somehow punished the French, whom he called 'the Froggies,' in a jocular, insulting tone. Hi's life now seemed to him a valuable gift that must not be wasted when so many had

125

died in French mud for reasons he still did not understand. He knew he had to get away from his family, from Tabletop with its relentless corn and quivering horizon. He wanted a frontier, though it seemed to him that the frontiers had all disappeared in his grandfather's time. He was, without knowing it, searching for a purpose that his spared body might carry out. Helen, nineteen years old and with long wood-brown hair, came into view as an island to the shipwrecked. They would make their own frontier.

*   *   *

Hi was counting on the corn and wheat prices staying up, and when corn dropped to forty-two cents and wheat plunged from three dollars fifty to a dollar, he was stunned.

'I don't understand how it could slide like that,' he said, for he had been too busy for many months to read *The Great Divide*. Now Helen pointed out an article warning that wartime demand had ended and that too many farmers, counting on continuing high prices, had overplanted.

'That don't make sense,' he said. 'There's still the same bunch a people in the world. They got to eat.'

Even if the prices had remained steady, they had to face the fact that neither the wheat nor corn had done well. Only the potatoes had

126

thrived, but potatoes were a cheap crop; anyone could grow them. In November of 1921, Hi went back to Iowa to see his father, not out of family sentiment, but to learn how to make potato whiskey.

They had, of course, to visit her family when they were in Iowa. They spent a bare half hour in the dismal house, then fled.

'See you are in the family way again,' her mother said coldly, went silent.

'How can they live that way,' mourned Helen on the way home. William had taken up egg collecting once more, not to align in rows in cabinets and on tabletops, but to sell to city collectors who did not have the time or location for egg forays. Soon he was making more money than any dairy farmer, such was the longing of fanciers in New York City and Philadelphia for the eggs of bald eagles, meadowlarks and trumpeter swans. His mother had made him move everything associated with eggs out to the old hen-house, now empty, as she would have nothing in the place that brought back memories of poor Ned. Rather than put up with his mother's icy hatred of what he was doing, William began to live in the henhouse himself, ripping the nest boxes off their support planks and throwing down his dirty blankets. Soon he smelled like a chicken, and looked like one, his clothes festooned with stray feathers.

'My poor brother,' Helen said and sighed.

'Huh,' said Hi. 'He's gone simple. Just a dirty gristle-heel chicken lover.'

*   *   *

The potato whiskey didn't work out. Hi was the kind of man who couldn't keep something quiet and within six months the revenuers were onto him. He had picked one of the old Indian caves under the ledges as his place of manufacture, throwing out the Indian corpse wrapped in deerskin and beads. He was cooking mash on a day of clouds smeared by thumbs of wind when the sheriff came in. The judge made him an example—six months in jail and a two-hundred-dollar fine. Helen had to borrow from William to pay the fine. She lied to Hi and told him she had raised the money selling the tractor. She had sold the tractor, but got only fifty dollars for it.

After he got out they moved over the state line to Wyoming in a region of steep pointed hills separated by deep gorges. The desert wilderness lay to the west; to the east the Sierra Madre rose like a great black wave. Helen's curly-headed sister Verla and her husband, Fenk Fipps, lived on one of the highest farms. Antip Bewley had showed and sold them the place.

'That man again,' said Helen. It seemed to her that Mr. Bewley had manipulated many lives; no doubt he thought of them as the little

128

people and himself as the puppeteer. All the settlers, dreaming the war prices would come again, grew wheat on the tops of the hills. The local ranchers were against them and there were rumors that two families had been burned out while they were up in Rawlins buying supplies. Helen thought it was a hard country with hard people and longed for their old place west of Great Divide although she had been glad to leave it.

1932

The children were making a tremendous racket, jumping on the beds it sounded like, and after a particularly violent crash a dead silence fell, followed by whispering. Helen went to the door and looked in. One of the beds had collapsed at one end and now resembled a cow getting up.

'For pity's sake,' she said. 'Your father will be here any time and what do you do? Smash up the furniture.' She looked wildly around as though for the stick with which she beat them.

'Listen! That's him!' said Mina, eleven years old and big in the same way Hi was big. The twins, Henry and Buster, were nine, slender and on the short side. Hi often teased them about their heights, urging them to eat plenty and put some meat on their bones. Little Riffie was the spoiled baby, the favorite.

They could all hear the chugging of the car

engine as it drew near the porch, and then Hi's feet on the steps, the door opening.

The boys raced for him, Henry already asking if he had brought them anything.

'Alls I could get was a roll a Life Savers. You got to share.' He held it out on his palm. Buster grabbed it and ran outside, the others snatching at his shirt.

Helen looked at him. He shook his head. 'I go in to Sharps, see, and say I heard he wanted a man. He didn't say a word, just pointed to where that big half-wit Church Davis was throwin bags a grain onto a wagon. His way of saying he already hired Church. Makes you blue to know a half-wit gets a job over you.'

Helen's stomach ached. What could they do? She didn't understand why the Depression was harming men who wanted to work. There had to be a way to get money.

*   *   *

From the front window Mina could see a throbbing plume of dust laboring up the hill through the heat. She knew it was going to turn in by the way it slowed.

'Ma! There's a car coming.'

Helen wiped her hands on her apron, slipped it off and went to the porch door. A heavy sedan crept up the drive. It was so dusty she could not see the color. Kind of maroon, she thought. The vehicle parked under the

130

cottonwood tree in the only piece of shade. The passenger window rolled down and a face appeared.

'Verla!' she cried and rushed down the steps. To the girls she called 'It's your aunt Verla!' The girls advanced, mincing across the gravel on bare feet. A half-grown puppy followed, biting at dress hems. Henry and Buster were a mile distant shooting prairie dogs with slingshots. Verla and Fenk stayed in their seats but rolled the windows down. Fenk's tight-jawed face displayed blackheads mixed with stubble. He had a low smile and dark, staring eyes like those of a marionette. Helen knew he beat his children with a strap and that he had slapped Verla around a few times. She shuddered to think of those wooden eyes painted with malice fastening on her sister.

'Out this way and thought we'd see if you was home,' whispered Fenk who had something wrong with his voice that threw it in a high womanish register. Whispering suited him better. Fenk generally let Verla do most of the talking. The story was that he had tried to hang himself as a boy and damaged his voice box. 'They get awful moody at a certain age,' his mother had offered as explanation, but his old father knew it was probably something else on the other edge of the great divide that separated men's and women's knowledge of sexual matters. He had caught the tail of some sniggered comment about coming or maybe going when he went into the metalwork shop, the informal meeting place for local farmers. Ray Gapes, who owned the smithy, had a large coffeepot and some stage of inky java was always on tap for anyone who could drink it.

Helen leaned into the passenger window, her arms on the hot metal, the breeze that moved always around the cottonwood fluttering the hem of her print dress.

'Where did you get the nice car?' she said. The car gave off a variety of ticks and pings as it cooled. The girls came up, Mina folding her arms across her flat chest, Riffie swinging on the door handle, and listened to the women talk. They too wore cotton print dresses but with puff sleeves and Riffie with a small lace-edged collar that Helen had tatted. Their pale legs were like peeled willow sticks.

'Fenk's makin good money catchin horses,' said Verla. 'That's how come us to visit.' She looked, not at her sister, but at Fenk, waiting for him to nod his head.

Hi appeared from behind the house where he had been grubbing up sagebrush. Helen wanted a kitchen garden and getting the soil in shape was work. He stood near Fenk's window.

Verla said, speaking for Fenk, 'Fenk wants Hi to throw in with him. The horses bring five or eight dollars and he has been getting good bunches.'

Hi shook his head. His work-enlarged

hands, crusted with soil, hung by his sides. 'Never done it,' he said.

Fenk had to speak. He whispered, 'It's good work. Some, like them Tolberts, runs them, some drives them into a box canyon, but we been makin night traps around water holes. That way you don't lose so many tryin to get out. You follow me? The money is good. I been workin with Wacky Lipe.'

'Wacky Lipe! Hell, he's got a wood leg.'

Verla spoke up. 'Yes, and it come off the other night. All the horses run out of the trap and now they're wise to it.'

Fenk added, pitching his voice down to alto, 'He hopped around pretty good, but wasn't no use. Wacky is all try and no luck.' He looked at Hi.

But Hi only said he'd think it over. Henry and Buster came in sight, lagging around the edge of the drought-burned wheat field. When they recognized the passengers in the car they began to run, hoping the male cousins had come. They were disappointed and showed it by punching their sisters and running.

'You boys better stop it,' said Helen.

*   *   *

Ten days later the old black Essex quit for good. Hi had made a hundred repairs over the years, had repaired the repairs, but now the entire engine had seized and he knew the thing

133

wasn't worth fixing. There was no money for it anyway, and so he had hoofed it to Fenk and Verla's and told Fenk he was in.

'I knew you'd come in,' murmured Fenk. 'Well, we're layin out a new trap tomorrow. We don't run horses—takes a lot of time and you need a bunch a riders. I'll leave that to the Tolberts. Old Jim there and his seven boys don't even need to talk they know each other's minds so good. Me and Wacky favor a water trap, you follow? Last month we found a spring the hell off in rough country, horse trails comin in from every direction. Hitched the wagon to the new car and hauled out the posts and cable last week and now we got a build the corral and the wings. Hard drivin out there. I about wrecked that car and Verla's pretty mad. There's deep washes and the stones are hell on the tires. I been thinkin about getting a set a them solid tires like the JO runs on their truck. I been thinkin about saw off the ass end and put a bed on her, follow me? I don't suppose you got a ridin horse these days?'

Hi shook his head. 'Just Old Bonnet. The kids ride him mostly. He's about a hunderd years old.'

'You can use Big Nose and Crabby.'

Hi nodded.

*　　　*　　　*

134

It was a rare day, windless, cool and clear. Fenk and Wacky had set up camp about three miles from the spring where they planned to build the water trap. They came to the camp in late afternoon, Fenk's sedan hauling the horse trailer, wallowing across the flats and washes. The country was rough, full of cliffs and arroyos, and Hi liked being out in it. The canvas tent at the foot of a sandstone bluff was stained red with desert dust and crowded inside with bedrolls, a stove, a crooked table and boxes of food. The stove was throwing off waves of heat. Hi threw his gear against the back wall. Fenk was unloading Big Nose and Crabby, putting them in the corral with the others. Wacky, who had stayed at the camp all week, had fresh coffee perking, antelope steaks frying and a pot of boiled potatoes. They ate outside where Fenk built a campfire and hit the hay before it was full dark.

'First light,' said Fenk softly, shaking him. Wacky was already at the stove cooking bacon and stirring the sourdough batter. They drank the coffeepot dry, saddled up and rode out. The hundred-mile sight line eased Hi's mind away from money worries.

The sun was up by the time they got to the spring. There were plenty of fresh horse tracks and piles of dung.

'They come for water after dark,' said Fenk in his woman's voice, 'with their tongues hanging out for a drink. You follow me? They

135

don't never come in the daylight.'

It took the three of them all day to dig four-foot holes and set the posts—old sawed-off telephone poles—and string the cable and wire. Wacky and Fenk built the wings while Hi hauled juniper and sagebrush to disguise them. It was late afternoon, about three hours before dark, the sky filling with braided clouds evasive in direction, when they finished. They went back to camp to pack up. Fenk whispered they would go home because it was going to rain and he didn't want to get the car stuck, let the horses have a week or two to get used to the change in the landscape, then they would come out, take their places before dusk and wait until night fell and the horses came to drink, then jump up and close the trap. They'd leave the horses there to fill up on water. They would be easier to handle the next morning that way when they'd be roping and hobbling them and driving them to the rail yard at Wamsutter, thirty miles distant.

'Then where do they go?' asked Hi. He guessed they would be rodeo stock.

Fenk sniggered. 'Mink farms. California pet food factories. Chicken feed. Follow me?'

Ten days later they caught seventeen horses. Fenk said it was a good trap, no telling how long they could use it; months, maybe. The hardest work was getting them to the railroad and into the hot, airless car. Those cars smelled like death, and Hi felt his stomach

136

roil. Horses kept coming to the trap and in between days they searched for additional springs and flowing wells.

Fenk had a dozen tricks to slow chicken horses down on the drive to the railroad. He would catch a horse, make a slit in a nostril, run a length of rawhide through and tie it closed, reducing the animal's oxygen intake. Or he would tie two horses together, or tie one to a broke saddle horse. A few got a big metal nut tied into their forelocks, the constant hit of the sharp-corner nut causing enough pain to slow them down. The ones who moved too quickly with front hobbles got side hobbles. And obstreperous horses that continued to fight to get free despite everything he gutshot.

'What the hell, Fenk!' cried Hi the first time his brother-in-law put up his rifle and shot a breakaway stallion. For two days the animal listlessly plodded after the other horses. It was still standing when they reached the tracks.

'They stay alive long enough,' murmured Fenk matter-of-factly. 'Hey, they're headed for chicken feed anyway, you follow me? What difference does it make? Still worth five or six bucks.'

But Hi thought it was an ugly business and when the day came that Fenk told him to shoot two of the fighters he quit. He said it as it came to him, without reflection.

'Well, you'll walk then. Go ahead. I'm not fixin to throw a fit over you.' Fenk's eyebrows pulled together in a black, hairy stripe. His whispering voice rasped like a file. 'You wasn't with us from the git-go, am I right? You're so lily-livered you can have a good long hike to think it over.'

'I thought it over.' Hi walked three miles to the tent camp, got his bedroll and necessaries and hiked through the night to the old stage road where, in early morning light, he caught a ride with Isidore the Jew peddler, riding in the back of his wagon and watching a handful of magpies chop the air into black and white flashes.

*   *   *

Helen put Mercurochrome on his blisters and bandaged his raw feet.

'I can't understand why you quit that way,' she said. 'What are we goin to do now?'

'Get out a this hellhole. Far as Fenk's concerned I'm sagebrushed for good. Wasn't makin enough to do much for the bank anyways. You might as well know they are takin the place. Move up to Rock Springs or Superior. We'll rent. I'll get a job in the coal mines. That's steady money and I won't have to shoot anybody in the guts.' He told her about Fenk's ways with wild horses.

'The poor things,' she said, for Helen had a tender heart. 'I guess Fenk has got a mean streak.'

'It's the money, I suppose. He's one will do anything to get it. You ought to see how he's wrecked the new car. Figures he can get another one easy.'

'Maybe he can,' said Helen. Fenk seemed to her now a cruel monster. She vowed never to speak to him again.

They were not hiring at Superior but he found work at the Union Pacific mines in Rock Springs. Even though the company house was more of a shack Helen liked the conveniences of town—electricity, running water. The kids could walk to school. There were plenty of people around, gossip and talk, a social life, handy food supplies. That pleasure sagged when little Riffie got sick with polio and had to be put in an iron lung. The doctor told Helen that it was living in town and going to school with other children that had caused it, that polio was contagious, and that in their old homestead out on the edge of the desert the child would likely have remained free of the affliction. Helen hated the doctor, not the town.

1940

The coal mines were hard for a man who'd once owned his place and worked all his life outdoors. Hi was surprised to find he missed horse catching with Fenk, riding through the chill high desert, the grey-green sage and greasewood, the salt sage sheltering sage hens, pronghorn, occasional elk, riding up on ridges and mesas to spy out bands of wild horses, plodding through the sand dunes, seeing burrowing owls in a prairie dog town, wheeling ferruginous hawks and eagles, a solitary magpie flying across the quilted sky like a driven needle, the occasional rattlesnake ribboning away. Seeking the elusive water flows and seeps had given him a private, solitary pleasure that he could not share with anyone. Not even Helen could understand the pull of the wild desert. And as much as he despised Fenk's ways, the man loved the wild country and it was a bond. Now, to go down in a metal cage with men in stinking garments unchanged for weeks or months, to work bent over in a cramped space in dim light was misery. He dragged home late, black with coal dust. Helen had a tub of hot water ready for him at night, a very great luxury. Because of the new war in Europe—they were calling it World War Two, demoting the Great War to World War One—the work held steady, he spoke less, went daily to the job as an automaton. Two years cranked by.

Helen mourned the separation from her sister but could not stomach the thought of Fenk. The children whined and belly-ached to see their cousins again. Verla wrote to her pleading, explaining and describing a Fenk Helen did not know, a sensitive 'deep' Fenk. It took time, but at last Verla wore Helen down and Helen gave in, persuaded Hi they had to make amends for the sake of the children and Verla. Thanksgiving was named as the day for reconciliation and rejoicing.

Verla and Fenk and their four children drove into town Thanksgiving morning in their 1939 Crosley, even Fenk, who was rough but bragged that he did not hold a grudge, keyed up. Verla balanced a packed basket on her knees and the girls clutched boxes of cake and jams. Immediately the country and town cousins ran down to the railroad tracks to throw stones at the bums in the hobo jungle and at the great huffing engines. The shining steel rails, surely the most polished objects on earth, awed the Fipps cousins.

'You got a penny?' asked Buster. The cousins shook their backcountry heads.

'Too bad. You put a penny on the rail, see, and the train comes and mashes it flat and big and skinny.'

'Yeah,' said Henry. 'And that ain't all. This kid in our school, Warren McGee, got his legs cut off. He was runnin on the ties and the train was comin and his sister yelled at him to get off but he tripped and the train got him.'

'Did he die?'

'Naw. He goes to school at home. The teacher comes to his house. He's got this wheelchair and his sister pushes him around.'

'Did he say it hurt?'

141

'What a you think? Course it hurt.'

The house was redolent of pies and simmering giblet gravy. Helen had raised two turkeys in the minuscule backyard, had slaughtered and plucked them two days earlier. She put them in the oven at seven, aiming at midafternoon. Verla brought side dishes and relishes—pickled black walnuts, red pepper relish, vinegar pie and a dish of Hattie Bailey, which she and Helen remembered from Thanksgiving at their paternal grandmother's house.

'Where did you get okra!' marveled Helen. Verla smirked and finally admitted a distant cousin had sent it in the mail and the pods had arrived in usable condition. The girls and women worked in the kitchen, punching down the dough for the rolls, grating carrots and cabbage for slaw, making celery curls and radish roses, arranging olives on a saucer with their red eyes glaring outward, all talking a mile a minute to catch up. Hi and Fenk talked politics at first, both hating FDR who had dragged them into this Hitler war. Fenk bragged about his Crosley which he claimed got better than fifty miles to the gallon. Hi said the coal mining business was changing.

'They're puttin in these machines for what they call "strip mining," put us old boys out a business.'

'Well,' said Fenk, 'oil is the direction to look, I think. Fella I know got in it two years

142

ago and today he is sittin pretty.'

'You still catchin horses?' asked Hi.

'Yeah. Well, not so much like we used to. I throwed in with Tolbert for a while after Wacky went up to Montana. So now I pretty much run em. Lot a fun, don't hurt them none. You got a dodge the oil geologists. Desert is crawlin with those bastards. You ought a come out with us, get out a that hole in the ground for a while. You used a be able to throw a loop. Do you good.'

Hi said it would sure enough do him good. He hated the underground. He said he would, and before the women called dinner he had agreed to ride out the next weekend with Fenk.

'If it ain't snowin a blizzard. Could start any day now.'

'We had that little swipe in September.'

'I got a real good horse you can ride. Little buckskin, come out a the Chain Lakes two years ago. Throws his head up real snooty like, so we call him "Senator Warren."'

Hi laughed.

*   *   *

The chase was exhilarating. He had missed the keen wind, the badlands and outlaw cliffs, the smell of horses, the distant pronghorn sentry alert and wound up, the whinnying dust cloud. Fenk flung his arm out. They went after the

143

band, cutting northeast at a sharp angle to head them off, but keeping two miles behind the rises to avoid showing themselves. They rode with Tolbert's two oldest boys, Hi on Senator Warren, his old rope coiled and ready. Fenk had built a trap in the heart of the badlands of casually interwoven sage and rabbitbrush to guide a herd into a box canyon with steep-sloped stone walls. But even as Hi rejoiced in the broken country, he could see changes had come in the two years he'd been digging coal. There were fences where no fences had ever been, and the old White Moon trail had become a county road, complete with culverts and ditches. There were wisps of wool in the sage and greasewood so he supposed the sheepmen had been using the desert for wintering their woolies.

Once inside the trap Fenk and the Tolberts leaped from their mounts and ran to close the opening with three heavy cables. They could hear the horses at the end of the trap coming up point-blank against the stone walls. The old stallion was screaming with rage, and even from the mouth of the trap they could see the powdery dust cloud that rose from frantic horses trying to scale unscalable walls. And yet somehow, almost beyond belief, one horse clawed its way up and began to run west.

Hi, outside the gate, was the only one mounted. Automatically he took up the chase, Senator Warren understanding the game well.

The escaped horse, a young bay, was hurt and exhausted. Climbing that thirty-foot almost sheer wall had taken a lot of the starch out of him. Hi built a loop and within a mile of the trap roped the escaped prisoner. But the terrified and furious horse drew on inner reserves of strength and fairly dragged Senator Warren with him. One of the new fence corners loomed. The wild horse dodged around it sharply. The sudden swerve broke the old rope. The bay staggered a step or two, then ran. Hi's end of the rope leaped back and wrapped around Senator Warren's ankles. The Senator began to buck, the rope tangling and twisting. Hi saw the fence coming closer and rather than get piled into it, he bailed out of the saddle, hit the ground and rolled. As he rolled one of Senator Warren's lashing hind feet clipped him on the thigh.

In a minute one of the Tolbert boys was there, catching up the Senator's reins. Fenk and the other Tolbert boy galloped up.

'Hell, I'm all right,' said Hi. 'Everthing's fine. Just my leg's a little bit busted. I guess I can get some time off from work now.' He laughed, and Fenk laughed with him, relieved that he wasn't bad hurt. The Tolbert boys sat dazed, dusty and wordless.

'Okay, just lay there,' said Fenk. 'I'm goin a get the Crosley and we'll get you into town, get that leg set.'

'Not much I can do except lay here,' said Hi.

'I promise I won't run off.'

Fenk went to get his automobile, and the Tolbert boys got down and squatted near Hi. They smoked cigarettes, lighting one for Hi. The oldest boy pulled out a half-empty pint of whiskey and offered it; Hi took a good slug.

'That was a good catch. Reckon your rope was old?'

'Hell, yes. Couple years I didn't use it. They say ever year you don't use a rope it loses half its strength. How about that old horse climb up that wall?'

Fenk was back with the Crosley after a wide hour and they loaded Hi into the backseat. There was no room for the Tolbert boys who rode back to the horse trap. Business was business.

*   *   *

All the way to Rock Springs Hi joked and laughed, said he had had a fine day, that he'd just as soon quit the coal mine before the strip machinery came in and go back to chasing horses with Fenk.

'Stop at the house first,' he said. 'I'll let Helen know I'm okay. Otherwise she'll be up at the hospital devilin everbody.'

Helen came out on the porch as Fenk pulled up. She had the fearful-woman look on her face. She leaned in, staring at Fenk, not seeing Hi in the back.

'What's wrong!' She knew it was bad if Fenk was alone. Her old dislike of her sister's husband, who caused harm to all around him, rose, flared anew.

From the backseat Hi called out that he was fine, and she cried a little, saying they really had her going there for a minute.

'They'll set the leg at the hospital and Fenk can bring me home. What's for dinner?' He laughed.

*   *   *

At the emergency entrance of the hospital Fenk parked near the door and walked in. It took him ten minutes to find anyone. He came back with Doc Plumworth whose mouth was so small only two teeth showed when he smiled, the cross-eyed nurse and a gurney. Doc opened the back door of the Crosley and pulled at Hi's arm.

'It's okay, fella, we'll get you fixed up,' he said in his crackery voice. He pulled again, turned to Fenk. 'Thought you said he was in good spirits. Thought you said he was conscious.'

'Christ, he is. Horse kicked him in the leg, that's all. I been kicked a hunderd times myself. Talked and laughed all the way in. Told jokes. Just stopped by his house to see his wife couple minutes ago.'

Doc Plumworth, half in the backseat, had

147

been examining Hi.

'Well, he's not telling jokes now. He's dead. Horse kicked him? I'll bet you . . .'

*   *   *

Helen heard Fenk's Crosley outside again. That was pretty quick, she thought. The coffee was perking and she was reheating the lamb stew. She opened the door to Fenk. He stood there, working his mouth, glutinously whispered something like 'clot,' then looked at her with his great staring eyes. Her mind snarled like a box of discarded fiddle strings. Civilization fell away and the primordial communication of tensed muscle, ragged breath, the heaving gullet and bent fingers spoke where language failed. She knew only what Fenk had not yet said and didn't need to say.

And shut the door in his face.

Deep-Blood-Greasy-Bowl

During construction of our house the builders unearthed an ancient fire pit. Carbon 14 testing indicated an age of 2,500 years, centuries before the Indians had horses or bows and arrows. Other fire pits, nearby tipi rings, projectile points and a chert quarry attest to long Indian presence on the land. Facing the house is a limestone cliff where a bison drive over the edge may have occurred in ancient days. Imagining the time and the hunt made this small story.

Gradually the familiar sounds of night and sleep gave way. A few men came awake at once and raised up on their elbows, listening to the change. The chill air presaged autumn. In the blue draw coyotes argued. A sated owl on the island hooted and the river choked through sunbaked stones. But these were common sounds, and had not wakened the men. Silence disturbed their sleep, the cessation of a voice. The shaman had stopped chanting. Night after night the thready monotone of his prayers and invocations had formed the solemn background of the band's dreaming. His beckoning, coaxing voice had become as elemental as chirring grasshopper wings or the rattle-stick cries of flying cranes.

149

Forbidden to eat during the ceremonial invocation the old man had grown gaunt and his voice had wavered almost to inaudibility. But now he was quiet, task completed, and into the vacuum of silence rushed excitement.

The men who had immediately wakened— the hunters—strained for the aural vanishing point, those sounds too remote for all but the inner ear. The need to put on fat, to store food against the hungry winter slinking toward them made them exquisitely sensitive to nuances of the natural world: strong clouds rubbing against the sky like a finger drawn over skin, the quiver of a single blade of grass in calm air showing subterranean movement. Some could tell by the briny smell of seaweed when storms were advancing from the distant ocean. A few branches of cottonwood leaves had already turned an urgent yellow; the first frosts hung over them like veils of thin rain not yet touching the ground.

Below their suspirations and heartbeats, they sensed the roaring of bison deep inside the earth, a bellowing that made bedrock quiver and promised that something long-awaited was about to happen. The shaman's silence allowed the promise to become a hot expectation of blood and meat, for bison, in their wandering journey through the world, were surely moving toward them.

The men rose and went outside to relieve themselves in the sagebrush, stared at the sky for its message. It was flat and colorless in the predawn as though rubbed by an antler polishing tool. It said nothing. It would be a hot, breathless day, affirming that summer still lay on them like a panting wolf on a red bone.

The hunters asked each other, How many? It was crucial to know how many.

It had been years since a herd had come within driving distance of the cliff, but because it had happened in the past at the end of one summer the band had continued to camp near the foot of the precipice, knowing it would happen again. The river lay between their camp and the pale limestone cliff. It was summer's end and the hard sun had incinerated all rain clouds until the river barely skimmed the gravel bars. At the base of the cliffs a strip of brushy ground fronted steep talus slopes, the millennial accumulation of debris from crumbling rock. The last time the driven animals had plunged into the terrifyingly steep chimney, some finally rolling down the talus slope, others piling up on it, a mass of kick-leg flesh. The butcher women had rushed at them with their biface chert knives, skinning and slicing tools, pitched the offal into the gulping river.

*   *   *

From the tipi camp on the south side of the river every detail of the cliff face and the lives

151

of the animals and birds who lived in and on it dominated their view. A small band of mountain sheep moved around the upper benches out of range, sometimes gazing haughtily down at them, sometimes still and bunched like pale fists. A pair of eagles and their two grown young played in the updrafts above the cliff, their thin, tumbling calls requests for prayers. As always, the young men made plans to capture them for their feathers, but they also begged the eagles to carry their wishes for a successful hunt to the spirits. There was a thrilling moment that sent chills down their spines when the eagles separated in the air and flew to the four sacred directions. Never had there been such a strong sign of the future.

In the spring one of the hunters, now a mature man but only a boy the last time the bison had allowed themselves to be driven over this cliff, had dreamed that this year they would come again. They would come through the east pass. They were coming, he knew it, a black mass pouring out of their deep hole into sunlight, stirring the powdery earth into dust clouds. He dreamed of spurting bright blood, slippery and strength-giving, coursing down the chins of his children, the yielding juiciness of fresh liver warm from a beast that moments before had been running out its life. He woke from the dream with the taste of liver and spicy gall in his mouth. The shaman also remembered that earlier hunt and said the man's dream was a true dream.

The intensity of the hunter's memory of the kill many seasons earlier had commanded attention from the others. Their tipi skins were old and patched, and so, in early summer they made the journey to that jump-off place. There were other reasons than bison to come here; innumerable sego lilies grew in a certain draw where in spring the women dug the bulbs with antler points; goosefoot and biscuit-root grew nearby. There was ricegrass around the sand dunes, fish, beaver and mink in the river, pronghorn and deer feeding along the waterway and the mountain sheep on the cliff. Countless birds and thousands of small animals lived in this rich riparian habitat.

On the great downslope atop the cliff the men and boys strengthened the old drive lines of stones with additional rocks, white lumps of limestone that showed even in twilight. Beside the western cairn marking the edge, the hunters dug a hiding pit for the shaman, who would pull the bison forward by incantation and the luring sound of his flute. When they finished, the heaps of stones extended out in lines from the top of the cliff toward the distant pass. The bison would come from that direction. It was the only possible direction. Near the top of the cliff a brushy draw, the upper end of the sego lily slope, angled toward the point where the drive line hooked inward to compress the herd. As the animals moved up the grade toward the drop-off, the flanking drivers would rise from hollows in the ground, from concealing sagebrush, and press them into panic. If the herd began to veer toward the shelter of the draw, the boys and young men concealed in that earth crease would rise up ululating and turn them irrevocably toward the edge. It was dangerous and beautiful, this death run with the bison. That was how it had been done in the earlier time. That was how they would do it again. It was what they had been born for.

Some men went to the chert vein that erupted along a ridge beyond the sand dunes, worrying the desirable nodules coated with white calcareous cortex from the earth. They would carry as many as they could back to the camp, bury them in the earth and build a fire on top for the slow heat treatment that made chert glossy and easy to work. Later, from the tempered chert they could strike good cores for making scrapers, projectiles and knife blades.

The hunter who had been a boy at the time of the previous hunt spoke again, as he had many times, of the sand dunes near the base of the great slope where the drivers had to work with the wind, not letting themselves be seen but guiding the keen-nostriled beasts between the drive lines by the presence of alien human odor. The others had heard all this and seen

154

the terrain each fruitless year when no bison came or only a too-small group that could not be driven. The hunter once more told them how the stampeders lying hidden behind sagebrush, badger tumuli and prairie dog mounds leapt up from the earth at the vital moment and confronted the bison. The terrified animals lost their reason, became mad creatures who rushed blindly forward, kicking up rocks and clods of threadleaf sedge with dark roots like tangled drowned man's hair, trampling snakes and grasshoppers, some stumbling, and the others rushing over animals trying vainly to rise. They were no longer bison but meat. That was how it had happened years before.

Again the hunters asked each other, How many? It was crucial to know how many.

Two young men said they would go and find the herd, determine its size, direction of travel and speed. A young boy of ten summers pleaded to come with them. When an infant his ears had frozen and the stubbed remnants gave him an animal appearance; he was Small Marmot. They headed east toward the mountain north of the pass at a distance-eating half trot. Was the herd large enough to be stampeded? Small groups did not succumb to mass hysteria. And the tipi skins were old.

*   *   *

155

It was late in the day when the young men returned. They had circled around, returning from the north where the precipice was low, allowing easy descent to the river ford and the camp on the far side. While still on high ground they stood looking at the camp below pressed by the stunning weight of light that hammered the earth's thin rind. The light seemed to pull at the tipis, pulling them loose to rise into twittering molecules of sky. The flood of brilliance offered a merciless clarity of view. In a few weeks autumn wildfire smoke would blur and erase the mountains, the wind would thicken with ash and dust, but now the still air was like pure water and all appeared as distinct as pebbles at the bottom of a spring. They heard a thin sound, rising and quivering like the kestrel hovering over prey. The old shaman had eaten and slept, regaining enough strength to play his flute, the sound that was even then ineluctably pulling the bison to them.

The stub-eared boy gazing down into the camp could see the fringe of shining hairs outlining a puppy's ears. As he stared the shaman's tipi seemed to tremble, losing its solid outline, becoming as transparent as new ice so that he could see everything inside. He could see the band's sacred treasure, a deep stone bowl that had come to them in the distant past. It was a soft and gleaming grey color veined with pale and dark streaks, and men said that to the touch it felt greasy. After a successful bison hunt it was rubbed with fat which further darkened the stone. Power emanated from the bowl. It craved blood. It needed fat. It was very heavy; two men were necessary to lift it even when it was empty. Because it was a spiritual treasure and because it had power, when they traveled they wrapped it in white deer hides with spiritual herbs, and it was drawn by dog travois. Small Marmot could feel its grey force pulling the bison closer, the bowl thirsty for the blood that would brim to its cold lip.

The young men and the boy told the hunters the bison were moving slowly toward the slope. It was a good herd. The three of them extended their fingers six times to show how many. The flute was drawing the animals. They could not help themselves. They were coming. They would be on the slope in the morning.

*   *   *

Now time began to mass together in the shape and color of bison. Nothing else had importance. The women examined their tipi skins, calculating how many new ones were needed. The waiting men struck long, slender cores from the cooled chert. Someone brought out a fine piece of obsidian from the northwest, the shining black stone responding to his touch as a child to his father. They finished and repaired thrusting spears, chipped fresh edges on skinning tools and knives. The young men, keyed up with excitement to the point of agony, wanted to get in place along the drive line before darkness fell. The hunters told them there would be time in the morning, that the bison would not arrive at the bot-tom of the great slope before the sun was high. Patience was essential in a hunt of this kind. Still, many lay awake all night, burning for the morning. Before they went on top of the cliff, the hunters, preceded by the shaman, carried the Deep-Blood-Greasy-Bowl to the butchering site where the bison would fall. They set it carefully on a large flat rock marked by an eagle feather.

As they came up over the cliff they could see the herd near the bottom of the slope. The evening before the bison had gone to the river and taken on huge quantities of water and were now recovering from the lethargy induced by deep drinking. The wind was out of the northwest. The shaman went to the declivity near the western cairn and began to call the herd on his flute. The men and boys took their places along the drive lines, in the sand dunes, behind burrowing animals' rubble heaps, in the sego lily draw. The sun stumped along the hot sky and the bison drifted slowly up the slope. They passed the sand dunes where the scent of the hunters hidden there

158

carried to them indirectly and faintly, just enough to make some of them slightly uneasy. Several bulls threw up their heads as though to get a stronger sense of it, but the herd kept grazing uphill.

When the sand dunes were behind them and they were a critical distance from the edge of the precipice, the men and boys at the rear of the drive lines stood up, shouting, flapping deerskins and running at the bisons' flanks. The startled herd veered west and twenty yelling men rose up. The animals at the front began to run, and when one ran, all ran. The herd coalesced, bunching up as the yelling boys and men flanked, moving faster until they were galloping upslope with staring but unseeing eyes, bumping each other, metamorphosing into a vast living animal with hundreds of legs.

Near the top the final group of hunters hidden in the west-hooking draw sprang up and forced the bison to pack together even more tightly in a galloping, insane crush from which it was impossible to escape. One of the young men dashed too close and was sucked into the hoofed landslide. The first animals went over the edge roaring and breaking off chunks of limestone, falling, flailing, flying, their legs still running as they tumbled through the air. Rocks fell with the bison in an earthquake of impact. Smothering clouds of dust rose. From below the hunters heard the shrieks and fierce cries of the women amid the dying bellows of broken bison. The last of the herd went over and the hunters dared to approach the edge.

Some animals had fallen on a projecting ledge where they tried to rise on broken legs or with shattered pelvises. Already a few magpies were pulling at open wounds and ravens spiraling down. Most of the bison had fallen or rolled all the way to the talus slope, killed by the impact; some even now were being eviscerated by the women. Men waiting at the bottom with spears and stone axes killed the survivors. None must live, for they would tell the secret of the invisible cliff to other bison.

At the top the hunters discovered the trodden remains of the young man who had gone too close to the running herd, now pulverized into bloody mud. His wife would not rejoice in the massive kill. But that news had not yet reached her and she, with the others, sliced and tore, cut still-pulsing throats and caught the blood in deerskin bags and clay pots. The hunters began scrambling down a precipitous cliff path some distance away, eager for the good rich meat.

The Deep-Blood-Greasy-Bowl stood on the eagle feather rock. To it the women brought their smaller containers of still-smoking blood, and the level in the stone bowl rose steadily higher. The stub-eared boy stood close and stared. Then it was full, so full the convex surface liquid rose slightly above the bowl's containing rim. A paw of wind ribbed the surface. The high blood and the ritual that followed twined into his lifelong sense of existence. The eagles cried sweetly and tenderly overhead, the old pair gliding down to feed on a broken animal on the high ledge. No one doubted that the birds remembered the last drive and would aid them in the next one.

Swamp Mischief

It was a fine summer morning, a day predicted to break all heat records. The Devil sat at his fireproof metal desk enjoying a Havana cigar and a triple espresso while he read *The New York Times, The Guardian* and the Botswana *Survivor* (asbestos editions). He asked Duane Fork, his private secretary demon, to open the windows so he could enjoy the fresh billows of sulfur from the pits and the stunning vista of multithousands of refineries, ship-breaking yards, oil wells and methane gas pads stretching to the horizon. On the wall hung a steel plate depicting the reverse image of Krakatoa exploding. When he had finished the cigar, the coffee and the papers, he checked his e-mail. As usual, no one had sent anything to Devil@hell.org except spammers promising a larger penis, hot stocks, cut-rate office supplies and surefire weight loss.

'Duane!'

'Yessir?' Duane Fork, obsequious and insolent at the same time, half secretary, half butler, was a heavy man with smoldering pants cuffs (when he wore pants) and raccoon eyes who walked as though climbing the steps of a guillotine. Like many shamblers he was a bad speller and so awkward that sometimes, when sitting, he missed the chair.

'Fetch some e-mail,' said the Lord of Darkness. Although he rarely received any messages himself, the Devil had ordered a few of his hackers roasting over eternal fires to collect strangers' e-mail from the Upper World. He had been bored the last few hundred years with very little to do but wait ever since he had put certain observations of steam kettles into the head of a young Scots inventor. The kettle epiphany had booted a species—selfish, clever creatures with poor impulse control, suited to hunt, gather and scratch a little agriculture—into a savagely technological civilization that got rapidly out of hand and sent them blundering toward The End.

'A few hundred years, they'll all be here with me,' he murmured. And while he waited for the self-reaping harvest he amused himself by manipulating those humans. He adored fashion, and got to as many designers' openings as he could. He it was who had inspired the butt-freezing Algonquin breechclout, the top-heavy Viking 'dilemma' helmet, the intestine-withering whalebone corset and, most recently, transparent nylon gauze trousers for men. He had the warmest feelings for Manolo Blahnik and had ordered a suite prepared for his occupancy with tiger-skin rugs, silver fittings, auk-down comforters and lead crystal decanters. The suite de luxe was equipped with a floor heated to 140 degrees F, and the only shoes waiting in the capacious closet were man-size copies of the master's own designs. If all went well the Devil had him marked for demon training.

One of the Devil's happier pastimes was to read and act upon other's e-mail messages as if they were addressed to him, to spread agreeable waves of havoc and confusion. For their retrieval services the hackers earned a little respite from their personal barbecues, and the Devil enjoyed the sensation of conducting important business.

'Yessir. What category—ordinary correspondence, World Bank messages or government correspondence? And if the latter, which governments?'

The Devil chose the day's category by randomly opening one of his many unabridged dictionaries and, eyes shut, placing his finger on a page. He had pointed up 'ornithologist.'

'Wonderful! Get me e-mails of ornithologists in Iceland— and America!'

'Including Canada?'

'No Canadian stuff today. I'm in no mood for their so-called civility. Get me stuff from the western states.' The Devil had felt himself a westerner ever since he noticed vain cowboys cramming their feet into tiny, high-heeled boots. Here was a fashion that suited the Hoofed One very well, and he had a rare collection of boots decorated with pitchforks, flames licking up from the insteps, an assortment that complemented his numerous bolo ties. (Readers who dispute the Devil's western identity have only to look at the maps—in Montana the Devil's Corkscrew, the Devil's Bedstead in Idaho, in Colorado his favorite Devil's Armchair and in California, of course, the Devil's Kitchen. His bathtub, filled with hot scratchy sand, can be found in Arizona.)

He was, in fact, something of a clotheshorse. After the Fall, the Devil, once the most beautiful of angels, changed beyond recognition. His rosy complexion metamorphosed into leathery grey sharkskin which kaleidoscoped constantly to thick yellow hair, to scales and exaggerated toenails, to heavy red hide or a dull blue dappled with sores. It was his vanity to show himself occasionally to mortal painters, and he was pleased that the walls of the world were hung with art showing him with antlers, with pronged horns, with tusks, with claws, with hair snakes and limp fuzz, with slavering red lips and goats' eyes. In his main closet hung tight silk skins in every color. Drawers of featherless wings, many of them enlarged bat wings in stainless steel and other materials such as vinyl or glue-stiffened burlap, lay folded neatly. In a locked bottom drawer to which only he had the key, covered by a gauze veil, reposed the sole relic of his heavenly past—a pair of exquisite butterfly wings. Two painters, Hieronymus Bosch and Brueghel the Elder, had not seen but dreamed them into paint. Jackson Pollock had also dreamed the Devil's wings, but the painting has been lost.

In the day's batch of e-mails there was little correspondence between Icelandic ornithologists, but a fairly rich harvest from the American west. Most of the messages had to do with an upcoming bird symposium on the theme of the evolution of delayed plumage maturation. His eyes gleamed, for along with fashion shows, rock concerts, amusement parks (he it was who gave Viliumas Malinauskas the idea for Stalin World), he delighted in symposia. He made a note of the date in his calendar.

A message from a biologist at a national park, someone who signed himself Argos, caught his eye. The Devil recalled Argos— Odysseus's dog, the only one who remembered his master after his grinding travels. He knew what most human historians did not—that Argos, who had never liked Odysseus, did not greet him with smiles and wagging tail, but lifted his black lip and growled.

The ornithologist Argos wrote to someone named James Tolbert:

Jim buddy, how goes it? Lousy here. Times I want to put Burton through the pencil sharpener. Another damn management meeting that went on for

166

three hours. They all treat me like I'm the janitor. Burton bows and flatters the wolf biologist, the mountain lion biologist, the bear man. Me? I'm just the bird guy, no power, no clout. The ones that count are the guys who deal with big animals that can kill people. What I need is a big dangerous bird. I'd sell my soul for a pterodactyl. They'd pay attention then you bet, especially after a couple tourists got carried off.

*   *   *

'*Carpe diem!*' said the Devil. 'Duane!'
'Yessir?'
'What do you know about pterodactyls?' He pronounced the 'p' very distinctly.
'I believe the pterodactyl was some kind of flying dinosaur, sir. I think it lived in the Jurassic.'
'You bet. Great times, the Jurassic. Dig out some background. Didn't we get the pterodactyl started on feathers?'
'I don't know, sir. That was before my time.'
A heavy envelope was sent up from Hell's research department and the Devil shuffled through the stack of photographs of skeletons and reconstructions.
'That one looks like my cousin.' He glanced briefly at his own reflection in his mirrored ashtray. 'Well, let's see. Maybe I'll give this

Argos a few sets of pterodactyls. Say about four to start. Go get one of those women who used to make the science films for the BBC so we can find out what pterodactyls eat. We might have to rearrange some of the habitat in Argos's park.'

The television woman, Malvina Sprout, came in at a half run. She smelled of charred hair and her hands and arms were black with soot.

'Sir?'

'You know what pterodactyls eat?'

'Pterodactyls? Is this a test? Do I get time off from the flamethrower if I get it right?'

The Devil frowned fearfully and the woman shrank back.

'I'm not sure. Ferns, maybe? Cycads? I think cycads?'

'Don't they eat meat?'

'I'm not sure. It's been a long time and I don't have any of my source material here. We never did much with pterodactyls.'

'Okay. Back to your flamethrower, sister.' He drummed his fingers, adjusted his chain-link tie. 'Duane!'

'Yessir?'

'See if we've got some dinosaur people here. Get me an expert. And check the bestiary, see if we've got any pterodactyls on hand.' He sucked at the end of his tail for a little pick-me-up. (The iconography of Hell often shows the Devil with a harpoon blade at the end of his caudal extremity, an error promulgated by ecclesiastical historians of yesteryear. In fact, the terminal of the Devil's tail is fitted with a carved ivory stopper, for the tail, like Toulouse-Lautrec's walking stick, is hollow, allowing the introduction of various liquids and sauces. The Devil keeps his tail charged with fine Spanish brandy.)

The summoned expert, Professor Bracelet Quean, was not the most reliable authority as he had earned his place in the Devil's simmering tar pit through plagiarism and fakery; he knew little about pterosaurs or any other extinct creature. But old rhetorical habits never die and he puffed and swaggered as though in possession of the most intimate knowledge.

'What did they eat? Well, let's just see now.' He paused for effect. 'I would say fish, they ate fish.' There was another pause.

'Snakes.' He was silent for nearly a minute. 'And ducks and birds. Insects—the giant dragonflies of the Jurassic, you know— and probably some plants. Cycads.'

'Cycads, eh?'

'Yes. Cycads are rather like giant carrots.'

'Make a note, Duane.'

Duane wrote down 'cicads.'

'And what sort of habitat?'

'Swamps. Heavy, moist, extensive swamps. And shallow seas. Very warm and moist climate.' The professor was cooking now.

169

'They'd skim over the seas snapping up ducks and flying fish. There would have been plenty of palm trees and giant horsetails. And the giant carrots.'

The Devil looked glum. It was one thing to throw together a few cacti and some scorpions, but an inland sea and extensive swamps called for advanced engineering and almost certainly a rearrangement of the yearly budget. Still, he had all those interstate highway engineers—he could put them to work. Perhaps they could skip the inland sea and make do with just the swamp. And if worse came to worst he would go to Plan B although it strained his powers.

'El visible universo era una ilusiôn,' he said, quoting Borges. 'Okay. Back to the book mutilation section, Professor. And snap it up!' His index finger released a stinging green ray that caught the academic on his left buttock.

* * *

The first to notice anything unusual was a retired hog farmer from Missouri. On his way out of the park he saw a ranger scraping canine ordure from the sole of his high-laced boot and stopped to talk.

'You know, I thought I was in Missoura there for a while—all them cicadas—just like in the Mark Twain National Forest back home. I didn't think you-all had cicadas out here.'

'We don't. Where did you see them?'

'Didn't *see* them. Heard them. Thousands and thousands. Up in that swamp. They don't live in swamps back home.'

'Swamp?'

'Yep. Show you on the map.' He pointed at the north corner where two lakes—Big Gramophone and Little Gramophone—were joined by a small stream.

'Thought I'd try a little fishing at the lakes here, and I hiked in, but there's no lakes, just a swamp. I seen a cowboy in there and asked him but he just took off. Guess you been in a bad drought situation?'

'It has been a little dry,' said the ranger, thinking that the lakes had looked high and full only two weeks earlier. Maybe the man had missed the trail. He tried to remember any swampy areas near the lakes.

'Well, I say you got some mighty powerful cicadas. Hope you get some rain and get those lakes filled up. It's probably globular warming. So long.'

'*Vaya con Dios,*' said the ranger, thinking he might take a run up to the Gramophones.

*　　　*　　　*

In Hell there was a commotion. There were no pterodactyls; a selection of English sparrows, the omnipresent birds of Hell, had had to be biologically modified and enlarged. Then these faux pterodactyls had to be recalled

171

when someone discovered they lacked serious dentition.

'Call these things pterodactyls?' raged the Devil, who cherished the image of shark-mouthed flying horrors in a Frank Frazetta painting. 'They look more like pelicans. Get some teeth in these things.'

The bestiary manager, who had run a petting zoo in the Upper World, said he thought this was the natural state of the creatures.

'They didn't really have much in the way of teeth, sir.'

'I don't care. We'll have our dentists do some implants. I want to see *teeth* before we send them out on their mission. The ornithologist Argos seems to think they had stupendous teeth. Fix them up.'

Most of the dentists had earned their way to the nether regions through multiple affairs with receptionists, assistants, hygienists and X-ray techs. Dr. Mavis Brooms had indulged in all of these venereal delights, with the UPS man thrown in for dessert. Still, she had been an excellent dentist and relished the chance to fit a few pterodactyls with teeth. She longed to take photographs of the procedure, write it up and send it to *Experimental Dentistry,* an impossible wish as the only mail that came to Hell consisted of bills for the inhabitants and no mail at all went out. There were computers, but they were programmed to crash randomly

172

five times a minute.

She spent considerable time working out a plan. Because there was no dental lab in Hell she had to persuade a farrier to hammer out the implants. The farrier was a cretin from Bessarabia who had died in 1842 from alcohol poisoning. It was difficult to make him understand what she needed. Anything beyond horseshoes seemed too much for him. In the end he whanged out something passable and Dr. Brooms put an automotive technician to work refining the shapes. The teeth were slightly more successful, fossil shark teeth stolen from a collection at a natural history museum in Valparaiso.

The pterodactyls were difficult patients and had to be strapped into the chair. They fought terribly and, as there was no anesthetic in Hell, moaned, but Dr. Brooms was hardened to moans, which rose from every corner and alley. The results were not good. The pterodactyls could not manage their shark teeth and constantly bit their own lips. Twigs and leaves stuck in the dental interstices. The Devil commanded that the creatures be whetted up on meat and took away their vegetation.

'Give them twenty-four hours' prey-capture training and get them up into that park!' shouted the Devil, 'while they can still chew.'

*   *   *

173

Park Superintendent Amelia McPherson, seven biologists (including Argos the ornithologist), the ranger and an unknown fellow with a deep sunburn in cowboy boots and bolo tie, presumably someone from Public Relations, gathered at the edge of the swamp. The din of cicadas was extraordinary.

'What about these cicadas?' shouted Fong Saucer, the wolf biologist, a big hirsute man with a nose like a kumquat and an electric yellow beard. 'What are they doing here?'

'They must have been introduced,' said the ornithologist with a poisonous glance, 'like your wolves.'

'This horrid swamp,' mourned Superintendent McPherson. 'Where are my lakes?' For a just-completed aerial survey had showed an extensive swamp but no lakes.

'What is *that?*' said the wolf man, catching sight of a pterodactyl with a thirty-foot wingspread, striking in crimson and green feathers, the primaries edged in black, the breast showing violet spots, gliding toward them through the dead trees.

'Hilfe!' shrieked Warwick the bear biologist (raised in Germany, where his father had been stationed) as the pterodactyl bore down on him. It snapped ghastly teeth and released a stream of pterodactyl manure from an oversize cloaca. It wheeled and came back again, its great claws curling for the grab. In seconds the

bear biologist was skimming over the swamp. The cicada din was terrific.

'Help me, Gott! Gott, *hilfe,* help!' bellowed the bear man and the pterodactyl dropped him like an oversize hot potato. The biologist fell headfirst into the swamp, sending up a gout of mud and gnawed sticks.

The creature sailed off into the dead snags at the far end of the swamp and they all heard the distant crack of branches as though something heavy had settled in dry limbs. The PR man moved back a little from the group. The shimmering horizon seemed to tilt slightly, as though the phantom cube of spatial balance in each viewer's mind had slipped a little.

'I think we just saw a pterodactyl,' said Argos calmly, feeling a tiny but odd grip inside his chest as though someone had nipped a paper clip onto a vague and minor part of his interior works. Then he shrieked, 'Just saw *a pterodactyl!* This is better than the ivory-billed woodpecker!' He began to caper and shake his arms. He rolled his head and hissed through his teeth, all the motions and cries one produces when confronted with fabulous impossibilities. A flash of scientific doubt shut him up.

'Got to get Reggie out,' said Superintendent Amelia, staring at the kicking legs of the bear biologist. She looked at the swamp. The black water was interrupted by great tussocks of saw-

175

edged grass. Below lay sunken logs slippery with green algae. In the distance something plunged. She reached for her cell phone.

'Hello, Security? I'm out at the swamp—where the lakes used to be. I said, out at the swamp. The noise? It's cicadas . . . Cicadas! Never mind that. Get a rescue helicopter out here. We've got a man drowning in a mud hole and can't get to him.'

But the bear biologist was far from drowning. His head and upper torso were wedged in the remnants of a beaver dam, and while it was not a pleasure retreat, the flow of water was minimal.

'It's the Final Days,' he whimpered. He prayed in German and English, for he was a religious man, a member of a group of hallucinated enthusiasts, Penecostal Grizzly Scientists, who met once a month in the back room of a taxidermist's shop. Now he drew heavily on his spiritual bank account, and it seemed to him that with every prayer he uttered the beaver dam structure gave way. In ten minutes he was able to pull himself out of the enmeshed branches. The swamp around him had cleared in a two-meter circle and a path of sparkling water stretched to the shore. He was gripping a log unusually large for a beaver dam, large enough, in fact, to be used as a watercraft.

'It's a miracle,' he said. 'Thank you, god.' Babbling prayers, he began to kick his way to land.

On that shore Argos was peering into the distance hoping to see the pterodactyl return. He wished badly he had brought a camera. He had to record what he was seeing. He owed it to science. He vowed to upgrade to a cell phone with a camera as soon as possible. With anxious hands he searched his pockets, found his folded paycheck and a ballpoint pen that skipped, began to sketch a clumsy impression of what he had seen. Or thought he had seen.

The superintendent was on the phone again.

'Security, cancel that helicopter. Our man is extricating himself. Here they come again!' The PR man took a few steps back.

All four pterodactyls, flying in formation, came quickly from the far end of the dissolving swamp. The park personnel clustered together.

'I don't believe it,' said Argos. 'This is not happening. This can't happen.'

'*Liebe Gott,* our Heavenly Father save us *now,*' muttered the bear biologist squelching along the shore. He could see the others in the distance, the PR man slipping away into the dead trees where, a few moments later, a column of steam indicated a hot spring.

Abruptly everything changed. There was a shower of shark teeth. Four sparrows flew over the lake. The bear man looked at the sky and wept. Argos the ornithologist stared at the

177

paycheck he held in his hand, the outline of a winged lobster scrawled on the back, the paper severely punctured by the point of the bad pen.

'I never believed it,' he said. But it was Warwick, the bear biologist, who had grappled with the searing truth when he understood in his marrow that demons were sprinkled throughout the world like croutons in a salad.

Back at his desk, Old Scratch tossed a metal token, a token such as those once used in whorehouses by customers with credit, into a drawer. Inscribed on it was Argos's name and a date.

'Illusions are a real bastard to hold steady,' he said. 'I'm beat.' He tapped idly with his long fingernails for a minute, then took out a pack of cards and began dealing himself poker hands.

'You got to know when to fold them,' he said. He shuffled the cards, producing a sound of whirring insect wings.

'The cicadas threw me off,' he said.

'Yes sir,' answered Duane Fork.

Testimony of the Donkey

Traveler, there is no path. Paths are
made by walking.
—Antonio Machado (1875-1939)

Marc was fourteen years older than Catlin, could speak three languages, was something of a self-declared epicure, a rock climber, an expert skier, a not-bad cellist, a man more at home in Europe than the American west, he said, but Catlin thought these differences were inconsequential although she had only been out of the state twice, spoke only American and played no instrument. They met and fell for each other in Idaho, where Marc was working as a volunteer on the fire line and Catlin was dishing up lasagna in the fire center cafeteria. After a few months they began to live together.

He had noticed her muscular legs as she strode along the counter snatching up pans empty of macaroni and cheese and asked her later if she would like to go hiking sometime. For the last two summers Catlin, against her parents' disapproval, had worked on an all-girl hay-stacking crew, and she had hiked Idaho's mountains since she was a child. She was strong and experienced. He knew an excellent

179

trail, he said. She said yes but doubted he could show her any trail she had not hiked.

He picked her up at four on Sunday morning and drove north. By sunrise she had figured it out: 'Seven Devils?' He nodded. And he was right. She had never been on the Dice Roll trail. It had a reputation for attracting tourists and she had always imagined it crowded by day-trippers tossing candy wrappers.

As they walked into the fragrant quietude of the pines she was suffused with euphoria, the old mountain trail excitement. Her earliest memory was of trying to clasp pollen-thick sunbeams streaming through stiff needles as she rode in the child carrier on her father's back. She associated the deep green canopy, the rough red bark with well-being. Marc smirked at her; he'd known she would like this trail. They moved in harmony. In midafternoon, her stomach growling with hunger, they reached a spectacular overlook into the chaos of Hell's Canyon. Marc's idea of lunch was two carrots, some string cheese and some fishy paste they scooped out of the container with the carrots. It didn't matter. They had shown each other their lapsarian atavistic tastes, their need for the forest, for the difficult and solitary, for what her father had called 'the eternal verities,' but which she secretly thought might be ephemeral verities. Yet Catlin's sensibilities tingled with a faint apprehension. She had never expected to meet such a person. Where was the catch?

Their time together stretched into four years. Catlin regaled him with family stories— her sleepwalking grandmother, the alcoholic cousin who fell off a Ferris wheel, her father's steady withdrawal from the family, her mother's generous humor. She told him about her only previous lover, a rapscallion type studying meteorology but now in Iraq. Their affair had been nothing, she said; they had slept together only twice before admitting a growing dislike for each other. Marc was quiet about his past and Catlin took him on lover's faith. His fine black hair rose in a Mephistophelian aura around his head when the wind blew—it was longer than the locals liked it—and his face bore an arched Iberian nose and narrow eyes with black irises and heavy brows. But in contrast to his darkly handsome face, he was rather short, with thick arms and small hands. He looked a little vicious, like an old artist whose eye is offended by contemporary daubs.

Catlin had been a plump baby with a face like a small pancake. Her adult face was still baby-round with fleshy cheeks and acne scars that gave her a slightly tough streetwise look. The hay-stacking job had made her muscular, an inch taller and ten pounds heavier than Marc. She had man-size feet that had never known high heels. Beauty salon visits lightened

181

and permed her limp blond hair into platinum waves that contrasted with her rough skin. She favored a blue-eyed, parted-lips look popularized by 1930s movie stars. She could hardly know that she resembled his mother.

At the end of the fire season they left Idaho for Lander, Wyoming, where Marc had the promise of a job with an outdoor climbing school. Housing was tight and they finally ended up in a drab single-wide trailer which Catlin said needed more color. She painted the walls cherry red, purple, orange. At a thrift store she found an old round table and sprayed it cobalt blue. A 1960s television set discovered in the shed behind the trailer became one of several shrines to her invented juju gods and fetishes—the Shrine of Never Falling, and the Shrine of Adventure.

'Very oriental,' said Marc in a tone that meant nothing. He was thinking of Tibet. After a few months he quit the job at the climbing school, saying only that he couldn't deal with so many flaming egos, didn't like the career life, the business of climbing. Still, he continued to climb with Ed Glide, his only local friend. He switched back to what he had done before firefighting—freelance work updating information on African countries for travelers' guidebooks, keeping track of insurrections, changing tastes in music and clothing, the whims of dictators. As a child he had lived in Ivory Coast and Zaire, then, as near as Catlin could make out, had spent his adult years in four or five Mediterranean countries. When she asked about that time he talked about plantains in fufu and other dishes. She changed the Shrine of Never Falling to a Shrine of Information for Travelers.

Their landlord was Biff, an elongated, chain-smoking old cowboy with a sweat stain on his hat that resembled the battlements of Jericho. Biff thought he'd discovered the secret of wealth by renting out his dead ex-wife's trailer. He did not like Catlin's color scheme.

'How in hell can I rent this place now? Looks like a carnival.' He was so thin he had to buy youth jeans. They were always too short. He stuffed the high-water ends into his run-down work boots.

'Well, you *are* renting it—to us.'

'When you're gone,' he said, rolling a fresh cigarette with maimed yellow fingers, squinting his triangular eyes against the smoke.

There was nothing to say to that. Only the day before she had asked Marc what he thought about building a cabin. She didn't want to say 'house.' It sounded too permanent. He only shrugged. That could mean anything. He had that evasive streak and it worried her. She asked once why he had come to Idaho and he answered that he had always wanted to be a cowboy. She had never seen him near a horse or a ranch. Was it a joke?

Catlin had been born and raised in Boise, the great-granddaughter of a Basque shepherd from the Pyrenees, and she sometimes told Marc that that made her European, although she had never been farther away from Idaho than Salt Lake City and Yellowstone Park.

The sheepherder ancestor had been ambitious. He became interested in the criminal physiognomy work of Bertillon and Galton and thought it was possible to make a composite photograph of the Universal Upright Man by overlaying photographs of respected men from every race. The project fell short when he could not find an Inuit, a Papuan, a Bushman or other Idaho rarities to photograph and coalesce. He became cynical about doing good in the world and turned his attention to money, opening a clothing store in Boise, a store that burgeoned into three, enough to provide the family with modest wealth.

Catlin had an allowance from her parents and could have scraped by without working, but she thought it would demoralize Marc. In Wyoming she found a part-time job with the local tourism office and they set her to puzzling out scenic motor tours for massive campers and RVs. That brought about the Shrine of Wide Roads with No Traffic and No Hills.

They maintained the fiction of independence because each owned a vehicle. The real focus of their lives was neither work nor clutching love, but wilderness travel. As many days and weeks as they could manage they spent hiking the Big Horns, the Wind Rivers, exploring old logging roads, digging around ancient mining claims. Marc had a hundred plans. He wanted to canoe the Boundary Waters, to kayak down the Labrador coast, to fish in Peru. They snowboarded the Wasatch, followed wolf packs in Yellowstone's backcountry. They spent long weekends in Utah's Canyonlands, in Wyoming's Red Desert Haystacks looking for fossils. The rough country was their emotional center.

But it wasn't all joy; sometimes the adventures went to vinegar—once when the snow came in mid-October, four feet of dry powder on bare ground, snow so insubstantial they sank through it until their skis grated on rock.

'Neige poudreuse. Give it a few days to settle and make a base,' he said. But it stayed cold and didn't pack, didn't settle, and that was it. The wind blew it around, wore it out. No more came in November, December, half of January. They were crazy with cabin fever, longing for snow. When Biff stopped by for the rent, he predicted, through a mouthful of chewing tobacco, a thousand-year drought.

'Happened before,' he said. 'Ask any

Anasazi.'

Then a line of storms moved in from the Pacific. Heavy snow and torrents of wind piled up seven-foot drifts. When they ran outside to load the skis and test the snow they could feel the tension, deep smothered sounds below indicating basal shifts.

'Today, no off *piste*,' said Marc. 'And we won't even try the trails. The old skid road is probably safe enough.'

On the drive up the mountain it began to snow again, and they passed men straining to push a truck out of the ditch. They crawled along in whiteout conditions.

They started skiing up the old logging road but in less than twenty minutes found it blocked by an ocean of broken snow. Looking up the east slope of the hill they could see the avalanche track, sack-shaped like the gut of a deer.

'Not good,' said Marc. 'No point going any farther. There's that terrain trap past the bridge.' They went home, Marc saying it was likely they could be called for avalanche rescue.

A violent wind battered the trailer half the night, the electric lights flickering. But the next morning the sky was milky blue. Marc squinted at it and sighed. They waited. By eleven the skin of cloud thickened. The left hand of the storm fell on them like a dropped rock. Marc's cell phone uttered an incongruous meadowlark call.

'Yes. Yes. Leaving now,' he said. Search and Rescue needed them. He reminded Catlin to put her radio transceiver in her jacket zip pocket.

'So we won't be part of the problem.' On the way he said that Ed Glide had remarked that the storm had brought out hundreds of people, who knew why? Well, because it had been a dry winter.

Catlin knew why. It was more than a dry winter. There was something about skiing in storms that thrilled certain people—climbers of dangerous rock at night, kayakers in ice-choked rivers, hikers who could not resist battering wind and hail.

At the trailhead excited people rushed around in the falling snow, shouting teenage snowboarders with huge packs on their backs, parents bellowing 'Get back here' at their children, skiers slipping through the trees, all disappearing into the bludgeoning white.

Ed Glide, beard as coarse as the stuffing in antique chair seats, dark nostrils reminding one of the open doors of a two-car garage, was standing in front of the billboard trail map using a ski pole as a pointer. The fresh rescue group listened, stamped around to keep their feet warm. Ed was talking about the lost snowmobiler rescued at dawn, naked and curled up under a tree.

'There's a shitload of snow in the

backcountry,' he said. 'And there's six damn kids on the Miner's trail. Snowshoes. They headed out this morning with one of the daddies to have a winter cookout at Horse Lake. There's that big cornice over the open slope along there. I doubt any of them's got enough sense to—' He had not finished the sentence when they all heard the heavy roar to the southwest. Even through the light snow they could see a vast cloud rising.

'Fuck!' shouted Ed. 'That's it. Let's go! Go!'

A mile along the trail they met two of the boys on snowshoes, stumbling along and repeatedly falling, red faces clotted with snow and frozen tears. The gasping boys said the group had almost reached Horse Lake when Mr. Shelman said the snow was too deep for a cookout and they turned back. They had barely recrossed the bottom of the open slope when the avalanche came. The others were under the snow.

The search crew spent the rest of the day looking for signs of survivors, probing, shoveling. None of the boys or Mr. Shelman had carried a transceiver. Distraught parents came postholing to the site and some of them brought the family dog. Someone found a mitten. The search went on through the night. It took two days to dig out the bodies, and forever to get over the sense of failure and loss.

'Cookout! What a fiasco,' said Marc. 'Poor

little kids.' He meant the two survivors, already stained with guilt at being alive.

*   *   *

Their best times were always their explorations into the remnants of the vanishing wild. They treasured discovering new country. She thought sometimes that they were seeing the end of the old world. She knew Marc felt it too. They were in such harmony that they had never had an argument until the lettuce fight.

They were leaving the next morning on a ten-day hike in the Old Bison range. The Jade trail had been closed for years but Marc relished the plan for an end run around the Forest Service. It was their practice to have a big dinner the night before they started an adventure, and then to eat sparingly in the wild, the feast a kind of Carnival before Lent. A little hunger, said Marc, makes the mind sharp. Catlin bought tomatoes, a head of lettuce, fillets of halibut at the local market. It was Marc's turn to make dinner. He was making aloko, an African dish of bananas cooked in palm oil with chile to accompany the fried halibut. And, of course, her salad.

Before he started cooking he took off his shirt, more efficient, he said, than putting on an apron. She knew it was because he didn't like the only apron in the house, a fire-engine red thing her mother had given her for a silly present. She said he would be burned by spattering grease. She said she didn't want to find chest hairs clinging to the lettuce.

'You worry too much,' he said. The oily smell of frying banana spread through the trailer.

She sorted gear for the trip. Why did he still prefer those antique primitivo boots studded with hobnails? 'Do you want a beer while you make the salad?'

'Isn't there any of that white wine left? Whatever it was.' He was cutting a red onion— the slices too thick. If he was so continental why couldn't he cut an onion properly? She found an opened bottle of the wine in the refrigerator, poured him a glass and stood watching as he finished slicing, waved the knife with a flourish and began hacking the lettuce.

'You didn't wash it,' she said. 'And you're supposed to tear the leaves, not cut them.'

'Babes, it's a clean lettuce, no dirt. Why wash it? Of course I would prefer a nice little endive, some mesclun, but what we've got is a big, tasteless, hard head of lettuce like a green cannonball. It deserves to be cut.' There was no doubt that he despised iceberg lettuce.

'Well, that's all they had. It came from California. Who knows if they sprayed it, or whether the one who picked it had a disease or TB or peed on it?' Her voice spiraled upward. Catlin was inclined to an organic, vegetarian

190

diet, a taste first professed when she was in her teens and designed to annoy her meat-and potatoes parents, a diet even more difficult to uphold in beef more-beef-and-potatoes Wyoming. She had considered herself sophisticated in food preferences until Marc. And although she usually gave in to him on whatever main dish he proposed, she insisted on the salad.

'Does everything have to be antiseptic? Does everything have to be done your way? It's only a salad, agreed, it is not a very good salad as we have only the most wretched of ingredients, but I'm making it, and you're eating it.' He, of course, would sniffily ignore the salad, gobble the bananas and chile heaped on the fish.

'Oh no. I'm not eating that salad. It's probably full of hairs.' He threw down the knife in exasperation.

There were a few more verbal jabs and then suddenly they were in a shouting match about fried bananas, Africa, Mexico, immigration policy, farm labor, olive trees, California. She said he was not only a filthy lettuce nonwasher but a foreign creep who would probably eat caterpillars. He was a freeloader (he was occasionally short on his share of the rent) and he couldn't even make a simple salad. He certainly didn't know how to slice an onion. And why wear those stupid hobnail boots that made him look like a nineteenth-century

Matterhorn guide? Maybe he'd like a pair of lederhosen for his birthday? He said he *had* eaten caterpillars in Africa and they were packed with protein and tasty, that the boots had belonged to his grandfather who had been a climber on serious Himalayan expeditions after the Second World War, that she had become controlling, headstrong, egotistical, provincial and unpleasant. Then came accusations of sexual failure and repulsive habits, of ex-lovers, of cheating and lying, the horrible wholesome flax-seed cereal she favored, his addiction to smelly cheeses and bread that had to be made because it could not be bought, and again the wretched hobnail boots. It was less argument than bitter testimony, as when, on the last night of Carneval in some towns in rural Spanish Galicia, a man presents the *testamento,* the rhymed and furious catalog of the village's sins in the past year, and fictionally apportions the body parts of a donkey to fit the sins. He had told her about this, and now he awarded her the donkey's flatulent gut as most expressive of her raving.

Hundreds of irritations and grievances each had kept closeted spouted from the volcanoes of their injured and insulted egos. Marc threw the salad bowl on the floor, the onion slices rolling on their broad edges. She threw his shirt in the salad. She poured olive oil on the shirt and said if he liked olive oil so much, why, here was plenty of it. She raced to the stove, seized the frying pan and dumped the banana-chile mess in the sink. When he tried to stop her she delivered him a head-ringing slap. She screamed imprecations but he was suddenly very quiet. The expression on his face was peculiar and familiar; anger and—yes, pleasure.

Then he recovered and as if to goad her began again. 'You American bitch!' he said, almost conversationally, but his voice sharpening with each word. 'You and this constipated place of white, narrow-minded Republicans with the same right-wing opinions. There's no diversity, there's no decent food, there's no conversation, there's no ideas, there's nothing except the scenery. And the Alps have more beautiful scenery than the Rockies.' He folded his arms and waited.

'Well, it's good to hear what you really think. Why don't you clear out. Go fuck old fat-legs Julia!' Her voice was a diabolic screech. Yet even as she yelled she was embarrassed by the florid theatricality of the scene. And he wondered how could she know anything about Julia. He had never mentioned her. Julia was his mother.

His lips infolded, he stalked through the rooms collecting his remaining clothes, his books, the maligned hobnail boots, his GPS unit and climbing gear, his skis, his African

193

mask collection, coldly packing everything into his truck. He said nothing while she continued to make caustic taunts. Striding through the kitchen he slipped on the olive oil and nearly fell. Humiliation deepened his anger. She noticed the bandage on his left hand was stained with pus and blood. A few days earlier, trying to strike flakes from a gleaming lump of obsidian Ed Glide had given him, he had driven a sliver deep into his hand. It must be infected, she thought with malicious joy.

The last thing he did was to rip down her poster of Big Train Johnson, the centerpiece of her Shrine to Idaho Baseball, showing the pitcher just after he'd hurled the ball, right-hand knuckles bent, an expression of mild curiosity on his plain face. Marc glared at her. It seemed to her he was presenting his face to get smacked again. She didn't move and abruptly he left.

Through the window she saw him get in his truck and drive away. South. Toward Denver, where, as he had said, there was more than one skin color, a cultural mix and an international airport.

She cleaned up the salad with his ruined shirt, crammed the greasy mess into a trash bag. Slowly she calmed and a brilliant thought came; she would hike the Jade trail without him. She didn't need him.

She slept only a few hours, waking twice to the knowledge that they had broken up. She got up with the first light, boiled a dozen eggs—good hiking trip food—and packed the Jeep. The phone rang as she was carrying out the last load.

'Catlin,' he said quietly. 'I've got two tickets to Athens on a flight tomorrow morning. I'm going to fight the wildfires in Greece. Will you come?'

'I've got other plans.' She hung up, then pulled out the phone cord. She tossed her watch and cell phone in the silverware drawer and rushed out the door. Somewhere along the way, not from *him,* she had learned that discarding the technology sharpened the senses, led to deeper awareness.

*   *   *

On the road driving north she felt she was once again in her own life. For miles she listened to music by groups he despised, reveling in the sense of liberation. He favored Alpha Blondy or monotonous talking-drum music on long drives. She could not stop thinking about the breakup, and after a while even her favorite tunes seemed to develop talking-drum backgrounds. Silence was better. She recalled the strangely pleased expression on Marc's face after she hit him, familiar but impossible to place in context.

It was dusk when she reached the town at the edge of the Big Bison National Forest. She found a motel. She did not want to miss the signless trailhead in evening gloom. The wind came up in the night, occasionally lifting her from sleep. Each time she stretched, thinking how wonderful it was to have the whole bed to herself. It was not until the morning that she discovered she had left the topo map back at the trailer in her haste to get out. At the local hardware store she found another, compiled from aerial photographs taken in 1958. It was better than the forgotten map as the Jade trail was clearly marked.

She found some paper in the glove compartment—the receipt for the last oil change—and with an old pencil stub that had rolled around on the dash for a year she scrawled her name, 'Jade Trail' and the date and left it on the seat.

Even in broad daylight the abandoned trail was difficult to find. Years before, the Forest Service had uprooted the sign and blocked off the entrance with fallen pines and boulders. Young lodgepole had grown up to shoulder height. The map showed that six miles north the trail flanked an unnamed mountain, then curled around half a dozen small glacier lakes. Marc had planned to fish those lakes. A disturbing thought came to her. He might not go to Athens but return to the trailer and find her gone, notice that all her camping gear was missing. He would know immediately that she had come up to hike the trail without him. He

196

would follow her. She would have to watch and dodge.

The first mile was unpleasant; the trail was rocky and the soil a fine dust half an inch deep. It was clear that many hikers ignored the 'Trail Closed' legend on the forest map and ventured up it for a mile or two before turning back. They had marked their passage with broken branches which clawed her arms.

Gradually the head-high trees disappeared as the trail led into the old forest. She walked soundlessly on the thick needle duff. The trail bent and opened onto views of forested slopes, showing thousands of deep red-orange trees killed by the mountain pine beetle infestation and drought. In open areas the trail was choked with seedlings reclaiming the ground. The young trees looked healthy and green, still untouched by the beetles. She wondered if the world was seeing the last of the lodgepole forests. If Marc had been with her they would have talked about this. The memory of his stained bandage came to her. He had determined to learn how to make stone projectile points. They had talked about prehistoric stone tools, and when he told her their edges were only a few microns thick and sharper than razors, she idly wondered aloud why terrorists did not arm themselves with chert knives that would escape airport detection. 'That's stupid,' he said.

After several miles of level ground the trail

began to climb and twist in a steep stairway of roots and rocks. Snowmelt had scoured it out to slick earth packed around bony flints. Around noon the trail broke into an explosion of wildflowers—columbine, penstemon, beautiful Clarkia, chickweed and Indian paintbrush. Delighted by the alpine meadow and a few banks of snow packed into clefts on the north sides of slopes, she looked down at a small lake. The scene was exquisitely beautiful. But even here it was not as cool as she had expected. The sun was strong and a cloud of gnats and mosquitoes warped around her in elliptical flight. She ate her lunch sitting in the shade of a giant boulder. She did not miss Marc.

She looked west at Buffalo Hunter, the highest peak in the range. Its year-round snow cover was gone and the peak stood obscenely bare, a pale grey summit quivering in radiant heat. Rock that had not seen sunlight in hundreds of years lay exposed. Another hot, dry summer, the sky filling with wind-torn clouds and lightning but no rain. Occasionally a few drops rattled the air before the clouds dragged them away. Next month the Arizona monsoon would move in with blessed rain, but now the flatland below was parched, the grasses seeded out and withered to a brittle tan wire that cracked underfoot. In the mountains the heat was almost as intense as at lower elevations, and the earth life-less gravel.

By late afternoon she was tired and reckoned she had hiked thirteen or fourteen miles. The Jade trail ran for another sixty-odd miles and came out on a dead trailhead near a mining ghost town. From the ruins to the main road was another four or five miles. She was sure she could do it easily in ten days. She pitched the little tent beside an unnamed glacier-melt lake. As she ate her hydrated tomato soup she watched trout rise to an evening hatch, the perfect circles spreading outward on the water, coalescing with other spreading circles. The setting sun illuminated the millions of flying insects as a glittering haze over the lake. Marc would have been down there matching the evening hatch, but he was probably in Greece by now. A grey jay, remembering the good old days when hikers had scattered bread crusts and potato chips along the trail, watched expectantly. She crumbled a cracker for him and gave him a name—Johnson, in honor of Big Train Johnson. The day left her a sky veneered with pink pearl, the black ridge against it serrated with pine tops like obsidian spear blades. She was not afraid of the dark and sat up listening to the night sounds until the last liquid smear of light in the west was gone. There was no moon.

She had slept on a stone and wakened stiff and aching in the vague morning. As soon as the sun came up the mountains began to heat, the few remaining snowdrifts melting to feed the gurgling rivulets that twisted through the alpine meadows. The snow patches lay in fantastic shapes, maps of remote archipelagoes, splatters of spilled yogurt, dirty legs, swan wings. There was no wind and the gnats and mosquitoes were bad enough that she slathered on insect repellent. She limbered up with a few bends and stretches, boiled water for tea, ate two of the boiled eggs in her pack and started off again. The eggs had picked up insect repellent from her fingers and the nasty smarting taste stayed in her mouth for a long time.

She hiked past half a dozen small lakes dimpled with rings from rising trout and thought of Marc. She could hear but not see a rushing stream under the willows, a stream that cascaded from the high melting snowbanks. Obscurant mountain willow grew thick wherever the water trickled. The shallow lakes, the color of brown khaki and denim blue, reflected the peaks and shrinking snowfields above. Some lakes were a profound, saturated blue shading out from tawny boulders at the edge to depths where the big fish rested in the coolest water. The waterlines marking shore boulders told that the lake levels once had been four or five feet higher.

The trail slanted steadily upward and was so badly overgrown that long sections melted into the general mountain terrain. Twice she lost it and had to scramble to a high point to see its continuation. She was close now to the height of land where the trail would run above tree line for seven or eight miles before starting down the west slope. This was country where great shelves and masses of shadowed rock displayed exquisite lichen worlds. She knew the lichen chemical factories broke down the rock into soil, some of them fanning across the stone like a stain, nitrogen-loving hot orange lichen where foxes had urinated. Marc had said once that lichens might have been the earth's first plants, that over millions of years they had converted the world's rock covering into the soil that allowed life; the lichens they saw were still devouring the mountains. On their hikes they had seen lichens in hundreds of shapes and colors—flames, antlers, specks and fiery dots, potato chips, caviar, blobs of jelly, corn kernels, green hair, tiny felt mittens, skin diseases, Lilliputian pink-rimmed cups. They always told each other that they were going to learn the lichens, and then, back home, never did.

The rocks themselves, wreathed to their knees in a foam of columbine blossom, were too beautiful to look at for long. One massive soft red rock, as large as three houses, was splotched with pea green lichen. She scratched at the lichen with her fingernail, but it was impervious to abrasion. Flowering plants grew on the rock's small ledges and shelves. This perfection of color and place, too rare and too much to absorb, induced a great sadness; she did not know why and thought it might be rooted in a primordial sense of the spiritual. In this wild place there were no signs of humans except the high mumble of an occasional jet. The solitude provoked existential thoughts, and she regretted the argument with Marc which fell steadily toward the importance of a fuzz of dust. But she was not unhappy to be alone. 'Puts things in perspective, right, Johnson?' she said to the grey jay who was following her.

*   *   *

On the next day around noon she reached a church-size rock about a hundred feet from a tan lake, really more cliff than rock, an interlocking system of glistening pink house-size chunks of granite cracked and fractured into blocks and shelves so huge a few young pines had found enough soil to keep them alive. Their forcing roots would split the rock in time. The ground between the cliff and the lake was littered with a talus of fallen boulders. A few miles away bare scree-covered slopes protruded from the gnarled krummholz, marking the trail's maximum height. She did not want to hike up there in late afternoon, to be forced by darkness to camp in the lightning zone. Even now torn grey clouds slid over the naked peaks. The map showed the tallest as 'Tolbert Mountain.' The sun was halfway down the western sky. She would quit for the day and camp here. She eased off her backpack and let it drop heavily to the trail. It made a hard clank. The trail here crossed a vast sheet of granite half a mile wide. To be free from the familiar weight was a luxury and she stretched.

High up on the pink cliff she thought she saw writing—initials and a date? Early miners and travelers had left their marks everywhere. She decided to scramble up and see what it was; maybe Jim Bridger, John Fremont or Jedediah Smith, or some other important historical figure. She felt a bitter dart of loss, like a thorn under the fingernail, that Marc wasn't with her. He would have shouted with joy at this beautiful trail and the pristine lakes, and he would have climbed directly to the inscription on the rock.

The bottom third of the cliff was a rubble of fallen breakstone encrusted with the nubby fabric of grey lichen. Then came fifty feet of climbable clean granite that gave way abruptly to an almost perpendicular wall of glinting stone bristling with jutting blocks. She was determined to get near enough to read the inscription, for she was sure the marks were weathered letters.

The climb was more difficult than it looked.

Several stones at the bottom wobbled a little, but so near the ground they seemed hardly a concern. Above them was a tiny trail formed by rain and snow runoff snaking down from an upper jam of more broken blocks, just wide enough for her foot. She inched up the tiny path as far as the lowest block and managed to claw her way around its side, not looking down. Now she was close enough to make out the letters daubed in black paint, JOSÉ 1931. Not a famous explorer after all—just some old Mexican sheepherder. So much for that.

Getting down was surprisingly awkward. Small rocks turned and slid beneath her feet. In one place she had to slide down a rough incline that rucked her pants uncomfortably up into her crotch. She was in a hurry to set up camp as soon as she got down. This would be the night to break out the pint of rum, maybe mix it with the bottle of cranberry juice she had lugged for days. She craved the thirst-quenching acidity.

Near the bottom she jumped eighteen inches onto the top stone in the jackstraw jumble. The stone swiveled as though it were on ball bearings. Her foot plunged down into the gap between it and another rock and with her weight off it, once more the huge stone shifted, pinning her leg. At first, while she struggled, she ignored the pain and thought of her situation as a temporary obstacle. Then, unable to move the rock or to pull out of its grip, she understood she was trapped.

It took a long time—several minutes—for her to grasp the situation because she was so furious. On the climb up that same block had shifted slightly with a stony rasp as though clearing its throat. Because it was less than two feet from the ground she had considered it inconsequential. She had not taken care. If Marc had been with her he would have said something like 'Watch out for this rock.' And if Marc was with her he could push or pry up the rock long enough for her to pull her leg out. If Marc was with her. If anyone was with her. She certainly knew the stupidity of hiking alone. She had climbed up there because that was what Marc would have done. So, in a causative way, he was there.

She kept trying to pull the rapidly swelling leg free. The rock pressed against her calf and knee. She could slightly move her ankle and foot. That was the only good news. As a child she had learned that those who did not give up lived, while those who quit trying died. And sometimes those who did not give up died anyway. She thought of her chances. If Marc went back to the trailer he would find the forgotten map on the kitchen table. He would see her camping gear was missing. He would know she was on the Jade trail and he would come. Unless, said her dark, inner voice, unless he was in Greece on some fire line. And if he was in Greece, would Forest Service personnel notice her jeep sitting there day after day? Would they see her note on the front seat, now six days old, and come looking? Those were her chances: to free herself; for Marc to come; for a Forest Service search and rescue. There was one more slender possibility. Another hiker or fisherman might take the closed trail. In the meantime she was mad thirsty. Her backpack was on the trail where she had dropped it, but because it was behind her she could not even see it. In it were the cranberry juice, food, the tiny stove, matches, a signal mirror—everything. In frustration she heaved at the rock which did not move.

As twilight advanced she cried angrily, raging at the tiny misstep that might cost her everything. Her tongue stuck to the roof of her dry mouth. Eventually, leaning against the cooling rock, she fell into a half doze, starting awake many times. Her trapped leg was numb. Thirst and the cold mountain air fastened onto her like leeches. Her neck ached, and she pulled her shoulders forward. She shivered, wrapped her arm around herself, but the shivering intensified until she was racked with deep, clenching shudders. Possible scenes rolled through her head. Could she get so cold the trapped leg would shrink enough to let her pull it out? She pulled again, the fiftieth time, and could feel the edge of the huge stone pressing down on the top of her kneecap.

Could she summon the strength to pull the leg relentlessly up even if the edge of the rock cut or crushed the kneecap? She tried until the pain overwhelmed. The effort eased the shuddering for a few minutes, but soon her muscles were clenching violently again. She prayed for morning, remembered how hot it had been every day. She thought if she could just get warm she would get back some strength, and if she had water, after she drank, surely she could get the leg out. She could pour water—if she had it—down her leg and perhaps the water would provide enough lubrication to let her get free. As she thought about this she realized that urine might both warm her and lubricate the trapped leg. But the warmth was fleeting and any lubrication went unnoticed by the rock, which had now passed from inanimate object to malevolent personality.

Between shuddering spasms she fell into tiny snatches of sleep just a few seconds in duration. Finally the stars paled and the sky turned the color of crabapple jelly.

'Come on, come on,' she begged the sun, which rose with interminable slowness. At last sunlight struck the ridge to the west, but she was still in cold shadow. An hour passed. She could hear birds. One perched on the edge of the cruel rock just out of her reach. If she could seize it she would bite its head off and drink the blood. But the air was slowly warming even if the sun rays were still not touching the rock. Her leg felt like a great pounding column. At last the blessed sun fell across her body, and gradually the shuddering slowed. The wonderful heat relaxed her and she nodded off for long minutes. But each time she snapped awake her thirst was a disease, enflaming every pore of her body, swelling her throat. She could feel her fat tongue thickening.

The sun's warmth, so pleasant and grateful, became heat, burning her exposed arms, her neck and face. The eagles screamed overhead. By noon her smarting skin and clamorous thirst over-shadowed the injured leg. Her eyes were scratchy and hot, and she had to blink to see the distant scree cones that seemed to pulse in the heat. By sunset those naked peaks had changed to heaps of glowing metal shavings. Several times throughout the day she imagined Marc's approach and called out to him. A fox ran up toward the snowbank with something in its mouth.

Now she took new stock of the object that was imprisoning her. It was an irregularly shaped block of granite roughly three feet long and two feet high, the top a sloping table with a scooped declivity a foot or so long and perhaps two inches deep in the center. She could just reach the declivity with her fingers.

The sun notched down the sky, changing the rock shadows. A curious marmot ran to the top of the adjacent rock and stared at her, ran down beneath it, reappeared from a different direction. Johnson, the grey jay, flew in and out of her vision so often he seemed a floater. There was nothing to see but Johnson, the marmot, the dots of black lichen, the eagles in the sky. There was only one thing to think about. Then, as the sun declined, there was another: night and cold.

The rock lost its heat slowly but with cruel inevitability. The sun crashed below the horizon and immediately a stream of chill air flowed down from the snow slopes. At first the coolness felt good on her burned skin, but within the hour she was shivering. She knew what was coming and so did her body, which seemed to brace itself. Far overhead she heard the drone of a small plane engine. Her mind raced to think of a way she could signal a plane the next day. She had a reflecting mirror in her backpack. If only she had worn her watch; if only she had brought the cell phone. If only she was not alone. If only she and Marc had not quarreled. If only he would come. Now. She thought that the sounds of his approach she had imagined during the day must have been a fox raiding her backpack. The night dragged and she dozed woozily for longer periods, minutes instead of seconds, bent over at the waist, for the rock made a kind of slanting table at just the height to cripple cotton pickers and short-row hoers. The leg alternated between numbness and throbbing.

The morning was bitterly familiar. She felt she had been trapped here since infancy. Nothing before the rock was real. She was a mouse in a mousetrap. Everything was the same, the brightening sky, the yearning for the sun's heat. Her tongue filled her mouth and her fingers were stiff. She mistook the grey jay, Johnson, standing two feet away from her on the far edge of the rock, for a wolf. The dull peaks at the height of land were very like monstrous ocean waves, and she could see them swell and roll. The surface of the rock holding her in its grasp was fine-grained, lustrous, dotted with pinprick lichens. The sky bent over the rock. Something smelled bad. Was it her leg or her urine-soaked jeans. Again her drying eyes went to the ocean waves, back down to the rock, to Johnson, who had now taken the guise of the sleeve of her grey chenille bathrobe, to the surface of the rock, to her cramping hands and back again to the naked scree slopes. She had not known that dying could be so boring. She fell asleep for moments and dreamed about the granite mousetrap, built with such care by an unknown stonemason. She dreamed that her father had pulled up a chair nearby. He said that her leg was going to wither and drop off, but that she could make a nice crutch from a small pine and hop back down the trail. She dreamed that a rare butterfly landed on the rock and an entomologist who looked like Marc came for it, easily lifting the stone from her leg and showing her the special mountain wheelchair he had brought to get her down the slopes.

When she snapped back to consciousness the sky hunched over the rock, the slopes, the high snowbanks oozed and sagged, undulating in rhythm with the bald knobs. Time itself writhed and fluttered. Johnson the jay was making thick booming sounds such as no bird had ever before produced. He was a drum, an empty oil barrel on which someone was beating a message, a talking drum. She almost understood. The sun seemed to go up and down like a yo-yo, splitting her eyes with light, then disappearing. Something was happening. She could just make out tiny lichens, transparent, hopping on the stone, on the backs of her hands, on her head and arms. She opened her mouth and the lichens became rain falling on her roasted tongue. Immediately she felt a surge of gratification and pleasure. She cupped her hands to catch the rain but they were too stiff. The rain poured off her hair, dripped from the end of her nose, soaked her shirt, filled the declivity in the top of the rock with blessed water that she could not quite reach.

She drank the downpour, feeling strength and reason return. When the storm moved away her head was clearer. The hard blue sky pressed down and the sun began to pull in the

211

moisture like someone reeling in a hose. She managed to get her shirt off and by making a feeble toss at the water-filled declivity, which held several cups of water, landed one sleeve in the precious puddle. She pulled it toward her and sucked the moisture from the sleeve, repeating the gesture until she had swallowed it all. Not far away she could hear one of the tiny mountain streams rattling through the stones. Her mind was lucid enough to realize that the rain might have only postponed one of the eternal verities. She could see other thunderheads to the east, but nothing to the northwest, the direction of the prevailing wind. The grey jay was not in her sight line.

She had sopped the declivity dry with her shirt, and now she pulled it back on against the burning sun. The gravelly soil had swallowed the rain. There was nothing to do but squint against the glittering world. The cycle started once more. Within an hour her thirst, which, before the storm, had begun to dim, returned with ferocity. Her entire body, her fingernails, her inner ears, the ends of her greasy hair, screamed for water. She bored holes in the sky looking for more rain.

In the night lightning teased in the distance but no more rain fell. The top of the imprisoning rock became a radiant plain under a sliver of ancient moonlight.

By morning the temporary jolt of strength and clarity was gone. She felt as though electricity was shooting up through the rock and into her torso, needles and pins and the numbness that followed was almost welcome, although she dimly knew what it meant. Apparitions swarmed from the snowbanks above, fountains and dervishes, streaming spigots, a helicopter with a waterslide, a crowd of garishly dressed people reaching down, extending their hands to her. All day a desiccating hot wind blew and made her nearly blind. She could not close her eyes. The sun was horrible and her tongue hung in her mouth like a metal bell clapper, clacking against her teeth. Her hands and arms had changed to black and grey leather, a kind of lichen. Her ears swarmed with rattling and buzzing and her shirt seemed made of a stiff metal that chafed her lizard skin.

In the long struggle to get her painful shirt off, through the buzzing in her ears, through her cracking skin she heard Marc. He was wearing the hobnail boots and coming up the trail behind her. This was no illusion. She fought to clear her senses and heard it clearly, the hobnail boots sharply click-click-clicking up the granite section of trail. She tried to call his name, but 'Marc' came out as a guttural roar, *'Maaaa . . .,'* a thick and frightening primeval sound. It startled the doe and her half-grown fawns behind her, and they clattered down the trail, black hooves clicking over the rock out of sight and out of hearing.

Tits-Up in a Ditch

Her mother had been knockout beautiful and no good and Dakotah had heard this from the time she recognized words. People said that Shaina Lister with aquamarine eyes and curls the shining maroon of waterbirch bark had won all the kiddie beauty contests and then had become the high school slut, knocked up when she was fifteen and cutting out the day after Dakotah was born, slinking and wincing, still in her hospital johnny, down the back stairs of Mercy Maternity to the street, where one of her greasy pals picked her up and headed west for Los Angeles. It was the same day television evangelist Jim Bakker, a found-out and confessed adulterer, resigned from his Praise the Lord money mill, his fall mourned by Bonita Lister, Shaina's mother. Bonita's husband, Verl, blamed the television for Shaina's wildness and her hatred of the ranch.

'She seen it was okay on the teevee and so she done it.' He said he wanted to get rid of the set but Bonita said there was no sense in locking up the horse after the barn burned down. Although Verl deplored the corrupting influence of television he said that since he was paying for the electricity he might as well get some use out of the thing. And saw danger, mystery, secrets and humiliation.

214

Verl and Bonita Lister were in their late thirties and stuck with the baby. If it had been a boy, Verl said, letting the words squeeze out around his roll-yer-own, he could have helped with the chores when he got to size. And inherited the ranch, was the implied finish to the sentence. Verl had named Dakotah after his homesteading great-grandmother, born in the territory, married and widowed and married again only after she had proved up on the place and the deed was in her name and in her hand. Later she was known for ridding the family of fleas by boiling the wash in a mixture of sheep dip and kerosene. In a day when the mourning period for a husband was two or three years and for a wife was three months, she had worn black for her first husband an insulting six weeks, then taken up a homestead claim. Verl treasured a photograph showing her with the precious deed, standing in front of her neat clapboarded house, a frowsy white dog leaning against her checkered skirt. She held one hand behind her back, and Verl said this was because she smoked a pipe. Dakotah was almost sure she could see a wisp of smoke curling up, but Bonita said it was dust raised by the wind. Since that pioneer time the country had become trammeled and gnawed, stippled with cattle, coal mines, oil wells and gas rigs, striated with pipelines. The road to the ranch had been named Sixteen Mile, though no one was sure what that distance

215

signified.

Bottle-blond Bonita (her great-grandfather had been a squaw man and black hair was in the genes) made an early grandmother. Ranch-raised and trained, she counted the grandchild as a difficulty that had to be met. She was used to praising thankless work as the right and good way, but what she was going to do without Jim Bakker's exhortation and encouragement she didn't know. First, an impaired husband, the endless labor and (sometimes forced) good humor that was expected of women, then a bad-girl daughter, and now the bad girl's baby to raise. Verl Lister was burden enough. He could not run the ranch alone and they often had to ask their neighbors to throw together and help out. Of course it was because he had been a wild boy in his youth, had rodeoed hard, a bareback rider who suffered falls, hyperextensions and breaks that had bloomed into arthritis and aches as he aged. A trampling had broken his pelvis and legs so that now he walked with the slinking crouch of a bagpipe player. She could not fault him for ancient injuries, and remembered him as the straight-backed, curly-headed young man with beautiful eyes sitting on his horse, back straight as a metal fence post. But a man, she thought, was supposed to endure pain silently, cowboy up and not bitch about it all day long. She, too, had arthritis in her left knee, but she suffered in silence.

216

Throughout the 1980s it was a puzzle where all the able-bodied labor had gone. During the energy boom, oil companies had sucked up Wyoming boys, offering high wages that no rancher, not even Wyatt Match, the county's richest cattleman, could pay. When the bust came there were still no ranch hands for hire. 'You'd think,' said Verl, 'with all them oil companies pullin out there'd be fifty guys on every corner lookin for work.' But the hands, after their taste of roustabout money, had followed the dollar away from Wyoming.

Verl was a trash rancher, said Wyatt Match, oyster eyes sliding around behind his gold-rimmed lenses that darkened in sunlight, and not so much because his land was overgrazed, but because there were fences down and gates hanging by one hinge, binder twine everywhere, rusting machinery in the pastures, and because the Listers' kitchen table was covered with a vinyl tablecloth showing the Last Supper. There was an old sedan with the hood up in one of the irrigation ditches. A defunct electric stove rested on the front porch. The Lister cows roamed the roads, constantly suffered accidents, drowning in the creek in spring flood, bogging in mud pots that came from nowhere.

Spring was the hardest time, the weather alternating between blizzards and Saharan heat. On a snow-whipped evening, Dakotah setting the table for supper, Verl said a cow who had tried to climb a steep, wet slope that apparently slid out from under her, had landed on her back in the ditch.

'Had me some luck today. Goddamn cow got herself tits-up in the ditch couple days ago. Dead, time I found her,' he said in a curiously satisfied tone, squinting through faded lashes, winking his eyes, the same aquamarine color as those of the wayward Shaina.

'Not every man would say that is luck,' said Bonita wearily. She pulled at a stray thread protruding from the leg seam of her pink slacks. It was an impractical color but she believed pastels projected freshness and youth. She went to the sink, stepping over Bum, Verl's ancient heeler crippled by cow kicks, and began scrubbing out the only pot large enough to boil potatoes in quantity, a pot she used several times a day.

'It is, in a way of speakin.'

She couldn't puzzle that one out, even if she had had the time. With Verl it was one thing after another. He went into the national forest to cut wood every fall, and she knew that he someday would cut himself in half with the cranky old chain saw. She almost hoped he would.

For Verl Lister everything turned on luck, and he had experienced very little of the good kind. His secret boyhood dream had been to become a charismatic radio man meeting singing personalities, giving the news,

218

announcing songs, describing the weather. All of this grew from a small, cheap radio he had earned as a boy selling Rosebud salve, riding ranch to ranch on an aged mare. At night, forbidden to listen past nine o'clock, he put it under the covers and turned it whisper low, listening to honey-voiced Paul Kallinger on a high-watt border station, the lonely hearts club ads, pitches for tonics and elixirs, yodeling cowboys, and, by the time he was in his teens, Wolfman Jack of scandalous sex talk and panting and howls. Yet he never wanted to be like Wolfman Jack. Kallinger was his ideal.

He had no idea how to get into the radio game, as he thought of it, and the plan faded as he grew into work on the home ranch. For fun he rode broncs, the source of his present miseries. He still kept the radio in his truck on constantly, had a radio in every room of the house despite the region's bad reception. Mostly he listened to the stations that featured songs about lost love and drinking, used car sales ads, church doings and auctions, stations that were pale imitations of the old border blasters of his youth. When NPR came to Wyoming in the 1960s, he judged it dull and hoity-toity. For him television was never as good as radio. He found that screen images were inferior to those in his mind.

*　　　*　　　*

Growing up, Wyatt Match had been given every advantage. He had good horses from the time he could walk, trips abroad, hand-tooled boots. He went to an eastern prep school and then the University of Pennsylvania. After graduation he came back to Wyoming with one or two ideas about agricultural progress and tried too soon to get into the legislature when the times favored conservative, frugal ranchers as political leaders, not spendthrift rich men, a label his father's private golf course had burned into an envious population. Over the years he had become a sharp-horned archconservative with a hard little mind like a diamond chip. After his youthful start flirting with useless ideas sown by the eastern professors, he had dedicated himself to maintaining the romantic heritage of the nineteenth-century ranch, Wyoming's golden time. Descended from Irish stock, he had a milky skin that flamed with sunburn, and his ginger hair had turned a saintly white. His pride was a blue neon sign—MATCH RANCH—near his monstrous post-and-lintel gate large enough to be the torii of a Shinto shrine. After years of trying he had finally made it into the state legislature. Local people were used to seeing his dusty Silverado bulge out onto the road and pass them on the right, throwing up a storm of gravel.

There was a tinge of superiority in all that he said, even in meaningless comments about weather. Match seemed to indicate that blizzards, windstorms, icy roads and punishing hail were for other people; he moved in a cloud of different, special weather. In the days when he was trying to push his way into the legislature with his radical ideas, a well-respected older rancher took him aside and told him, stressing his words, that Wyoming was *fine just the way it was.* Gradually he learned the truth of that statement.

His political value increased after he married Debra Gale Sunchley, a fifth-generation Wyoming ranch woman, a hard worker with a built-in capacity for endurance who dressed in crease-ironed jeans, boots and an old Carhartt jacket. The first Sunchley had come to Wyoming with the 11th Ohio Volunteers to fight Indians after the Civil War. Stationed at Post Greasewood on the North Platte, he deserted, hid out with a Finn coal mining family in Carbon and eventually married one of the daughters, Johanna Haapakoski.

Debra Gale Sunchley Match was secretary-treasurer of the Cow Belles, and member of the Christian Women's Book Circle. The Book Circle, always striving to do good and become better, favored memoirs by old cowboys and ranchers who personified grit and endurance. Debra Gale had read no more than ten books in her life but knew she had as much right as anyone to give her opinion. After Wyatt divorced her to marry Carol Shovel, whom he had met on a California golf vacation, Debra Gale and her brother Tuffy Sunchley stayed on as joint ranch managers. Match built his ex-wife her own house on the property, a simple one-story ranch with a big shed for her nine dogs. He paid her a wage. She was a good worker and he wasn't going to let her go.

*　　　*　　　*

As Dakotah grew up the Lister ranch staggered along, Bonita making ends meet, worrying about money and Verl's health. The only free time she had was kneeling at the side of the bed saying her prayers, asking for strength to go on and for her husband's well-being.

'Don't let yourself get old before your time,' she said impatiently to Verl who seemed to look forward to old age. It took half an hour in the morning for him to limber up his joints. It irritated her that the child, Dakotah, had little interest in riding or rodeo, resisted 4-H meetings. Bonita could always think of some task or job for the girl, whether collecting eggs, picking over beans or discovering the section of broken fence where the cows got out. Scraping the burned toast for Verl was the most hated task. Verl insisted on toast but would not part with the money for a toaster.

'My mother made good toast on the griddle.

222

It come already buttered,' he said. Bonita often burned the toast as she tried to cook eggs and hash, forgetting the smoking bread. Dakotah rasped the charcoal into the sink with a table knife.

Once, moved by some filament of need for affection, Dakotah tried to hug Bonita, who was scrubbing potatoes in the sink. Bonita briskly shoved her away. Once in a while Dakotah wandered around the ranch on foot, usually heading for the steep pine slope with a tiny spring, the ground littered with old grey bones from a time when a mountain lion had her den beneath a fallen tree. Bonita herself never went for a walk, a wasteful dereliction of duty. She worked spring branding with the men and still managed dinner for all hands, was again on a horse at November sale time overseeing the cows prodded into cattle trucks with Swiss-cheese sides while Verl cut winter wood in the forest. Verl walked nowhere, was always in his truck when he wasn't in the reclining chair he favored. He would come into the house and sigh.

'Well, I had me some luck today,' he would say in his plaintive voice.

She waited. This might be one of his slow unwinding stories that went nowhere, wasted her time.

'Filled up the gas can, got up there in the woods and damned if the can hadn't tipped over and spilled out all the gas.'

Yes, it was. He was speaking in his portentous, I've-got-grave-news voice. She nodded, scraped carrots, making the orange fiber fly. She was still in her red pajama bottoms, had pushed the heifers out of the east pasture, mended a broken section of fence, got the mail, fed the bum lambs and was now cooking dinner. There had been no time to pull on a pair of jeans. She wasn't going to town anyway.

'And then I got to workin awhile and the chain broke.'

'Well, you surely had problems.' Once, oppressed by Verl's self-pitying complaints, she had considered poisoning him. But they carried no insurance and how she could manage alone she didn't know and gave up the idea. Then, too, she never forgot the joyous winter when they were courting, the long freezing drive in from the ranch in a truck with a broken heater to meet him at the Double Arrow Café. Her teeth chattering, she would walk from the snowy street into the wonderfully hot and noisy bar, Russ Eftink punching G5 again and again to make 'Blue Bayou' play continuously, and Verl, the tough handsome cowboy, slouching across the room toward her and pulling her into the music. Into the pot went the carrots and she started on potatoes with an ancient peeler that had been in the kitchen since Verl's great-grandmother's day. The wood handle had broken away

224

decades earlier. Most of her kitchen tools were old or broken—an egg-beater with a loose handle bolt that fell into the mixture, a chipped and rusted enamel colander, warped frying pans and spoons worn to the quick.

His voice lifted. 'And my chest didn't hurt today the way it done yesterday.'

'Uh-huh.' She rinsed the potatoes and cubed them so they would cook faster.

'I supposed to go see her, that doctor, tomorrow mornin at ten minutes before eight. I don't know if I should now. Seein it didn't hurt today.'

'Well, Verl, it might a been a matter a luck, don't you think? That it didn't hurt and you workin so hard.'

He squinted at her, trying to tell if she was being sarcastic. 'It's just I don't want a leave you all alone, and me dead of a heart attack,' he said sanctimoniously.

She said nothing.

'So I guess I better go.' It was what he'd intended to do from the beginning.

*   *   *

Wyatt Match thought Verl Lister's dilapidated place gave Wyoming ranchers a slob name. He personally thanked heaven that Lister was not on the main road. He often quoted Robert Frost's line 'good fences make good neighbors' without understanding the poem or the

225

differences of intent between those who made fences of stone and those who used barbed wire. He had picked the Listers to criticize, and whether it was Verl's work habits or the way he never looked straight at anyone except in the left eye, or Bonita's aqua rayon pantsuit, Wyatt Match made them out to be the county fools. In truth, Verl Lister's cows were wild and rough because they were rarely worked; they suffered parasites, hoof rot, milk fever, prolapses and hernias; they were shot by rifle and bow and arrow, they fell on tee-posts, ate wire, coughed and snuffled, fell into streams and drowned. Verl referred to Match as 'him and his click. Them bastards pretty much run things the way they want.' Yet if he met Match at a cattle sale or the feed store, he would smile and greet him cordially. And Match, in his turn, would say, 'How'r you, Verl?' But if they crossed on the back roads in their trucks, Verl lifted three fingers in salute while Match, face bright with sun color, stared straight ahead. Pete Azkua, the grandson of a Basque sheep rancher, put it simply: *'Nahi bezala haundiak ahal bezala ttipiak,'* which he said meant the big boys do what they want, the small fry do what they can, which accounted for certain sour faces around town.

Verl resented Match, but it was Match's second wife, Carol Shovel, whom he truly detested. She was a California woman with red eyebrows and foxy hair, clothed in revealing dresses and garnished with clanking bracelets. She considered herself an authority on everything. She was a smart-mouth. No one knew why she had married Match. Of course, they said, he did have money, not from ranching, but through the Cowboy Slim Program, his father's patented weight-loss mail-order plan. Carol Match had endless recipes for Wyoming's betterment: bring back the train or start up a bus line for public transportation; invite black people and Asians to move in and improve ethnic diversity; shift the capital to Cody; make the state attractive to moviemakers and computer commuters. It got around that she had said Wyoming people were lazy. *Lazy!* Verl was outraged. Although he himself avoided as much work as he could, it was because he was half-crippled and work was bad for his heart. The whole world, except this California bitch, knew that there were no more frugal, thrifty, tough and hardworking people on the face of the earth than those in Wyoming. Work was almost holy, good physical labor done cheerfully and for its own sake, the center of each day, the node of Wyoming life. That and toughing it out when adversity struck, accepting that it was not necessary to wear a seat belt because when it was time for you to go, you went. Not being constrained by a seat belt was the pioneer spirit of freedom.

'I'd sure tell *her* where to set her empties,

but you can't tell nobody like that nothin,' he said to Bonita. 'She is too ignorant. It would just be water off a duck's ass.'

One day in the auto parts store, where Carol Match was checking to see if their order for a side window sunscreen for the restored 1948 Chevy half-ton had come in, he listened to her talk to Chet Bree behind the counter. She was wearing a tiny blue skirt with a hem just below her fatty buttocks and a silky top that showed off her robust tanned breasts.

'They have *got* to put a traffic light at that intersection. Somebody is going to get killed one day.' Her bracelets rattled.

'Always been okay the way it is. Just got to be a little bit careful. People here never had no trouble with it.' Bree looked at her chest for a few seconds, then looked away, then again let his gaze slide down into the cleft. Verl almost had the view of her bum.

'The place needs some new people,' she said.

Verl understood that she didn't just mean importing strangers. She meant an exchange. For every ignorant California fool she brought in, a Wyoming-born native would be . . . removed. He was sure she had a list and that he was on it. Bree said nothing, and that, thought Verl, had probably got him on the list.

'Wyomin is fine just the way it is,' said Verl to Bonita. 'They come in here and . . .'

For Dakotah, kindergarten was packed with revelations. On the first day the teacher, a fat woman with a pink, hairy sweater, asked each child for a birthday date.

'We'll have a party each time it is somebody's birthday,' she said with false excitement. One by one the children named dates, but Dakotah, who had never had or heard of a birthday party, was confused. The boy next to her said, 'December nine.'

The teacher looked expectantly at Dakotah.

'December nine,' she whispered.

'Oh, class! Did you hear that? Dakotah has the same birthday as Billy! That's so wonderful! We'll have a double birthday party! Two children have the same birthday! We'll have two cakes!'

Riding home in the truck with Bonita, Dakotah asked if she had a birthday and if it was December nine.

'Well of course. Everbody has a birthday! Yours is April first, April Fools' Day. That's when you play mean tricks on somebody. Like the April Fool trick your mother pulled on us. Why do you want to know?'

Dakotah explained that the teacher wanted to make many parties at school for birthdays with cakes and games. And she didn't know her birthday. And there was a song.

'Well, we never went in for that birthday

229

stuff. We don't do such foolishness. No wonder the school is always runnin out a money if they spend it on cakes.'

She knew she could not tell the teacher her birthday was an April Fool.

In school she learned again what she already knew; that she was different from others, unworthy of friends.

The Listers did their duty, raising Dakotah, Bonita making peanut butter sandwiches for her school lunch while listening to *Morning Glory,* the pre-sunrise program of advertisements, a little news of the sensational kind, prayer and weather reports. The radio voices roared in the bathroom where Verl crouched on the toilet with chronic constipation. His chest pain, which often migrated to some remote interior organ where it pulsed and gnawed, had long baffled the young woman doctor from India who tried to fit into the rural life by uncomprehendingly attending the local amusements of fishing derbies, calcuttas, poker runs and darts tournaments.

'You see Jimmy Mint catch that three-hundred-dollar fish?' she asked to put him at ease. He preferred to describe his torments in exquisite detail, drawing the devious path of a pain with his finger, tracking across his chest, down to his groin, around to the side and back again, rising to the throat.

*   *   *

At last the doctor sent Verl to Salt Lake City for advanced tests. Bonita went with him after arranging for Dakotah to stay with Pastor Alf Crashbee and his wife, Marva.

Dakotah, then seven years old, stood shyly in the hallway while Bonita and Marva Crashbee talked. Mrs. Crashbee spoke in emphatic phrases to set up her salient points. She puffed her cheeks and her nostrils flared. As Dakotah waited to be told where to go and what to do, she fell in love with a candy dish. The single piece of furniture in the hallway was a long, narrow table. On its gleaming surface rested Mrs. Crashbee's car keys. On the farthest end was a small blue plate, close to a saucer in size, and shaped like a fish. On it were seven or eight watermelon-flavored Jolly Rancher candies. It was the amusing shape and color of the dish that entranced, variegated blues ranging from cobalt to flushes of teal. Mrs. Crashbee noticed her gaping and told her to help herself to Jolly Ranchers, thinking that the poor thing probably never had much candy. After Bonita left she said it again in a spasm of urging.

'Go *ahead!* Help your*self.*'

Dakotah took one and unwrapped it, not sure where to put the wrapper. The pastor's wife led the way into the kitchen and pointed

231

at a chrome can. When Dakotah tried to lift the lid, the pastor's wife motioned her away, trod on a foot pedal, and the lid flew open. This, too, was novel. She blushed with shame because she had not known about the foot pedal. At her grandparents' house, trash went into a paper grocery bag sitting on a newspaper, and when it was full, the sides grease-stained, the bottom often weakened by wet coffee grounds, it was her job to carry the bag out to the burn barrel. This was the only time she was allowed to light matches, which she did with the gravity of one lighting a vestal hearth, then ran from the stinking smoke.

Bonita came alone to pick her up. She told Mrs. Crashbee that Verl's tests showed serious arthritis in his joints and lumps of bone where old breaks had healed badly, but that not much could be done. He needed a whole new skeleton and his heart was weak. A bull had stepped on his chest when he was twenty and bruised his heart. They told him to take it easy.

'He's at home resting this very minute,' said Bonita.

In some way Dakotah's coat sleeve brushed the blue dish off the hall table. Jolly Ranchers skittered along the floor like pale red nuts.

'For pity's sake,' said Bonita, bending down to pick up the pieces, 'clumsy as a calf.' Mrs. Crashbee, shaking her head and thrusting out her chin, said, 'It is *noth*ing, just an *old cheap dish*,' but her tone implied it had been part of a set of Royal Worcester. Bonita gave Dakotah a good leg whipping when they got home.

Mrs. Crashbee had a microwave oven that had magically heated the soup for lunch. When Dakotah described this marvel to Bonita a few days later, Verl, who was listening from his chair in the living room, snorted and shouted that he guessed he would stick with the good old kitchen stove. It was a way of saying there would be no microwave oven for Bonita, who had shown some interest in Dakotah's description.

*   *   *

Thin and with colorless brown-grey hair and greyish eyes, yet with a boy-size nose and chin, no trace of her mother's vivid beauty, in school Dakotah hunched over and kept to herself, considered somewhat stupid by her teachers.

In the fourth grade Sherri Match brought four kittens to school.

'They're for free,' she said. 'You can choose.'

Dakotah instantly wanted the tiny black one with white paws and a diminutive tail that stood straight up. She smoothed him and he purred.

'You can have him,' said Sherri grandly, the dispenser of munificence.

Dakotah brought the kitten home under her sweater, where he scratched and wriggled,

233

terribly strong for such a small creature. In Bonita's kitchen she gave him a doll's saucer of milk. He sneezed, then drank greedily. Bonita said nothing, but her expression was chill.

'Where'd that cat come from?' demanded Verl at supper.

'Sherri Match was givin kitties away.'

'I bet she was,' said Verl grimly. 'Well it can't stay here. Cats give me asthma. I'll take it back to them goddamn Matches,' and he picked up the kitten and strode out to the truck.

At school the next day Dakotah mumbled to Sherri that she was sorry her granddad had brought the kitten back. 'He said cats give him asmar.'

Sherri looked at her. 'He didn't bring it back. He didn't come to our house. What's asmar?'

*   *   *

As she approached her teens the leg whippings stopped. Bonita seemed to soften through time or remorse. Yet as Dakotah filled out her grandparents became very watchful. She was not allowed to go to anyone's house, or to walk to and from school. Social nights were out, and Bonita told her there would be no dating, as that was the way her mother had been ruined. All around them the gas fields opened up and Verl squinted down the road to see if EnCana or British Petroleum was coming to free him from poverty.

*   *   *

Dakotah was curious about her mother. 'Didn't you save any of her stuff?' she asked Bonita after a secret rummage through the attic.

'No, I didn't. I burned those whorish clothes and the stupid pictures she pasted on the walls. She was kind of crazy is what I come to figure. Always makin some mess or doin some outlandish thing. She never did nothin in the kitchen except one time she cooked a whole pot a Minute rice, caught a trout in the stock pond and cut off a piece a that raw trout and laid it on the rice and *ate it. Raw.* I about gagged. That's the kind a thing she did. Crazy stuff.'

*   *   *

Dakotah, knowing herself to be unattractive, was too eager to please, hungry beyond measure for affection. She was ready to love anyone. Sash Hicks, a skinny boy dressed perpetually in camouflage clothing, with a face and body that seemed to have been broken and then realigned, noticed her, attracted to her shy silence. She responded with long, intense stares when she thought he wasn't

235

looking and daydreams that never went farther than swooning kisses. One day Mr. Lewksberry, the history teacher, in an effort to make his despised subject more interesting, pandered to the local definition of history by assigning his students an essay on western outlaws. In the school library, turning the pages of the *Encyclopedia of Western Badmen,* Dakotah came on a photograph of Billy the Kid. It seemed Sash Hicks was looking up from the page, the same smirky triumph in the face, the slouched posture and dirty pants. Sash immediately gained a lustrous aura of outlawry and gun expertise. Now in her daydreams they rode away together, Sash twisting back in the saddle to shoot at their pursuers, Verl and Bonita. In real life Dakotah and Sash began to think of themselves as a couple, meeting in hallways, sitting near each other in classes, exchanging notes. She felt he was her only chance to get away from Bonita and Verl, that the distance between them could be bridged by grappling. She loved him. At home she kept Sash a secret.

In the beginning of their senior year Sash Hicks made up his mind. No judge of character, he gauged her a biddable handmaiden who would look to his comforts. He said, Let's get married, and she agreed. She expected her grandparents would boil with rage when they heard the news. She said it quickly at the dinner table. They were pleased.

She had not realized that they shared her feeling of unjust imprisonment from their own perspective.

'You'll get along good with Sash,' said Verl, jovial with relief that she would soon be off his hands.

'Too bad Shaina didn't think a that, might a saved her,' mumbled Bonita, who never gave up on the subject. Their approval was the closest to praise they had ever bestowed on her.

Dakotah dropped out of school a few months before graduation. The school counselor, Mrs. Lenski, middle-aged and with murky blue eyes outlined in brown, tried to persuade her to finish. 'Oh, I know how you feel, I completely understand that you want to get married, but believe me, you will *never never* regret finishing school. If you should have to get a job or if trouble comes—'

No, thought Dakotah, you don't know how I feel, you don't know what it is like to be me, but she said nothing. She found a waitressing job at Big Bob's travel stop. The pay was minimum wage and the tips rarely more than dimes or quarters but enough for them to rent a three-room apartment over the Elks lodge.

*　　*　　*

Otto and Virginia Hicks and Verl and Bonita came with them to the town clerk's office on

Dakotah's day off. After the brief ceremony, aware that some kind of celebration was proper, they went to Big Bob's and sat in a booth, surrounded by truckers and gas field workers. Mr. Castle, the manager, gave them free drinks and his best wishes. Sash picked at a sore on his upper lip and ate three Big Bobbers with a quart-size milk shake. Dakotah ordered hot chocolate with whipped cream. Mrs. Hicks spilled cola on her lilac skirt and became impatient to get home and sponge it off.

'I hope it don't stain,' she mourned.

The Hickses were famous for their card parties at which canasta was the game of choice and the first prize was one of Virginia Hicks's pecan pies, for she came from Texas and prided herself on them. Otto Hicks had met her when, as a young man just out of college, he went to Amarillo for a job interview with a drill-bit manufacturer. He wore his cowboy hat and boots and barn jacket and did not get the job. Yet he persuaded Virginia, their head receptionist, to walk out without notice and come with him to Wyoming, and that was some satisfaction. As an added revenge, when he walked past the personnel manager's parking space he had scratched the door of the man's car with a hoof pick that he had in his pocket. Back in Wyoming, Otto got into the snow fence business, subcontracting for the state highway department.

Bonita and Verl, leaving their balled-up greasy napkins on the table instead of putting them in the disposal bin, also hurried away as Verl felt his old pain encroaching, moving stealthily toward his heart. None of them knew what it was like having a serious medical condition, Verl thought, or what it was like waking in the morning and never knowing if he would see the yard light come on at twilight. He had given up on the clinic doctors and now followed the local practice of consulting a chiropractor, the most favored Jacky Barstow, a fat man with steel rod fingers. The chiropractor told him his problem was in his spine, and most ailments, including cancer, were caused by bad, jammed-up spines. Verl's spine, he said, was one of the worst he had ever seen. Verl slid out of the booth and Bonita followed. Dakotah, unable to shake off her job training, picked up after them, threw the cups and paper wrappers in the trash bin, something Sash Hicks (and Mr. Castle) noticed with approval. No one had paid for the food, and Mr. Castle told Dakotah he would deduct the cost from her next paycheck.

*   *   *

Sash Hicks was not the first naked man Dakotah had seen. When she was fourteen Bonita fell down the porch steps because of

239

her arthritic knee's stiffness and pain and broke her left arm. The new doctor at the clinic, a slab-sided fiftyish woman, after talking on the phone with Bonita's regular doctor, who was treating her for the arthritis, ignored her furious glare and said it was the ideal time to get that recommended knee replacement as she would be laid up for weeks anyway.

'You're not getting any younger, Bonita,' she said, showing her the X-rays. 'The right knee looks pretty good, but the bones are very worn and diseased in the left. It can't get better by itself, especially if you persist in ignoring the situation. The replacement will let you get around pretty well. You'll have years of pain-less movement.' Bonita protested, but Verl said she should go ahead with it, and after her arm was set they moved her to a hospital room for knee surgery.

Verl came home from the hospital around noon carrying bags of groceries and several bottles of whiskey. He said that Bonita would be back home in ten days encased in two casts.

'So you'll have to pretty much take care a the kitchen.'

He seemed a little excited, putting steaks in a Pyrex dish and shaking Tabasco and Texas barbecue sauce onto them, sprinkling coarse salt and pepper. He made a long, rectangular fire on the ground, cowboy style, saying it would burn down to a good bed of coals. He told Dakotah to get some potatoes ready for baking. Dakotah caught some of his excitement; it was a vacation from Bonita and her rules, a kind of picnic for her and Verl. But around four o'clock the real reason for the steaks showed up—Harlan, Verl's brother who worked for the Bureau of Land Management in Crack Springs. Harlan was short and muscular and very quiet. His hair was longer than Verl's. He wore brown plastic-framed glasses. Whenever he visited conversation died away and they all stared at the curtains or picked at their cuticles until someone, usually Bonita, said, 'Well, I got to get somethin done,' rose and left the room. But now, without Bonita, a kind of conversation sprang up between the two brothers, a discussion of an old schoolmate who had been indicted for embezzling the town's Arbor Day tree fund. While the fire sank into shimmering coals they sat on the ground and drank the whiskey, then Verl laid the two steaks directly on the coals. Clouds of fragrant smoke spread out and after a minute he stabbed the meat with a long-handled fork and turned it over. Black coals and ash stuck to the charred steaks. Harlan held out a tin pie pan and Verl got the meat onto it. They went into the kitchen. Neither of them said anything to Dakotah until she put the baked potatoes on the table with the butter dish. She had figured out that the steaks were only for the men.

'Still hard in the middle, dammit,' said Verl.

'Don't you know how to bake a potato?' But they ate them and then, ignoring her, went into the living room to watch television crime shows and drink more whiskey. She made herself the old reliable peanut butter sandwich.

During the night some unfamiliar sound like an Indian whoop woke her, but she heard nothing more. She got up to go to the bathroom, tiptoeing in the dark past the guest room where Harlan would be sleeping. But the door was open and the moonlight shone on an undisturbed bed. Maybe, she thought, after all that whiskey he was sleeping on the couch. She turned the corner toward the bathroom, switched on the hall light as the door to Bonita and Verl's bedroom opened. Harlan came out. He was naked, his eyes dazed. His sexual parts looked large and dark. He seemed not to see Dakotah and she fled back to her room and down the back stairs, going into the yard rather than risk the path to the bathroom again.

*   *   *

Sash Hicks discovered her quiet demeanor masked gritty stubbornness. After a few weeks, when they weren't rolling on the new Super-Puff mattress, they were fighting over issues petty and large.

'Chrissake,' said Hicks, who was still in

school working toward his goal of becoming a computer programmer, 'all I asked was for you to get me a beer and some a them chips and the salsa. That goin a break your arm?'

'Get it yourself. I been bossed around since I was a kid. I didn't agree to be your maid. I worked a full shift and I'm tired. You should be gettin *me* a beer. You act like a customer. Go on, talk to the manager and get me fired!' She surprised herself. Where had this hard attitude come from? It was something in her, and it must be from her rebellious, unknown mother. And maybe also from Bonita, who had her own raspy side when Verl wasn't around.

Hicks, aggrieved at her stubbornness, saw he had made a dreadful mistake. Plus she was flat-chested. After months of her obstinate refusals to bring him tools or beers or to pull off his stinking sneakers, they had it out. He said he was through and she said good, but she was keeping the apartment since she paid the rent. In a flare of accusations and blames they agreed to divorce. He moved back to his parents' house and indulged in a debauch of drinking and partying to celebrate his new freedom. When he failed his final exams, he joined the army, telling his father that the army would train him in computer programming and he'd get paid for it, too. It was even better than his original plan—it really would let him be all he could be. He used the enlistment bonus for a down payment on a new truck which his family would keep for him until he came back.

*   *   *

But before he left for basic training, Dakotah discovered she was pregnant.

'Oh my god,' said Bonita. 'You get hold a Sash Hicks right now.'

'What for? We are gettin a divorce. He's goin in the army. Me and Sash are through.'

'Not if you are havin his baby. You're not through by a long shot. You better call him up right now and stop this divorce mess.'

But Dakotah would not call him. Why, she wanted to ask Bonita, didn't you and Verl stop me from marrying him? But she knew that if they had protested she would have run off with Sash to spite them.

The months went by. Dakotah kept working at Big Bob's, enjoying the apartment, having all that room to herself. Sometimes she talked to the absent Sash Hicks. 'Get me a glass a champagne, Sash. And a turkey sandwich. With mayo and pickles. Run down the store and pick up some chocolate puddin. What's the matter, cat got your tongue?' She planned to keep the apartment after the baby came. She had not considered who would take care of the baby while she worked.

One day Mrs. Lenski, the school counselor, came into Big Bob's and sat in a booth by herself. She pulled a tissue from her purse and blew her nose, sopped at her watery eyes.

'Why Dakotah. I wondered where you were these days. I see you and Sash are expecting. Excuse me, I think I'm getting the flu.'

'I'm expecting. He don't even know. We broke up. You were right. It would of been better if I graduated. Get a better job than *this.*' She gestured at the booths, at the cubbyhole where the orders from the kitchen came out, Adam and Eve on a raft, axle grease, Mike and Ike, and Big Bob's super burger, called a 'bomb' in the kitchen.

'It could be worse,' said Mrs. Lenski. 'You could have been a school counselor. Heartbreaker job.' She gave Dakotah her card and said they would stay in touch. She came in once a week after that and always asked what Dakotah was doing, planning, thinking of for the future, those questions that adults believed occupied the thoughts of the young. Dakotah had no plans for the future; the present seemed solid.

Mr. Castle asked her to come into his office, a windowless hole that barely contained his desk. A huge tinted photograph of his wife and triplet daughters took up most of the desktop. Boxes of paper cups were piled up in the corner. Mr. Castle had a red, jolly face and a store of mossy jokes. He got along with everyone, calmed difficult customers as a snake charmer soothes irritable cobras.

'Well, Dakotah,' he began. 'I don't have no problem with you havin a baby, but the company got a policy that no lady more than six months gone can work here.'

'That's not fair,' said Dakotah. 'I need this job. Sash and me split up. I'm on my own. I work hard for you, Mr. Castle.'

'Oh, I know that, Dakotah, but it's not for me to say.' He cast a husband's practiced eye over her. 'That baby is expected pretty damn soon, right? Like in a few weeks? You can't fool me, Dakotah, so don't try.' All the jolliness had dried up. She understood she was being fired.

The boy was born six days later, and Mr. Castle winced as he realized how close they had come to having a delivery during noon rush hour. He sent a potted chrysanthemum with a card saying, 'From the Gang at Big Bob's!'

*   *   *

Dakotah had somehow expected the baby to be a quiet creature she would care for as one cared for a pet. She was unprepared for the child's roaring greediness, his assertion of self, or for the violence of love that swamped her, that made her shake with what she knew must come next.

'I guess I got a put the baby up for adoption,' she said to Bonita, then broke down and bawled. 'I had money saved up for the doctor, but now I don't have my job and can't pay the rent.' Bonita was aghast. The boy was legitimate, though deserted by his father. She could almost hear the Matches sneering that Bonita and Verl would not care for their own flesh and blood. And he was a boy!

'You can't bring more shame on this family. It's almost as bad as what your mother done. You come up with some support money from that no-good bum you married and your granddad and me will take care a the child. We'll have to do it. Your mother's sin unto the second generation. I want you to call up Mrs. Hicks and tell her that her precious son skipped out on his child. Tell her that you are goin to the child support people and a lawyer. I'll bet you anything he give the enlistment bonus to his folks.'

Dakotah did telephone Mrs. Hicks and asked for Sash's address.

'I spose you want a squeeze money out a him,' said Mrs. Hicks. 'He is in the army and we don't know where. Someplace in California. He didn't tell us where they was sendin him. Probably Eye-rack by now. He said he was bein deployed to Eye-rack. But we don't know for sure. He didn't tell *me*.' There was bitterness in her voice, perhaps the bitterness of the neglected mother or of someone wishing to be in the land of fresh pecans.

Bonita sighed. 'She's lyin. She knows where he is. But them Hickses stick together tighter than cuckleburrs. We'll have to take care a him. You name that baby Verl after your granddad. That'll make him more interested to help the boy.' She sighed. 'Does it ever end?' she asked and in her mind phrased a prayerful request for strength.

Among the privileges of western malehood from which the baby benefited were opened dams of affection in Bonita and Verl. Dakotah was amazed at the way Verl hung over the infant's crib mouthing nonsense words, but she understood what had happened. It was the same knife slice of lightning love that had cut her. He wanted Dakotah to change the child's last name to Lister, but she said that although Sash Hicks was a rat, he was still the legal and legitimate father and the baby would stay a Hicks.

Nor could Sash Hicks be located. He had been at Fort Irwin National Training Center and had sent home a cryptic letter. 'I learned some Arab words. Na'am. Marhaba. Marhaba means hello. Na'am means yes. So you know.'

Neither Bonita nor Verl would hear of Dakotah going on welfare or accepting social services, for the Matches would rightly condemn them as weak-kneed sucks on the taxpayer's tit. They talked it through at night, the yard light casting its corrosive glare on the south wall. She could go back to Mr. Castle and beg for her old job. Bonita and Verl would care for the baby. Or—

'Way we see it,' said Bonita to Dakotah, 'is *you* ought a join the army yourself. They take women. You can support Little Verl that way. Finish your education. And find out how to get through the red tape that will track down Sash Hicks. Me and Big Verl will take care a him until you get through with the army. A job at Big Bob's don't pay enough.'

Verl added his opinion. 'When you come back you can get a real good job. And if you can get one a them digital cameras cheap at the PX, we'll take pictures a him—' He nodded at the baby sleeping in his carry chair.

She could not believe how solicitous they had become. It was as though their icy hearts had melted and the leg whippings had never happened, as though they were bound by consanguineous affection instead of grudging duty in obeisance to community mores. She marveled that this change of heart was rooted in involuntary love, a love that had not moved them when they brought her as an infant to the ranch.

Her grandfather himself drove her to the recruitment office in Crack Springs, harping all the way on duty, responsibility, the necessity for signing the papers so child support could come to them. He also drove her to the Military Entrance Processing Station in Cody. He had even picked out a

249

specialty for her: combat medic.

'I checked around,' he said, winking his pinpoint aquamarine eyes, which, as he aged, had almost disappeared under colorless eyebrows and hanging folds of flesh. 'EMTs make good money. You could get to be a medic and when you come back, why there's your career, just waiting.' The word 'career' sounded strange coming out of his mouth. For years he had ranted against wives who worked out of the home. On the ranches the wives held everything together—cooking for big crowds, nursing the sick and injured, cleaning, raising children and driving them to rodeo practice, keeping the books and paying the bills, making mail runs and picking up feed at the farm supply, taking the dogs in for their shots, and often riding with the men at branding and shipping times, and in mountainous country helping with the annual shove up and shove down shifting cattle to and from pasturage leased from the Forest Service, and were treated with little more regard than the beef they helped produce.

It was almost spring, last night's small snow spiking up the dead grass in ragged points, balling in the yellow joints of the stream-side willow, snow that would melt as soon as the sun touched it. She was joining the army, leaving behind the seedy two-story town, the dun-colored prairie flattened by wind, leaving the gumbo roads, the radio voices flailing

250

through nets of static, the gossip and narrow opinions. As they drove through the town, she saw the muddy truck that was always parked in front of the bar, the kid named Bub Carl who hung around the barbershop. The sun was up, warming the asphalt, and already heat waves ran across the road as the old landscape fell away behind her. Yet she felt nothing for the place or herself, not even relief at escaping Verl and Bonita, or sorrow or regret at putting the baby in their care. As for the child, she would be coming back to him. He would wait, as she had waited, but for him there would be a happy ending, for she would return. She picked him up and stared into his slate blue eyes.

'See? I'm comin back to get you. I'm coming back for you. I love you and will come back. Promise.' She just had to get through the dense period of life away from the ranch, away from Wyoming, away from her baby who gave the place its only value.

*   *   *

She went to Fort Leonard Wood in Missouri for basic training. The first thing she learned was that it was still a man's army and that women were decidedly inferior in all ways. The memory flashed of a time when she had gone shopping with Bonita in Cody. Bonita favored a pint-size mall that featured Cowboy

Meats, Radio Shack and a video store. Dakotah chose to wait in the truck instead of trailing after Bonita, who was a ruthless and vociferous shopper for the cheapest of everything. Dakotah watched a man and his two children outside Grum's Dollar Mart, where there was a tiny patch of grass. The man had a hard red face and brown mustache. He was dressed in jeans, dirty undershirt and ball cap, but wore ranch work boots. He was throwing a Frisbee gently to the boy, a slow toddler unable to catch it. Against the Dollar Mart wall stood the girl, a year or two older than the boy, but the father did not throw the Frisbee to her. Dakotah hated the way he ignored the girl's yearning gaze. She smiled at the girl staring so fixedly at the father and son. At last Dakotah got out of the truck and walked over.

'Hey there,' she said to the girl, smiling. 'What's your name?'

The child did not answer but flattened herself against the grimy wall.

'What d'*you* want?' said the father, letting his arm down, the Frisbee sagging against his leg. It was a nylon Frisbee, the kind dog owners favored.

The toddler was yelling at the father. 'Frow! Frow!' When the man did not throw the Frisbee, the boy began to whine and blub.

'Nothin. Just sayin hello. To the little girl.'

'Yeah. Well, here comes your granny. Git

252

home and don't be botherin my kids.' The little girl gave her a look of pure hatred and stuck out a long, yellow tongue.

Bonita wedged the bags of groceries between two bags of garbage she intended to drop off at the landfill. 'What're you doin talkin a him?'

'I wasn't! I was sayin hello to the little girl. Who are they?'

'He's Rick Sminger, one a Shaina's old . . . friends. Least said about him the better. I was you I wouldn't ask no questions. Get in and let's get goin.'

*   *   *

The worst thing about the army, the thing she knew she could never get used to, was the constant presence of too many people, too close, in her face, radiating heat and smells, talking and shouting. Someone who has grown up in silence and vast space, who was born to solitude, who feels different and shrinks from notice, suffers in the company of others. So homesickness took the shape of longing for wind, an empty landscape, for silence and privacy. She longed for the baby and came to believe she was homesick for the old ranch.

She made a low score on the aptitude test, edging into the borderline just enough to continue on. She thought about Verl's suggestion she become a combat medic. She had no other ideas. At least she would be helping people. She named it as her choice of a Military Occupational Specialty. During basic training she heard that becoming a combat medic was very tough. Candidates went crazy, they said, because of the enormous amounts of information they had to memorize. But she had learned CPR in sophomore gym class and thought she could study enough to pass a few tests.

After basic training she went to Fort Sam Houston in San Antonio for EMT training, and the immediate future loomed like a cliff. All of her fellow volunteers seemed to have been practicing medicine since kindergarten. Pat Moody, a wiry blonde from Oregon, was the daughter of a doctor and had heard medical talk for years. She was excited about training at Brooks Medical Center because of its famous burn unit and planned to become a doctor after she got out of the army. Marnie Jellson came from a potato farm in Idaho and had cared for her sick mother for two years. When the mother died she had enlisted. Tommet Means had been an EMT since high school. Chris Jinkla came from a family of veterinarians and had accompanied his father on calls a thousand times.

'I grew up bandaging paws,' he said.

She and Pat and Marnie became friends. Pat played the guitar and taught Dakotah enough chords to string together 'Michael, Row the

254

Boat Ashore.' Marnie had a collection of movies that they watched on weekends. Marnie had a potato tattooed on her left calf and knew dozens of potato jokes. Both of them talked about their families, and finally Dakotah explained that her grandparents had brought her up, told about Sash and the breakup and the baby.

'You poor kiddo,' said Marnie. 'You've been through a lot.'

'How can it be,' Dakotah asked them, 'that you feel homesick for a place you hate?' She thought of the neutral smell of dust like stones or old wood, of summer haze from distant forest fires, of rose-rock outcrops breaking from the rusty earth. She thought of the rundown town, every other building sporting a weathered For Sale sign.

'Maybe it's the people you are homesick for, not the place,' said Pat.

And of course it was. She saw that right away. Not just Baby Verl, but even closed-up Bonita and Verl hitching along on his bad legs.

She bought a camera and sent it to Bonita and Verl, begging them to take photographs of Baby Verl. She taped the dozens of them on her wall. She wrote long letters to the baby, covered the margins with symbols of kisses and hugs. She and Pat and Marnie raided the PX for baby toys, miniature blue jeans, pajamas imprinted with tanks and planes.

They went to dinner at restaurants and

255

Dakotah learned it was bad manners to stack the empty dishes. 'I was just helpin the waitress out,' she explained. It was what ranch people did after finishing their burgers at Big Bob's.

At a Japanese place one night Pat persuaded her to try sushi.

'What is it?' she asked, looking at the hump of rice with an orange slice of something on top.

'It is salmon and rice, and that is wasabi, a kind of grated horseradish. It's hot.'

She ate it, and the texture of the salmon startled her. 'It's not cooked!'

'It's not supposed to be cooked.'

'It's raw! Raw fish! I ate it.' Her stomach heaved but she kept it down and even ate another. A day later she remembered Bonita describing Shaina putting raw trout on some Minute rice. Was it possible that her mother had heard somewhere about sushi and decided to try it—Wyoming style? Was it possible her mother had been exhibiting not craziness but curiosity about the outside world? She told Pat and Marnie about it and they decided that was it—curiosity and longing for the exotic.

*   *   *

As the tsunami of reading material, lectures, slides, videos, X-rays, computer tutorials on anatomy, diseases, trauma, physiology, obstetrics, pediatrics, shock and a bewildering vocabulary of medical terms swept over the group, Dakotah did not think she would pass the EMT Basic Registry Exam. And even if she did, then came primary care training and the horror courses in chemical, explosive and radiation injuries.

'I will never get to Whiskey level,' she said calmly to Pat, thinking of needle chest compression and clearing airways, both of which she dreaded.

'Come on. You'll make it,' said Pat, who aced every test. 'Those are situational exercises, which makes it real interesting.' Dakotah passed the EMT test, but at the bottom of the class. Marnie flat-out failed.

'Suggest you think about changin to military police,' said the squinty-eyed, spotted-banana-skin instructor to Dakotah. 'Medicine is not your thing. I know I'd sure hate to be lyin there with my guts hangin out and here comes old rough-hand Dakotah tryin to remember what to do.'

*   *   *

Pat went to Fort Drum in New York for training at the medical simulation center, where darkness, explosions and smoke mimicked realistic battlefield situations. She sent Marnie and Dakotah a letter describing Private Hunk, a computerized patient-simulation mannequin who could bleed, breathe, even talk a little. He was complete in the last detail, constructed for countless intubations, tracheotomies, catheterizations. He suffered sucking chest wounds, hideous traumas. He bled and moaned for help and on occasion shrieked an inhuman birdcall like a falcon. He was hot or cold, at the instructor's wish, could run a fever or suffer severe hypothermia.

'He's got a cute little dick. I'm in love with him,' wrote Pat. Dakotah answered the letter, but they never heard from Pat again.

There were many letters from Bonita, the words looping downhill across the page and ending with a two-line prayer. She always began the letter with news of Baby Verl's progress with cutting teeth, crawling, standing up, how Verl's old dog Bum had taken to him, following him everywhere and letting Baby pull his ears, how Verl had got another dog, Buddy, because Bum was getting old, and how Buddy loved the baby even more than Bum, and only when she had detailed every wonderful thing Baby Verl had done did she report on local events. Her sister Juanita had come from Casper for a visit and to show off her new husband, who worked in the gas fields for Triangle Energy. The first husband, Don, had worked for the same company. He had believed fall-protection gear was for pantywaists and died when he reached for a hoist-lifted pipe and missed. Big Verl, Bonita wrote, had quit his chiropractor and was now going to a fat woman who gave massages and charged terrific prices. 'At least she advertises they are massages. If Verl wasn't Verl I would think it was something else.' Dakotah felt a rare and even painful rush of affection mixed with pity for Bonita, although she suspected she was only writing out of a sense of duty.

A few letters came from Mrs. Lenski, alternately sardonic and cheerful. It seemed to Dakotah that as soon as she had left, the town started dying off. One of the Vasey twins had been killed and the other severely injured in a car crash at the intersection where everybody knew to slow down. Some truck with Colorado plates had blasted through and T-boned them. And, wrote Mrs. Lenski, two lesbian women with a herd of goats had bought the Tin Can house and planned to make cheese and sell it locally. Dakotah was shocked to see the word 'lesbian' on the page of a letter like any ordinary word. Tug Diceheart and two other hands riding for the Tic-Tac had been caught making meth in the bunkhouse and arrested. Juiciest of all, Mrs. Match had left Wyatt and returned to California to become a real estate agent. Dakotah wondered if Verl was gloating.

*   *   *

Both Dakotah and Marnie changed their MOS

to Military Police. They had become closest friends, closer than she had ever been to Sash. Dakotah, for the first time in her life, had someone to talk to, someone who understood everything, from rural ways to failing at tests. Marnie said maybe they were in love. They talked about setting up house together with Baby Verl after they got out. One day they were in a Humvee, Dakotah clutching a machine gun, on their way to a checkpoint to search Iraqi women.

'Yup, here we are with the fuckups. MP is where the dumb ones end up. Supposed a be the stupidest part of the entire army.'

'Don't you think some of the officers could get that prize?'

'Yeah. So probably MPs come second. Second dumbest, something to brag about.'

They had learned that the checkpoints were intensely dangerous, and after a few weeks Dakotah developed a little magic ritual to keep herself alive. She rapidly twitched the muscles of her toes, heel, calf, knee, hip, waist, shoulder, eyebrow, elbow, wrist, thumb, fingers on the right side and then repeated the series for the left side. Bonita had sent her a silver-plated cross that she recognized. It had always been in the second drawer of the kitchen dresser with a tortoiseshell comb, a pot holder too nice to use, a pair of small kid gloves that had belonged to Verl's famous great-grandmother, a red box with a sliding lid filled with old buttons. She wore the cross once, but it tangled with her dog tags and she put it away.

She hated searching the Iraqi women, knew that they hated her doing it. Some of them smelled, and their voluminous, often ragged and dusty burkas could conceal everything from a black market radio to baby clothes to a bomb. One young woman had six glossy eggplants hidden under her garment. Dakotah pitied her, unable even to buy and carry home a few eggplants without an American soldier groping at her. Never had the world seemed so vile and her own problems so mean and petty.

On the day the IED exploded under the Humvee she had not completed the left side of the protecting muscle twitches, choosing a third cup of coffee instead. It happened too suddenly for anything to register. One moment they were traveling fast, the next she was looking up into the face of Chris Jinkla.

'Moooo,' she said, trying to make a cow joke for the veterinary's son, but he didn't recognize her and thought she was moaning. She felt nothing at that moment and tried her magic muscle twitch sequence, but something was wrong on the right side.

'I'm fine, Chris. Except my arm.'

The medic was startled. He peered into her bloody face. 'My god, it's Pat, right?'

'Dakotah,' she whispered. 'I'm Dakotah. I'm fine but I need my arm. Please look for it. I can't go home without it.' She turned her head and saw a heap of bloody rags and a patch of skin.

'Marnie?'

Her right arm was still there though cruelly shattered, and the best they could hope for, said the doctor at the field hospital, was to amputate and save enough stump to carry a prosthetic. 'You're young and strong,' he said. 'You'll make it.'

'I'm fine,' she agreed. 'How about Marnie?' She knew as she asked.

The doctor gave her a look.

She was shipped out to Germany with other wounded, gradually aware that there was some awful knowledge hovering, something worse than her mangled arm, which had been amputated, something as bad as losing Marnie. Maybe they had discovered she had cancer and wouldn't tell her. But it was not until she was sent to Walter Reed that she heard the bad news from Bonita herself, who stood at her bedside with a curious expression of mingled sorrow and, looking at the stump of her arm, a ghoulish curiosity.

'Oh, oh,' she whispered, and then burst into streaming tears. Never had Dakotah seen anyone cry that way, tears pouring down Bonita's cheeks to the corners of her mouth, splashing from her jawline onto her rayon blouse as though her head was filled with water. She could not speak for long minutes.

'Baby Verl,' she finally said.

'*What?*' Dakotah knew instinctively it was the worst thing. 'Ridin in the back a Big Verl's truck—' And the tears began again. 'He fell out.'

The story came slowly and wetly. The eighteen-month-old child had loved riding with his great-grandfather, but this day Verl put him with the dogs in the open truck bed. Big Verl was so proud to have a boy and wanted him to be tough. The dogs loved him. She said that several times. The rest of it came in a rush.

'See, Verl thought he'd just sit with the dogs. They done it before. But you know how dogs hang over the edge. Baby Verl did that too, near as we can tell, so that when the truck went down in one a them dips it threw him out. It was a accident. He fell under the wheels, Dakotah. Big Verl is half-crazy. They got him sedated. The doctors are fixin it up for you to come home.'

Dakotah threw back her head and howled. She snapped her teeth at Bonita and began to curse her and Verl. How could he be so stupid as to put a baby in the bed of a pickup? The shouting and crying brought an irritated nurse, who asked them to keep it down. Bonita, who had been backing away, turned and ran into the corridor and did not come back.

*   *   *

263

'It takes a year, Dakotah,' said Mrs. Parka, the grief counselor, a full-bosomed woman with enormous liquid eyes. 'A full turn of the seasons before you begin to heal. Time *does* heal all wounds, and right now the passage of time is the best medicine. And you yourself must heal physically as well as spiritually. You need to be very strong. What is your religion?'

Dakotah shook her head. She had asked the woman to write to Mrs. Lenski for her and tell her what happened, but the woman said it was part of the healing process for Dakotah to face the fact of Baby Verl's passing and tell Mrs. Lenski herself. Dakotah wanted to choke the woman until she went blue-black and died.

She glared furiously.

'There are other ways for you to communicate. The telephone. E-mail?'

'Get away from me,' said Dakotah.

*   *   *

At the end of the summer she was still there, in a grimy old motel somehow connected to the hospital, getting used to the prosthesis. She sat in the dim room doing nothing. Dreary days went by. She struggled to understand the morass of papers about disability allowances, death allowances, Baby Verl's support. One of the official letters said that support payments for baby Verl Hicks should never have been

264

paid for, by or through Dakotah, but through the child's father, SSgt Saskatoon M. Hicks, currently at Walter Reed Hospital recuperating.

That Sash was somewhere at the same hospital amazed her. That she had learned about it amazed her more, for the legendary confusion and chaos of lost patients was like the nest of rattlesnakes Verl had once showed her, a coiling, twisting mass under a shelving boulder. He had fired his old 12-gauge at them and still the torn flesh twisted.

One afternoon a volunteer, Mrs. Glossbeau, came to her. Dakotah saw she must be rich; she was trim and tanned and wore an elegant raspberry-colored wool suit with a white silk shirt.

'Are you Dakotah Hicks?'

She had forgotten they were still married. Sash's divorce action had gone dormant when he left for basic training.

'Yes, but we were gettin a divorce. And then I don't know what happened.'

'Well, your husband is here in the complex and his doctors think you ought to see him. I should warn you, he has suffered very severe injuries. He may not recognize you. He probably won't. They are hoping that seeing you again will . . . sort of wake him up.'

Dakotah said nothing at first. She did not want to see Sash. She wanted to see Marnie. She wanted Baby Verl. She half-believed he was waiting to play patty-cake. She could feel his small warm hands.

'I don't really want to see him. We got nothin to talk about.'

But the woman sat beside her chair and cajoled. Dakotah breathed in a delicious fragrance, as rich as apricots in cream and with the slight bitterness from the cyanide kernel. The woman's hands were shapely with long pale nails, her fingers laden with diamond-heavy rings. Because it seemed the only way to get rid of the woman was to agree, in the end she went.

*   *   *

Sash Hicks had disintegrated, both legs blown off at midthigh, the left side of his face a mass of shiny scar tissue, the left ear and eye gone. It was almost like seeing Marnie, whom she knew was dead, although she kept on hearing her voice in corridors. Sash's nurse told her that he had suffered brain damage. But Dakotah recognized him, old Billy the Kid shot up by Pat Garrett. More than ever he looked like the antique outlaw. He stared at the ceiling with his right eye. The ruined face showed no comprehension except that something was terribly wrong if he could only know what.

'Sash. It's me, Dakotah.'

He said nothing. Although his face was

ruined and he was ravaged from the waist down, his right shoulder and arm were muscular and stout.

She didn't know what she felt for him—pity or nothing at all.

Words came out of the distorted mouth.

'Ah—ah—eh.' He subsided as though someone had unscrewed the valve that kept his body inflated and upright. His moment of grappling with the world had passed and his chin sank onto his chest.

'Are you asleep?' asked Dakotah. There was no answer and she left.

* * *

The trip to the ranch was hard, but there was nowhere else to go. She dreaded seeing Verl; would she scream and punch him? Grab the .30-.30 on top of the dish cupboard and shoot him? She felt a scorching rage and at the same time was listless and inert, slumping on the backseat of the taxi. Sonny Ezell's old vehicle moved very slowly. Her prosthesis was in her suitcase. She knew they had to see the arm stump to believe, just as she had to see little Verl's grave.

They passed the Match ranch, unchanged, and turned onto Sixteen Mile. The days were shortening, but there was still plenty of light, the top of Table Butte, layered bands of buff, gamboge and violet, gilded by the setting sun.

The shallow river, as yellow as lemon rind, lay flaccid between denuded banks. The dying sun hit the willows, transforming them into bloody wands. Light reflected from the road as from glass. They seemed to be traveling through a hammered red landscape in which ranch buildings appeared dark and sorrowful. She knew what blood-soaked ground was, knew that severed arteries squirted like the backyard hose. A dog came out of the ditch and ran into a stubble field. They passed the Persa ranch, where the youngest son had drowned in last spring's flood. She realized that every ranch she passed had lost a boy, lost them early and late, boys smiling, sure in their risks, healthy, tipped out of the current of life by liquor and acceleration, rodeo smashups, bad horses, deep irrigation ditches, high trestles, tractor rollovers and 'unloaded' guns. Her boy, too. This was the waiting darkness that surrounded ranch boys, the dangerous growing up that canceled their favored status. The trip along this road was a roll call of grief. Wind began to lift the fine dust and the sun set in haze.

When she got out at the house the wind swallowed her whole, snatching at her scarf, huffing up under the hem of her coat, eeling up her sleeve. She could feel the grit. Every step she took dried weeds snapped under her shoes. Sonny Ezell carried her suitcase to the porch and wouldn't take any money. Someone inside switched on the porch light.

She did not attack Verl. Both of her grandparents hugged her and cried. Verl thudded to his knees and sobbed that he was sorry unto death. He pressed his wet face against her hand. He had never before touched her in any way. She felt nothing and took it to mean recovery. There was a large color photograph of little Verl on the wall. He was sitting on a bench with one chubby leg folded under, the other dangling and showing a snowy white stocking and miniature sneaker. He held a plush bear by its ear. They must have taken him to the Wal-Mart portrait studio. They had sent her a print of the same picture.

Bonita brought out a big dinner, fried chicken, mashed potatoes, string beans with cream sauce, fresh rolls and for dessert a pecan pie that she said Mrs. Hicks had sent over. She said something about Mrs. Hicks that Dakotah did not catch. It was a terrible dinner. None of them could eat. They pushed the food around and in hoarse teary voices said how good everything looked. Verl, perhaps trying to set an example, took a forkful of mashed potato and retched. At last they got up. Bonita wrapped the food with plastic film and put it in the refrigerator.

'We'll eat it tomorrow,' she said.

They sat in awful silence in the living room, the television set dark.

'Your old room is made up,' said Bonita. In

the quiet the kitchen refrigerator hummed like wind in the wires. 'You know, them Hickses couldn't afford to go to Warshinton and see Sash. They need to know about him. They can't find out a thing. They telephoned a hunderd times. Every time they call that hospital they get cut off or transferred to somebody don't know. They need for you to tell them. It's bad, them not knowing.'

She could not tell them how much worse it was to know.

*   *   *

The next morning was somewhat easier; they could all drink hot coffee. Mourning, grief and loss were somehow eased by hot, black coffee. But still no one could eat. At noon Dakotah left Verl and Bonita and went for a walk up the pine slope. A new power line ran through the slashed trees.

At supper the welcome-home meal reappeared, heated in Bonita's microwave that she had bought with some of Dakotah's money. They finally ate, very slowly. In a low voice Dakotah said that the chicken was good. It had no taste. Bonita made more coffee—none of them would sleep anyway—and cut Mrs. Hicks's pecan pie. Verl gazed at the golden triangle on his saucer, seemed unable to lift his fork.

There was the creak of the kitchen door and

Otto and Virginia Hicks came in, tentatively. Bonita urged them to sit down, got coffee for them. Mrs. Hicks's red eyes went to Dakotah. The older woman's hand shook and the coffee cup stuttered against the saucer. She suddenly gave up on the coffee and pushed it away.

'What about Sash?' she blurted. 'You seen him. We got that official letter that says he is coming home. They don't say how bad he was hurt. We can't find out nothing. He don't call us. Maybe he can't call us. What about Sash?'

Bonita looked at Dakotah, opened her mouth to say something, then closed it again.

The silence spread out like a rain-swollen river, lapping against the walls of the room, mounting over their heads. Dakotah thought of Ezell's taxi rolling slowly past the bereft ranches. She felt the Hickses' fear begin to solidify into knowledge. Already grief was settling around the tense couple like a rope loop, the same rope that encircled all of them. She had to draw the Hickses' rope tight and snub them up to the pain until they went numb, show that it didn't pay to love.

'Sash,' she said at last so softly they could barely hear. 'Sash is tits-up in a ditch.'

They sat frozen like people in the aftermath of an explosion, each silently calculating their survival chances in lives that must grind on. The air vibrated. At last Mrs. Hicks turned her red eyes on Dakotah.

'You're his wife,' she said.

There was no answer to that and Dakotah felt her own hooves slip and the beginning descent into the dark, watery mud.

.